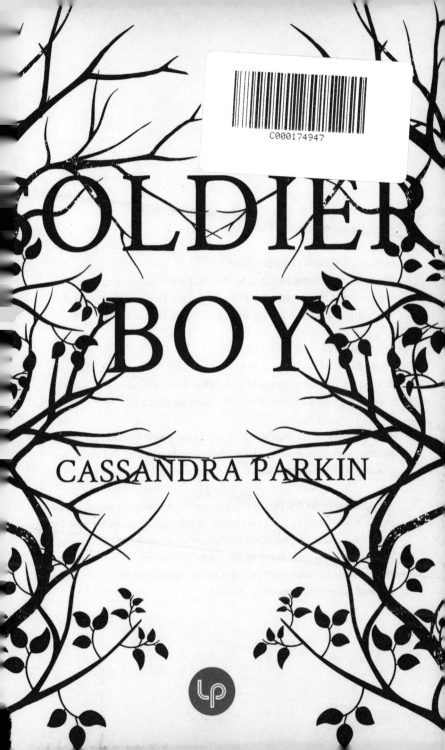

SOLDIER BOY

CASSANDRA PARKIN

Legend Press Ltd, 51 Gower Street, London, WC1E 6HJ
info@legendpress.co.uk | www.legendpress.co.uk

Contents © Cassandra Parkin 2020
The right of the above author to be identified as the author of this work has
been asserted in accordance with the Copyright, Designs and Patents Act
1988. British Library Cataloguing in Publication Data available.

Print ISBN 978-1-78955-1-174
Ebook ISBN 978-1-78955-1-181
Set in Times. Printing managed by Jellyfish Solutions Ltd
Cover design by Kari Brownlie | www.karibrownlie.co.uk

Cassandra Parkin grew up in Hull, and now lives in East Yorkshire. Her debut novel *The Summer We All Ran Away* was published by Legend Press in 2013 and was shortlisted for the Amazon Rising Star Award. Her short story collection, *New World Fairy Tales* (Salt Publishing, 2011) was the winner of the 2011 Scott Prize for Short Stories. *The Beach Hut* was published in 2015, *Lily's House* in 2016, *The Winter's Child* in 2017, *Underwater Breathing* in 2018 and *The Slaughter Man* in 2019. Cassandra's work has been published in numerous magazines and anthologies.

Visit Cassandra at
cassandraparkin.wordpress.com
or follow her
@cassandrajaneuk

For Harry
Shine bright, like the star you are

CHAPTER ONE

(DECEMBER, NOW)

standing in the bright light and harsh disinfectant scent of the grimy toilet block, staring at her reflection in the mirror.

Alannah's used to the dull discomfort that comes with looking at herself. Each day begins before the mirror of her practice barre in her bedroom; most afternoons end with time in ballet class. Weekends are dominated by this relentless study of her own face and body, stretching and smiling through the pain, disciplining herself not to lick the sweat from her upper lip, taking and applying the corrections, watching for flaws, finding the ways she can improve, and the occasional moment of shock – *that girl looks quite good – wait, that's me...*

This mirror lacks the brutal clarity of the studio. It's nothing more than a small polished patch of steel, its dim surface made cloudier by the angle of the glaring pinkish lights and the dried swirl of a cleaning cloth smeared across it. If she approaches it carefully, letting her gaze slide over it without ever quite snagging and pausing, her image becomes a blur, as if she's watching a confident, comfortable stranger. Someone who looks and doesn't feel the inevitable stab of *no, not good enough, not right*, but instead thinks, *yes, quite nice.*

Perhaps if she looks long enough, she'll call the other girl out to her, let her climb into Alannah's skin and walk around in it.

Neither she nor the girl in the mirror are supposed to be here. She's meant to be in a car with three other girls and their ballet teacher, Mrs Baxter. On their way to a hotel room and tomorrow to the theatre, where they'll rehearse and rehearse and finally dance for an audience, alongside what her sort-of-friend Lucy refers to as *actual proper ballet dancers*. Christmas lights gleaming through dark evenings; the sensation of winter in the air. One night with her parents watching, three nights with Granny Jane. Back at home, the tree trimmed and pretty in the living room, waiting for her to return in triumph. Instead, she's in a roadside toilet block, her dad waiting in the car, both wondering where they might go, what will happen next, how all of this will end, neither of them daring to speak about any of it.

In her hand are her mother's scissors. She's not supposed to have them. They're fabric shears, from the top drawer of the sewing cabinet. Her parents don't agree on a lot of things, but her dad has always approved of the way her mum keeps her sewing supplies. Each drawer carefully ordered. Fabric folded into cubbyholes and sorted by type, colour and pattern. Scraps in a large but not-unattractive cotton sack, regularly sorted and purged. Cotton-reels with their ends tucked under. The sharp things – needles, scissors, seam rippers, the rotary cutter with its frightening circular blades – in the top drawer, a legacy from when Alannah was too young to be trusted not to touch, and too small not to try and touch anyway.

"We'll be out of here in ten," her father had told her, taking clothes from drawers and shelves, packing them into his kit bag, swift and focused. "One teddy if you absolutely must. Warm clothes. And bring your duvet. It might get cold." Knowing she had only moments to choose her reminder, she crept into the sewing room, slid open the drawer and found the cool sleek touch of the scissors. This is how she wants to remember her mother – the way she is when Alannah

8

is most afraid of her. She's sharp and bright, dangerous if handled wrongly, able to make anything, repair any damage, cut through any challenge. (*I'm a witch*, her mother croons in her ear, *I've said it three times so now it's bound to come true*. Remaking Alannah into the daughter she truly wants.) In the mirror, Alannah can see the throb of blood in her neck.

Dad'll be worrying, she thinks. *Stop dreaming and get moving.*

("Don't overthink it, Alannah," her ballet teacher endlessly tells her. "Let yourself *feel* the music..." No, she doesn't want to *feel*, she doesn't dare let herself *feel*, that's the whole point. If she stops for a moment to *feel*, who knows what's going to happen?)

Stop dreaming and get moving, she repeats to herself, hearing the words in her dad's voice because this is something he often says. Or when he's in a better mood, he puts on a Yoda voice and intones, *Do. Or do not. There is no try.* Better moods were more common when he went to work, most common of all when he was still in the Army and they were living in the gone-and-here rhythm of Dad Going Away and Dad Coming Back. But he's been out for two years. Hasn't had a job for four months. Hasn't been in a better mood for a long time. *It's not his fault. Things will get better.* She's heard the words so many times, they run on a loop in her head. None of it's his fault. Things will get better.

So why is everything getting worse?

Her vision's adjusting now; she can see herself more clearly, commence her search for flaws. There she is, her muscles hugged tight against her bones, her limbs slender, her posture correct, her neck long, her shoulders held in place. Good enough for now. But who knows what the next year will bring?

Mrs Baxter, brisk and firm. "You're growing up now, you'll start becoming women. That means your bones will harden, and then, *if* you're ready, we can think about pointe work." And in the changing area and in the corners of the studio, the other, darker murmurs from the older girls. "She got too tall," she heard one whisper to another, a little scornful, a little disgusted, as if getting too tall was a mark of weakness. Another time, another two girls, talking casually about a rival: "Don't worry about her, her boobs are massive, she'll never be the right shape." The thought of what's coming, the storm of hormones about to ravage her body, turns Alannah cold. What if she gets too tall? What if her boobs turn out massive? What will happen to her then?

Her mother has told her over and over again not to worry, she doesn't have to have the perfect body, doesn't have to be a dancer, and she'll be proud and happy whatever her daughter chooses. But how can Alannah believe that, when everything her mother does shows her it isn't true? What's the meaning of all the pretty custom-made clothes, the cute little hair decorations, the exquisite dance costumes, the hours her mother spends grooming her, and the endless, endless praise of her hair, her face, her slenderness, her grace, if it's not *I only love you when you're perfect*? Alannah knows what's really going on. Her mother doesn't like ugly things. What if Alannah ends up ugly?

She didn't always feel this way. She's seen photos of herself as a baby and then as a toddler, romping confidently about the house and garden, comfortable in her shape. She can dimly remember being small, not thinking about her body, not caring how it looked. She's done her best to hold it at bay, working diligently at home and in class, eating as little as she can get away with, trying to discipline her body into thinness and smallness, to make time stand still. But her future's written into her genes. There's no escaping what's coming.

"Get on with it," she says out loud. Her voice echoes off the walls and makes her jump. She's glad she's alone, even though the place itself is spooky – a pebble-dashed hut in a rain-soaked layby, drainpipes painted in thick drips of bottle-green, spindly spiders flattening themselves against the walls, and a stink of pee and disinfectant that rolled out like a hug when she tugged on the door. She'd thought it might be locked, was prepared to use the bushes, but it opened, and inside were three cleanish cubicles, two wall-mounted *things* with buttons to dispense soap and water and warm air, lights bright enough to see clearly by. And no other girls or women. And a mirror. And her mother's scissors, slithering in the pocket of the black combat trousers her mother made, blade tips pricking and jabbing at the meat of her thigh.

The feeling inside her is demanding and terrible. She's tried to keep it down but it's too strong. She has to act or else she'll burst. Lying in bed at night, she's found herself terrified by the thoughts of what she might do. Thoughts of burning, of smashing, of destroying. Of tearing through the kitchen like a whirlwind, flinging plates and glasses to the floor. Of taking these scissors and slashing every single thing her mother has ever made for her into a snowstorm of snipped fabric. Of unscrewing the car's petrol cap and lighting a match and flinging it inside. But she knows she doesn't dare. Her parents would never forgive her, and who will ever love her if they don't? The only thing she owns, the only thing in this universe she can express herself with, is her body.

She can't stand here staring into the mirror any longer. Her dad's waiting, everyone's waiting, this is her cue. If she doesn't move, they'll all be trapped forever in these three moments of separateness, waiting for someone to move them forward. Alannah in this grotty little bathroom. Her mum looking blankly out from the window of the bus as it passed her on the street. Her dad, alone and upright in the driver's seat of the car.

She raises the scissors to her neck. The blades part like lips. She takes a deep breath, closes her eyes, opens them again, and in that moment becomes ready.

("Don't overthink it, Alannah." Mrs Baxter again, the words like a refrain. "Let yourself *feel* the music...") No, she's finished with *feeling*, she needs to *do*. She whimpers in fright, but the blades are sharp and eager. There's a faint satisfying *shhhh* sound as they draw together, slicing

CHAPTER TWO

(DECEMBER, NOW)

slicing through the rain, backwards and forwards across the windscreen in a steady two-second rubberised beat. Liam's counting in his head, trying to work out if it's time to check on Alannah and make sure she's all right, or if this is simply that typical female thing of taking longer in the bathroom than most men find sensible. What if something's happened to her? What if there was someone in there already? No, there can't be; the layby was empty when he pulled in. She's been gone for eight minutes and twenty seconds now.

Stop worrying. She's fine. There's nobody in there with her. But what if there is? What if Alannah's talking to them? What might she be saying? *My mum's left us and Dad and me have run away. He's taken me away because my mum's gone mad.* No, she wouldn't say that, of course she wouldn't. But what if she has?

But she hasn't, he tells himself firmly. *There's no one in there and she wouldn't say anything anyway. She's doing whatever it is women do in bathrooms. Get yourself in check.*

Eight minutes and fifty seconds. It's fine. He knows it's fine. The imaginary woman interrogating his daughter is nonsense, something his brain's inventing to account for the way he feels. Retro-fitting circumstances to emotions. Adrenaline sings in his ears.

He's in that state of alertness where he's thinking at least three moves ahead, planning out contingencies and countermoves in a long branching chain of possibilities. *What if she doesn't come out after ten minutes? Go and look for her. What if someone sees me going into the Ladies? Irrelevant: there's no one here to see. What if someone arrives before the ten's up? Tell them the truth; you think your daughter might have locked herself in and you're going to check. What if she is locked in? Ask her to describe what kind of lock, then make a plan to get it open. What if someone pulls into the layby while I'm in there and sees me coming out of the Ladies? Hold Alannah's hand so it's clear I'm meant to be with her, make sure I'm talking to her as we come out. What if someone on the road sees me going in or out and they know I'm going into the Ladies and they think it looks suspicious? Check the sightlines from the road and move accordingly. What if someone sees me and recognises my face? Don't be so fucking ridiculous, you've not been gone three hours and Emma's gone off somewhere and for God's sake, you have to remember you're in charge here, all of this is legitimate. Alannah's your daughter and you're her father and you're entitled to take her away overnight if you fucking want to.*

It still feels wrong, but that's only because it's different. A break in the pattern. A break that Emma initiated by walking out, leaving him to keep the household going while she swanned off and did whatever she fancied, leaving him behind like a dog outside a shop, not knowing if she's coming back at all.

He'd said these words to her, or something like them, knowing even as they were spoken what her answer would be. *What do you think it was like for me when you were deployed? What do you think it was like, waiting and waiting, hardly hearing anything, watching the front door every minute, worried sick every time the phone rang? How did I ever know you'd come home?* She'd thrown that one at him in the kitchen, a few hours and about ten million years ago. And he'd replied –

(shouted)

"For God's sake, I'm not shouting! I'm putting my point across! Why do you always say I'm fucking shouting when I'm not?"

She always says that, it's her winning move. Any time they get into it, when he thinks he's finally getting through, after he's waited and waited for his turn to speak, finally putting his side of the story…

("You're not right in the head, Emma, this shit isn't normal. You're messing up Alannah with the way you behave. I'm not having it, do you hear? You need to get some help, right fucking now, or—")

every time, Emma pulls her ace out of her sleeve. ("You're shouting. You're frightening Alannah and you're frightening me. Stop it.") Of all the things she says that wind him up, her telling him he's frightening her is the worst of all. Mostly because he can see perfectly well she's *not* frightened. He's been in battle; he knows what *frightened* looks like. And besides, nobody could be frightened when they're as in control as Emma always is.

Nine minutes and fifteen. It's fine. It's fine. He'll wait until ten minutes. That's the plan, there's no new information since the plan was formed, therefore no reason to change. Instinct isn't always your friend. Lock yourself down. Alannah's fine.

And, and, and – if the sound of them arguing frightens Alannah, then why does Emma pick the fights in the first place? Emma only says it to make him shut up. She knows he's not shouting, it's simply his natural speaking voice, and the only way for him to stop "shouting" is to stop speaking. Knuckle under and accept whatever she wants him to agree with. That he's the one in the wrong, he's the reason their marriage is going sour, she's not mad and he's not right and everything is his fault and always has been and will be until the end of fucking time.

14

And then, when he gave in, when he did exactly as she asked and stopped talking…

(*Stopped shouting*, Emma insists in his head, that insidious little voice that will never, ever go away, he can already tell that even if he never sees her again, he'll be listening to her voice for the rest of his life.)

Then, she hit him with it. She was leaving. Arms folded. Face calm. Royal flush laid out across the table. Game over. A game he hadn't even known they were playing. Oh, she said it wasn't forever, she said it was only *so she could sort her head out*, but he knew what it meant. What woman or man ever left their spouse for two weeks right before Christmas, to *think*, and then came back and declared that everything was fine and they were still solid and they could all go back to normal and enjoy turkey and presents? This was the first stage in her plan, that was all. She might be as mad as a box of frogs but she could still get herself organised. All those days and nights she must have planned this, all those times they'd lain side-by-side in that bed, their daughter asleep on the other side of the wall, all those nights he'd thought they were all right, that Emma was the one thing in his life he could count on, the one stable point he could build the rest of his existence around, and all that time she'd been planning…

Nine minutes and thirty. How did it come to this? How has he let her do any of this to him? But he'll show her. He'll fucking show her. He'll show them all.

His bravado sounds stupid even inside his head. He'll show them all, will he? And who's *they*, then? He's not going to get through any of this with swagger and bluster. He needs to be cold and logical. Cool heads win wars and stay alive and go home safe to their…

Keep it together, Liam. Keep it locked down.

Nine minutes and forty. He's got a stopwatch running on his phone, but that's just to check his old skills are intact. He's always been good at timekeeping, the counter in his head keeping perfect, effortless pace with the movement of

15

the universe. They'd been told in training that at times of stress, their heart rate would rise and time would seem to slow down, because humans keep track of time by the beat of their heart. It had been a joke among the lads that he always knew exactly what time it was, no matter how much stress they were under. Mr Data, they called him at first, and then, more wittily, Hannibal ("because your pulse never gets above eighty, mate, even when you're eating her tongue"). Girls in pubs sometimes edged away when they heard the explanation for his nickname. Emma hadn't, though. She'd laughed and said she loved serial killer movies, and which was his favourite? Nine minutes fifty. He checks the stopwatch and sees the numbers flick over in perfect synchronicity.

"What's your favourite serial killer movie?" she'd asked, and he'd said *"Saw,"* not because he particularly liked it but because he very much liked this girl with the pretty face and the tough attitude, and *Saw* was the first one he thought of. She'd told him *Saw* wasn't a serial killer movie, it was a slasher movie, not flirty-argumentative but firm and corrective, someone putting a small child straight about something important, and somehow that was the sexiest thing he'd heard a woman say, ever. He'd even had that specific thought, *you're not a pretty girl, you're a sexy woman.* She'd reeled him in that night, sunk her hooks in so deeply he couldn't even feel them. Ten minutes. Check of the phone, yes, definitely ten. Time for a recce.

He's about to unfasten his seatbelt, but then a set of headlights sweep across the layby. He forces himself not to duck, not to do anything that would make him look as if he's trying to hide. *What if it's a woman who gets out and she goes into the toilets and Alannah's stuck in there? Use it; get out of the car and ask her if she'd mind checking if your daughter's all right. What if you end up on the news and she remembers meeting you in the layby? So stay in the car and wait it out. What if it's a woman and she goes in there and Alannah's locked in and she remembers you not going to check on her*

and that sticks in her mind more than if you asked her to check?
No, wait, it was only turning round, it's gone. Ten minutes
and twenty. Where's Alannah? What's she doing? Don't panic.
You've got a plan, no, it's all right, there she is. She's put her
hood up, walking as if she's crossing a stage. That posture
trained into her from years and years of dance lessons.

(Does she even enjoy it? Emma swears it's Alannah's
passion, the one thing she loves beyond all others, but he's
never been sure what to call the look on his daughter's face as
she works at the barre he'd screwed to the wall of her room.
The relentless repetition, her face and back gleaming with
sweat. The pitiless way she looked at herself in the mirror.
That expression in her eyes. What was the name for that
expression in her eyes?)

"Everything all right?" And what if it's not? What then?
He's in charge of her welfare, he has to know what questions
to ask. He's got a girl to care for, a girl on the cusp of puberty,
and what the fuck does he know about the things that might
be going on in her tight little body?

"I'm fine."

"You sure? You were a while."

"I'm fine."

She's not fine. She looks as guilty as sin. What's she been
doing? What what what? He's thought for a while now that
there's something not right with Alannah and the way she
looks at her own body. He's not an idiot, he knows these
things happen. Emma keeps telling him it's nothing, he's
imagining things, that Alannah's a dancer and dancers have to
be body-conscious, have to be critical, and does he really think
he knows better than she does given all the time he's spent
away from them both? (And when he pointed out that he'd
been out for almost two years now and he spent more time
around the house than she did, what did Emma say? "Stop
shouting, you're scaring me and you're scaring Alannah.")

"Nothing you need to tell me?" His voice is louder than he
meant it to be, he'll admit it this time, but that's not because

he's angry, it's because he doesn't want to make Alannah feel ashamed. "If there's something wrong you need to let me know, all right?"

"I'm fine."

"Not got your period unexpectedly or anything?"

"Dad!" Her face is crimson. "I haven't… I don't—"

"Hey, I'm only asking. Eleven isn't too young these days, is it? Nothing to be embarrassed about. Happens to half the world once a month." She's shut her eyes. He's pretty sure she wants to stuff her fingers down her ears too. "I do know about this stuff you know, I'm—"

His throat closes. Is he still married?

"All right." He's had enough of arguing with women tonight. He's had enough of arguing with women to last the rest of his life. "Sure there's nothing you want to tell me? Then get in. No, not the front this time, the back. You'll be more comfortable."

He can tell she'd prefer the front, but he wants her to go to sleep. If she's right next to him, even if she sits in total silence, she'll stay awake for longer, and he won't be able to think. Acting as if you expect to be obeyed without question is the best way to ensure you're obeyed without question. He looks at her and waits. Sure enough, within a couple of seconds, Alannah's climbing out of the front seat and opening the door to the back.

"Good girl," he says. "Wrap up in your duvet. That's it. You need to sleep. It's really late."

He lurks at the layby entrance, then joins the flow of traffic. He has no idea where they're going, but he has to keep moving.

("And don't think you're getting Alannah if we split. She's coming with me." Emma's parting words to him as she left him in the hallway. As if Alannah was not a person with thoughts and desires of her own, but a chip in the endless card game their relationship had become. As if Emma could see into his head, see all the thoughts he'd kept tightly battened down, thoughts about Alannah's dancing and Alannah's bitten nails and Alannah's barely touched dinner plate and the way Alannah looked at herself in mirrors, the sideways glance and flinch for ordinary times, the aggressive pitiless stare at the practice barre in her bedroom. As if Emma knew she was being judged as a mother. As if she understood what he would do, even before he did it. Mad, but not too mad to plan. "Don't think you're getting Alannah." She'd said these words to him as he was still trying to process the unbelievable fact that his wife, his *wife*, was in her coat and holding a large bag that wasn't quite a suitcase and standing on the wrong side of the doorstep. She was already three moves ahead of him.)

Well, she's not going to win that one. She's not going to beat him. He's going to get ahead of her. He has Alannah now, she's in the car with her dad and she chose him and whatever comes next, they're in it together.

His foot itches against the accelerator. The gap in the right-hand lane isn't really big enough but he drives into it anyway, changing down two gears and gunning the engine. The Vauxhall that's now behind him slams on the brakes and flashes its lights in protest, but he raises one hand to the driver in a gesture that could be an apology or a threat, and the Vauxhall backs off and after a few minutes of driving, turns off at a roundabout and disappears. *That's right, pal. Don't mess with me.* In the back seat, Alannah is almost asleep, soothed by the slow rhythm of lights that flick over her skin and fade, flick and fade, flick and fade. He's not sleepy at all; he's perfectly awake, prepared for whatever the rest of the night throws his way. He's combat-ready and he's going to win. He and his daughter are going to be safe.

You fucking coward. His contempt for himself has Emma's voice. He'd like to put the radio on but he's afraid of waking Alannah. The hum of the road creates the illusion of peace, and as the sodium-lit night folds around him he feels himself sinking into a silence so deep

CHAPTER THREE

(DECEMBER, NOW)

so deep I'm not entirely sure it's real.

I'm in a room I suppose I can call mine. I have a card with the room number and my name, *Emma Wright*, that I can use to charge things, which surely means it must, in some way, belong to me. I'm lying on a vast white bed. I'm trying not to move too much because the perfectly ironed linen is so intimidatingly beautiful. If I sit up – carefully, preserving the arrangement of the scatter cushions – the low-set window with the frame like a cartwheel will lead my gaze across the emptiness of the park. Right now, the space beyond the buildings is inky-black, but when the Sun rises I'll watch it soar over the land where the deer used to walk, perfectly bisected by a tree-lined avenue. New arrivals can be seen long before they actually arrive. This must have been useful for the people who lived here, in the days before it was a hotel. Not for me, though. I don't need to keep watch. Liam won't be looking for me. That's one thing I know deep in my gut.

And even if anyone tries to seek me out, I've covered my tracks pretty well, I think. I booked the time off, but I told the headteacher I was needed to chaperone Alannah, and she gave me permission because it looks good for the school to have a pupil doing something so prestigious. My laptop's in my overnight bag, my phone's switched off and shut away in my bedside table at home, and I've cleared my browsing history from both. My credit card statement's online only, and password protected. I'm cocooned in secrecy. I wonder who I'll be when I leave the chrysalis.

I haven't left Liam. That's the truth I need to hold on to. This isn't an end. It's a pause. A ceasefire. A chance for everyone to regroup, for the casualties to be cleared off the battlefield. At some point the ceasefire will end, but that doesn't mean straight back into outright war. We might choose something completely different. We'll have to. We can't go on the way we have been. It's so quiet here I can hear the air pressing against my eardrums.

I never thought I'd be nostalgic for the days when Liam disappeared for weeks or months at a time, while I held my breath until he returned. Being a military wife – he's been out for two years but I'm still a military wife, just as Liam is still a soldier – wasn't how lots of people imagine. My house didn't become a beautiful man-free haven; I didn't float blissfully on a cloud of sisterhood. I was the same as any other single mum – juggling work with childcare, keeping the cogs of the household turning – but with the added bonus of that constant background anxiety, a lurking shadow that licks the cream off everything you're doing, every small moment of joy. *What if today's the day?*

Watching the news never frightened me. By the time it's broadcast, everyone who matters already knows. Instead, I was acutely conscious of my own front door. I knew the shapes to dread, the tall figures in full uniform, very clean car parked discreetly outside. I paid close attention to delivery estimates from shipping companies, and once swore in the face of two Mormons whose neat silhouettes momentarily stopped my heart. I looked forward, then, to the day it would end, when Liam would get his papers and find his next adventure (an ordinary one this time, retraining as a teacher or a plumber or an accountant, the possibilities dizzying when I lay awake and tried to picture our far future) and we'd all become civilians.

My belly's full of fish, which I chose because I don't like cooking fish and so don't often get to eat it. Langoustines to start with, giant orange monsters with their eyes black and beady, claws saluting outwards from the bowl. I tore their heads off before peeling off their shells. After that, I gorged on baked sea bass, sopping the juices with the extra bread they offered me without prompting. I was glad to have been seated in a corner.

At the table in the centre of the room was a young couple. A man with thick fair hair and premature windblown creases around his eyes, and a woman. He was attractive, but I spent more time watching her. Her hair looked as if she'd spent no time at all styling it, as if she'd simply run her brush through it and it had miraculously fallen into that shape, a thick, ordered fall tumbling to the base of her slim shoulder blades. For her starter, she ordered something in a terracotta pot, and dipped hunks of bread into it. When she offered some to her partner (he ate straight from her fingers, and looked at her with such innocent longing) the ring finger of her left hand glittered like a tiny star.

I wanted them to be loud and obnoxious and spoiled and entitled, but they weren't. Their words carried only enough for me to catch the drift of their conversation. Of course I eavesdropped. Who ever ate a meal on their own without eavesdropping?

They were excited, giddy with it, thrilled to bits with this outrageous pre-Christmas treat. Her dress was slightly too formal and he wore his suit as if it was strange to him. They talked about the food, about their room, about the extra hours they'd worked to afford them, about the days off they'd sacrificed in return, both of them taking shifts over the Christmas weekend. (I heard *shifts* and imagined a bar, but it could have been a warehouse or a hospital or a call centre or a supermarket.) They laughed about their scruffy little car, out of place in the car park. They wondered at the spa treatments they'd chosen, said how strange it must be to be *one of those people*, who can regularly pay a stranger to wrap them up in warm towels and plaster them in mud. They ate two courses each, studied the dessert menu with unselfconscious intensity, then ordered a cheese board to share. They were *perfect*.

I wonder if they even noticed me. I know I'm not here to be noticed. I'm here to hide, dress my wounds and regroup. But still, I do wonder if they noticed me, noticing them. I hope not. I don't want to be that weird woman in the corner who stared and stared.

It's probably fine. It's easy to disappear when you're alone. In the earlier versions of this fantasy, before *The Nutcracker* had given me a blessed way out, I'd imagined bringing Alannah. Girl time, we could call it, time to bond as mother and daughter. But when you've regularly spent time in the loving claustrophobia of just you and your daughter, you don't crave time together the same way. (Instead you long for time alone, truly alone, in a room that's not yours and contains nothing you're responsible for.) And besides, Alannah wouldn't enjoy watching the beautiful girl with her beautiful lover.

Lying on the bed I'm calling *mine*, I can picture Alannah's reactions as clearly as if we'd sat together in that restaurant, as clearly as if she was lying beside me. She'd order tomato soup to start, because Alannah's made nervous by food and prefers to stick to something she recognises. (The soup would be thick and garlicky, flecked with basil, not the familiar orange goop, but she'd force herself to eat some of it anyway, taking a few token mouthfuls and stirring the rest around the bowl with her spoon.) Like me, she would have noticed the couple in the centre of the room. Like me, she'd find herself compelled to unpick the delicate beauty of the girl.

She'd begin with the face: well-defined cheekbones freckled with sunlight, long neck, slim sharp shoulders, hands and fingers with blunt, unpolished nails, tiny diamond on her left hand, marking her as beloved. She'd trace the curve of the young woman's spine, the effortless lift of her waist rising out of her hips. She'd gaze at the small fold of the girl's stomach, neat and discreet, the small difference between bag-of-bones-thin and slim-but-curvy. And I would feel my own tension rising like a flame, because I would see on Alannah's face the anxiety that haunts her. My girl, my girl who loves to dance, my girl who is strong and talented and so beautiful. My girl, who's on the cusp of becoming a woman. My girl, who's terrified of her own body.

What might I have said to Alannah? *Your hair would look nice that way.* Or perhaps, *I could make you a dress like that.* A change of subject maybe. *Do you want a pudding? Go on, just this once won't hurt, you're so slim anyway it won't make a difference* – when all the while the only words I want to say lurk at the edges of my mouth – *for God's sake, you're beautiful, you're skinny and beautiful and you have nothing to worry about, so where does all this fucking self-hatred even come from?*

Why am I worrying about this? I've come here specifically to get away from trying to manage other people's feelings. Let Liam and Alannah cope without me for once. I'm sick of both of them.

No, that's not true. I'm not sick of them, I love them. I'm just… sick. Sick, and tired. I have nothing left in me to give, no more kind words to apply to their wounds, no more patience to tell them that they're being too hard on themselves, they're fine the way they are, and everything will be all right in the end. They've leaned on me and leaned on me and leaned on me until I'm thin and flat. I'm used up, squeezed dry of empathy. I need to recharge. I can't stand being strong a minute longer. Only two weeks. That's all I need. Two weeks to get my head back together. Liam called me mad, and while I don't think he's right, he's maybe not completely wrong either.

(Except this isn't a cost-free exercise. This will change things, upset the balance, do damage. All the protections I made for them, all the ways I kept them both safe, unravelling. Whether they sink or swim without me, when we're reunited, none of us will be the same.)

I don't want to think. I didn't come here to think. I came here specifically to *not think*. Bed rest for the mind. I thought that meant resting my body too, but now I'm thinking that keeping still is the opposite of what I need.

There's a pool, because of course there's a pool. A limpid pseudo-Grecian haven, half of it under glass and the other half open to the sky.

(How do they keep it clean? Not my problem, of course. I need to stop thinking about the mechanics of how everything keeps going, learn to rely on other people to take care of the details for me. That's the whole point of this week – for me to find a way to relax and let go, or as Liam would probably put it, to become less of a control freak. If he thought I was going to be less "controlling" when I came back, would he throw his support behind my little jaunt? Does he realise that if either of us is in the driving seat of our marriage, it's him?)

Like most women I know, I hate shopping for swimwear. Unlike most women I know, I have the skills to make my own. The practical black one-piece is one of the projects I'm most proud of, because it's exactly what I wanted. It's plain, it's simple, and it fits. When I put it on, I disappear into the background. Nothing to see here. No gaping or crushing in the cups, no wrinkles or sagging at the waistline, no slipping straps. No endless pulling up or pulling out, no gestures that scream *this isn't what I wanted but it was the closest they had.* Just a woman in a swimsuit.

Will it be busy in the water? They're good at creating the illusion that you're the only guest, but even they can't magically empty the pool. However, when I collect my towel from the smiling receptionist, the changing room's deserted. (It's a smooth bland underfloor-heated space of travertine tiles and blonde wood, a style that's a little past its time, but so immaculately clean it can still be interpreted as luxury.

How often must they clean it to keep it free of stray hairs and shampoo smears and water streaks? Are there cleaners hiding in the lockers, waiting to wipe away traces of my presence? Stop it, Emma, it's not your problem.) The texture of the warm tiles feels good against my toes. (I wish I'd painted my toenails, pumiced my heels. But there's never any time, never any time – *stop* it, Emma! No one gives a damn about your feet. Get in the shower and get in the pool and get swimming.)

The vaulted roof and marble columns give me the feeling of a temple. Apparently it used to be a ballroom. The few Christmas lights they've allowed themselves are elegant and discreet. There's a man in the poolside hot tub; a woman swimming slow meditative lengths, tight against the wall. Not empty, but close enough. No danger of being approached and talked to.

I walk down the wide steps and bisect the space between the man and the woman. There's only one way to swim that's appropriate here, a slow dignified breaststroke that barely disturbs the water. The reflections on the ceiling quiver and fracture, then resettle into a new shape. The three of us float in our pods of silence.

This is the opposite of Liam's idea of fun. He likes waterparks, splashing jets and sudden soakings, tubes to fling yourself down, slides ending with a sudden drop into cold water. He likes noise and physical challenge. His idea of hell is to sit still in a clean room and do nothing. The pool's one of the reasons I chose this place; it's something I can't have unless I leave Liam behind.

And Alannah? What would she like? She doesn't particularly like waterparks but she wouldn't like this place either. She'd cringe through the ordeal of the changing room, forcing herself not to cower when the mirrors caught her reflection. Then she'd turn her swim into an exercise, the way she turns everything into an exercise. Building stamina, stretching out muscles, minimising body fat, as focused as if her swim is a mandatory school project.

If she was here, I'd be trying to validate her, telling her how perfect she looks. She'd listen, but then she'd look at me, her eyes travelling over my figure, which isn't bad considering I'm almost forty and I've had a baby but is definitely not a dancer's body, and I'd see her thoughts in her face. She'd be thinking, *is that my future? What if that's my future? What if...*

My stroke's getting jerky and angry, and I'm starting to splash. I force myself to slow down and move smoothly. Stop thinking, Emma. Stop thinking. Alannah's not your problem now. She's safe in her performance bubble. Liam's safe at home. No need to worry about either of them.

I left him on his own. This thought is so sharp and clear, I feel as if I've spoken it aloud. It doesn't matter that I wanted a break, that Alannah and Liam between them have driven me to the cusp of that madness Liam insisted I'd already tumbled into. *I left him on his own.* I can't even claim I did it in the unbearable heat of the moment. I planned every aspect of what I've done, and what I've done is...

Stop thinking, Emma. Liam can manage. He'll have to manage; that's what grown-ups do. Like that time he was deployed and Alannah and I came down with norovirus, and I couldn't ask friends for help because then they'd catch it too. So we sat it out, she and I, and it was gross and exhausting and unbelievably hard but we got through it, and afterwards I actually felt quite good, because as it turned out, I was much tougher than I thought I was. I woman-ed up and I got us both through. That's what Liam has to do now. He's got to woman up. Get through his time of waiting and hoping. And then afterwards, we'll see.

The curtain screening the entrance to the outside section of the pool is the first unattractive thing I've seen here. Between the thick plastic ribbons that separate us from the night sky, slices of cool air creep through. They've done their best, it's free of mould and embossed with plastic diamonds, probably the most attractive plastic strip-curtain available, but some things are incapable of prettiness. I push past it quickly, disliking the way it clings to my hair, and break through into the air.

If the inside is like a temple, the outside makes me think of the fountains at Versailles. I've never been, but I've seen them on screen so often, I feel as if I have. (If Liam was gone from my life, I'd have freedom. I could disappear anywhere in the world. Stop thinking, Emma.) The lip of the pool forms an achingly gracious curve, swelling out from the left-hand cheek of the wall, returning to kiss it at the right. And I'm alone, me and the spotlights and the few stars bright enough to stand out against them. I turn onto my back and float, not caring that my hair is soaking in chlorine and will need thoroughly washing afterwards. I'm invisible because I'm alone, I'm unfindable because no one's looking for me, I float because I'm weightless, and I'm weightless because I have left all my responsibilities behind. I will not think. I will not. I will simply... be.

For a single sacred minute, the illusion holds.

Then there's a rustle and slap of plastic. It's the young man from the restaurant. His skin's smooth and golden, and his hair looks good wet and tousled. A moment later, the girl follows him. Her hair's caught in a knot on the back of her head, held in place with a single hairband so when she takes it down again, one simple gesture will spill it out around her shoulders. A fantasy hairstyle that exists only in movies and TV programmes and occasionally, when the Fates align and the Gods are smiling on you, on beaches and at swimming pools.

I want them to do something out of place, to splash and shriek and giggle, to fumble and rummage at each other's flesh. But they were perfect in the restaurant and they're perfect here too; they swim reverently to the edge and then gaze and gaze, first at the sky, then at the grounds, and then at each other. They look so right; I think I might be sick.

It's silly to feel such envy. They're young and in love, but that won't stop the tide. They love each other right now, but a year from now or ten years from now or maybe in a couple of weeks, that might end. And even if they stay in love, their lives won't be an idyll of country hotel retreats and stars gleaming down on their flawless faces. Their car will break down or one of them will lose their job or the boiler will go in the middle of winter, and they'll worry about how to pay for it. They'll have children and those children will get ill and cost money and need new shoes. They'll get older and fatter and greyer. If they're lucky, none of that will matter, because they'll still be a couple, still love each other enough to hold hands in public and turn towards each other in bed. But they won't be a couple people look at anymore; they won't be the ones who I spot from across an expensive restaurant and feel an instant clench of envy in my calves. They'll simply be ordinary, like me.

I tell myself this, but I don't believe it. What I secretly believe is that they've been blessed in a way I was not, and now will never be. They'll float through their lives on the crest of a shining wave of happiness. Even when they're my age, even when they're older, they'll always be the couple everyone looks at and thinks, *I wish I was them.*

They're still at the edge of the pool, their backs to me. They look like a painting. The girl's head falls onto the boy's shoulder for a moment. It's tender and understated and perfect.

Moving stealthily, I swim back towards the curtain and slip between the plastic fronds. The man and the woman have swapped places. Now he's swimming laps while she takes possession of the hot tub. I wonder if they've swapped places by mutual agreement. I take care not to make eye contact. Back in the changing room, I carry my clothes into a cubicle and hang my towel over the saloon doors. I dress as quickly as I can. I'd planned a nightcap in the bar afterwards, but now all I want to do is get back to my room. I turn the fat iron key in the lock, open the door, then pause.

The whole room looks subtly distorted and disrupted, as if someone's been in here while I've been away. The bedding's rumpled, the scatter cushions disturbed. There's a handbag on the bedside table, and the clutter of possessions beside it look scruffy and unattractive. Someone's been in my room and messed it up, and my sense of outrage is so entire and unquestioning that it takes me a moment to realise what the problem is.

I've paid to be here. It's my room, my bed to mess up, my space to occupy. But now that I'm here, I feel as if I'm intruding. I want this room to exist, I want it to be mine, but as soon as I've come into it, it's spoiled. My overnight bag is the wrong style. My clothes aren't pale or floaty enough to hang convincingly in the wardrobe. My shoes are ugly. My toiletries bag is marked with make-up. My presence is the problem.

Are you sure you should be here? It's so quiet here I can't block out my own thoughts. *Are you sure*

CHAPTER FOUR

(1988)

"—you sure you know where we're going?"

"Course I am." Frank is always relaxed, always calm, even when there's really nothing to be calm about. It's one of the reasons why I married him, and now it's one of the reasons why I sometimes think of leaving him. Not the biggest reason, of course. But one of them.

"I could look at the map." In the back seat, Liam looks hopeful. Liam's good at map reading, enjoys being able to follow along with where we are and where we'll be going next. It's easy for me to forget that he also enjoys Frank's freewheeling delight at getting deliberately lost, going somewhere he barely knew existed before he arrives there. Our son needs us both. That's one of the reasons I stay, keeping the façade in place, keeping my mouth shut. That, and the fact that I'm not yet certain, and until I'm certain I won't do anything to change how our lives are.

"We're fine, I know the way. Well, roughly. I'll know the right road when I see it. It's a bit difficult to describe." He puts a warm hand on my thigh. "I know, I'm being annoying. I promise it's worth it."

He's sometimes disarmingly perceptive, this man I

married. I let his hand remain in my lap. The way it makes me feel is another reason to stay. Each time the scales tip, he says or does something that tips them back again.

If it was just Liam and I making this journey, I'd have planned out the route the night before, listing each road and junction in a spiral-bound notebook. Liam would sit where I am now, road atlas spread across his skinny knees, reading out instructions and following our progress across the pages. He'd be watching the road signs, getting ready to tell me when the next turning's coming up. We'd be a team. With Frank in the driving seat, we're both reduced to the status of passengers, no responsibilities but also no control. Am I happy with this? Is Liam? He's watching the road even though he doesn't have a job to do, looking for clues.

"Are you hungry yet?" I'm not bothered for myself, but it's almost one o'clock, and Liam's entering the ravenous bottomless-pit phase the mothers of older boys have warned me about. "Frank, we'll need to get some lunch soon."

"Okay." Frank's smiling and humming, enjoying the bright day and the clear view. "I'll keep an eye out for a café or something."

And here we go again. The slip and slide of weights in the scale. I've let Frank be in charge, and he's not up to the job. If Liam and I were on our own... No, this is ridiculous, I can't leave my husband for this. If I'm going to leave him, let it be for the bigger things, the ones that make me sweat with terror in the night...

"I don't think there'll be a café."

"Something always turns up."

"Look at the road. It's barely two lanes wide. Nobody's going to open a café down here. What kind of trade would they get?"

"Jane." I marvel at his expressiveness, placating and anxious and exasperated all at once. It's amazing how much he can cram into a single word. He should have been an actor instead of a salesman.

"It's all right." My voice sounds tight. Maybe I need to do some breathing exercises. "I've packed sandwiches. Stop in the next layby, it'll be fine."

"What did you do that for? You didn't have to."

"Well, it's a good thing I did because I don't think we'll find anything else, do you?" I don't want to be like this, I don't want to be the nag who points out his failings, but sometimes I can't stop myself. "Find a layby."

"Hey, look at that." Frank brakes and points to a sign by the side of the road. I instinctively glance in the rear-view mirror to see if there's someone behind us. My eyes meet the reflection of Liam's. He's doing the same thing. Is he being forced to grow up too fast? Or am I passing on my lack of trust to my son? "The Rumbling Tum. Layby, two miles. There you go."

What sort of food will they sell at The Rumbling Tum? Will it be somewhere you go inside and sit down? Or will it be a van, handing out bacon sandwiches from above? Will Liam like the food? No, it'll be fine. If it wasn't for Frank, I'd never do anything new. I'd never be doing this, driving through winter sunshine knowing no more than to *pack for the beach*. Who knows what will wait for us at the end? A week in someone else's caravan, perhaps. Maybe a small hotel. I'd prefer the hotel, but I don't like to get my hopes up.

"There you go." Frank points over the steering wheel towards the layby that curves away from the road behind a thick verge of grass. "The Rumbling Tum café. Perfect. Okay, quick pit stop here and... Oh no, hang on... it's closed. As you were."

"Stop here anyway and we'll have the picnic instead. Oh for God's sake."

"Sorry." He's already accelerating onto the road again. "Too late to stop."

There was plenty of time to stop. I don't say these words aloud, but I can see from Frank's uneasy sideways glance that I don't need to. Frank always says I'm telepathic, that he can read my thoughts from half a street away. Sometimes I'll reach the corner of our road and think, *And I bet even though he's home early, he hasn't bothered with the washing-up.* Then I'll come into the kitchen and find Frank standing uneasily at the sink, elbow-deep in suds. But then there are the other times, when I come home and he's waiting at the door and he kisses me until my knees turn weak, and we go into the bedroom without saying a word and this is one thing he's so damn good at, so intuitive, so *skilled.* When the time and tides are right, this man of mine can send me literally out of my mind, my head empty, my body singing with pleasure, and for the whole of the evening and well into the next morning I don't think about anything at all; I only feel. His hand is on my leg again. Maybe he knows what I'm thinking about. How could I live without that in my life? How could I live without him?

What if Frank is thinking about leaving me?

"There'll be another layby soon," Frank says.

For forty long minutes, there isn't and isn't and still isn't another layby. I sit silent, breathing slowly and steadily. I'm trying, I am. I'm trying so hard. Liam watches from the back seat. My guilt's like a fist around my heart. When finally, another layby appears, both Frank and Liam heave semi-secret sighs of relief.

"Sorry about that," Frank mutters to me as we climb out of the car and stretch. "Should have listened to you, shouldn't I?"

"It's fine," I say. "We don't mind."

Yes, I think. *You should have.*

I spread a waterproof blanket on the grass and lift the picnic from the boot of the car. The freezer-block in the bag means the drinks have stayed cold and the margarine hasn't soaked into the bread. The sandwiches are ham – Liam's favourite – salmon mashed into a paste with a splash of vinegar – which Frank adores – and cheese. There are crisps and fruit and bars of chocolate. I can see how pleased they both are.

This is my family, I think. *We're happy. We're happy*

because we're together. Of course I can't leave Frank. Without each other, we'd both be lesser. I would never have planned this adventure. He would never have remembered to make a picnic. We're a team, picking up each other's slack. We sit on the grass and eat our food, then take it in turns to pee behind the hedge.

After lunch, Liam drifts in and out of sleep for the rest of the journey, the window sweat-sticky where he leans against it. I rest my hand against Frank's neck, and am rewarded with his lovely, lovely smile. The air's growing softer. We must be near to the sea. What has he booked? Will we like it? Can we really afford this? How on earth are we going to...

"Don't worry," Frank says, and I wonder again how it is that he can read my thoughts so accurately. "Trust me. Please, love."

All right, I think. *I will. We'll do this your way.* I close my eyes so I can't see the road, or the signs, or the clock. I give up trying to guess. I surrender myself to sleep.

When I wake, it's to the crunch of braking tyres and the small jerk as the car comes to a stop. The car is hot and disgusting. I'm glad to be getting out of it.

"Liam." Frank is leaning over into the back, patting at Liam's shoulder, as excited as a child. "Wake up, love. We're here." He opens the passenger door so Liam can tumble clumsily out onto the path. "What do you think?"

What do I think? It's hard to say. We're outside a long, low wooden bungalow, set in its own suburban-looking garden with a square lawn surrounded by flowerbeds. The wooden window frames are very neat and white, the wooden walls are very dark brown, and I can smell the creosote from the side of the road – a thick, antiseptic, vaguely comforting smell that reminds me of the local Scout hut.

"It's fabulous," I say, because Frank has done something special for us, and of course he won't want to hear his grand surprise described as *like the Scout hut*. It's an unlikely-looking holiday cottage, but maybe the location's more important. "Can we go inside?"

"Of course we can!" I must have sounded convincing, because Frank's laughing with pleasure. "Let me find the key. I've got it here somewhere... it's on a piece of string with a label on it..."

As Frank rummages through pockets and cubbyholes, I take a moment to size up the house, looking it all over and trying to see it the way my husband obviously does. I need to be careful of my own prejudices here. In general, I don't like surprises. The one time Liam managed to really enrage me was when, aged six, he crouched behind the door of my bedroom and leapt out at me, roaring and grabbing for my legs. The bellow of fury that came out of me terrified us both. *I thought you were going to eat me*, Liam sobbed on my lap afterwards, and I cringed in shame. *I could have been carrying a cup of tea*, I told him, when his sobs had finally faded to a slow snivel and he was calm enough to hear me again. *I might have burned you.* But even though he was only six, he must have understood that the true source of my rage was that he'd managed to startle me. He must have understood this, because he never did it again.

In Frank's hand, the key quivers on its string like a divining rod. He's like a horse on the morning of a hunt, or a fox when it hears the first blast of the horn. Why does this week by the seaside mean so much to him? He holds it out to Liam. "Liam, you want to do the honours while we get the suitcases out?"

"Can he manage?" I ask Frank anxiously.

"Of course he can, woman." Frank kisses my hair. "He can work a key. He's tall enough to reach, look."

And he is. Our son is tall enough to reach the Yale lock of the front door. I slip my hand into Frank's. Of course I can't leave this man. If I left him, who would ever share these moments with me? The key turns and opens up into an oddly spacious hallway that bisects the house like a spine. Liam charges over the threshold. The wooden floor is adorned with a rag rug, slightly askew.

"It's so well-kept," I say. My voice sounds false. I try again. "Has it been freshly creosoted? It looks like it has."

"Yep. Won't need doing again for at least a year. So you do like it? I know it's a bit of a shock, but the deal came up and—"

"Yes, it's lovely." I say, and then, as my brain catches up with my ears, "Sorry, what did you say?"

"Jane, it's ours. For keeps. I bought it. It's for us. It's our holiday cottage."

The shock roots me to the doorstep.

"I… Sorry, what?"

"I bought it for us. Early Christmas present. It came up at auction. Couldn't resist. And wait till you see inside, Jane! It's immaculate. The old fella who had it before, he died, he was very proud of it, apparently. His children were thinking of keeping it on, but they decided they'd prefer the cash. And now it's ours!"

"I… My God, I don't know what to—"

"Fixtures and fittings included," Frank says. "Go on in, love, look around."

Sick and disoriented, I force myself to go inside. It's still so full of its previous occupant that I feel as if I'm breaking in. I open a door and find a lounge with a goldy-browny three-piece suite. Across the hall from the lounge is a dining room, and next to that, a thin little kitchen with a table crammed underneath the window. Beyond the kitchen, beside the back door, is the bathroom. A tiny corridor barely wide enough to walk down separates the lounge from the two bedrooms: one big, one little. The little bedroom has twin beds in it. The bigger one has a bed that would once have passed for a generous double, but now looks almost disturbingly intimate. Frank and I will have to sleep pressed together.

"We don't have clean sheets," I say. I sound so ungrateful, but I can't help it. The least of my worries is the very best I can manage.

"Don't worry. The old fella was very clean. Look at the place!" Frank runs a finger along the top of a picture (a sketchy watercolour of boats lying in mud at low tide) and shows me the clean, pink skin. "Spick and span."

"But other people's sheets, Frank." It's not what I really want to say, but everything else is too huge to squeeze past my teeth.

"There'll be some clean ones around somewhere. There's a washing machine as well." He's watching my face, waiting for a smile. "So what do you think? Bit of a bargain, it was."

"Oh, Frank." I can't get my face in order. I put my arms around him instead, hide my expression against his chest. "How can we even afford this?"

"Christmas bonus."

"Big enough to buy us a holiday cottage?"

"Shifted that office block at last. You know the big one? Wouldn't call it a cottage exactly. It's more of a bungalow. It went to auction, we handled the sale, no one bid but me, we got the deal of the century. Don't worry, all right? I just got lucky."

"But there'll be rates and bills and so on. We could have paid off a chunk of the mortgage—"

"Where's the fun in that? I swear to you, it's fine. If it doesn't work out we can always sell up. But let's have some fun while we can, yes?" He kisses the top of my head. "You worry too much."

"Well, you don't worry enough."

"So between us, we're even, aren't we? Let's get unpacked. Liam, you'll be in the little bedroom, all right?"

I should help Frank with the suitcases, but I can't. Instead I hover outside the bathroom while Liam uses it, relieved to hear that the toilet flushes without any fuss and actual water comes from the taps. Perhaps it might be all right. Perhaps if I try hard enough I can make all of this all right. Frank has done an amazing, astounding, miraculous thing for us. He has bought us, of all things, a holiday cottage. We're a two-home family. We're doing fine, doing brilliantly. There's no need for the sickness that's growing in my belly.

"This is ace," Liam says, coming out of the bathroom.

"Very ace. Is there soap in there?"

"Yep."

I peer in anyway to make sure. A cracked bar of green, marbled soap rests in a china dish on the side of the basin.

"You know," Liam says, "the last person who used this soap's probably dead now."

I try not to shiver. I'm being ridiculous. Liam's not going to catch *dead* off a bar of soap, is he? And besides, maybe the old fella's children came in here after he died. I wonder if this was their holiday home too, their retreat when they were small. Perhaps this might be a happy place after all.

In Liam's room, there are two beds to choose from. The one against the wall has a long shaft of winter sunlight warming a woollen blanket and a thick, faded eiderdown. The other one is under the window, which makes me think of draughts. I watch Liam lie experimentally down on the one by the wall, trying it out for size. It's higher and narrower than his bed at home, squeaking and creaking with his movements.

"You can swap each night if you want to," I tell Liam, even though I know that for Liam, choosing a bed is one of those decisions that can never be undone, and this bed against the thin wooden wall will be the one he sleeps in for the rest of time. There's a picture hanging there: a girl with an outsized head and huge cow eyes, dressed in a ruffled pink dress and ankle socks, petting a fat kitten in a way that shows her knickers. Frank rattles around in the hallway, grunting as he drags in our suitcase. How much did he pay for this place? Is it even remotely feasible that he could have bought it with a bonus?

"And you know what else?" He's standing in Liam's doorway now, high and giddy with what he's done. I'll get no sense out of him for hours. I'll have to bide my time. "Walk down the road for five minutes, and you get to the sea. We can come back for Christmas Day if you like. Sandcastles and swimming at Christmas, Liam. How about that?"

It's way too cold for sandcastles and swimming, I think, but do not say, because that would be mean. Without intending to, I catch Liam's eye. He looks sad, as if he's glimpsed something he'd rather not have spotted.

"We can walk down there once we've unpacked," I say. I sound almost natural.

"Unpacking? What's the matter with you, woman?" Frank catches me around my waist and twirls clumsily, knocking a picture askew. "Let's go now!"

The early winter darkness is folded around our new house. We're in the living room; Liam's in his new bed. He's tired, but small sounds tell me he's still awake. Before he can relax enough to sleep, he'll have to let his skin grow accustomed to the smooth cold slither of the eiderdown, let his ears tune out the tick and click of the pipes in the bathroom next door and the soft wooden creaks as the building settles down for the night. I know this because Liam's like me, and in a few hours, I'll have to do the same.

Does the bungalow like its new owners? Is it pleased to have people in it again, eating fish and chips from the paper at the kitchen table, washing-up in the sink that's positioned at the short end wall, so if someone opens a cupboard behind you, you're trapped? ("The old fella built this place himself, apparently," Frank told me as he struggled with the kitchen window, finally flinging it open with a grunt of triumph, and I couldn't quite stop the reply that came to me – "I knew this kitchen had been designed by a man." It could have gone either way, but we were both trying, both determined to be kind, and after a tense second we were laughing, Frank opening all the cupboard doors to shut me in.)

"Bedtime." Frank's eyes are bright and wanting. Desire uncoils in my belly.

"Liam's still awake."

"No he isn't."

"Course he is, he's gone quiet. Come on, I'll show you."
Frank leads me down the corridor. His hand is warm and dry,
delicious against my own.

"See?" He's so confident his son's asleep, he doesn't even
bother to lower his voice. "Spark out. I told you."

"He never sleeps well the first night in a strange place."

"Well, that's a sign this place isn't strange then, isn't it?
We're going to have fun here, Jane, I promise."

"Where did the money come from?" My question's quick
and sudden, perfectly timed to catch Frank out, and I hate
myself for doing this, for not being the kind of wife who
simply accepts her own astounding good fortune. And then a
fraction of a second passes and now I'm not sorry anymore,
because in that moment before he answers, I can hear Frank
getting ready to lie.

"I told you. Christmas bonus at work."

"Which work?"

He laughs uneasily. "What do you mean, which work?"

"You know bloody well what I mean. I'm your wife. Tell
me the truth."

"Oh, Jane…" He's trying to hold me, one hand on the back
of my neck, his thumb caressing the spot I like just below my
ear, and it's hard to stop myself from melting. "Don't be like
this. Can't you be happy for what we've got?"

"You promised me. We *agreed*. No more risky deals."

"It wasn't a risky deal. It was a single transaction, cash
job, I knew everyone involved and they're all good blokes,
so nothing to worry about, all right?"

"There's everything to worry about. What about Liam?"

"They don't even know Liam exists, love." His voice is
low and eloquent, but it's his hand that's really doing the
talking here, stroking and smoothing, making me breathless.
"They barely know *you* exist. I'm just a dull name and a nice
suit and a reliable set of wheels. That's why they pay me. I

41

don't look like the type, so I can pull it off. And they're like that too, d'you see? We fly under the radar. That's why we do so well. Come on, don't spoil tonight. We've had a lovely day, haven't we?"

"You promised," I say again. "You promised, and you broke that promise. What am I supposed to do now?"

"I didn't break any promise. I promised nothing risky, and it wasn't. I promised nothing dangerous, and it wasn't. A nice little bonus, that's all it was. A nice little bonus. And now we've got a nice little holiday bungalow. Early Christmas present." This is Frank; always relaxed, always calm, even when there's nothing to be calm about. "With a nice little bed where we'll be squashed up close."

"And a dead man's sheets."

"He died in hospital."

"And he changed the sheets before he went in?"

"Come to bed, love."

And because his hands are so knowing, so coaxing – because today, we walked on cold sand and paddled briefly in the freezing sea – because Liam's in the bedroom next to us and I don't want him to hear us shouting – because Frank is sure and I am not sure – I do as he says. The soundproofing's much worse than at home. We'll have to be quiet and careful.

Then Frank's hands are inside my clothes and I don't know if I can manage to be either. It's like the tide coming in, washing everything away and leaving only blank sand behind, and we're united at last, making our mark on this new-old bungalow, filled with a dead man's possessions, that's somehow come to be ours.

And if I could fall asleep as fast as Frank does, maybe that would be all that happens. But instead, I lie awake and stare at the ceiling, and as Frank slumbers beside me, I feel the words taking shape inside my head:

How dare you – how dare you – how fucking dare you.

Frank's breath is warm against my shoulder. I try not to let myself dwell on how cold it will be when he

CHAPTER FIVE

(DECEMBER, NOW)

when he wakes, it's because of the cold. He thought he'd
be all right with his coat and the blankets he grabbed from
the back of the sofa as they left. Liam's slept under canvas
plenty of times, under the stars plenty of times more. With
Alannah in the car, adding extra body heat, he should have
been fine. He'd forgotten that mysterious trick cars can pull,
the interior somehow growing even colder than the air outside.
And he'd forgotten how soft he's got since getting his papers.
The chill's deep in his flesh, a chill that will take hours to shift
and may not shift at all before it's time to face their fourth
night in the car.

His internal clock tells him it's just before eight in the
morning. The sky between the trees is turning orange. Thank
God no one's disturbed them in the night. He'd been half-
prepared for a torch through the window, an angry landowner
ready for battle with the trespasser who'd parked his car
behind his hedge, but they seem to have got away with it. At
least this is better than last night's layby, when he'd barely
dared sleep for fear of someone trying to rob them.

Alannah's bundled deep inside her duvet, breathing softly
in a way that's not quite a snore. Is she cold too? She's tied

her hoodie tight around her face, and he can only see her nose and her forehead. Perhaps he should wake her. But then, what comes next? What will they do after this?

He's trying to ignore it but he can't; he absolutely has to pee. Will he wake Alannah by moving? Nothing he can do about that. He inches the door open, wincing as the interior lights come on. Alannah stirs and sighs. When he comes back to the car, she's sitting up, peering out from inside her hoodie like E.T., her duvet around her shoulders.

"What time is it?" she asks.

"Right on eight o'clock."

"Is that the sunrise?"

"What else would it be?"

"Dad…"

"Yes?"

"I need the toilet."

"Go behind the car. Same as usual."

"Won't the farmer mind?"

He can feel himself getting angry, and he knows he can't afford to. She's not trying to be irritating, she's only a kid.

"He won't mind. Rabbits don't have toilets, do they? Or foxes? Or cows? Go on."

"And you won't look?"

"Why would I want to—" he stops, takes a breath, softens his voice. "I won't look. I never look. Off you go."

She hops out of the car, gone before he can tell her to put her shoes on. She always insists on taking her shoes off before sleeping. Now she'll have wet socks. Another problem that could have been avoided. His mouth aches for coffee. He makes do with a can of Diet Coke from the bag of supplies. Alannah hops back inside, teeth chattering.

"The grass is wet," she says. "Did it rain?"

"It's probably dew." What can he give her for breakfast? A Mars bar and a bottle of water, or cold baked beans eaten straight from the can? Which is the least bad option? Alannah's

44

starting to look grimy; they both are. This isn't sustainable. None of this is sustainable.

"What's dew?"

If they had a camping stove he'd have brought that, but of course they don't bloody have one. Catch Emma going camping. "It's water that settles on the grass at night. Don't worry about it." He's supposed to be *good* at this, for fuck's sake. Coping in less than ideal conditions is a core skill for a soldier. But then, he's never been in a situation where he didn't have his kit on him, never had to drag along a small child into the bargain.

"How does it get there?"

"Alannah…" He's trying so hard to manage his anger, but he's tired and hasn't eaten properly, and he has to choose between *keeping his temper* and *achieving absolutely anything else*. He imagines a cooking pot, perilously over-full, lid jumping with steam. "Please stop asking me about the dew. I need to think, all right? Stop talking and get some layers on." He points at the bag of supplies. "Oh, and we need to eat as well. Have a look in there and see what you fancy for breakfast."

Alannah reaches for her rucksack. Is she going to cry? He can't deal with tears. He turns away, telling himself he's giving her privacy. The Sun is cresting the tops of the trees, turning from thick orange to fierce yellow. A good day for a march, a day to get warm and then hot and then power on anyway, striding out with heavy boots and a heavy pack. Instead he's trapped in a field, he and his daughter growing dirtier by the hour and nothing but chocolate and baked beans for breakfast. Her duvet's spilling into the grass. He bundles it back onto the seat before it can soak up too much water.

"Dad."

"What?"

"Am I supposed to take off my dirty things first?"

"No, you'll be fine. But put on some layers."

"But—"

45

"Alannah." *Keep a lid on it.* The pot in his chest, spitting water and steam. Treat it like a job. You can't always enjoy your job. Suck it up and do it anyway. "Put on extra stuff over what you're wearing now, it'll be fine."

"But Mum says—" she stops herself before she can finish the sentence. "Don't I need clean stuff?"

Sudden flashback to peeling his kit off at the end of a week-long march. The way the dormitory smelled when he left to have a shower, then came back in again. He makes himself smile. "You haven't been wearing them long enough to get them properly dirty. Keeping your clothes on keeps you warmer at night and saves time in the morning."

"Is that what you did in the Army?" Alannah's face is hidden by the edges of her hoodie. It's easier to talk to her when she's not looking at him.

"On base you have to be neat and well-presented. Out in the field it's different." There, Emma. See that? My daughter asked me a question and I answered it. She's fine with me. We're fine together. We don't need you.

"But you'd be wearing a uniform," Alannah says, to herself rather than to him. "So you put on the same thing every day."

"There's different kit for different occasions. Like, an everyday uniform and a dress uniform. Different kit for different environments. So if we were deployed to the Arctic, for example, we'd have cold-weather gear." For when they were *in theatre*, that's what the brass used to call it. War as performance. There's a connection here, a way to bond with Alannah. "Kind of like when you go to classes, you have your sweats and leotard and such, and then for a dance show…"

His words trail off into the silence of the dew. Alannah keeps her head down, concentrating hard on pulling up extra leggings over the taut muscles of her legs. He knows what she's sacrificed to be here with him. Should he mention it? No, best not. What's done is done. Let sleeping dogs lie. Alannah reaches for her trainers.

"No, take off your wet socks and put clean ones on. You're

better off naked than with wet clothes. And especially not wet socks."

"Why are wet socks worse?"

"If your feet are wet for too long you get trench foot." His legs are growing stiff. He stands up to stretch them. "When I was... Ah, shit—"

It's just the tiredness, that's all. Tiredness and hunger and tension, joining forces with low blood pressure on a cold morning and conspiring to clobber him over the head. It's nothing sinister, nothing wrong with his brain, all of that's behind him where it belongs. He's tired and dizzy, his vision contracting, his knees letting him down a bit, his brain soaring off into a place he doesn't want to be, but it's nothing, he's fine, he only needs a minute.

"Dad, it's all right." Alannah panicking, because of course she is, she's been brainwashed by Emma. He reaches out to pat her reassuringly, makes a connection. "Ow, ow, Dad. It's all right, it's me, I won't hurt you."

He's all right, he's all right, it's fine. It's passing. He can see again. He's leaning on the car door in a field in a cold clear English dawn. It's fading, it's simmering down, it's going away now. He's all right. He's all right. He and Alannah are both all right. She's standing beside him, patting awkwardly at his arm. It's all fine, a blip, nothing more. How can he make sure she knows not to worry?

"Sorry about that." His voice sounds tight and clipped, but at least there's no panic there. "Just felt a bit... Stood up a bit fast."

"Is it to do with—"

"Alannah. Please listen to me. Forget all that nonsense your mother told you, she's the—" No, he won't sink to Emma's level and start badmouthing her to their daughter. Even if Emma is clearly insane. "Stop worrying, okay?"

(Overheard on the stairs one day: his wife and child, conspiring in the utility room. "Alannah, listen. Your dad's... Look, I don't want you to worry about this, that's my job. But I need you to – if he says anything strange, or frightening, you let me know, okay? So I can sort it out." Alannah, sounding confused, "What sort of things?" And Emma's reply: "Anything you don't understand. Don't stress about it, you don't need to worry, you only need to concentrate on your dancing. But, if anything ever worries you, you let me know. I'll look after you. I promise." He'd forgotten about that moment, simply tucked it out of sight and walked away. If he'd gone downstairs and confronted her instead, would everything have been different? Is there no end to Emma's betrayals?)

"I was a bit dizzy, but I am *fine*." Alannah's expression suggests she doesn't believe him, but also doesn't quite dare to argue. For God's *sake*, why does no one listen when he says there's nothing wrong? Her hood's caught on her ears, messy-looking. He pushes it down impatiently. She flinches as if he's gone to hit her, then lifts her chin and looks at him.

There's something strange about her appearance. Something different. Something at once small and gigantic, almost too big for him to see. Has she put on make-up? No, that's not it.

Then he sees what's happened and he feels a great hollow shock, because she's cut her hair off.

"Alannah." He raises one hand to her newly exposed neck. "What the... When did you do this?"

"On the first night. In those toilets. You remember? When you said I'd been ages."

"The first *night*? You've had your hair like that for *three days* and I didn't..." He's not sure who he's angry with. Alannah for doing this and not telling him. Himself for not noticing.

She shrugs. "It's been cold. I kept my hood up."

"But..." He isn't sure how to even begin. "I mean, why?"

Alannah has always looked like Emma to him, and Emma's face has always been closed and serene, mysterious. With her hair gone, Alannah looks more like him, but he still can't read her expression. What does it matter anyway? *Why* isn't important. Kids do stuff like this without ever really knowing why.

"What did you use?"

She hesitates, then takes the scissors from her pocket. He pushes aside his first two reactions, which are *For God's sake Alannah, these are your mother's dressmaking shears* and *Jesus Christ, Alannah, you could have had your eye out*. He and Emma are no longer a team and he has no obligation to worry about her stupid scissors anymore, and Alannah *didn't* have her eye out with them so there's no point dwelling on what she might have done but didn't, and besides, he's been in places where children her age are trusted with far more deadly things.

What would Emma do? She'd lose her mind, no question. Best do the opposite of that, then.

"It's a bit scruffy," he says. "Needs neatening. Keep still and I'll have a go."

Standing in the shivery orange of the low dawn light, he does his best with the remains of his daughter's hair. She's given herself a sort of bowl cut, with a couple of long strands hanging down like rattails at the nape of her neck. He snips and shapes, shortening it around her ears, trying to keep it even. It's dry and wispy, hard to cut. If he'd thought this through, he would have dampened it down first, run a comb through it to get it into shape. There's still time to do this, it would still be worth doing, but he'd rather stay put and struggle. This is inflexible thinking, a sign that he's not coping as well as he could. He's failing to adapt to the situation and acknowledge his own shortcomings. He's making poor decisions.

He moves onto her fringe, glancing cautiously at her expression. She has her eyes closed, her face serene as a cat being petted in exactly the right spot, as if this is a holy moment, as if she's praying. He hardly ever gets this close to her. Hardly ever has the chance to. Emma's in charge of getting Alannah ready each day, brushing and grooming and adorning her until she's ready to be presented to the world, the perfect embodiment of all Emma's work and care. Now, he's remaking Alannah into an image that suits him instead of his wife. He hacks away, taking it shorter and shorter and still shorter until she's left with a roughly uniform couple of inches length all over the top of her skull.

"You all right?" He pats her shoulder. She nods, but keeps her eyes shut. "Okay. You're done."

She opens her eyes with caution, sliding her gaze sideways towards the ghostly reflection of herself in the car window. Shorn of its length, her hair looks darker, more ordinary. Guilt jabs him hard in the stomach. He holds himself rigid against it.

"There," he says. "That's better."

"I look really different." She's looking at herself, turning her head critically from side to side. "I couldn't see it properly before."

Does she regret it? She's a dancer. Dancers have long hair. It's part of the look. Isn't it? Emma has always cherished Alannah's hair, brushing and combing and styling and curling, gloating over the thick shiny waves. No wonder Alannah was more Emma's child than his. But now he'd shown her. No more hair for her to fondle and fawn over.

"It looks fine," he says. Should he be more effusive? Of course he shouldn't, *fine* is exactly how it looks. If she wanted *pretty* she'd have left it alone. "Get in the car. Seatbelt on. That's it."

"Dad, where are we going?"

It's a fair question, which is why it's so much less okay that his immediate reaction is anger. He swallows it down, pushes the lid back down on the pot. He's in control, not his emotions.

"You sure you're okay about your hair?" Good deflection, but stupid question. What's he going to do if she says *no*? Stick it back on her head?

"Yes, but, where are we? Are you allowed to tell me? I won't tell anyone."

She's only eleven. When he was eleven, he still secretly thought he might grow up to be a low-key British version of Spiderman, tearing around his neighbourhood with his coat buttoned around his neck and a bandana over his face, saving strangers from dangerous situations. Is it fair to tell her the truth?

"I'm not sure," he admits, and finds he doesn't have a name for the way it feels to say these words out loud. "You see, Alannah, the thing is…"

She turns around in the seat so she can face him. Her trainers scrape against the upholstery and leave a long smear of wetness.

"Well, you know Mum's gone away for a few days?"

"To have a little break. Because she hasn't had a break for a long time and she needs to get away." He hates the sound of his fumbled explanation, pouring out between Alannah's little parrot lips. "And she's going to—"

"All right, Alannah, I'm talking now." She stops speaking instantly, her eyes fixed on his face. "That's right. That's what I said. She needs a break, to sort her head out."

"Has she got mental health problems?"

(The words sound incongruous coming from such an unformed, innocent face. Where has she even heard them? As if he doesn't know. *See how you like it when it's being said about you, Emma. You fucking cow.*)

"Well. Yes. A bit. I mean. You saw all that…" He swallows, not sure what to call it. "Stuff. That stuff she had. On the kitchen table." Alannah tries not to flinch, and fails. Well, good. He doesn't want to talk about any of it either. "Look, don't worry about it. None of it, okay? She'll be fine. But she needed a break. And so I thought we could—"

(*do a bunk while she's not looking, because no fucking way will I leave you on your own with her, no way will she turn me into a useless fucking deadbeat waste of space like my dad was, no fucking way will you grow up without me in your life*)

"—have a bit of a break too. Me and you. An adventure."

For a minute, he remembers the adventure she was supposed to be taking, and feels guilty. "The only thing is, I didn't exactly plan it, so—"

"We could go to a hotel?"

They're not going to a hotel. Where would he get the money? He hasn't thought anywhere beyond the moment that he won't even be there to witness. The moment when Emma will walk back into the perfectly nice and normal life she's trying to shove him out of, to find her nest's been raided, her treasure stolen away. Bitch. *Bitch.* He'd give anything to be there to see it. Imagining it is almost as good.

(And what will she do next? He can hear her on the phone to the police, her voice cool and taut with anxiety. His name pinging away on computer systems – bank transactions, credit checks, CCTV in hotel lobbies, requests for identity. Will they look for him? Of course they will. One thing he knows in his bones: no matter what the law says, no matter how much talk of equality he hears, when it comes to children, the mother is in control. He'll be tolerated in Alannah's life only as long as Emma allows him to be there. "My husband has disappeared and he's taken our little girl.")

(*Fuck off out of my head Emma, fuck off fuck off fuck off. You don't belong here and I'm fine and I'm in charge.*)

He clenches his fists, then relaxes them as he breathes slowly out again. When he opens his eyes, Alannah is watching him. Is he frightening her yet? She doesn't look frightened; she's just watching him with that patient stillness they must have taught her in dance class, waiting for her next cue. She'd make a good soldier, he thinks. No whining or chuntering. Calm under pressure. Not like her mum.

"We could go to Granny Jane's?"

"Nope." His mother, pure and ruthless, who drove her husband away because she'd decided he wasn't good enough for their son. (Of course, his dad was weak and pitiful, because he *let* her do it. But that's not important right now. He won't be the same as his dad.) If he went to his mum, would she be on his side? Can't be sure. Best not risk it.

"But she—"

"No. Look, it's not your job to think of where we're going, all right? Trust me. I'll think of something."

"Okay." Alannah is looking at herself in the mirror again, frowning at her own newly exposed face.

For Christ's sake, Liam, he thinks. *What do you think you're doing? She's supposed to be in the theatre right now, rehearsing. And where is she instead? Wearing dirty clothes, sleeping in a car in a field, her hair in a mess, and you're so tired you're like a dead man*

CHAPTER SIX

(DECEMBER, NOW)

dead man's possessions that have somehow come to feel like his. When he first bought the place, Frank gave no thought to the man whose home he was taking over, but over the years his interest has grown.

He knows the dead man's name (or at least, he knows where he's put the documents that would remind him of the name), but he's not interested in tracking down his history, stalking a dead stranger. Instead, he's preoccupied by what his predecessor was *like*. Frank knows he appreciated quality – the three-piece suite that was here when he moved in is still going strong, the cushions firm and rigid, no real signs of wear on the old-fashioned golden-brown velvet. The curtains have resisted fading in the sunlight. The beds creak, but they're sturdy, mattresses undeformed by the pressure of human bodies over ten thousand nights and more. The brogues he found in the cupboard under the stairs, unworn and exactly his size, are the brogues he wears today sometimes when he wants to look smart and put-together.

A wooden home takes much more maintenance than a brick-built one, but he doesn't mind that. Necessary jobs are a useful anchor. Some days as he stands on the ladder, meticulously re-creosoting the walls, he wonders if there's anyone still living here who knew his predecessor, if they even realise he's a different man to the one who came before. Some days he wonders if he's been possessed by the spirit of the man who used to live here. Some days he wonders what will happen to all this stuff when it's his time to leave.

Did the man who came before him live in this same bubble of silence? Did his wife break his heart and destroy his life too?

Until the day Jane took herself and Liam away from him, he hadn't appreciated how much noise other people made simply by being alive. With someone else in the house with you – even if the someone else was angry with you – you had their footsteps, upstairs or in the next room. Doors opening and shutting. The brush of their clothes as they moved, the small disturbances in the air. The rise and fall of their breathing. Now he's on his own, and he sometimes has to fight the urge to break a window or to smash a cup against the wall, simply to hear the sound and remember he's alive.

Of course, he hasn't been entirely isolated. His hyena wife has occasionally been replaced by women who wandered into his life like visiting cats, eating the food he provided for them, stretching themselves into long ecstatic shapes when he stroked them, sometimes clawing at his skin, before making themselves at home on the pillow beside his. At these times, he's woken to the sound of someone else's breathing, to the scent of someone else's sweat. (If he added all this time together, what would it come to? Would it be into the years? Or has he had only months?) But each time he let himself imagine permanence, the woman would get bored, or irritated, or maybe take up an offer of better food or a better sleeping spot or a warmer place in the sun, and wander out again.

Or perhaps the problem was that he was thinking of them as cats rather than as adult human females. It was Jane's fault – or rather, not Jane's fault exactly, but definitely a consequence of having known her. She'd broken his heart and stolen his child and driven him out of his own life, but she was a hard act to follow.

But didn't I do my best, Jane, didn't I? Didn't I do everything I promised? Didn't I buy us a home? Didn't I stay faithful and true, give you a child, make a good life for us, a life with everything we needed and most of what we wanted? And when you decided to kick me out, didn't I do everything you asked of me even then? Didn't I complete the paperwork without any fuss? Didn't I agree not to contact Liam unless he contacted me first? That last one nearly killed me, by the way, but I did it, because I never broke a promise to you, not once. Not even when I could have. Not even when you broke yours.

Is he being too kind to himself, too harsh to Jane? He doesn't think so. He'd played his part, giving her the child they'd both wanted, keeping her in the style she liked. He'd done his job even though he hadn't had any of the benefits he'd expected in return (awkward bear-hugs from a teen grown newly gawky; man-to-man conversations in cars on the way to and from unimportant destinations; understated farewells on doorsteps; a chance to embarrass his son and himself on his son's wedding day).

So, what would Jane say if she was here? She'd say she'd taken as little as she could from him, and been fine without him. She'd point out that she hadn't sat around and eked out the money he sent, but had gone to college and got her teaching certificate. She'd tell him she'd raised their son without him, successfully and well. She'd remind him that she'd even sent occasional updates about what Liam was doing – or, being strictly accurate, what Liam had done, to avoid the risk of Frank turning up unexpectedly. He hadn't seen her for decades but he could still conjure her voice, fill in her side of the argument. (God, what he'd give, even now, for her to be here, arguing with him.)

In the beginning, he'd had fantasies where Jane would lose her job or become very sick – perhaps both, the details weren't important. (Perhaps she would lose all her money to drink or gambling. Perhaps she and Liam would be driving in his neighbourhood after dark for some reason, and she would crash the car and flee to the only door she knew to come to. Perhaps her house would burn down.) He'd open the door and there she'd be on the doorstep. She'd throw her arms around him and beg him to take her back. (Of course he'd take her back, instantly and forever. He wouldn't torture her. *Until death do us part.* He'd keep his promises.) As the years have rolled past, he's winnowed this extravagant nonsense down to its simple essence: a longing for Jane and Liam to return, and *see him.* That's all he wants from life now; to be seen, by the only two people whose opinions still matter.

"There's still time," he says to the clock that ticks on the shelf in the kitchen. The clock was made by a company called Westclox, in a style called Baby Ben. It has a cream casing and large friendly numbers, its face so familiar he could draw it in his sleep. "It could still happen." He knows it won't happen, but he also knows he can't afford to stop dreaming. "Maybe one day." Baby Ben Westclox is a sturdy piece of kit, but he needs winding each day. Frank takes the clock down from the shelf and begins to turn the key.

Jane and Liam are always on his mind when he does this. He's careful not to look, but he can't avoid thinking about the box, tucked onto the shelf behind Baby Ben Westclox. In that box are the few letters and photographs Jane has sent over the years. When the last one came, over a decade ago, he was unprepared for the shock of that scarlet, shrivelly, unformed, beautiful face. He fell to the floor and lay with his cheek pressed against the cool black-and-white floor tiles and sobbed, lay there until Baby Ben stopped ticking and the house turned dark. He hasn't dared look at it again. But there's no unknowing what he knows. Somewhere out there is his grandchild. He, Frank, is now a grandfather.

What have they called it? He feels uncomfortable calling his grandchild *it*, but *them* seems even more peculiar. Is it a boy or a girl? Jane didn't say. The lack of detail was part of the complicated equation she kept running in her heart at all times, balancing off what she felt she owed against what she felt she could get away with not paying. He can picture Jane frowning as she seals the envelope, hesitating by the post-box to double check; *is this definitely right? Have I done enough to keep my conscience sweet, just enough and not a shred more? Yes, yes, it's definitely fine,* and she lets the envelope drop and it begins to make its way towards him.

Somewhere out there is his grandchild. He can see the box where the evidence lies, safely hidden but there. One day he'd love to… His fingers falter on the key at the back of the clock. Best not to think about it while he's holding something delicate. He finishes winding the clock and puts it back on the shelf. Now he can't see the box anymore, so he can let himself finish the thought.

One day he would love to see his grandchild. Nothing big or complicated, no grand gesture. Only to see the face. Perhaps to kiss it. Perhaps to say…

No. Best not to wish for too much. One glimpse, that's all. There's still time. He's still young, or, all right, he isn't *young*, he hasn't been that for a while now, but he feels young inside and surely that counts for something. The number of years he can expect to live is still well in the double digits. He looks after himself. He's strong. He'll last a long time.

What time is it? He's been standing here dreaming for far too long. There must be some task or other he needs to complete. What he'd really like is some work to be getting on with. He still works regularly, although he'd wondered if he'd find himself forcibly retired as the younger kids came into the business. As it turned out, they liked him precisely because he was nothing like them. They enjoyed his incongruity. *You see, Jane? I never broke my promise. I told you I'd never get caught, and I never ever have been. It's as safe as houses as long as you're careful. And I'm always careful. Always. I have to be. I've got a family to look after.*

His mobile phone buzzes against his thigh. When he

takes it out, there's a message waiting for him. They change platforms and communication methods with dizzying speed. Once it was messages passed from ear to ear or hand to hand, muttered phrases and slips of paper. Then there was the era of pagers, then SMS texts, then emails. Today, it's a WhatsApp message. He feels the buzz building in his blood. Thank God for work. It's kept him sane for years.

Because he lives alone and spends most of his time in his house, he's attuned to the sounds of his neighbourhood. He knows the engine-note of everyone's cars, the schedules people follow and the routines they've developed. He can pick out the clatter of new arrivals staying in the holiday cottages scattered along the street, and within a couple of days, he'll often know their names. He's not got as far as identifying the individual songs of the birds in the garden, but he's not far off. The sound of a car pulling up outside his house isn't a surprise, exactly – he does *get* visitors, even if most of them are Jehovah's Witnesses or people selling tea towels – but it's enough of an event to draw him to the window. *Curtain twitcher*, he thinks ruefully, and wonders if his visitor will see him peering and blinking, unable to wait five or six seconds for the gate to open, for the knock at the door.

First out of the car is a tall man in his late thirties (or potentially wildly younger or ludicrously older – Frank's never been good at guessing). There's a child with him. A boy, from the look of his fairly terrible haircut. Both the man and the boy have a scruffy air, as if they've spent the night somewhere uncomfortable and haven't had a chance to clean up. The man looks tense and exhausted, and he's sizing up the house in a way that looks familiar, a set of movements and actions that belong to a different body. Frank's heart knows the truth long before his brain does; he can feel it thumping away against his ribs like a warning, and he has to lean against the window frame.

"Fuck," he says out loud, and then he laughs at his own incongruity – what a stupid thing to say at a time like this!

– and then he has to wipe his face with a tea towel because he's crying at the same time, and he only has a couple of seconds to get himself in order before they'll be at the front door. *Oh, thank you God, thank you Universe, thank you thank you thank you.*

An awkward blur of arrival, Frank not sure what to do with his hands or his face. What words did he speak to ask them inside? He'll never remember. His hands shake as he fills the kettle and takes two mugs from the cupboard. One of them is dusty. When he rinses it, he almost drops it.

His son! His grandchild! Side-by-side on the oversized couch in his living room! The house is ablaze with the new life that's walked in over the threshold.

No tea for the little one, obviously. He takes down a glass and fills it with water, wishing he had something nicer, more fun, to offer. He's dreamed of this day a thousand times, so why didn't he buy a bottle of squash in preparation? The old fella left him a tray, its bluish still-life print of grapes and glasses, still fresh and clear.

His son is here. *His son has come back to him.* Frank wants to hold him close against his heart and smother him with kisses. He wants to sob out all the words he's held inside, to explain himself, eloquently and perfectly, so Liam will understand. *Do you know I sent money? Do you know I looked after you even though she wouldn't let me see you? Do you know I forgive you for not wanting to see me? Do you know how much I love you?* It's hard to stop the tea from slopping over the rims of the mugs.

Liam and the child are sitting where he left them. Liam is tall and bulky, giving the impression of masculine sprawl even though he's sitting neat and straight, taking up no more space than is reasonable. If only he could take his son's face between his palms and stare into it, rediscover the boy he lost.

How did the tall, serious, beautiful ten-year-old boy turn into this frowning hulk of manhood?

"Here you go," he says, and holds out the mug of tea. "Two sugars, wasn't it?" He knows damn well it's two sugars; he's not about to forget the first piece of new information he's had about his own son in over a decade. But what else can he say? Jane would be so much better at this than he is. Things like this are easier for women.

"That's right. Thanks." Liam takes the mug gratefully and swallows down the first inch in a single gulp.

"And, um." Frank realises he hasn't yet been introduced to the child. He isn't even sure if he's looking at a girl or a boy. The hair suggests *boy*, the features are like Liam's at that age, but still he's not quite confident. The clothes aren't much help, since girls and boys all seem to dress alike these days. Does Liam think he knows already? "I've only got water, I'm afraid. Sorry."

"Thank you." No clues in the voice either. The smile is shy and tight. How can he get them through these opening moments? What can he do? What can he say?

"So, I gather you're in the Army," Frank blurts out. (Is he supposed to know this? Will Liam be angry that he knows?) On the sofa, the child draws in a quick apprehensive breath and looks towards Liam.

"Was," says Liam.

"Time to get out and do something new, hey?"

"Something like that."

"Good idea. You been out long?"

"Two years and three—" Liam stops himself so sharply Frank can see the small jerk in his neck as he clamps down on the words. "Not long."

Weeks? Months? Years? What was it going to be? Doesn't matter. I know how you feel. I have a clock like that too. It tells me that it's been twenty-nine years, six months and seventeen days since I last saw you. That's one thing we have in common; that little clock in our heads. Say it. Say it. Break through.

"And what are you up to now?"

"Could I please go to the toilet?" The child stands up. Water fountains over the side of the glass and throws itself across the golden carpet.

"For God's sake, be careful!" Liam takes the glass from the child, puts it down on the tray. "You're a guest, remember? Now apologise."

"I'm sorry."

"I should think so. Go out into the hall and down the corridor. It's the first door on the right."

The child looks uneasily at Frank. *Yes*, he thinks dizzily, *stay there and keep still, let me stare at you. Let me look for traces of myself in your bones. Are you scared? Please don't be scared. My God, what's your dad told you about me? Did you even know I existed before today?*

"I'll mop up the water."

"It's all right about the water, honestly." Frank longs to touch the child in some way. A pat on the head. A stroke of the shoulder. "Don't worry. It'll dry in no time."

"I don't mind doing it."

"Just go." Liam's voice, not a shout, but a command given in utter expectation of obedience. Shades of Jane, who rarely shouted because she rarely had to. No wonder she became a teacher, no wonder her son became a soldier. The child scurries off instantly.

"Sorry about the mess," Liam says as soon as they're alone.

"It doesn't matter, honestly. It'll dry in."

"I know, you said. Still doesn't make it okay."

"Kids are clumsy sometimes. Nothing to worry about." Frank can hear the click of the bathroom door opening and closing. If Jane was here, they wouldn't be talking about a splash of water on the carpet. How are they supposed to do this without a woman to help it all along?

"Um." He isn't sure how to phrase it. "Is, um. I mean. Your mum told me you, um. Told me you were. Is there, um, anyone else joining us?"

"It's only us." Liam's hand is rubbing anxiously against the soft pile of the sofa's arm. Frank only notices because Liam glances down at his hand, frowns, and stops.

"Well, it's great to see you." That false, hearty uplift in his voice, as if he's trying to bring a tedious conversation to a close. Why did he say that? None of this is what he means.

"You've got things to be doing." Liam's on his feet instantly. "No problem. We'll get off."

"No, please! Don't go, you've only just got here. At least stay for lunch."

"Don't be daft. You don't have to feed us."

"Stay and have something to eat. It'd be a pleasure after all this…"

The words *after all this time* hang in the air between them. It's a ridiculous phrase. As if they're faint golf club acquaintances who've met, awkwardly and with little true pleasure, in a railway-station pub, knowing they'll eat a single meal together, then never meet again. The space is too vast. He doesn't know this man standing in front of him. They're never going to connect.

What would Jane say? Something real, something true. A rope thrown across the abyss. The first stage in building a bridge between them.

"We could get fish and chips," he says. "Do you remember? From down the road. It's still there. We could eat them out the paper. They always taste better out the paper."

"We'd better make a move. We might stop there on the way past though. Thanks for the tip-off."

From the bathroom, the sound of the toilet flushing is muffled but audible. The tank refills with a slow sucking gurgle, finishing with a distinctive slurp. The last woman who came here (what was she called again? Karen? Kimberley?) said she didn't know how he could live with it. He wasn't embarrassed then, but he's embarrassed now. What must Liam think of him, living in this place for so long without bothering to fix the cistern?

"I remember that sound," Liam says. His expression is soft and bewildered, and for the first time Frank looks at this strange grim man and sees traces of his lost boy. "I remember lying in bed and hearing that sound."

Holding his breath, terrified he's going to do something wrong, Frank reaches out and puts his hand on his son's arm. The muscles beneath the thin crumpled t-shirt feel like iron.

"Do you need help? Let me help. What's the matter?"

"I can handle it." The softness is gone, but that doesn't matter; Frank's seen an opportunity, a way in. They're on home territory now, familiar ground. He's not much good at emotions. But a problem that needs fixing, a challenge with a definite solution? That he can deal with. "It's nothing major."

"But what's happened?"

"We're taking a break." Liam looks directly at Frank as he says this, as if he's daring his father to pity him. "My wife and me, I mean."

"Oh. I'm sorry."

"Don't be. I'm not."

Yes, you are. Oh, my little son. Yes, you are.

"It's all right," Frank says. "I know how that one goes. Bloody hurts, doesn't it?"

Liam grins. "Bloody does and all."

"Does your mother know?" A mis-step. He shouldn't be asking this. It's too needy, too close to the bone.

"Christ, no!" Liam laughs. "She'd tell me to get my arse back home and sort it out."

"Women."

"You're not wrong."

A connection built on a shared understanding that women are despicable traitors. *Well, tough luck, Jane. I've got a chance to get my son back. You've had him for all this time. Now it's my turn.*

"Need somewhere to stay?"

"No need for that. We'll be fine."

"Don't be daft. I've got room."

"You're busy. We'll find a hotel or something."

"Don't be daft, it's Christmas, they're all booked up. Listen, you working at the minute?"

Liam flushes a dark crimson. "Not right now."

"Good. You can help out around the place, then. Get that cistern fixed."

"Are we staying here?" The child has come back without either of them noticing, and is standing in the doorway, watching them with wide eyes.

"That's right." Liam nods curtly towards the door. "Get your things in."

"If that's all right by you," Frank adds, feeling his heart quail in his chest. Why can't Liam be a little bit tender? Just a hug? A ruffle of the hair? The poor kid must be so confused. But no, the front door's already opening, the small slim figure going down the garden path. That walk, held up from the small of the back like a dancer. A girl after all?

"Thanks for this." Liam places an awkward hand on his dad's shoulder, and Frank prays for the moment to stretch out so he can savour it. "We slept in the car last night."

"Daft lad, you didn't need to do that. You should have come here straight away." *You should have come before, this should be a place you know as well as I do* – no, it wasn't Liam's fault. It was Jane's fault, all of it. *Are you watching, Jane? Do you know our son came to me and not to you?*

"Wasn't sure you'd even be here," Liam admits.

"Where else would I be?" Frank smiles, stretching his face wide and tight so there'll be no room for the tears to leak out. "Last place I was happy was here."

For a quick, shy moment they're connected again. They're getting dangerously close to honesty. It's a relief when the child stumbles back into the house, dragging a rucksack.

"Don't scrape the paintwork." Liam's instantly there, correcting, adjusting. "Pick it up and carry it properly."

"Can we introduce ourselves formally?" Frank steps into the hall, falsely hearty because he's afraid this moment will pass and he'll have missed his chance to find out, once and for all. The child looks at Liam. Liam nods. A small hand is held out. He hesitates, takes a risk.

"What's your name, son?"

"I'm Alfie," the child falters.

So he'd guessed right. Thank God. The picture resolves; the ambiguity settles into place. Frank reaches for his grandson's hand.

"And I'm your grandfather, Frank," he says, feeling the smooth skin under his fingers, squeezing

CHAPTER SEVEN

(DECEMBER, NOW)

squeezing the block of soap between her fingers to see how far they'll sink in. The outer layer's soft, but inside is a solid core.

"It's nice to meet you, Alfie," Alannah whispers to her reflection in the bathroom mirror, then glances guiltily over her shoulder. Soon she'll have to explain herself to her father. How can she explain what she doesn't understand herself? She hadn't meant to tell that man Frank that she was a boy, any more than she'd *meant* to cut her hair off. It was as if *Alfie* had been waiting inside her head, waiting for his cue. *What's your name, son?* And she'd opened her mouth and Alfie had simply… come out. To that man, Frank. That man who's her grandfather.

Is he really, though? Could there have been a mistake? She'd once been transfixed by a nature documentary, where an old man with a comforting voice described animals who had babies without finding a mate. For years afterwards, she'd believed Granny Jane had produced her dad spontaneously, something rare but known. (If anyone could do this, it would be Granny Jane. Alannah loves Granny Jane fiercely, but she's also slightly afraid of her.)

Now, she's going to be sleeping under her grandfather's

roof and her grandfather has a name, Frank, and a face that looks a little like her father and a lot like a stranger's face, and the first thing she's told him is a lie.

Has anyone realised they've gone yet? Probably not. It feels as if huge amounts of time have passed since they left, but in fact what's passed is a huge amount of *stuff*, crammed into an incredibly busy few days. Her dad told Lucy's mum that there was an unexpected family emergency (*no, no help needed thanks, no, we're fine, right, I'll let you go now*) so no one from the theatre will be looking for her. Her mother won't know because she's gone on her break. And she won't care anyway. She'd seen her mum's face, as blank as the bus window.

No, she won't think about that. Her mother's on holiday. What sort of holiday? *City break*; a holiday when you go to a city and walk around it. (How can that be fun? It sounds *awful*.) *Holiday cottage*; when you borrow someone else's house. (Better, possibly, but still a bit pointless.) *All-inclusive*, with pools and water slides and the same buffet each day. (They actually did that once. Only once, though.) *A week in the sun*, when you go somewhere hot and come home suntanned. How can her mother be doing any of these things without them?

She can't get used to her own reflection. She's spent so much of her life being groomed and plaited and curled. Now all she'll have to do is dunk her head in her bathwater, and rub it dry with a towel. Probably she doesn't need a hairbrush anymore. Will her mother even recognise her? Let alone still love her?

"What's done is done," Alannah whispers. *What's done is done*, a phrase her grandmother Jane is fond of using.

"Are you in there?" Her father rattles the door handle.

"Yes."

"Finish up and come out here."

She's not ready for this, she hasn't got her story straight, but she can't hide forever. The bar of soap is a squidged-up mess. She reshapes it as best she can, wipes long streaks of soap off on the towel and unlocks the door.

"Your room's down here." Her dad takes her by the shoulders, steers her down the corridor. Is it good or bad that he wants privacy? Her room has two beds, high and old-fashioned, but she doesn't have time to notice anything else because the interrogation's begun.

"All right. Why did you say you're a boy called Alfie? What a bloody stupid thing to do."

"You haven't told him?" She doesn't want to sound afraid. Her dad despises weakness. She makes herself stand up straight and square her shoulders. (*Slip your shoulder blades down your back*, Mrs Baxter always tells them. *Grow tall. Grow long.*)

"I'm not the one who's a liar. Why should I explain? You can do it yourself."

"No! Please don't make me…" She's doing this wrong; she can see it. Her dad doesn't want to be begged and pleaded with. He likes her when she's strong and capable,

(the way she was in the garage – no, she can't think about that now)

arguing her point rather than pleading for mercy.

"He'll think you're insane," her dad continues remorse-lessly. "Is that what you want? Do you want him to think you're insane?"

"Well then, maybe we could carry on calling me Alfie?"

"And why the… Why on earth would we do that?"

"Because," Alannah says, suddenly inspired, "when they start looking for us, they'll be looking for a little girl with long hair."

"What are you talking about?" Her dad's trying to laugh but it comes out more like a yelp, as if he's a dog someone has trodden on. "Why would anyone be looking for us?"

"Because we've run away." There, she's said it. Now what happens? "Haven't we? That's what we're doing, isn't it? I thought we were running away from home."

He's about to deny it, he's about to lie. Part of her wants him to. ("Don't be silly, of course we're not running away, this is a little holiday, the same as Mum. A little adventure.")

"Yes," he says instead. "We're running away."

She swallows the truth like a pill, forcing herself not to retch. "Because Mum's left us."

"…Yes."

"And you think she won't let you see me anymore."

His shoulders are slumping a little. "Yes."

"Because of… because of—"

"No!" It's almost a shout but not quite, her dad remembering just in time they're in someone else's house. "Alannah. Leave it. It was an accident. Understand?"

"But—"

"But nothing. It was an accident. Okay?" She nods. "Say it out loud so I know you understand."

"It was an accident."

"That's right. Nothing to do with any of this."

She desperately wants to believe him.

"But when Mum comes back she'll be angry," she persists. "She'll want us to come home. And if they look for us, they'll be looking for a man, and a girl with long hair called Alannah."

"For God's sake. I'm your dad, I'm allowed to have you."

"Dad."

"And it's not like my… It's not like Frank doesn't know my name, is it? If he hears about us somehow, he won't think, *oh well, it must be some other bloke with that name and that face and a kid about the right age* and switch over to *EastEnders*, will he? What? *What?*"

"I…" Alannah says, and then stops. Does she dare? *I want to keep you safe. I want us to be able to hide. I want…*

"Come on. Don't play games. Say it or shut up."

"I want to stay with you."

She doesn't know the name for the expression on her dad's face. His hands clench into fists, then relax again.

"Alfie?" It's her grandfather, knocking at the bedroom door. "Am I all right to come in?"

"Yes."

She can feel the vibrations in the floor as her grandad moves closer to the door. The boards must go right under the wall.

"I brought you a towel," he explains as he comes in.

Alannah takes the towel guiltily. She'd assumed she was meant to use the one hanging on the radiator. Was that a special towel that she'll be in trouble for using?

"Shall we go for fish and chips, then?" Her grandfather's looking at them both as if he's expecting them to disappear. This must be so strange for him. Like something from a fairy tale. She knows this because it feels the same for her. She's been whisked away from the life she thought she was living and dropped into a strange new land...

"I'll walk down with you," her dad says.

"Want to come along as well, Alfie?" Her grandfather half-raises his hand as if he'd like to take hold of hers.

Her dad's watching her, waiting to see what she'll say, what she'll do.

"Maybe I should unpack my things," she says.

"No problem. I mean, if that's all right with your dad?"

Her grandfather is looking at Liam. Liam is looking at Alannah. Alannah makes herself meet her dad's gaze. *Drop your shoulder blades down your back. Be tall. Be long.* Are any of them saying what they really want to say?

"All right." Her dad gives her a nod. "No messing about though, mate, you hear me?"

She can hear their footsteps echoing down the corridor. The floor feels good under her feet, the boards offering less give than the floor of the studio but more than her bedroom at home. Somewhere in a parallel universe, she's in a studio right now, wearing her girl's name and her long hair, practising until her legs tremble, and Granny Jane is coming to see her perform three nights in a row and her parents are coming for the last night and her mother is sane and loves her. In this reality, her mother has left them, and Alannah has short hair and a name that's not really hers and her dad is with her and a strange man is telling her he's her grandfather and somehow, somehow she has to hold herself together.

There's a chest of drawers in the corner. She opens her rucksack and starts putting things away.

The fish and chips are divine. It's disgusting to eat them, she knows it is, but they taste so good and she can't stop herself. Her grandfather watches approvingly, nodding as if there's nothing wrong with a dancer shovelling a week's worth of fat into her mouth at a single sitting. Afterwards there's a box of Celebrations, which she manages to refuse. (Sometimes when she listens to her ballet teacher talking about the plot of *The Nutcracker*, she thinks about being sent to the Land Of Sweets and wonders what it would feel like – surrounded by all that sugar, unable to eat any of it because she'll put on weight and be too heavy for pointe work and look dreadful in her costumes.) In the bath, the skin of her belly presses outwards, gorged with food. She ought to make herself sick. She's done it before when she's been coerced into eating something she knows she shouldn't, but she's afraid they'll hear her.

But at least she's clean. (God, how *disgusting* was the bathwater when she let it out? She hadn't known water could go that colour.) And now she's going to sleep in a proper bed. She cleans her teeth in the basin, and puts her toothbrush in the glass. (Will that be all right? Will her grandfather mind his toothbrush sharing space with hers?) Still wrapped tightly in her towel, she scuttles into her bedroom.

Does she like this room more or less than her bedroom at home? The two spaces are so different from each other, it's like trying to decide if she likes tigers more than elephants. The walls are white and wooden. There are two beds. There's a picture on the wall, a little girl with a giant head petting a kitten. There's the single chest of drawers that holds her clothes. There are no books. There's a squat metal oblong in one corner that clicks and ticks and sends out waves of heat, looking simultaneously like a modern addition, and like a piece of technology from a long-forgotten time.

What should she wear to bed? Her pyjamas are cream flannelette with a print of ballet dancers. Alannah could wear them. Alfie can't possibly get away with them. She puts on a long baggy t-shirt and leggings with a neutral print of skulls and crossbones. It's fine, boys can wear leggings too.

"You ready yet?" Her dad sticks his head around the door. "Well done. Into bed. I'll tuck you in."

She's too old for being tucked in, but she lets him do it anyway because everything feels so strange, and if she doesn't have at least one familiar thing she might float away into space. She climbs into the bed beneath the window. Her dad presses the blanket tight against her, pulls the slithery thing like a duvet up to her chin, and runs his hand over her shorn head.

"All right in there?" Her dad's hand presses down a little as if he, too, is afraid she'll float away. "Warm enough?"

She nods.

"Did you leave your dirty clothes in the bathroom? No? You sure? Well done." He hasn't called her *Alfie* yet, settling instead for the neutrality of *mate* or *kid*, but he hasn't given her away yet. "How about your towel? Did you pick it up?" Her stomach drops. "It's all right. Just this once – *just* this once – I'll sort it out for you. But remember in future, all right? We're guests here." His words are stern but his face is smiling, as if he's happy to be here. Because he looks so calm and peaceful, she decides to risk a question.

"Which bed did you sleep in when you were little?"

"The other one, actually. Why?"

"I only wondered."

"Well, now you know. Need a glass of water?"

"No thanks."

"Okay, then. Night night." He goes to the door, flicks out the light switch.

"Dad." It's easier to ask for things in the dark.

"Yes."

"I need some new clothes."

"What? I told you to pack—"

"I only have girl's socks and girl's knickers and girl's pyjamas."

"Alannah—"

"Please, Dad." She could say, *It's nearly Christmas*, but she won't. She won't mention Christmas at all. Her gift to her dad will be not to remind him of what he's taken her away from.

Her dad's sigh is heavy and deep.

"I'll think about it. Now go to sleep. And no messing around. You hear me?"

She's alone in the dark, but not really, because she can hear the deep rumble of her dad and her grandfather talking, the chatter of the television in the background. She wonders what they're talking about, whether they're finding it easy or difficult. They have a lot to catch up on, but she knows how hard it is to start a conversation with your dad when you haven't seen him for a long time.

Her bed's far more comfortable than the car, but she's at the point of tiredness when even falling asleep requires more energy than she's got. Heat throbs out from the box in the corner, and a smaller, thinner wave of coolness creeps in from outside. Turning onto her side, she finds a small place in the wall where a knot has fallen from the wood. When she pokes her finger through it, the cool night air licks at her skin.

Alannah scoots down and presses her mouth to the hole, imagining she can taste the sea. She stays there until she falls asleep, breathing

CHAPTER EIGHT

(2002)

breathing as quietly as I can, not wanting Liam to know that his mother's hidden behind her own garden fence, listening in to his driveway conversation with the girl he's brought to meet me.

"Why have you brought a plant in a pot?" Liam asks, and I can hear that while he isn't exactly mocking, he's surprised by this girl – Emma – doing something so strange and exotic. He's been raised by me and me alone; he ought to be attuned to female behaviours. But as he's grown up, he's put on a veneer of puzzled masculinity that now feels like it was always a part of him. ("Mum, why do you have five different pots of cream for your face? Why have you got a box in this drawer full of brand new birthday cards? But what kind of emergency would it be where you'd need a birthday card but you wouldn't be able to go to the shops?") He shows his love by gentle teasing. Now he's teasing Emma, whose face I haven't even seen yet, as they stand on the doorstep before ringing the doorbell and I stand mouse-still behind the fence and listen.

"It's a Peace Lily," Emma says.

"But why have you got it?"

"It's for your mum."

"But you don't even know her. It's not even Christmas yet."

"It's good manners. She's giving us dinner so I'm taking her a plant. What's so funny?"

"Will you bring a plant every time we see her?"

"No! I don't know, maybe not a plant. And not every time. I just want her to like me."

"She'll like you. Why wouldn't she? And why would it matter if she didn't?"

Emma keeps quiet, but I know what she's thinking. *Because she's your mum and she raised you and you love her.* Her anxiety parallels my own. Emma wants me to like her for the same reason I want her to like me: because we're going to be in each other's lives a long time, and that will be much easier if we actually get along. She's brought me a plant even though she didn't have to for the same reason I've cooked delicately flavoured roast chicken with fondant potatoes and raspberry mousse for dessert (even though I didn't have to). A mutually good first impression is important.

There's no point saying this to Liam. My lovely boy has grown into the most uncomplicated man you'll ever meet. The subtexts and undercurrents and passive-aggressive conversations – all the little psycho-dramas between women who love the same man in two different ways – are about as real to him as Santa Claus. He's heard about them, seen them on television and in movies, but he doesn't believe they happen in the real world.

But Emma's brought me a plant. I've made her dinner. We've already decided to like each other, so this is going to be fine.

It's time for me go to inside, put on my official meeting face, begin this official meeting. Still, I linger a moment longer, because this is my last chance to spy.

"Is it weird, coming to see her in a different house?"

"Nah. The other place was only a building."

("Home's about people, not buildings," Liam said when I told him I was thinking of selling his childhood home.

He's unsentimental about houses. A good trait in a soldier. Something Emma will have to learn too, if they make a go of this. They'll be moving a lot, taking their home with them. And where will I be? Waiting here, for them. Waiting to be invited. Waiting for visits. I'll be fine. That's as it should be.)

I creep through the back door, scurry through the kitchen, the dining room, the sitting room, into the hall. The inside of my house is very quiet. It never seems possible that we're so close to the motorway, that there can be people walking around among traffic that six minutes ago was thundering along at eighty miles an hour.

I will my heart to slow down. Am I about to meet a friend and an ally? Or am I about to start a war? I open the door. On the doorstep is Liam, and beside him a tall young woman with long brown hair, a pretty face and a determined expression, holding a plant in a pot. Our eyes meet.

"Mum." Liam puts his arms out and folds me into them. "Nice to see you. This is Emma."

She's no delicate princess or shrinking violet, not one of those candyfloss bits of fluff Liam once had such a weakness for. She's a woman and not a girl, and that's a good thing, because I can see from the look on Liam's face that Emma is the one. Emma and I smile at each other, and I look at her smile and her capable hands and her gift of a plant that she's holding out to me, and I think, *this one is strong*.

"Is this for me? It's lovely. Is it a Peace Lily?" My fingers caress the leaves. "I'm Jane. Come and sit down. I'll make us a drink."

I can decorate my house exactly how I want it, no man to please, and the result is a room that I know Liam finds overly feminine. The sofa is chintzy and floral, saved from Laura Ashley horribleness by bright Scandinavian scatter cushions and a pair of gingham easy chairs. Will Emma admire my taste? Or does she think I'm a silly old lady? I'm turning into a silly old lady, lurking behind the door while the kettle boils, wanting to hear what's being said when they think I'm not listening.

"Don't do that," Emma says, and I know exactly what Liam's doing. He's never seen the point of scatter cushions.

"They're in the way. What else am I supposed to do with them?"

"You lean on them, of course." They're teasing each other, I can hear it in their voices. They love each other enough for arguments like this to be playful.

"They're not compulsory."

"It's rude to put them on the floor though."

"How can putting my mum's cushions on the floor be rude? No, come on, tell me. I really want to know."

Emma's laugh is low and sweet. "Okay, then. I don't want her to think I'm the kind of woman who approves of a man who puts other people's cushions on the floor."

"You what?" Liam's laughing too now, both of them laughing together.

"When you take on a man, people judge you for the stuff he does. You must know this."

"You're mad."

"And you're an idiot."

"And rude. Don't forget rude."

"Come here, rude boy."

The silence must mean they're kissing. In the kitchen, the kettle bubbles wetly, and clicks.

"She's lovely," I tell the mugs, quietly even though I'm two rooms away and they'll never hear me speaking. "She's lovely. She's lovely. And we're going to get on brilliantly." I load everything onto a tray – milk, sugar, teapot, mugs. I'm used to carrying my own heavy objects. Single parenthood and single living toughens you up in all sorts of ways you don't expect.

Still, it's nice to get back to the living room and find Emma opening the door for me.

"Thank you. Liam, clear the books off that coffee table. That's it."

There's a neatly-stacked pile of cushions on the floor by the sofa. I know already who made them neat, treated them with care. And if I hadn't known, the way Emma bites her lip as she looks at them would tell me anyway. I could be cruel or kind here. There's no question which I'll choose.

"I know," I say quietly as Liam obediently gathers up the books and stacks them on the floor. "I know what Liam's like about cushions. He's been driving me mad with it for years, and now he'll drive you mad with it for years too. Unless you can manage to train him out of it. I never did, but he'll take more notice of you, I expect."

And it's a risk, I know it's a risk. I don't want her to think I'm strange or that I've been listening at doors (even though I have been listening at doors and, after years of living by myself, I probably am a bit strange). But it pays off. Emma responds to my conspiratorial smile like a plant to sunlight. We want to like each other. We do like each other. Our mutual relief sits in the room like a third guest.

Because Emma and I are women, we seal our alliance by talking and talking and talking. Emma tells me she's a teaching assistant. I could assert my dominance (*oh, it's good not to have too much responsibility, isn't it? I was a teacher before I retired...*). Instead I say how much I appreciated my own TAs, how unfair it is that they're paid so little. Then I say, "Anyway, Liam says you have a business too. Handmade clothes, is that right? If I say it's your *side gig*, will you laugh at me?" because I want her to know I've paid attention, that Liam's talked about her and I've listened. We talk about online marketplaces and photography and costing and pricing, about people who think *handmade* might somehow mean *cheaper*, as if the whole point of the Industrial Revolution was to make things in a more expensive way. I've already guessed that she made the dress she's wearing, but I let her tell me that anyway, and exclaim in delight. I'm a teacher; I'm good at giving praise that people value.

We talk our way through lunch, carefully trading information, stressing over and over to each other *I'm on your side, I'm not a threat, there's room in Liam's life for both of us.* She briefly mentions her mother, the lightest possible touch – "I don't really have any family so I decided I'd pick the nicest city I could afford." What she's really saying is *do you know my parents are still alive but my dad left us for someone else and my mother fell apart at the bottom of a pill bottle and now I don't see her anymore?* I do know this, and I tell her so – "I did the same, it was only me and Liam so we only had ourselves to think about," which really means, *yes I know, I know and I do not judge, I understand what hard times look like and you can trust me not to pry.* I can almost see a chunk of prickly armour fall away.

Does Liam hear any of what we say between the words? Of course not. He's somewhere else by this time, doing the washing-up, I think, or possibly cleaning the kitchen, happy because we're getting along, not really considering that we might not have. Emma and I are looking at photographs. She lingers and murmurs over Liam in his various childhood forms. It pleases me, her hunger to get to know him so thoroughly. The album ends on Liam in uniform.

"The rest are on the mantelpiece," I say, and although I haven't invited her to do so, she's so confident in her welcome that she goes to look for herself, hands reaching for the first frame so she can examine it more closely, and then…

The noise that comes out of my throat is undignified. Uncivilised. A muffled banshee screech that I have to smother behind my hands. Emma looks at me, her lips parting in shock. Has she seen it?

Yes, she's seen it. I can see it through her eyes, how it must look, the insanity of it. An odd assortment of dusty, dirty things, out of place in this clean little room. Behind the photo of Liam's passing-out photo, arranged in a little pile like an offering. A scrap of fabric. A twist of hair, tied with wool that was once red. A yellowed baby tooth.

What does she think of me now? Mad, a mad old woman, making charms and keepsakes to protect my boy, when he goes out into those places in the world that want to eat him whole and spit back his bones. It feels as intimate as if she's been through my underwear drawer, as if she's seen me naked.

She looks at it, and then at me, and she knows, we both know, what's at stake in this moment. She could give me away to Liam, tell him *do you know what your mother's got on the mantelpiece?* She could relegate me in a few words. She could drive a wedge between us, take control of him.

But what she says is,

"Is it true Liam bleached his hair once? I can't imagine him blond. Do you have any pictures of it?"

And what she means is, *it's all right. I understand that this is something secret and sacred, something that must be done but never spoken of. We are two women together, and I will never, ever tell.*

And I take a deep breath, and reply,

"I think I might do somewhere. Let me have a look."

And what I mean is, *thank you.*

Then Emma's on the sofa beside me, the moment passed, the two of us turning pages of photographs, lingering on one of Liam dripping with water, his hair an ill-advised shade of platinum. And I say, "I got him with the garden hose, he was complaining about being too hot," and Emma asks me when that would have been, and I tell her and she nods and she asks something else and I don't really hear her but it doesn't matter because what we're really doing is burying the bad moment, layering on good, skilled, civilised moments to disguise the brief minute that was neither of those things.

And when Liam finds us flicking through the album and laughing at him, he has no idea that anything important has happened.

"You hang on to this one," I tell Liam as they leave, and although I'm murmuring to Liam, Emma and I both know that I want her to hear too. "She's a keeper." And Liam – who, man that he is, will never understand the secret ways women have of speaking to one another – murmurs back, "Mum, I'm going to marry her if she'll have me." And I chuckle against his cheek and pat him kindly on the arm and wave them off.

As they climb into the car and turn around towards the motorway I think, *yes, yes, marry her. Marry this one. This strong lovely girl who you've brought to my home and who's seen the things that must be done to keep you safe and who didn't laugh or look away. She's the right one for you. She'll take care of you. You think you're strong, my darling son, but you still need looking after. The idea that men are stronger than women is the biggest lie*

CHAPTER NINE

(DECEMBER, NOW)

lie here forever on the cushions on the living room floor, bored out of his mind. Is he the only one awake? Liam doesn't want to move until he knows his dad's ready to start the day too. The big downside of a wooden bungalow: when someone moves in one room, everyone else feels it happen. He won't give his dad the chance to be kind about getting up before he really wanted to.

He hears the creak of Alannah's door. She obviously doesn't share his worries. What's she doing? Maybe getting herself some breakfast. After three days of roadside café food and Mars bars, she must be craving genuine nutrition.

Before leaving the living room, he rebuilds the sofa, folds up the blanket and pulls back the curtains. The weather outside is yellowish, greyish, watery, uncertain: rain or sunshine, could go either way. The kitchen's empty, as is the bathroom. He hurries past Frank's bedroom door, uneasy at the intimacy of hearing his father, the stranger, drawing deep breaths that are not quite snores. Alannah's bedroom door is open a crack.

She's dragged the heavy swing mirror away from its corner and improvised a practice space, because of course she has. The wooden towel rail from the bathroom has been moved and is now a makeshift barre. Her phone is stuffed into the back of her leggings, the wire of her earphones threaded up beneath her t-shirt as she dances to music only she can hear. The effect is eerie, made stranger by the shape of her shorn head.

Liam's seen her dance before. He's survived endless ballet recitals, endless minutes of *other people's children* prancing around before the golden moment of *his daughter* as she hopped onto the stage in bunny ears or skipped across the boards like a lamb or leapt in some stiff netted skirt thing and flung her arms over her head. But it's been a while – *how long has it been?* – and in the interim, something's changed.

She's really good at this, he thinks to himself. *Shit. When did that happen? What have I done?*

She's supposed to be in a studio, with her friends, rehearsing for her role of Clara's brother in *The Nutcracker*. Instead, she's dancing in front of an improvised mirror to music from her phone, in a crappy wooden hut in a fading seaside town. But there'll be other chances, there must be. He'll find a way to make it happen. His daughter, oblivious, dances on. Will she ever forgive him? Of course she will. She doesn't mind, *she doesn't mind*, it was her choice.

He can hear his father stirring now, the creak of the bed and the movement in the floorboards and the slow scrape of the door. Frank comes to stand behind him, watching the child he thinks is his grandson, lost and absorbed, sweat soaking through the back of the t-shirt, working harder than either of them can imagine to make each movement look effortless. The look of soft surprise on Frank's face is a mirror of his own feelings.

"I didn't realise," Frank murmurs, and then stops. "I mean, I know I'm being old-fashioned."

Liam keeps quiet.

"Silly really, isn't it," Frank says. "Boys can dance too, can't they?"

"Yup."

"Does… um, does he want to do this professionally?"

"We'll see."

Alannah stops dancing, wipes sweat from her face and neck, flings the towel onto the bed. Fumbles with her phone. Begins again.

"Hard-working little bugger, isn't he?"

Liam doesn't like the way Frank sounds. Possessive, proud, affectionate. As if he has some right to Alannah. Is a genetic connection really so powerful? Alannah turns, dips her arm to one side, looks up and sees them watching, and the spell's broken and she's clawing her earbuds out of her ears and blushing and apologising and a few minutes later they're all in the kitchen, eating cereal from bowls and trying not to crunch too loudly because the silence between the three of them is hard to sit with.

"Got plans for today?" Frank asks at last, placing his spoon in his cereal bowl.

A plan. Yes. He needs a job. A place to live. A school for Alannah to attend. A whole new life, set up in the few short days before Emma comes back and finds out what he's done. That means he has to make a plan, quietly and calmly. Failure to prepare means preparing for failure.

"Got some life admin," he says. "You?"

"Thought I'd walk down to the beach maybe. Then you can have the house to yourself."

"It's your house. You don't have to go out."

"Don't be silly, I don't mind. Do me good to get some fresh air."

"We could all go," says Alannah.

"Oh." Frank looks from Alannah to Liam. "Well, if you'd like to."

"If *you'd* like," Liam says, passing the burden of gratitude back Frank's way.

"Would you like that, Alfie?" Frank's looking at Alannah in that soft, fond way again, and Liam swallows a blade of wild jealousy. *Don't you let him in, Alannah*, he thinks, *he*

85

might act fond, but he won't hang around if things get difficult, he's not to be trusted – but Alannah's nod seals the deal.

For fuck's sake, Liam thinks. *I've got things to do. I really have. And now we all have to go to the beach.*

The strip of shops is as shoddy as any he's seen, but the beach is flat and clean, dotted with people even though it's almost Christmas and the sky is freezing. Bereft of their womenfolk, the three of them walk out onto the sand in silence. Liam in the front. Frank in the back. Alannah the buffer between them. A solemn parade.

Out on the flats, they fumble to a halt. A fine thin wind peels off the dusty top layer and scatters it over their clothes and faces. There's something else that has to happen now, some action that kick-starts this trip and turns it into something other than two men and a girl standing in a row, staring speechlessly out to sea. Liam doesn't know what it is yet, but in a minute, he'll think of it. Men can do this too, of course they can. It's not the absence of both their wives that's creating this bizarre pool of silence.

Frank pats Alannah's shoulder. "If you go down to the wet sand and write a wish, if the sea washes it away before anyone can read it, it might come true." Alannah smiles politely, but doesn't move. "Trust me. I know what I'm talking about."

"Did you ever try it?" Alannah asks, and Liam has to swallow a chuckle at the polite-old-lady tone that comes out of her mouth. She sounds like the Queen meeting a commoner.

"I did," says Frank, poker-faced.

"And did it come true?" *And what do you do for a job?* Liam thinks. *And do you enjoy that? Splendid...*

"Course it did. In the end."

"That's nice," says Alannah, still not moving.

"Why don't you give me and your grandad some space," Liam says.

"Oh!" Alannah blinks. "Sorry."

"No," Frank protests. "I didn't mean that."

"Yes, you did," Liam says. Alannah's already gone, jogging obediently down towards the water.

"When you were little, there was this theory that boys do better with direct instructions." Frank scuffs at the sand with one toe. He's wearing jeans and industrial-looking boots. If his dad wore dark brown brogues, slightly scuffed, and a pair of well-pressed trousers, Liam would feel as if the world was as it ought to be. "Maybe there's something in it after all."

She's not a boy, Liam thinks, already weary of the thought.

"Do you remember coming here when you were little?"

In the months following the separation, Liam relived those two days so obsessively that for a while, they felt more real than reality. Then he locked it away in a quiet place in his head and moved on. "Not really."

"I know it probably wasn't the happiest..."

"No, it wasn't that." He doesn't want his dad feeling sorry for him. He doesn't want his dad feeling anything about him. "It was a long time ago, that's all. Why?"

"That second day..." His dad is smiling to himself, as if he has a pleasant surprise for them both. Liam draws himself together, wary. "Oh, look at that. He's writing a wish."

Down at the waterline, Alannah's bent double, carving at the sand. What's she wishing for? She'd had what Emma had insisted was her heart's desire, but when it came to it, she chose him.

Then he hears voices, a clatter on the road above them, and Alannah stares up the beach, and for a slippery treacherous minute, he's a small boy again and his father is his God and he can't stop the smile from invading his face, because he remembers, he remembers, he does. The way they looked. The way they ran. The dull thunder against the sand.

There are seven of them today, a raggedy assortment illustrating the sheer range of shapes and sizes horses come in. A feathery-hooved piebald giant, with a Roman profile and a noble curve to his neck, who picks his feet up high and snorts into the breeze. A nervy red chestnut with delicate legs, prancing like a child before being brought back into line by his rider. A sturdy grey mare, the matriarch of the group, ridden by a sturdy grey woman who matches her perfectly. Another, smaller, grey with the pretty head and graceful form of a circus pony, who puts her ears back and nips when other horses enter the patch of beach she's deemed her personal space. A fat black barrel with stumpy legs and an attitude the size of a planet, who even the nippy grey mare keeps a wary eye on. A patient-looking brown horse who watches wearily from the sidelines as the others flounce and squeal. And bringing up the rear, a shining black mare with a ridiculously long mane and a thick tail that almost touches the sand. *If horses made porn, that horse would be a star*, Liam thinks, and wonders what's the matter with him to have such a thought.

"Now do you remember?" Frank murmurs, and although Liam shakes his head stubbornly, he does, he does. The way they looked. The way they ran. Being scooped up by one of the riders, solid arm holding him tight...

"Alfie!" Frank is waving to Alannah. Alannah starts obediently up the beach towards Frank, stopping to gaze longingly at the horses as they walk in sedate single file down to the waterline.

"They're beautiful," Alannah says breathlessly as soon as she's within earshot.

"They're from the local livery stables. They come at low tide for a gallop. Apparently it's good for their muscles."

"You know them?" Liam hadn't meant to ask.

"A bit. You know how it is when you live somewhere a long time."

Liam's never had this, because he's never lived anywhere long enough for it to happen. Emma would say she'd never had that either, but she had it easier than he did. Whole swathes of time when he was on deployment and she was at home, building her own network, making herself independent of him. Preparing for the day when she could pull the rug out from under him.

"They're beautiful," Alannah repeats. "Oh!"

"What's the matter?"

"They're going to run over my wish."

"It doesn't matter," Frank says. "Having it trampled by horses is as good as having the sea wash it away."

Alannah bites her lip. "I don't want them to read it."

"Horses can't read," Frank says, not laughing.

"No, the riders."

"They'll be moving too fast to read anything in a minute. Yep, see, look at that."

The horses have broken into a flowing run, necks stretching, tails streaming. At first they're bunched together, and Liam wonders if they'll collide and fall. Then the nervy-looking chestnut takes the lead, and the others stream out behind him like the tail of a comet, the stumpy pony labouring mightily to stay close to the rest of the herd. *You go for it, mate*, Liam thinks, admiring its determination. They tear along the sands, then just as suddenly slow down again, the riders sitting straight and bouncing in their saddles, pulling tight on the reins. The horses are like children, nudging at each other with their long noses, tossing their heads and breaking into short little bursts of purposeless direction. He can hear the laughter of the riders, the exasperated shout as the littlest one takes a mean nip at the plump brown bottom of the only horse that's behaving itself.

"That was lovely," says Alannah fervently.

"I'd better go down and say hello," says Frank, and Alannah catches her breath. "No need to come with me, I won't be a minute."

"Could we go too?" Alannah almost whispers it, as if asking is forbidden. "To see the horses."

"All the way down there again?" Frank laughs. "You'll be worn out."

Liam can see Alannah's incredulity. It's barely a hundred feet to where the horses are standing. *Old man*, he thinks, with some satisfaction. *My daughter's a dancer. She could run up and down twenty times and not get tired. We both could.*

"Besides," Frank says, frowning towards the horses, "I don't know how safe they are. They're very excited, look at them jumping all around."

"Oh, come on," says Liam, impatient. "You let them take me for a ride when I was—" he clamps his mouth shut, but it's too late. He's let the memory go free. Frank is turning towards him, his expression tender with amazement and pleasure, and Alannah is looking at him too, a wild hope growing behind her eyes.

"Well, then," says Frank, and that seems to be the signal for all three of them to file off down towards the waterline.

The group of horses is becoming less organised. Two of the riders direct their horses into the sea, the horses pushing eagerly into the waves as if they've done this before. The red horse is being made to trot a figure of eight, while another rider looks on and calls out instructions. Liam can't see why a horse that can trot a figure-of-eight shape would come in useful, but presumably it's part of a wider training plan.

"Frank." The rider of the large sensible brown horse raises one hand, sweeps his gaze over Liam and Alannah with well-mannered surprise. "How are you keeping?" He has exactly the sort of plummy, authoritative voice Liam would have predicted.

"Good. You?"

"Can't complain. *Stand*, Sergeant." The brown horse stops pulling on its reins and stands like a statue. "And, um –?"

"Liam, this is Hugh. He runs the livery stable and riding school." Frank hesitates. "And this is Liam. He's my son," he adds, sounding almost aggressive, as if Hugh might not believe him. "And the little one's Alfie."

"Pleasure," says Hugh. Liam takes the offered hand and shakes it, telling himself that Hugh isn't trying to be condescending. It's not the other man's fault that he is, quite literally, on his high horse. Hugh turns to Alannah and puts one finger to his hat. "Pleasure, young man."

"Hello." Alannah is looking at the horse. The horse looks back, and lowers its nose in a friendly manner.

"Hold your hand out," Hugh instructs. "Nice and flat. That's it. Let him have a sniff. There you go. Now stroke his nose." Alannah dabs cautiously at the pink velvet muzzle. The horse accepts this graciously. "Nice and gentle. That's the way."

Alannah strokes the horse's nose one more time, then steps back as if she's completed a precarious task and is afraid of upsetting something. There's a strange little pause whose meaning Liam can't quite unpack, Hugh and Frank looking at each other as if they're both waiting for something to happen. Is Liam intruding somehow? No, that's stupid.

"Want a ride?" Hugh offers abruptly in Alannah's direction. Alannah catches her breath. "Thought so. All kids like horses." He turns in his saddle and waves across the beach. "Shauna! Shauna!"

You'd do all right on the parade ground, Liam thinks to himself. He's used to people shouting but he doesn't enjoy the plumminess of Hugh's voice, ringing with generations of quiet privilege. *Posh twat. No, stop it. He's being nice to your daughter. Don't be a fucking misery. Keep it together.* He offers Hugh a smile that feels artificial even to himself. Fortunately, Hugh's looking in the other direction. The enormous war-horse-looking creature trots towards them. The rider's thin and whippety, with a hard, pretty face and thick hair in a short bob.

"Take the kid for a quick turn around the sand, would you?" Hugh points down to Alannah with his stick. Liam feels his hackles rising. "Lift him up as far as you can and let Shauna pull him on. Don't worry, Jupiter's a gentleman."

Just do as I tell you, my man. Let me give your child a little treat to lift it out of its working-class gloom for a moment, so

I can go home and feel good about myself as I scrape up my foie gras pâté from my plate with my enormous silver spoon. Liam takes his revenge by grasping Alannah under the armpits and lifting her effortlessly up towards the woman on the horse, earning a surprised eyebrow from Hugh and a smile of pride from Frank. *And Jupiter is a fucking stupid name for a horse and all.*

"You all right there?" Shauna's smile is small and cold. "What's your name?"

"Alfie." Alannah is either so thrilled she can hardly speak, or so terrified she can hardly move. "We're really high, aren't we?"

"Don't worry, I've got you. Grip with your calves and grab onto that strap there. Got it? Don't worry, he won't do anything unless I tell him to. Ready?" A small nod. "All right then."

At some invisible signal from Shauna, Jupiter steps out across the sand, arching his neck and lifting his feet high. The prints he leaves behind him make Liam think of dessert plates.

"Bloody comedian," Hugh remarks, bafflingly. "Walk down after if you like. Shauna won't let him do anything too dramatic."

Off you go, peasant, and leave your father and I to talk. Liam's half-tempted to stay just out of spite, but then he'd have to listen to Hugh talking. He follows Jupiter's tracks down to the water, and amuses himself by imagining all of the ways he could achieve Hugh's death, using only what's available right now. Frightening the horse would be a good one. Get it to rear or bolt, something sudden enough to dislodge Hugh from his saddle, and then keep chasing so it dragged him along the ground. Or if he came off cleanly, he could grab Hugh before he had a chance to get himself together and strangle him. Although strangling was tricky. Easy to think you've finished the other guy off when they're only unconscious. But once he was out for the count, he could drag him to the water, leave him face-down in the waves…

Jupiter and his passengers have reached the water now, and turned so they're facing along the beach. Liam can see Alannah, small and vulnerable in front of Shauna. For a moment, they stand motionless, a noble silhouette against the horizon. Then Jupiter springs forward, and they're racing across the sand.

What is that stupid fucking woman *thinking?* Alannah's never *been* on a horse before. She'll never stay on, she'll be off in a minute, and then, those terrible pounding hooves, and Alannah's head, not even wearing a helmet…

He runs after them, no plan in his mind beyond *get to Alannah*. If anything happens to his daughter, he will shoot that horse through its pitiful pea-brain and eat its heart, paint himself in its blood and build a bonfire and burn Hugh and Shauna to death.

And then, as quickly as the gallop began, it's over. Jupiter slows to a jouncing trot. Alannah tossed into the air with every step, Shauna's arms steadying her – then he's walking, and then standing still, and Alannah is fine, not falling, not crumpled and trampled, but perched in front of Shauna on the high saddle. He slows his run as he gets closer, not wanting this strange woman to see his panic.

"Enjoy that?" There's a glint of laughter in Shauna's eye. *Once I've got my daughter back*, Liam thinks, *I could spook that fucking horse so fast and so badly you'd be off in a second. Think you'd enjoy that? Because I would.* "Slide your leg over his neck and turn sideways. Steady on, don't kick him. That's it. Now jump down and let your dad catch you."

Another moment, and Alannah's beside him. Shauna lets the reins go and Jupiter stretches his neck, blows a deep rattling sigh through his nostrils.

"Thank you." Alannah's voice is filled with emotion. He still can't tell if she enjoyed the ride or not.

"Easier to sit to a canter than a trot," Shauna says. "Well done on not falling off." She gives Liam a small smile. "He did all right for a first go. Maybe bring him up to the stables some time for some lessons."

"We don't live here," Liam says. "Thanks for the ride though."

"Can I stroke him?" Alannah is looking at Jupiter longingly. "To say thank you? He is a boy, isn't he?"

"Sort of," says Shauna. "He's a gelding."

"What's a gelding?"

Shauna looks at Liam. Liam deliberately doesn't catch her eye. *You started this. You deal with it.*

"A female horse is a mare. A male horse is a stallion. But stallions are a nuisance, they fight and boss the mares around and argue with you. So most male horses have an operation, and, after that, they're geldings, and they stop fighting and wanting to mate and can start earning their keep."

"So, they have an operation and they… stop being boys?"

"Not really. He's a different kind of boy, is all. I'd better get moving, he's getting fidgety." Shauna picks up her reins and clicks her tongue. Jupiter, who was showing no signs of fidgeting, moves obediently off. "Maybe see you again."

Over my dead body, Liam thinks. *Or maybe over yours.* His dad and Hugh have finished talking, and Hugh's horse is trotting towards the main group.

"That was amazing," Alannah says. "I thought I was going to fall off. But then Jupiter went all smooth and fast and it was lovely. Have you ever done that, Dad?"

"Only once."

"Did you like it too?"

Yes. The memory is suddenly complete in his mind, bright and demanding. *Yes, yes, exactly that.* Different horse, different rider, but the same beach, the same kind of weather, the same kind of sensation. The same exhilarated terror. It's too easy to remember here. And with the memory, something else. From the depths of memory, Hugh's face, much younger and atop a different horse, talking to his father for a few moments, then looking at Liam. *Want a ride?* How weird that he's still in the area. How weird that he and Alannah have this in common. Frank is waiting for them, watching and smiling paternally.

"Reckon the sea's got your wish yet?" Frank ruffles Alannah's hair.

Alannah looks at the sea.

"I think so."

"What did you wish for? Another ride on the horses? No, don't tell me or it won't come true."

The horses have already left, leaving a churn of sand to mark their passage. Alannah is watching the sweep and retreat of the waves. Frank and Liam begin the slow stump up the beach's subtle incline.

"Funny," Frank says thoughtfully. "I couldn't tell if he was excited about that horse, or petrified. Wonder what he did wish for?"

"No idea." He's got plenty of ideas, but he won't share. He won't let Frank see anything. As a teenager, he'd lie awake at night and picture fierce reunions, create impassioned and eloquent speeches detailing every aspect of his pain, speeches that would make his father weep with remorse, before showering Liam with gifts and affection. But he's an adult now.

"What's her name?" Frank asks. "Your wife, I mean."

"Does it matter?"

"I only wondered. If you don't mind telling me."

"She's called Emma." No need to be childish. Even if he wants to be.

"And is it definitely all washed up now?"

"I... Why would you think—"

"It's all right, son," Frank says, and for a terrible minute Liam thinks his father's going to pat his arm. "Nothing to be ashamed of."

"It's not like that," Liam says, unsure what he's even talking about. (*What's not like what? What does that even mean? Can't you talk to me properly for once?* Emma, still in his head even though he's left her. She was the one who got on the bus, but he's the one who's got their child. He's the one in control.)

"But she has left you," Frank says, as if he's trying to explain something to a very small child. "I mean, that's why you've come to see me now, isn't it?"

"Actually, no she hasn't. She hasn't left me." Liam can hear his voice rising. He forces himself to slow down. "It's the other way round. I've left her."

"I'm sorry."

"Why? You never met her."

"Did your mum get on with her?"

"Like a house on fire." Liam laughs, trying to break the tension. "Sometimes I think she prefers Emma to me."

"That's why you came to me, then."

"Well, it wasn't because of the incredible job you did being a father," Liam says before he can stop himself.

They fix their gaze on the small figure of Alannah, scribbling messages in the sand for the ocean.

"That's fair," Frank says at last. "I wasn't up to much."

"Doesn't matter. Mum did everything."

"I did send money."

Liam considers replying to this, but silence seems more satisfying.

"I was only going to say," Frank says. "If you needed some space. You and Emma, I mean. If it's not definite. If you need some space to be alone. Talk things through."

"We've got a house." Well, now Emma has a house. She can take over the lease and live there alone, fill it with pretty blankets and scatter cushions until she suffocates. One advantage of renting; it's easier to cut ties.

"But somewhere neutral. You can borrow the bungalow, is what I'm trying to say. I'll clear out for a bit. You can have a holiday."

"Why on earth would we want to—"

"Okay. Sorry. Offer's there, if you want it, is all. But not if you don't."

"Cheers."

Down at the shoreline, Alannah is still writing in the sand. Watching her is easier than looking at his father.

"You got the most important thing right anyway," says Frank.

"What?"

"You know what," says Frank with a wry smile. "Smarter than me, you are. Does she know where you are?"

"Nah." He doesn't want to open up, wants to keep everything locked down and secure, but he can't help the little bit of pleasure that sneaks out across his face. "Gone off on her own for a bit."

"She'll not be happy when she gets back though."

"Probably not."

"You know," says Frank. "I'm on your side. No matter what happens. I've got your back."

"Great," says Liam, then feels ashamed. "I mean. Thanks. That's... that's nice."

"It's good having you here. Both of you."

How is he going to stand being around his dad if his dad's going to try and be kind? Alannah's finally finished writing. Now she's balancing on one leg and facing the ocean. Liam wonders what she's thinking as the waves

CHAPTER TEN

(DECEMBER, NOW)

waves at Liam as he walks past the car, a friendly acknowledgement from a stranger with a dog to a fellow human being
out in the dark. Liam had been braced for conflict – a strange
man, sitting in a car, staring out at the ocean, long after this
would count as respectable – but no, the other man simply
gave him that cheerful wave and moved on. He'll take that
as a good sign.

He doesn't have to be doing this. He could have done more
or less what he told Frank he was going to do – found a pub,
got a drink, maybe even had a chat with someone – but he
likes the freedom of nobody knowing where he is. He'd rather
be here, in his own little haven. He has to be back at the
bungalow by the morning, but right now he could do anything.
Go anywhere. No one will know or care.

And so, here he is, back in his car. A quick trip to a petrol
station, and he has all he needs. A thick blanket to wrap
himself in. Gloves and a hat to keep his extremities warm. A
bottle of vodka and a bottle of water and a bottle to piss in.
A selection of snacks. A view of the ocean. What more could
anyone want?

It's good to have time to think. Being around his dad

is exhausting. Both of them playing a part the whole time. Being so carefully polite, not saying anything real, competing between themselves to prove who could be the most considerate, the cleanest, the tidiest, the best cook, the fastest washer-upper. Alannah, playing out her strange charade of being a boy called Alfie, growing more comfortable in her role; and isn't it weird that Alannah's the only one who seems genuinely happy, when she's doing the most pretending of all? If nothing else, a night in the car will give him a chance to sort out his thoughts about his daughter ("Those jogging bottoms are filthy. Put them in the wash and put something else on."

"I don't have anything else that's right."

"What are you talking about? You packed clothes; I know you did."

"Girl's clothes."

"Well then, that's what you're going to be wearing, isn't it?"

She doesn't speak, doesn't look at him. Just waits. It's infuriating because he knows she's learned it from him.

"We don't have money for new clothes."

"I've brought my birthday money."

"You need to save that for—" He can't think of what she ought to be saving it for. "You're not spending your money on—" That's ridiculous, boy's clothes for a girl are about as far from *essentials* as it's possible to get. "For God's *sake*."

"There's a big supermarket. I could get some clothes there."

"How do you know?"

"I asked… him." She'll call him *grandad* to his face, but when they're alone he's only *him*. Is she simply picking up on Liam's reluctance? Or does she share it?

"They won't be like what your mum makes, you know. They'll be cheap crap."

"I don't mind."

But you ought to, he thinks. *You're supposed to give a shit about stuff like that. Isn't that what being a girl's about? No, I can't say that, I don't really think that. Emma might think that but I don't. Alannah can dress how the fuck she likes.* And, disarmed by his righteous pleasure at being unlike his wife, he'd driven them both to the supermarket and let Alannah choose what she wanted.)

The car is warm and snug, its comfort insidious. He'll be asleep in a minute if he's not careful. Not that it matters. He's allowed to sleep. He just can't shake the feeling of being out on patrol.

He opens the window. Lets the air coil in to nip at his ears and cheeks. He *wants* sleep, but he doesn't *need* it. He can make himself wait. It's satisfying to find he can still resist the demands of his own body, stay awake and alert in case… in case he…

The temperature's dropping rapidly now. He'll have to put the engine on for a bit, get some warmth in his bones before he lets himself rest. A sign outside tells him he's breaking a by-law sleeping here, but he's pretty sure that if the police were going to bother him, they'd have done it by now. He'll wake bright and refreshed and ready for battle.

(Are you warm and comfortable right now, Emma? Sleep comfortably in your luxurious crisp white linen, my darling. Once you come home, it'll be the last good night's sleep you'll have for a long time.)

He turns the key in the ignition, tips the seat back and pulls the blanket up to his chin. He'll let the thoughts wash over him like waves, simply accept them and then let them drift away like clouds, the way that fucking mindfulness madwoman had gone on about, just accept whatever comes into his head.

That afternoon in the bungalow. He'd been passing the bathroom. The door was open by a crack. Found himself glancing in. No particular reason, certainly no expectation of seeing anything interesting. Simply the way his gaze had happened to fall. He'd seen Alfie – no, damn it, *Alannah*

– standing in front of the toilet, trying to pee standing up. He'd stopped for a second, appalled by the thought of the mess, and then appalled for a different reason.

He'd seen women do that for a laugh, of course he had. He'd been a soldier. He'd seen *everything*. But his own daughter? In a house where she was a guest? And besides, there was something disturbing about it, firm little buttocks clenched in effort, boy's underpants pulled down at the front, boy's trousers around his daughter's ankles. *Five minutes and fifty quid*, he told Alannah sternly as he stood at the entrance to the supermarket clothing section, and five minutes later she'd emerged with a basket full of cheap long-sleeved tops and utilitarian jogging bottoms. He hadn't spotted the boy's socks and boy's pants until they were already at the till, Alannah packing them away with scurrying movements that looked like theft. Took the coward's way out and pretended not to notice. Handed over the cash. Refused to think about what he'd seen. Actually managed to forget it until he saw his daughter, standing at the toilet bowl, looking like… looking exactly like…

He'd walked away, of course. Some things a mother could do that a father simply couldn't, and one of them was walking in on his daughter while she was peeing (even if she was doing something so weird he wasn't sure how to process it. Even if she was, almost certainly, spraying everything around her with pee). But the thought had got into his head and he'd had to go in there himself five minutes later and scrub the seat and the bowl and the floor, even though there was no real sign of a mess. The rage he'd felt as he completed this self-imposed task refused to dissipate, growing in him like a black flower, until he knew he had to get out of the bungalow for a while otherwise it would simply burst out of his chest and destroy him and everyone around him. *Yes, of course*, Frank had said as Liam abruptly asked him if he'd mind watching Alannah for the evening while he met a mate to talk about a possible job. *Take your time, son. No problem at all.*

And what was Frank doing with his evening? Liam can definitely let that one go, let it drift by like a cloud, because the truth is, he doesn't really care. What's Frank to him other than a DNA donor? Frank might think they're building bridges, but this is nothing more than a brief sharing of quarters. When the time comes, he and Alannah will be off into the night like smoke, and Frank will never know who he had in his house. The car is warm and snug, but he won't sleep, not yet. He'll stay awake a little longer, thinking his thoughts in peace.

It's a comforting feeling, the knowledge that he's getting away with something. That's one thing he definitely misses about the Army. The awareness that you were allowed to do stuff that was utterly forbidden to civilians. The constant, unspoken feeling that you were *getting away with something*.

Sudden sharp noise by his ear. Face looking in at him. Adrenaline shocks him awake like he's been defibrillated, out of the car before he knows what's happening. Squawk of surprise from whoever's attacking him. Good. Liam's not going gentle, not going down without a fight.

Brief struggle, brief bit of flailing, but whoever it is doesn't know who they're messing with here. A fierce few moments, exhaust fumes swirling around them, and then it's locked down. Got a nice strong grip on his opponent. Got them pressed against the car, face first. Liam's knees pressed against the back of theirs. One arm pulled high up their back, nicely twisted so all they can think about is the pain in their shoulder. The crook of Liam's elbow against their throat. Could choke them off if he needs to, no problem. If he had a knife he could finish this right now.

"Please." Whoever it is wheezes frantically, and Liam's lip curls. Why start something you can't finish? "Please, I'm sorry."

"Are you?" Liam keeps his voice conversational. Twists the arm up a little higher. Presses his knees in a little harder.

Feels his enemy buckle. "That's nice. What d'you think you're playing at, pal?"

"You left your engine running," the man pants. "I thought – you were – you know – doing something daft – I only wanted to check – ow, please, I'm sorry, I'm *sorry*."

Oh.

Oh.

Oh.

Liam lets go slowly and carefully, in case it's a trick. Backs off from the knees first, tense and ready in case his opponent uses the opportunity to buck into him, trying to regain the advantage, but the red mist is clearing. He removes his arm from the throat, hears him take a frantic sip of air even though he hadn't been properly restricting his breath, not really, not like he *could* have done. Releases the arm, slowly. Holds onto his readiness. Watches as his captive pulls himself slowly back together. He's older than Liam, younger than Liam's dad, that hinterland where you're past your prime but haven't yet tipped over into *old*. Should have known better.

"Shit." The other man is stretching out his arm now, gently rotating the shoulder, checking everything still works. "I thought you were going to kill me. Are you a policeman or something?"

Liam takes a risk, reaches inside his car. Turns off the engine.

"Army."

"That makes sense. Shit, that *really* hurts, I think you broke something."

"If it was broken you'd be screaming."

"What the fuck did you do that for anyway? Jumping out at me like a madman, breaking my shoulder." Liam can hear tears in the other man's voice, thinly disguised beneath anger. "I was checking you were all right!"

"Yeah, you said. Maybe next time don't go around banging on strangers' windows when they're trying to grab ten minutes of kip, yeah?" Liam feels not an ounce of guilt, even though the man probably was only trying to be kind. You go around

103

poking your nose in other people's business, bad stuff is going to happen to you. The adrenaline's wearing off now and there's a fine tremor in his limbs. That's okay. It'll pass.

The strange man is looking Liam up and down, still wary but with something else in his face now. "So you were in the Army?"

"S'what I said."

"Um. And. You… you're not living in your car, are you?"

"Course I'm fucking not."

"Okay. Okay. No offence, I'm only asking." The man is making strange movements with his hands, patting at the air as if he's calming an invisible animal. "Only I know it's tough for veterans sometimes. That's all." He glances at the exhaust pipe. "And I saw the engine running and the window down a little bit and I thought…"

More than anything in this world, Liam wants to punch this man in his stupid mouth and then keep punching until his jaw splinters and his teeth spill out and he never says anything else, ever again. It's an impulse, that's all, nothing real, nothing he has to act on. He can let the thought pass. Liam keeps his breathing even. Keeps his hands still. Waits for the image to float away.

"What are you doing out at this time?" Liam asks, to divert them both from his thoughts.

"Oh." The man laughs. "Had a row with the missus. She told me to get out. So I thought I'd walk around in the dark for a bit. Give her a chance to calm down. You married?"

"Not sure," says Liam before he can stop himself.

"Yeah. I know how you feel."

No, Liam thinks grimly. *You don't. You really don't. You need to go away before I do something we'll both regret.*

"If you need any help," the man says.

"I'm fine."

"You've got somewhere to go? Somewhere warm?"

"I'm *fine*." Doesn't this stupid guy know that Liam

almost killed him just now? Doesn't he know Liam still wants to kill him?

"All right, then. I'll, um…" He shakes his head. "I'll let you get on. Um. Take care."

Liam keeps breathing slowly and evenly as the stranger limps out of sight. Fucking civilians.

It's half three in the morning, the worst of all times to be awake. All he wanted was a single night's undisturbed sleep away from his responsibilities, but he's clearly not going to get that, so there's no point complaining about it. He walks down to the beach instead, looks at the sea. That fucking maniac, banging on the window, thinking Liam was… thinking he was…

And then suddenly the memory of that man's utter terror (*he knocked on the window! And then I jumped out of the car and grabbed him!*) is the absolute funniest thing Liam has ever thought about, ever. He laughs until he can't breathe, until he falls to his knees, until he thinks he might genuinely piss himself, until he's sobbing. It goes on and on, and then suddenly it's over, and he's kneeling on the freezing sand, wiping tears from his cheeks, feeling good. Feeling cleansed. Maybe this is what he needed after all.

The tide's been in and is making its way out again. He can see it retreating, thin little sheets of water laced with foam that creep in and back away, each reaching its highest point a little bit further away from his feet than the last one. The waves are so small, as if the ocean's taking it easy now the night's fallen.

And like that, he's ambushed again, not by anyone wanting to get in, but by a memory in his head that insists on getting out.

A time with Emma, after their marriage but before Alannah. Not in a car but outside, breathing air that was warmer and softer, side-by-side in the dusk on a bench, watching another patch of sea meeting another patch of land.

"The waves are always smaller in the evening and at night," she'd said. "Have you ever noticed that?" Her smile, so sweet and mischievous. "I think they switch it all off after the tourists go home." He'd been utterly charmed, then, by the sheer weirdness of her belief; had spent several enchanted minutes interrogating her about who *they* might be, where they were located, what kind of machinery they had, how they worked it so that the waves went off at different times all around the world, and what happened when there was a storm out at sea? She'd had an answer for everything (*they* were the Bureau of Sea Management; they had a submarine base just off-shore, about where the headlands gave way to open water; the machines were some sort of turbine thing although it was hard to describe exactly; they had different branches for every coastline; the Bureau were only for the coastline and not the open water, so what happened further out was left up to Nature).

And he'd laughed. He'd been fucking *delighted.* The Bureau of Sea Management! Where on earth had she come up with that? How glorious was it to discover that even after several years together, his wife, his beautiful, sexy, fuckable wife, could still surprise him with what went on inside of her head?

He's on the beach, in the dark, awake, alone, sad maybe, but not crying. This isn't him denying reality: it's a simple physical fact. Tears are a waste of effort. Yes, they were happy once, but that was then. This is now. In *now*, Emma is the enemy. That's how it happens sometimes. You think someone's a friend and then, for some reason or other, they turn on you. When it happens, it hurts. It's correct to acknowledge that. But he can deal with that later. Right now he has a battle to fight.

So, here's the situation. Emma got the jump on him, but

she's made a tactical error. She thought she'd cleared Alannah off the gameboard, but she hadn't. Alannah's here with him, and as long as Alannah is with him, he's winning. His job now is to make sure it stays that way.

Coming to his dad's place is a brilliant move, but they can't live here forever. *I'll be back for Christmas*, Emma said, and that's it, that's his ticking clock. Emma, the mother, has the natural advantage, but he'll find a way around that. He needs to get his head together, is all. That's why he's out here, on the beach, and not going slowly out of his mind as he and Frank sit together in the living room and gaze at the screen with fixed smiles, locked into the polite fiction that they're a father and a son sharing time together.

He's tired, that's the problem. Living on adrenaline, making short-term survival decisions. What he needs is what he's given himself. A space of his own.

It's good, out here on the beach. He'll stay here until morning. He'd like sleep, but he doesn't need it. He'll be fine. He's strong. He's gone through worse than this and come out fighting.

When he goes back to the car, the lemony sunlight sparkles off waves that are, indeed, a bit bigger than in the night. The Bureau must have switched the machine on nice and early this morning. That's an Emma thought, but he'll forgive himself. It's the last one he'll allow himself today.

He climbs into the car, pisses into the empty bottle, gets out again and throws it in the bin. He's had a night off and he hasn't slept much, but at least he's had time to clear his head. Today he'll make his plan. He needed a break, that was all. Time to sit in the front seat of his car, doing nothing and thinking of nothing, letting the warmth take him somewhere safe and far away. Somewhere he doesn't have to be in charge, somewhere he can let go and stop worrying…

He's moving into dangerous territory here. He clamps

down on the thought before it can take hold, holds tight, breathes out, sends it away. Nothing to worry about. Nothing to worry about at all. His mindfulness teacher would be proud.

Right. Quick trip to McDonald's for breakfast and a wash in the bathroom, and then he can go back home and tell lies about where he's been. He's ready for it. He's ready to take on the world.

The front door is open, not merely unlocked but slightly ajar, as if the concept of danger from the outside hasn't even occurred to Frank. Liam tries not to mind. It's not his house after all.

"Did it go well last night?" Frank's bustling aimlessly around in the way Liam absolutely can't stand, wandering in and out of rooms, picking things up only to put them down somewhere equally unsuitable. *Only touch each thing once.* The tidying mantra, instilled into him by his mother, reinforced by his time in the Army. *No*, Liam tells himself, *let it go.*

"Yes, fine. Met up with Paul." *Did I call him Paul yesterday? Doesn't matter. Act as if that's what I called him and I'll get away with it.* "Had a good chat. Went down the pub for a bit. Looked at the sea."

"Sounds nice. You sleep all right? You look all in."

"I'm fine."

His dad's hovering around him now, which is even worse than the twittering-about performance. "Fancy a coffee?"

"I'll make it." The living room's frowsty and cluttered, curtains half-drawn against the sunlight, plates and glasses and bottles littered everywhere, a loaded ashtray, a discarded takeaway. He retreats into the kitchen like a sanctuary, wishing he could shut the door. Coffee for himself, and coffee for his dad too, even though he's pretty sure the old man prefers tea. Let him live with the drink his son's made him. It's not Liam's fault if he has no idea what his father's preferences are.

He can hear Alannah rattling around the bathroom, the distinctive slow hiss of the cistern refilling. She must have only just woken up. It's not like her to sleep late. She usually gets up early, squeezing in time at the barre before school. (Ten thousand hours, he'd heard once, ten thousand hours to get really good at something, and his daughter seems determined to put in every one of those ten thousand hours before she hits her teens.) When he looks up from the coffee mugs, Alannah stands in the living room, dressed for the day but with her hair unkempt even though it ought to be too short to get that way, and blinking like an owl.

"Alfie." Frank smiles in pleasure, and Alannah smiles at him in return, a sweet unguarded smile that she doesn't produce often enough. How much she's enjoying her deception. The heroine, who cuts off her hair to protect her dad from being found. Even down to the *underwear*, for God's sake. His little girl, dressed in boy's pants. The thought feels squirmy inside his head, even though he knows it doesn't matter, it's only clothes, she's still herself underneath them. Why she felt the need to take it all the way down to the underwear…

Forget it. It's weird, but kids are weird. She'll get over this phase soon enough.

"Was there a party last night?" Alannah asks.

Frank laughs a little too loudly. "What makes you think there was a party?"

"It looks like a party," Alannah says. She looks at the empty bottle of wine, at the delicate glassware, smeared with fingerprints. "A fancy party."

"If it had been a party we'd have got through a lot more than two bottles and a couple of beers," Frank says. He's not quite looking in Liam's direction. Liam takes the coffee and puts it into Frank's hand, just to get into his space a little, just to make sure Frank remembers he's there, listening. "I had a friend over for a few hours. That's all."

A friend, thinks Liam.

"Like a playdate for grown-ups," Alannah says to herself,

then returns to her interrogation. "So, did you go to bed without tidying up?"

"Oi," says Liam.

"No, it's all right, let him ask. No point ruining a good night with washing-up. Leave it till the morning, I say."

"I thought that was only for parties," Alannah persists. "Like when you have loads of people over and the music's really loud, and everyone stays over. Grown-ups sleeping all over the house."

(Where is Alannah even getting this from? But no, there *had* been times when he and Emma were like that, there really had. When Alannah was small and he'd been home on leave. They'd fill up their house with noise and alcohol and laughter, put everyone's kids in Alannah's room, DVDs and mountains of snacks until they fell asleep in a heap like puppies. Meanwhile the adults danced and talked and drank until the Sun came up. The serene chaos of the morning after, feeding small children and childish adults through a haze of tiredness, frying up mountains of bacon and eggs while Emma manned the kettle and the toaster. It was like looking into another life, lived by another man. Had they really done that? How had he stood it?)

"Now that does sound like a party," Frank says. "But I'm a bit old for that now. It was just a friend over."

"Was he nice? Did he know you've got me and Dad staying? Is that why Dad went out? Or was it a lady?"

"Enough," says Liam. He's curious himself, but he'll find out in his own way. "Get some breakfast." He picks up the dirty glasses, unable to help himself. They're thin and frail between his fingers. If he squeezes too hard they'll crack. He's always thought *breaking easily* should be a mark of poor quality rather than the opposite. The first time he'd taken Emma to bed he'd seen her look of proud defiance as he unwrapped her thighs, daring him to comment or complain. He'd looked at the muscles, the soft dimpled skin, this beautiful strong woman who was willing to let him into her bed and into her body, and thought he'd never seen anything more fucking beautiful in his life…

For God's sake, why is Emma in his head so much today? He fills a bowl of hot water and adds washing-up liquid. How Frank could get to sleep with this shit all over the house, festering and stinking.

"Leave it," Frank says from the living room. "Have your coffee at least."

"Dad likes things to be clean," says Alannah. Liam frowns.

"Nothing wrong with that at all. How about you, mate? Do you like things to be clean?"

"I quite like this sort of mess," Alannah says. Liam can hear glass clinking. Alannah must be rearranging the bottles on the table. "It looks sort of… like in a film when they're in a really old house and it's not tidy, but it still looks nice."

"Bohemian?" Frank suggests. "Decadent?"

"Bring the rest of the pots through, will you?" It's really annoying to be standing here at the sink, scrubbing like a skivvy, while Frank and Alannah debate adjectives among the clutter. He's talking to Alannah, but it's Frank who appears at his elbow with the few remaining bits. There wasn't as much as he'd thought, after all.

"It's all right, I'll do it." Frank's trying to elbow Liam out of the way. "Come on, son, you don't need to wash up after me."

In among the clutter is a glass ashtray. He's never seen his dad smoke. Of course, it might have been for his guest. His *friend*.

"I mean it, let me sort it out."

Frank's growing more determined, but Liam is bigger and younger and he's not moving. Not until he's had a proper look at that ashtray.

"Seriously. Out the way. Make yourself some toast."

Liam stirs the ashtray with his finger.

"It's nothing," says Frank.

Liam looks at him.

"Helps with arthritis," says Frank.

Frank's hands are smooth and unknotted. Liam just looks at him.

"It won't even be illegal in a few years," says Frank, and then, incredibly, he laughs. "Come on, son. If you know what you're looking at then you've done it yourself. Want another coffee?"

Liam wants to say, *you're breaking the law, you stupid old man.* He wants to say, *with Alannah in the house?* He wants to say, *I fucking trusted you to be in charge.* But he can't say any of that, because he's a guest in his dad's house and he has nowhere else to go and he can't afford to leave until he does. He's been outmanoeuvred and it fucking annoys him.

"Could I help?" Alannah's arrived in the kitchen, crowding the long thin space. With one smooth motion, Frank tips the ashtray into the bin.

"You want to wash up? Well, why not? Come and stand in front of me and I'll show you what to do."

"I know how to do it." Alannah slides her lithe body into the space between her grandfather and the sink. Now Liam's trapped at the end, unless he's willing to squeeze intimately past the other two, which he isn't keen on doing. "They showed us how on Pack Holiday."

"So you're a – Cub, is it? Good for you."

"N-yes," says Alannah. "I mean, I was a Cub, but once you're ten you have to go to Scouts." She's going to slip up eventually, but for now she's staying on top of the deception, covering her slip-ups with the practised smoothness of a serial liar. Liam isn't sure if he's impressed or appalled.

"And do you still do badges and that? And Bob-A-Job? Do you still have Bob-A-Job?"

"Sometimes we do car washes. And bag packing in supermarkets."

"Good money, I bet. Rinse the glass off, it'll dry more cleanly. That's it. I had a friend once who was a Brown Owl. You know, for the Brownies. She said they raised almost a thousand pounds doing bag packing."

"Is she still your friend?" Alannah is scrubbing the inside of a mug. Liam keeps still, not wanting to give away that he's interested.

"I see her from time to time," Frank says.

"Did she come to your party last night?"

"No, that was someone else... We didn't disturb you, did we?"

"No. I didn't know you had anyone here."

"It was only a couple of people. Just for a few hours. All finished? All right, now empty the bowl out. Leave it upside down to drain. There we go. All done for now."

"It needs drying and putting away," says Alannah. "Dad likes things to be tidy."

"Dad's right here," Liam says. "You can talk to me if you like."

"Sorry." Alannah looks stricken.

"Don't be hard on him, son." Frank's voice is casual. An effortless correction by the family patriarch. The way he might sound if this was one of a thousand times they'd crammed together into this kitchen. As if he'd been Liam's dad for the whole of his life, and not simply until he lost interest. Frank sounds like *Jane*. Frank must sense this too, because he looks at Liam uneasily. "Sorry, not trying to interfere. Alfie, you've done a great job of the washing-up, mate. Why don't you go and watch television or something?"

"Or go out in the garden or something," says Liam. "Get some fresh air."

"I'll go out in the garden."

"He looks up to you," Frank says when they're alone again.

"Yeah?"

"Boys need their fathers," Frank says, as shocking as if he'd unexpectedly cursed. "Liam, can I say something..."

"Forget it," says Liam. He'd like to get out of the kitchen, but with Frank in the centre of the galley there's no way past without shoving his dad out of the way.

"Please. I wish I'd been there. While you were growing up."

"I wasn't stopping you." Now he's the one cursing, the forbidden words leaking out of the side of his mouth. "You knew where we lived."

"It wasn't that simple."

"Wasn't it? All right then."

"I know you don't want to hear this, but I need to say it."

"You don't need to explain. It's in the past."

"It still matters. It wasn't my choice, Liam, do you understand? I... I don't want to have a go at your mother—"

"Then don't."

"—but she said it would unsettle you. She said it was too far for you to visit. Said you'd be confused. Spending every other weekend out here in the back of beyond."

"Doesn't matter now." He wants to say, *I would have bloody loved coming up to see you every other weekend.* He wants to say, *I bloody loved you.*

"I always sent money, though."

"Thanks."

"I know that wasn't the same as being in your life."

"Forget it." He wants to say, *How can you possibly think money makes up for anything?* He wants to say, *How could you let Mum push you out like that?* He wants to ask, *What kind of a man are you?*

"Don't let Emma do that to you," Frank says, and Liam can feel his lip curling in disbelief. "Okay? She'll try and push you out, but don't let her. Things are different now. You've got rights too."

"It doesn't... I don't..." He wants to contradict his father, but he can't do so without contradicting what he himself believes.

"It's the way they're made," Frank says. "They give birth to them so they think they own them. But don't you let her."

Liam's mouth is a doorway, words all jostling to squeeze through. Which is the best way to tell his dad to shut up? He's gaping like a fish, glued to the spot. This isn't how he was trained. He needs to get a grip on himself.

"All right if I play a bit of footie with Alfie?" Incredibly, Frank's going to leave before Liam has a chance to speak. "Sit down and drink that coffee, son. You really do look tired."

That's because last night, I had three hours sleep and then almost killed a stranger. He could tell his father the truth. But what good would that do? He's not letting his dad in. He won't give him that. He hasn't earned it.

His dad's outside already, scuffling around the lawn in Crocs. He kicks the football in Alannah's direction. She fumbles the stop, takes a wild swipe with her right foot, misses the ball entirely. Her next attempt connects with the ball, but most of the power goes into taking a large muddy divot out of the lawn. The ball trickles over the grass and stops at Frank's feet.

"Don't worry, mate," Frank says. "You've got plenty of power. You just need to direct it. Look, I'll show you."

This is familiar. Why is this familiar? It takes Liam a while to place the memory, mainly because he's lived his life by the mantra of *not looking back*. Then he has it. He's in the garden of his childhood home. The privet hedge is green and dank, the lawn neatly mowed but the flower beds untended. This must be soon after they moved in. There's a football at his feet. His dad stands over him, a benign giant. *Look*, he says. *I'll show you.*

And now his dad's out there on a different patch of grass, teaching a different small boy how to kick a ball. Except it's a trick, he's being deceived. He'd know that if he'd stayed in Liam's life. But he didn't. His dad is a stranger.

Fuck that, he thinks. *I won't let that happen to you, Alannah. I'm not leaving you behind. You're staying with me. Whatever it takes. Whatever it takes. I'll do right by you, I promise, I swear.*

While his father and daughter shriek and call to each other on the lawn, Liam moves around the living room, neatening cushions, straightening curtains, sweeping away the last traces of whatever his dad was doing last night. He'll never understand how anyone can go to bed leaving their place in a tip like this. It's no way to live. The sight of all this mess makes his skin crawl and shiver

CHAPTER ELEVEN

(2014)

shiver in the air, that excitement you find in lots of places, but especially at the train stations of London. Waves of energy, flowing with the crowds as we bundle down the platform. Rush rush rush. Some because we've got somewhere to be. Some because we're meeting someone we love. The rest of us because everyone else is rushing, and there's that herd-member fear of being left behind. Liam's taken the lead, which makes sense because he's the biggest and has the strongest presence. It can't be the way he looks that makes people get out of his way, because most of them have their backs to him. Maybe it's some sort of pheromone he gives out.

Emma hurries in his wake, and I can see from the shape of her back that she's enjoying watching my son – her husband. She's thinking about how much she loves him; how glad she is that he's hers. That's good. It's partly why I suggested this trip, so Liam and Emma could have a little fun. Some might call it interfering, but I know I'm not. I'm only nudging things in the right direction. You can only push people where they want to go anyway.

Emma's caught up with Liam now, and taken his hand, each of them pulling one suitcase. He's glad to have her by his side. She's glad to be there. They're enjoying their synchronicity, the way their feet move in time without them having to work at it, the way they automatically fall into step. Strange how expressive a back can be. Strange to think I once felt that way about Frank. What if Emma falls out of love too? No, she won't, there's no reason for her to. I spent years shaping my son into a man I could be proud of. He's nothing like the man whose genes he shares. Beside me, Alannah's holding very tight to my hand.

This is the other, secret reason I suggested the trip.

"All right, sweetie?" I stroke her fingers with mine. She could have been holding her mum's hand but she chose mine, and I'm glad. It's nice to be chosen. Of course it's not a contest, Alannah has plenty of room in her five-year-old heart for us both. Nonetheless, I do sometimes feel that competitive urge, that desire to be the *one and only*, the way I was in those long, hard, glorious years when my sole focus was Liam. I won't give in to it, though. It's good that he has a wife and a child to love. It wouldn't be healthy otherwise.

It's strange to be so connected to another woman like this. Liam came from my body, but he belongs to Emma now. And Alannah came from Emma's body, but a quarter of everything Alannah is comes from me.

We make our way through the small irritations of travel: the crowds, the diesel fumes, the suitcases caught in the barriers, the queue for the taxi. Liam and Emma suggested the tube, but I told them I'd pay for a cab. ("I can afford it," I told them firmly, "and it's nicer for everyone.")

Before the station's even out of sight, the taxi divides in two. The front half's for the men, Liam turning his mouth towards the partition to talk to the driver, about war and fighting and terrorism and security measures. They exchange words like *Helmand* and *IED* and *freedom*, liberally filled out with gestures and laughter. Is the taxi driver ex-Forces? I'd like to ask but if I do, I'll break the flow between the two of them, make everything awkward.

And so, three and a half thousand miles away in the back of the taxi, Emma and Alannah and I talk to each other. What clothes we've brought with us. The museums we'll visit. The food we might eat. The shows we'll see (*Les Misérables* for Liam and Emma, *The Nutcracker* for Alannah and me). Occasionally we both glance at Liam, checking in with our boy. We try to time our glances so we don't catch each other doing it and feel as if we're competing. Emma and I have stuck to our pact to like each other, and part of that liking is not treading on each other's toes.

Alannah looks out of the window, whispering to herself. Is she looking at the Christmas lights, blaring out like sirens? No; she's counting buses. Emma hasn't noticed and may never notice. Even Alannah doesn't know I know. It's something for me, a crumb of insight to hold tight against my heart. My body swells with love. She's such a strange little scrap sometimes.

At the hotel, Emma joins Liam at the check-in counter while Alannah and I look at the leaflets in the rack. There's no point to looking – our days are tightly planned – but Alannah likes taking the leaflets out and slotting them back again.

Check-in takes a while. The clerk apologises that our rooms aren't adjacent. Liam, tight-jawed, explains that this is how it's supposed to be. There's a touch of tension in the air as everyone processes why a man and his wife might want some distance between them and their relatives, Liam standing a little bit taller than he needs to, determined not to look embarrassed. This could sour the whole trip, but there's nothing I can do.

Nothing I can do. Something Emma can do. Hidden from the clerk but visible to me, I see her fingertips reach for Liam's where they rest against his hip. Her thumb makes a slow circle of his palm. Presses against it. Releases. His fingers hesitate, then reach for hers. Such a tender, lewd, intimate gesture.

I shouldn't be watching, so after a moment, I don't. Alannah tugs on my arm and I bend over. She whispers, so softly I have to bend down and ask her to repeat it.

"I like it when Mummy and Daddy hold hands," she says. She's right. It's a good thing. The little ripples of tension I sense between them are no more than that, simply a breeze ruffling the surface. The quiet depths of their marriage remain untouched. They're going to be all right. They're going to be all right. Everything's as it should be.

The rooms are boring and comfortable, nothing worth spending time in, which is exactly the point of them. We're all keen to get out and see London, but we have to unpack first. Emma thinks Liam's insistence on unpacking before anything else can happen comes from his Army training, but she's wrong; I taught him myself. I unpack, then help Alannah to do the same, disciplining myself not to linger over the sheer *prettiness* of her wardrobe. Soft jersey dresses in bright colours. Beautifully finished leggings. Perfectly spaced gathers. French seams. What a talented woman my son married. He must hold on to her. She must hold on to him. They must stay together.

Liam knocks at the door, says he's come to inspect Alannah's unpacking, an activity that's half a game and half serious.

The inspection goes well, as I knew it would. Of course Liam wouldn't have been cross with Alannah if she'd made a mess. Of course his displeasure wouldn't have put a dampener on the day. That's only me being silly. I notice Emma realising that I must have helped Alannah, and then notice her noticing me, and we silently enjoy our shared successful deception of Liam. We should bring Alannah into it too, a three-way conspiracy against the male in our lives. But no, she's only five, still liable to blurt out the truth over dinner. (*Dad, did you know it was actually Granny Jane who made my clothes so tidy?*)

Oh, and also, I shouldn't encourage Alannah to think of her dad and her mum as being on opposite sides to each other, or to think of men as people who you have to deceive and manage and generally get around. Things are different now. Times have moved on.

Emma is a little protective of Alannah, a little on her guard whenever Liam speaks to their daughter. I won't worry about this; it's only natural. When Liam disappears into the Army capsule, Alannah becomes all Emma's. It must be difficult to let go again when he returns. Of course, being a single parent was even harder…

But none of this matters, because Emma loves Liam an astonishing amount. She loves him with tenderness and ferocity, with gentleness and with strength. She has enough love to keep him safe for a lifetime. It's just that sometimes, you can lose track of that love for a while, the way you can take a ring off and forget where you've left it and work yourself into a panic, until you find it again and get it safely back onto your finger. Their lives aren't perfect because nobody's life is perfect, but they make it work. They're a successful couple. I'm doing my part at keeping them both together. It's not meddling to lend a helping hand.

The afternoon passes. We visit the Natural History Museum, take an open-topped bus ride, stand in a London Eye capsule and stare at the view. By the time we get back to the hotel at five thirty, Liam and Emma are relaxed and happy but Alannah's dropping with tiredness, tetchy in the way only a young child can be. This is another potentially risky moment, when the good mood between them could be soured, but because I'm here I can smooth everything out and make the evening perfect. Liam and Emma will go out. Alannah and I will order sandwiches from Room Service and take a nap, and when she wakes I'll dress her in the party frock Emma made and take her to Covent Garden and we'll lose ourselves in the ballet, and then we will come home again and I'll bathe her and put her to bed with a mug of warm milk and a handful of biscuits.

I haven't planned this only for me. It's for Liam and Emma too. Thanks to me, they'll have dinner. The theatre. A night in a strange bed. It's inappropriate to follow them any further, but I was married once too, and I can feel the shape of it. Leaning against each other on the tube ride back to the hotel. Their fingers, intertwined. The liberating peace of a hotel room where no one in earshot knows or cares who they are. I could go further, look deeper, but what comes next is not for my eyes.

The weekend, they'll say, has done them both good, and I'll agree, as if *the weekend* has a mind of its own, as if there was no one in the background, pulling the strings. Emma's clever at sewing clothes, but my skill is sewing the two of them back together, repairing any small damages. They'll have their evening alone, and I'll get precious time with Alannah, and tomorrow morning I'll see the happiness leaking out of all three of them.

On her bed, Alannah snuffles and stirs. She's slept for slightly under an hour. Enough to recharge, not enough to draw her too deep for waking, only to resurface in the early hours, body clock hopelessly askew and the whole day after ruined. It's time to wake her for our stolen evening, when I will be in sole charge of her and we can do exactly what we like without feeling as though I'm treading on Emma's toes.

Londoners are supposed to be withdrawn and private, but in the plush lobby we find ourselves showered in smiles. We look like who we are: a loving grandmother and her beloved granddaughter, out for an evening of magic. The programme's expensive but I buy one anyway. The usher guides us to our places, and we cram into velvet seats in the winter dark of the theatre. Alannah presses against my arm and slowly turns the pages, studying the photographs.

Did I choose well? To me, the ballet at Christmas has always been the height of luxury, but what if Alannah disagrees? Would she have preferred the cinema instead? It's too late now, the money's spent, the doors sealed. If we leave now they won't let us back in. The music of a years-dead Russian floats up from the pit.

How does it take me so long to notice Alannah's gradual and consuming rapture? At first I think she's merely happy. The curtain scrolls upwards to reveal the set, glittering and layered, hard to make sense of, and Alannah gasps. Clara dances onto the stage, her dress coincidentally the same colour as Alannah's; I see her incredulous smile. The mice make their entrance, and Alannah stops leaning against me and sits forward in her seat. The curtain drops for the interval, and Alannah looks at me in panic and asks, *is that the end? Is there any more?* She follows me to the toilet, waits in the queue, goes into and then out of the cubicle, declines my offer of an ice-cream, leads the way back to the auditorium, climbs into her seat and sits with her gaze straight ahead, all in utter silence, as if she's afraid words will shake away the glory inside her head.

What Alannah is experiencing is greater and more painful than happiness, but I don't see it straight away. Not when the curtain rises again and Alannah's eyes grow wide. Not when the dancers pour on and off the stage, each in their turn, the Spanish dance and the Arabian dance and the Chinese dance and the Russian dance. I don't see any of this, or rather, I see it but I don't understand it.

Not even when the theatre grows quiet and expectant and the Sugar Plum Fairy takes her place in the centre of the stage.

Her beauty is frightening, a grace almost too perfect to look at. Her limbs have that slender, disarticulated look that displays both effortless ease and endless, relentless strength. She floats onto her toes and *smiles*, as if nothing could be more natural than to balance the whole weight of your body on a single joint, brutally compressed against a block of stiffened card. The sight makes me shiver, and I remember the many, many fairy tales where women are punished with shoes.

She's twirling and spinning around the stage now, making it look so *easy*, as if this is a natural thing for a human being to do, as if she's immune to the pull of gravity, as if she feels no pain. Her body is a kinetic work of art, a paradox of elegance and power. She is so utterly confident in her own skin, no defensiveness, no hint of apology. She knows how glorious she is, and every woman and man in here knows it too.

She's thin, her cheekbones sharp, her arms and legs like wires, but nonetheless she's the strongest person in the theatre. This is not a crude analogy but a simple truth. In any trial of strength or endurance, this woman would win. She's stretched her joints and muscles beyond their natural limits, disciplined herself through years of pain and repetition, learned to smile as her nails crack and her feet bleed. This moment, this magic she's creating on the stage, is her reward. Her beauty has elements in common with the languid doe-eyed models who drape themselves across every page, every billboard, every screen, but what she's performing is not sex. This is female power, made manifest. *This* is what we should all look like. This is what we should aim for, but will never reach. We can only sit and gaze and worship. Would the dancer look this beautiful if we met her on the street? It's impossible to say. I only know that she has the whole theatre corralled into a single animal, all of us focused on the vital task of watching this savage loveliness, this impossible physical cruelty that has somehow been transmuted into pure beauty.

I'm so transported that I completely fail to notice what's happening to Alannah.

She's quiet in the taxi home, leaning on my shoulder and blinking sleepily at the lights. Back in our room, I'm about to say she doesn't need a bath, but she's in the bathroom before I can speak. Then there's the thunder of the taps running and when I open the door, she's tipped in half a bottle of Matey and the room's filling up with foam and Alannah herself is sitting in the water, eyes round with exhaustion.

"It's all right," I say, and kneel at the side of the bath among the spilling bubbles. "Don't worry. I'll sort it out."

She doesn't really speak as I scrub her flannel over her pink little body, her limbs as passive and heavy as a doll's as I shimmy her into her pyjamas. She drinks from the mug of milk in slow breathless gulps, licks biscuit crumbs from her lips, stands quietly as I clean her teeth. There's something unspeakably dear about a sleepy child. I carry her to her bed, slip her down between cool sheets, tuck her in. I'm tired myself, glad to hose away the remaining foam and finally take a shower.

I'd thought Alannah was already asleep, so it's a shock to come out of the bathroom and find her standing at the end of her bed, shucked pyjamas crumpled at her feet, staring at her naked self in the mirror. I wonder if she's sleepwalking, but her gaze when she looks up at me is clear and focused.

"Granny Jane," she whispers. "My body's all wrong."

"What? What are you talking about?"

"I don't like the way my body looks. It's not right."

"Alannah, you're being ridiculous. Your body is *perfect*. Do you hear me? Absolutely perfect." My voice is too brisk and sharp, my urge to defend her soft, pudgy, silken five-year-old self getting out of control. I force myself to soften it. "Has anyone said anything that's upset you?"

Alannah shakes her head violently. A tear flies loose and flicks onto the floor.

"It's not anyone else, Granny, it's me. *I* don't like me. I'm wrong."

"Well, what is it you think you're supposed to look like?"

Alannah's gaze falls on the programme from the theatre, open to a page showcasing their prima ballerina. My heart thumps in my chest.

"She looked happy," Alannah whispers.

What should I say? *There are so many different ways of*

looking beautiful, that's just one way. Or, *she doesn't look like that in real life, she's wearing a ton of make-up and a special costume.* Or, *why does it matter what you look like? Beauty comes from the inside.* Is it even my place to have this conversation? *You're a little girl and she's a grown woman, of course you don't look like her yet, but you'll see, once you grow up...* I'm frightened of saying the wrong words, putting the wrong ideas into her head. Is it right for me to disturb her universe?

"Well," I say slowly. "You know, that ballerina... she wasn't *born* being able to do that. She didn't, I don't know, wake up one morning and know how to dance. She had to learn."

"Could I learn that?"

Be cautious, be cautious. It's a dangerous thing to plant a dream in a child's head. "She's worked at it all her life. She's trained and studied and fallen over and had blisters and torn muscles and had to soak her feet in ice for hours just to get her shoes on so she can keep going. She had to transform every single part of her body. Do you know what *transform* means? It means—"

"Could I learn that?"

"I... maybe. I don't know. It's not easy."

Alannah is studying herself in the mirror again. She lifts one arm, examines the effect. "I'd like to learn that."

Alannah's body works perfectly. She's never had a serious illness, never spent a night inside a hospital since the day she was born. She hit all of her physical milestones exactly on time. She has no genetic conditions. She's broken no bones. She is five years old, and her body's already dodged a million invisible bullets fired from the scattergun of chance and bad luck. Why can't that be enough? Why does she, so young and tender, have to face all the angst and insecurity that comes with being born female?

"Can I learn?" she asks, sweet and hesitant.

I think about the ballerina, the taut curve of her body,

the smile on her face. The strength of her. The glory that comes, not from make-up and adornment and meekness and stillness, but from skill and effort and power. Her beauty's unchallengeable, but I can't tell if it's an act of compliance, the ultimate expression of an impossible physical standard, or simply a gigantic *fuck you* to the world.

"If you still feel the same in a couple of weeks, I can get you some ballet lessons as a Christmas present," I say, not yet realising that I've started

CHAPTER TWELVE

(DECEMBER, NOW)

started to get comfortable, the waves of sleep dragging him under, he'll find himself lurching awake again. If he isn't careful, Liam could let this become A Thing, hyper-alertness signalling the start of true insomnia. But he'll be careful; he doesn't need to worry. He knows how to manage his own brain.

For a civilian, lying on his father's living room floor would be slumming it, a reason in itself to be unable to fall asleep, but not for him. He's slept in a rut in the ground on Dartmoor. In a canvas cot where his feet and half of his calves hung off the end. In the tipped-back driver's seat of his car, his daughter beside him. A row of cushions on a flat surface, covered with a clean sheet, is comfort.

His dad doesn't like him doing this – he'd prefer Liam tucked away in the spare bed in Alannah's room – but Liam knows what Frank does not, and it's not right for a father to share a bedroom with his daughter. He's much happier here, in his own improvised little nest. He's good at adapting to unusual places. Small adjustments have a big impact. Like the way he's wedged the cushions across the floor so they're held in place by the heavy furniture, for example. A civilian might go for aesthetic appeal, lining up their bed in a way that matches the straight lines of the walls or the orientation of the fireplace. Liam knows better.

As always, closing his eyes in a place that's still unfamiliar acts as a temporary stimulant to his ears. The wooden walls, heated during the day and now releasing that heat, make small organic sounds that make him think of insects. This triggers a memory of Out There, of the camel spider that lived in the last cubicle of the toilet block, of how they'd grown quite fond of it as the days passed. That time when Taff found a live mouse in his boot and picked it up by the tail and threw it to the spider, and the cheer that went up as the spider tore out of its corner and caught the mouse in its jaws… It was good to have a pet, even if the pet was objectively a bit horrifying. Who made the rule that humans were only allowed to be fond of fluffy things?

The kitchen clock's ticking, but if he lets himself listen he'll start to fixate on it and he'll never get to sleep. He needs a distraction. His hand creeps across his thigh towards his groin… but no… he won't do that here. He's a grown man, not a schoolboy. The trick is to accept the ticking clock as part of what's happening. He's slept through worse sounds in worse places.

Tick, tick, tick. Tune it out. Think of something else. Where was he a minute ago? Oh, yes, the camel spider. It was there for weeks, then one day it was gone. They'd joked about it going to join the enemy, but they were all uneasy. A giant spider that lived in a specific spot and took no notice of you was all right. But a giant spider that roamed at will and might be anywhere, at any moment… In the end, someone found its corpse in a corner and put it in Jammer's locker. When he opened the door and it fell out towards him, he'd shrieked like a girl, then cursed up a blue streak and wrestled the nearest three watchers to the ground, one after another, all of them half-helpless with laughter. Good times. This is what no one who hasn't done what he's done will ever understand. The sheer, inexplicable *fun* that sometimes came with the business of going to war.

The kitchen clock's still ticking, but now he's found a memory to attach to it; the lad who had the cot next to him, Paul, who made this weird clicking noise when he slept on his back. He imagines he's back in the barracks, Paul clicking away, the breaths and snores and mumbles of the other men around him.

Within minutes, memory becomes haziness becomes a dream. Cocooned by the soft noises of his comrades, he turns carefully onto his side, tucks his feet inside the blankets in case the camel spider decides to visit, and lets the darkness take him.

Some time passes, in which he's off in his head somewhere, no one's business but his own, and then he's awake with a start.

Something wrong. He's needed. He fumbles out of the blanket, conscious that he's moving clumsily, knocking things over. Doesn't matter. He has to get up, get onto his feet, get alert and ready.

What's happening? Ticking noise. An IED? Need to get everyone out of here. Everyone else gone. He's the weak link. On his feet now, no time to think, only to act, feet in boots and then *go*, get moving, get out of here. Corridor outside, doesn't look familiar but that's nothing to worry about, you notice things differently when you're in the grip of adrenaline. Keep moving. Find the door. Door locked, what the fuck? What fucker locks a door in a barracks? Scrabble for the latch. Yale lock. Doesn't make sense. Never mind.

Get the door open. Out we go. Cooler than he'd expected. Grass outside. Wet against his ankles. When did it last rain out here? Has the grass grown in the night? Where the fuck is he? Where the fuck is everybody? Is Emma here? He'd like her to be here, her hand on his back, rubbing and patting, pressing him back through the veil and into reality. Something he ought to remember about Emma. What was it? Is she dead? Fuck no, of course she's not dead, he wouldn't forget his wife's death. What else, then – Alannah, he's left Alannah inside, has to get to her...

Someone in the way, telling him it's all right, stop, calm down, it's all right, son. He's coming down from it now, falling back into reality, braced for landing. Assume the position. Bend over, head between your knees, and kiss your ass goodbye... no one sure if this does any good, or if it's a way of keeping you in your seat so they can match you to the seating records afterwards. They tell you that's not true, but they would, wouldn't they? Can't trust anyone but yourself and your mates... and Emma...

No. He can't trust Emma, that's what he's doing here. Of course it is. She left him. He's in his father's house. Outside his father's house. Standing on the lawn. And the stranger beside him is...

"It's all right, son." Hands on his shoulders, annoying him. "I'm here. You're safe."

It's raining, not that bullet downpour that drills into the ground and batters the world into submission but a slow, cold soaking that turns the lawn to mush and rots the dead leaves and creates puddles that are only a few hours from freezing. An English rain in an English winter. He's in England. Of course he is. And even though he's absolutely fine, all of this is only reflexes that he hasn't quite let go of yet, his dad is acting like Liam might die right there in front of him. *Civilians.*

"That's it. Calm down now. There you go." His dad is still patting and stroking. He's in a strange garden, in boots and t-shirt and boxers, being patted by a man he hardly knows. As if he's ill, dying, rather than simply performing the soldiering version of waking up for work at the weekend. If he wasn't so embarrassed, he'd be laughing.

"I'm fine." Liam directs his gaze at his father's eyebrows,

grey and wiry. Keeps his voice brisk and cheery. "Didn't mean to wake you."

"Were you dreaming?"

"Um… what? I dunno, maybe." Why the fuck is his dad asking about his *dreams*? The space between his ears is his own. "I'll just have heard a noise, that's all. It's nothing. Number of times they wake you in the night, after a while you react on autopilot."

"Do you want to come inside? You're getting cold."

It's actually quite nice out here, despite the chill. But Liam looks at his dad, who like him is wearing a t-shirt and boxer shorts, but barefooted too and beginning to shiver, and realises what his dad is really saying is *I'm getting cold*. He stamps firmly down on his incipient smugness. Nothing to be proud of in being tougher than a man decades older, with no training.

"You go in. I'll stay out here for a bit." Liam licks rain off his lip. "Nice to be a bit cold for a change." Pretending he's fresh from deployment, somewhere hot and faintly hellish. Does his dad know how long it's been? He can't remember.

"Fancy a drink to warm up? I can make coffee. Or I've got some vodka somewhere. Maybe some whiskey."

"I'm fine. You go ahead."

"If you're sure." His dad is beginning to shiver.

"I'm fine."

That's right, Dad. You go inside and be the weak civilian who can't stand the rain on his skin. Liam watches the old man go back inside, then walks out across the lawn, relishing the cold green squelch of it beneath his feet. Connecting with the earth. He thinks about the breathing exercises they taught him. Breathe in and stretch your arms out side-to-side as you stand up tall. Breathe out and bring them together in prayer. Breathe in and stretch up to the sky. Breathe out and fold forward as you rain your fingers down. *It's a yoga technique*, the mindfulness woman said, and he could see her wondering if he'd protest. As if he hadn't spent years teaching his body to take on whatever meaningless shape it was ordered to. He won't do the exercises now, but that's because he doesn't need them. He's fine. He's doing fine. Nothing to worry about here.

Something's happening in the porch. It's his dad, wearing a waxed jacket and a pair of trainers, ineptly dragging a motley collection of things. Two folding wooden chairs that pull against his forearm and leave gouges in the lawn; a spare anorak; a couple of trailing blankets; an umbrella hooked over one of the chairs, bouncing and rattling with every step; a bottle of something tucked under his arm; two steaming mugs, precariously pinched between his fingers. Thirty seconds of planning would make the job way more efficient, but civilians never plan.

"Thought I'd join you," he huffs as he reaches Liam. Another consequence of his poor planning is that he has no idea how to put anything down. Liam unhooks the umbrella and drops it to the ground, unfolds the first chair and begins stacking things on top of it so his dad's hands will be free. "Good thing you're here. I'd have dropped the whole lot on the grass… I've made coffee but we can warm it up a bit with this if you like? Help you sleep after."

He doesn't want to sit out here and drink vodka-laced coffee with his estranged father, but he's smart enough to know he's got to. He's staying in his dad's house. Now he has to pay his rent. He unfolds the second chair and ushers his dad into it. Wraps the blankets around the old man's shoulders. Adds a generous slug of vodka to one mug, and passes it over. Spikes his own drink. Puts on the spare anorak. Sits down beside him. Opens the umbrella and offers it to the older man. *D'you see, Dad? I don't run away from my responsibilities.*

"You have the brolly," his dad says immediately.

"I'm fine, don't worry about me." *I'm younger and tougher. Don't try and keep up with me.*

"I'd rather you were dry than me."

"That's ridiculous."

"You're my son."

"No, I'm not."

The words are so toxic he imagines the air turning green.

"No," his dad says after a minute. His voice is stiff with pain. "No, that's fair. I know I wasn't there for most of your childhood. I don't get to expect anything now."

"I didn't mean—" Liam begins.

"I looked in on your little lad, by the way. Hope you don't mind."

"Sleep through a war, that one."

"You used to sleep like that too." His dad takes a thoughtful sip of coffee. Holds it in his mouth for a minute. Swallows. "Not a peep out of you from dusk till dawn. If we move these chairs closer we can share the brolly."

He doesn't want to get closer to his dad, but he does it anyway. He lifts his chair, shuffles a foot and a half across the grass, sets it down again. Now he can smell the faint afternotes of his father's aftershave. *Scent can be a trigger*, they told him. He's never found one that takes him back to the desert, but this one drags him on a more treacherous journey. He's small, he's sleepy, he's being held by someone who's carrying him off to bed…

He will not let this soften him. The man next to him donated money and chromosomes. Nothing else. It takes more than that to be a dad, and he intends to do everything the job asks of him. He'll never, ever leave Alannah.

"Does that happen to you a lot?" His dad scuffs at the place on the lawn where the turf is scraped up. "Waking up and thinking you're back at work, I mean?"

"Does it matter?" The question's harder to avoid because they're side-by-side, not face-to-face. He can't recast this as a confrontation.

"No, of course not. I just wondered."

"I…" Lying is for weaklings, and he won't be a weakling. "Not *a lot*, but sometimes. No big deal. Sleeping in a strange place, that's all." He hates having to ask but he has to know. "Was I… um… was I yelling or anything?"

"No, nothing like that. I heard you in the hallway. Why? Were you having a nightmare?"

"Not really."

"Do you get a lot of them?"

He can feel his irritation rising. "Not especially."

"You must have seen some sights."

Ah, here it is. The invitation ex-soldiers are always offered. *You must have seen things I'll never see, must have seen explosions and blood and horror and triumph. Tell me all about it so I can enjoy a second-hand thrill. Let me revel in your trauma and make sympathetic noises about how brave you are, while still feeling a little bit pleased that my hands are clean. Show me the dark side. Tell me a horror story. Make my skin crawl.* He's had it from strangers on trains, from servers in bars and restaurants, from Emma's friends, even from Alannah's ballet teacher. Why would his dad be any different?

It's okay, though. He knows how to do this. No such thing as a free lunch. If his dad wants paying in war stories, Liam can oblige.

"It was pretty spicy sometimes."

"So you were… deployed? In combat?"

"That was the job."

"Where did they send you? Are you allowed to say?"

"Not really." He is allowed to say, but he doesn't feel like it.

"I'm sorry."

Liam shrugs. "It's what I signed up for."

"I know, I know. But, I used to watch the news. I mean, I know there's always wars, everywhere, I don't know if you were even in the ones I was looking at. But I used to worry."

The thought of his dad watching the screen, thinking he had the right to worry about the boy he abandoned, makes Liam angry. He forces himself to sit still, show nothing. "No point joining if you're not prepared to do the job."

"Did you have to kill people?" The question shocks him

135

into looking his dad full in the face. "Sorry, it's none of my business."

"I was a soldier. We're not just hired killers, you know." He won't get irritated. It's a rude question, but most people don't think before they speak. "Quite a bit of it was local relations. Training programmes. Rebuilding projects. That kind of thing."

"Quite a bit of it?"

"Most of it really."

"But not all of it?"

"I'm sorry, what?" Most people would have backed off by now. Even Emma knows that when he uses that particular tone, it's time to stop asking. But his dad is a persistent old bugger.

"Is that why you had to leave?"

"I didn't *have to* leave; I chose to leave. Time to do something else." What the hell is his dad thinking, winding him up like this? It's taking everything he's got to keep sitting in this chair, keep looking out at the rain and the grass and the road, keep his hands where they belong, which is wrapped around his coffee mug, and definitely not smashed into this stupid old bastard's face. The blanket rustles as his dad turns in his chair. Don't look at me, you daft cunt. If you fucking look at me I'll drive my fucking fist right through your nose and into your fucking brain.

"I'm so sorry for whatever happened to you," his dad says, and despite the ferocious warning signals Liam is diligently sending out, despite the tensed shoulders and the tight fists and the rapid breathing and the general air of *I am a dangerous man and you need to get away from me right now*, he puts an arm across Liam's shoulders.

He can't control the quiver in his muscles. The wall isn't going to hold. The dam's going to breach. He can't afford to look behind it. He can't afford to let it out because he's a man and it's his job to keep the defences secure.

But it's all right. It's okay. The moment's passing. It's passed. He's in charge again. And apart from that single moment, that seismic tremor of weakness, there's nothing to show for it.

"No need." A brisk, clipped word, easy to get out. He focuses again on his dad's eyebrows, creating the illusion of eye contact. "It was the job. Nothing serious." *Switch the focus. Change the script.* "It's cold. You go in and I'll clear this lot up when I'm done." *Go to bed and we can pass this whole thing off as an eccentric little escapade. Go to bed before either of us says something we regret.*

"I'll stay with you. If you don't mind, I mean."

"No need." He does mind, he wants to be out here alone so he can reconstruct himself and get ready for sleep, but he can hardly say so.

"It's okay. I'll stay."

So this is the job right now. Sit in rain with the old man and let him pretend we're building relationship bridges. Well. Easier work than building genuine relationship bridges. Or actual real bridges.

"You're not drinking that," Frank says, nodding towards Liam's mug.

"I'll get to it." He won't be intimidated into drinking something he doesn't want. He's a grown adult. He's been as polite as he needs to be.

"Prefer something else?"

"I'm fine."

"You know," says Frank tentatively. He's fumbling in his anorak pocket, pulling out a plastic bag that can't possibly be what Liam thinks it is. "If you want…"

Liam looks at the bag, at the tiny white rolls nestled next to the lighter.

"I just thought," Frank says. "If you'd prefer."

What the hell would Emma say if she knew?

"Ah, come on." Frank's voice is warm and reassuring. "You know I do and I'm sure you *have*. What's the harm?" The hand holding the bag is firm and steady. "Only if you fancy it. Not compulsory."

137

Fuck it, Liam thinks in amazement. What's he getting so uptight about? His dad's right. It *is* just a bit of weed. He *has* done it himself, plenty of times. And why the fuck not? Bet Emma's been drunk plenty of times without him; bet there've been plenty of nights when she's gone to bed with her head full of stars. He picks out the lighter and the fattest of the joints, lights it up. Takes a long draw of thick resiny smoke and passes it on to his dad. Holds it in his lungs. It's been a while, but he'll do this without coughing.

Crammed together beneath the umbrella, mellow and giddy, they sit side-by-side and watch the rain. It's awkward at first, neither of them with anything to say, and then gradually something begins to ease between them as the understanding grows that they don't have to talk. They're two men alone without their women, getting pleasantly high in the rain together, and somehow this makes the silence

CHAPTER THIRTEEN

(DECEMBER, NOW)

silence has a different quality tonight, as it has for several nights, because there are strangers under his roof. Strangers who Frank should know as well as he knows his own self. Maybe it's guilt keeping him half-awake (the righteous shell of *Jane it was your fault you did this to me* finally cracking, letting in the light that forces him to see the man he's been). Maybe it's having a child in the house. He remembers so well those first few weeks with Liam, both exhausted but also unable to sleep, terrified that if they let themselves relax, something would happen to their son. Maybe it's merely the sound of their breathing. Never mind. He'll take it, this uneasy half-awakeness. An early Christmas present from the universe.

There's a crash from the living room, a flurry of movement, then someone scrabbling frantically at the back door. He knows instantly who it is, knows he isn't being burgled or attacked. It's Liam, who insists on sleeping in there even though there's a perfectly good bed in Alfie's room. (What's behind this strange refusal? He'd love to insist, but Jane took away his right to pull fatherly rank on Liam decades ago.) Liam, stumbling around and dragging the door open in a way that's instantly recognisable as a man who's still half-asleep, not properly back in his body yet, his brain wandering somewhere Frank can't picture.

Frank's somehow expecting to find a little boy, lost and compliant. Instead, here's this strange man – too big, too strong, too watchful – who the boy Liam has secretly become. How does he touch him? Is it all right to touch him? Liam's clearly in the grip of a nightmare, eyes frantic, limbs flailing. He pats tentatively at Liam's shoulder, murmuring the words all humans say to each other at moments like this: *it's all right, don't worry, you're fine, everything's fine*. Feels the tension in the muscles, the quiver in the bones. Will Liam think he's dangerous, try to attack him? Surely not. He keeps patting, keeps murmuring. Liam calms down. Wakes up. For a moment, they're looking at each other. Is this a connection? Are they reconnecting? Is he going to rediscover his son? Is he…

"I'm fine," Liam says, eyes blank, face closed. "Sorry for waking you."

A dismissal. *Go back to bed and leave me alone. I don't need anything from you.* And that's definitely what Frank wants, now that first fierce instinct has slunk off back to its lair. So why are the next words out of his mouth not the required response of *no worries, see you in the morning*, but instead this shockingly intimate question:

"Were you having a nightmare?"

And for a second, there's a crack in the shutters, a chink of orangey hell-light glinting through, and he tries not to flinch at this glimpse of the inside of Liam's head.

My son needs me. He remembers this part of his brain switching on, when he held Liam, purple-hued and smeared with that *stuff* nobody warned you about, slick and disgusting and with its own primal smell. He's less clear on when it finally stopped clamouring and fell silent. Sometime around the fourth or fifth year after Jane left him, maybe. And now, here it is again. *I have to look after you. This is my duty.* It's only a whisper, easily ignored over the sound of Liam's voice, telling him to go inside, get warmed up, leave him alone, he'll be fine.

And Frank wants to walk away; he almost manages it. He doesn't want to sit in the rain with Liam. It's exhausting enough sharing living space during the day. They're men. They don't come with the emotional skills for personal revelation.

Nonetheless, back inside, he puts the kettle on and then finds himself pushing his feet into his trainers, puttering through cupboards and closets, finding two chairs, a spare coat, an umbrella, a couple of rugs. He knows he shouldn't bring vodka, alcohol won't help anything, but he tucks it under his arm anyway.

And now here they are, side-by-side in chairs in the rain, an absurd sight if anyone happened to be looking. (*Jane, can you see me now? Can you see us? Can you see the mistake you made, shutting me out? Is it your fault he's damaged? He came to me for help, not to you. That has to mean something.*) His breathing feels weird, as if his automatic functions have been switched off. He doesn't know how to sit in this chair, either, or how to be with this angry stranger who his brain insists he's responsible for. And the worst thing is, he's done this to himself. He's chosen to be here, watching Liam glowering into the darkness.

Now what happens?

"Does that happen a lot?" The question feels clumsy. He's way out of his comfort zone. "Dreaming about being back in the field?"

"Every now and then. No big deal. It's sleeping somewhere strange that does it." A small flicker in the relentless flatness of Liam's poker face. "Did I yell or anything?"

"No, no, nothing like that." It's not true but it's surely what Liam wants to hear. What Frank himself would want to hear. Frank can only see his son's profile, and it feels as if they're sitting in a car. Frank's on the right, so he's technically in the

141

driving seat, which is a bit of a shame because he has no idea where to go or how to get there. Should he try and get Liam to talk? Is that what he's meant to do? He's going to make a mess of this, he's going to do some damage. There's no intimacy here to build on.

What if he pretends Liam is some bloke he's met in a pub?

"You must have seen some things," he says. Vague and casual. *Tell me your best war story.*

"It was pretty spicy sometimes."

"So you were deployed?"

"Course I was. That was the job."

He knew anyway, but it's still a shock. His son, his little boy, sent to those places where for centuries white men have gone to discover that they're killers.

"It's what I signed up for." His terrible casualness shakes Frank's heart. "No point joining if you're not prepared to do the job."

"Did they make you... Did you have to..." The look on Liam's face turns him colder than the rain. "I'm sorry, it's none of my business."

"We're not just hired killers, you know."

Frank tries not to let his fear show. *Not just* isn't the same as *not*.

"Some of it was helping the locals," Liam continues. "Rebuilding stuff. Education."

"Quite a bit of it?"

"Most of it really."

"But not all of it? Is that why you had to leave?"

Poking the bear, that's what he's doing. There's a dangerous killer bear in the seat next to him and he's poking it with a great big pointy stick. No, Liam isn't a bear, he's a man, and the man was once his boy. Frank's heart pounds, but he's not sure what he's feeling. Could be love. Could be terror.

"I didn't *have* to leave; I chose to leave. Time to do something else." Frank can feel the potential for violence here now. It's a hard thing, for one human being to hurt another, but training and conditioning make it much easier. *This is my boy. My lad. My little lad. I'm supposed to help him.*

"I'm so sorry for whatever happened to you," he makes himself say. Makes himself put his hand on Liam's rigid back. Feels the quiver and flex of the muscles there, as if a creature is stirring beneath Liam's skin. *Oh shit*, he thinks, braces himself for whatever's coming. There's a mask, but now it's coming off, and who knows what he's going to see behind it? Is he going to be hit? Does Liam think Frank might hit *him*? What's going on inside his son's head?

And then, abruptly, the mask is back in place. Whatever it was, is gone again.

"It was the job. Nothing serious." He feels his dad shiver. "You go in now. It's cold."

"I'll stay out here with you. If you don't mind, I mean."

"No need."

But there is a need, there is. *My son needs me.* What's a father for, if not to keep the demons at bay?

"It's okay. I'll stay."

They sit side-by-side in the falling rain. Liam holds his mug of coffee but doesn't drink from it. He looks tense. Why isn't he drinking it? *Because it's coffee and it's night-time and he wants to sleep, you dozy old fool. You should have brought something else.*

He has something else, actually. Something more medicinal. Something that's almost a medicine. Something kinder, gentler, sweeter. He could…

He shouldn't. Jane would…

He's already reaching into his pocket.

There's a moment when he thinks he's misjudged this, but then Liam takes the bag from him, lights up the joint and inhales, and it feels like a victory. His son was in need and Frank's given him something.

Or, alternatively: his son had a nightmare and Frank's pressed him into taking mind-altering drugs.

But it can't be the first time. Liam knew what it *was*, for

143

goodness sakes, he knew what to *do*. Is this really any worse than giving him caffeine or alcohol? Liam looks a little looser, a little less anxious, but he's still not speaking. Frank looks at his son's profile and thinks, *Which is more terrible? The thought of you killing people and being broken by it? Or the thought that you've killed people and come home unchanged, feeling nothing at all? If I stay here by your side, will I be able to fix you? Or do you not want to be fixed?*

The silence is terrible, and Frank wants to run away from it, but he won't let himself do it. Whatever it is that's happening out here, he'll see it through to the end. *You're a father*, he thinks, *you're supposed to be*

CHAPTER FOURTEEN

(DECEMBER, NOW)

supposed to be asleep long ago, but her grandfather woke her when he opened the door to peek in, and then she heard the shout of her father waking and her grandfather following him outside and now they're both sitting out there in the dark, doing something mysterious Alannah can't quite make sense of. She won't sleep again until her father's safely back inside. So instead she's watching the rain, kneeling up in the darkness so she can follow the droplets on the glass.

A rainy night means a dry day tomorrow, her grandfather said over dinner, but how on earth can he know? Even the weather people get it wrong most of the time. That's what her parents always say. *Shall we go out somewhere tomorrow? The weather forecast says it'll be nice. Well, they always say that, don't they? They get it wrong most of the time.* Alannah always means to check for herself, to remember what the prediction was and match it against reality, but she can never make herself concentrate. Instead she gets lost in trying to find places she likes on the map. If she spots somewhere she likes the sound of – Aberystwyth, or Edinburgh, hard to spell but satisfying to look at – she knows tomorrow will be a good day.

If she sees a place name she doesn't like, she braces herself for a bad one.

There are three layers to what she can see, depending on where she focuses her attention. If she looks outwards, she sees the dim shape of two men, side-by-side beneath an umbrella. (She doesn't like seeing them out there, and certainly doesn't want them to see her. She's glad their backs are towards her.) If she brings her focus closer, fat blobs of water merge and separate, making their way down the pane. They move like children playing Grandmother's Footsteps; pausing and gathering themselves, growing fat with anticipation, then leaping forward to the next milestone.

And if she pulls back slightly from the window and turns her head, she sees the ghost of her own reflection, soft and uncertain beneath her new boy's haircut.

"I'm Alfie," she whispers to the face looking back at her.

Will her mother recognise her with her new short hair? Sometimes she uses Alannah as a model for her online mini-shop. Alannah's always hopeful the photos will tell her something important, help her connect with her own body, but they give her the same feeling she always has when she looks in the mirror. The girl in the photographs is pretty, graceful, feminine, and somehow *not her*.

She's used to transformations, to pretending. *Alannah, you'll be a snowflake. A lamb. A robot. A snake.* And the one that made her heart swell with something she couldn't truly name: *Alannah, you'll be dancing the part of one of Clara's brothers.*

Dance is about illusion. Playing a part, a performance with her whole body. More than that: it's about pretending that what's happening on the stage is natural, effortless, that every moment is spontaneous and nothing hurts. That it's easy to become someone she isn't. A snowflake. A lamb. A robot. A snake. A boy.

An illusion. A performance. That's how it ought to feel, being Alfie, saying this new name out loud in the dark to a rain-smeared reflection. Instead, there's a sense of rightness. Something's falling into place. The journey's been going on for a while now, but suddenly the destination's clear. "I'm Alfie."

The words make a cloud on the glass. It's Alannah who speaks them, but Alfie who watches as the patch of mist fades away. He's finally made sense of it, uncovered the mystery, brought it into the light. He knows who he is, and it's as if he's always known. He's Alfie. He's Alfie. He's found himself. He draws a deep breath and feels whole inside his skin.

So that's what it is, he thinks, a little dazed.

He's been afraid for so long. There are still so many things that he's afraid of. He's afraid of being here, in this house he hardly knows yet, when he was supposed to be in another city, dancing. He's afraid of his parents – his mother who left him, his father who's stolen him away. He's afraid of the blank future that lies on the other side of Christmas – where will they live, what will they do, what will any of them be? But right now, it's enough to have solved the puzzle of himself.

"I'm Alfie," he whispers again. There. That's three times. What does his mother always say? *I'm a witch and I've said it three times, so now it's bound to come true.* Can a boy be a witch? Perhaps he can cast this spell with the last trace of his girlhood, before he leaves it behind forever.

If I can only have this, he thinks, *I'll put up with anything else. Anything at all. Please let me have this.*

Outside on the lawn, he can still see the shapes of his father and grandfather. How will he tell them? Perhaps his dad already knows. Perhaps his grandad will never need to hear it said out loud. Perhaps he can simply get on with being himself, quietly, with no fanfare. Maybe all they'll need

CHAPTER FIFTEEN

(DECEMBER, NOW)

need, if we're going to dig a really good hole," his grandfather says as they mark out the circumference of their project, "is a steep beach with good, damp sand. If the beach is too shallow, you hit water too quick. If it's too dry, the hole caves in. If it's too pebbly, it's hard to dig and it won't hold its shape. But this sort of beach is perfect."

Alfie scrunches his bare toes into the sand and nods. It's cold enough to make his feet hurt, but he's used to his feet hurting. He's used to every part of him hurting. That's part of the deal. Perfection hurts.

"That's it. Nice and big. Don't dig it too narrow. Remember, you always want angled walls, not straight ones. Just in case the sides collapse. People have died that way."

Alfie imagines digging a hole so dangerous it could kill someone. He isn't sure if it would feel good, or terrifying.

"Don't worry. We won't die." His grandfather's smile is sincere and lovely. "I'm a world-class hole-digger, I am. You'll see."

"You don't have to wear yourself out doing that." His dad sounds cross, as if either Alfie or his grandfather has done something wrong, but Alfie thinks maybe the person

148

his dad is angry with is himself. Because he hadn't offered to help, maybe? The silly thing is, Alfie's too old to want to muck around like this, too old for digging holes and building sandcastles, and the weather's all wrong for it anyway, it's nearly *Christmas*. But he doesn't say any of this. He made a bargain – *if you let me have this, I can cope with everything else* – and so far, the universe has kept its side of the bargain. If he starts pointing out the fractures in the way his life is right now, who knows what's going to break?

"I don't mind. Do us both good." Frank smiles at Alfie, ruffles his hair with a sandy hand. "Got to get you built up for lifting those girls up if you're going to be a dancer, hey?"

If he's going to be a dancer. He's never thought of the word *if* before. Being a dancer has been his plan for as long as he's had one. *If he's going to be a dancer.* Will he still be able to? Have there been any dancers like him before? Will he even be allowed to go back to *class*? Mrs Baxter will be furious with him for missing his spot in *The Nutcracker*. On the other hand, she's always complaining that there aren't enough boys. Will she accept him as himself? Surely she'll accept him as himself. If his dad can be okay about it…

Is he, though? He calls him *Alfie* in public, but still *Alannah* in private. He's been hoping his dad will maybe forget, after a while, slip into the habit of using his true name. It hasn't happened yet. Will it ever? Alfie glances at his dad. He's stretched out but tense; Alfie can see the rigidity of his dad's shoulders, the clench of his jaw.

The hole isn't an interesting project, but he keeps working at it because it's easier than sitting down and watching his dad trying to sit still and his grandfather not knowing what to say. It's dull and joyless, until he's waist-deep in a cold sandy pit, and then suddenly it's enthralling. Look what he's done. Look how much sand he's shifted. How deep can he go? Could he dig down far enough to find water?

"That's pretty big."

Alfie squints up through low-lying sunshine. A boy about

his own age peers over the edge, assessing the hole with a connoisseur's eye.

"It's just getting started really." Alfie tries to copy the boy's stance. The stranger's wearing jeans, a hoodie tied round his waist, a t-shirt that's the same as the one Alfie wore yesterday. If they were girls, they might have a conversation about this – *I have that t-shirt too, I like it with that hoodie* – but he isn't sure if this is something boys do, or not. His grandfather's watching with a smile.

"Want to give us a hand?" Frank holds out his spade.

"Um..." The boy does want to help, Alfie can see, but he also doesn't want to look too eager.

"It'll go quicker with an extra digger," Frank says. "I was going to take a break anyway. So there's a spare spade if you want it. Is that your mum over there?"

From inside the hole, Alfie can't see the other boy's mum, but Frank waves and points and makes gestures that must have been okay, because a minute later, Frank's surrendered his spade and gone to sit on the rug. Now it's only the new boy, and Alfie.

"I'm Noah," says the boy. "Can I get in too?"

Alfie feels a tingle pass over his skin that could be either excitement, or fear. His dad knows the truth and his grandad's old and the people in the shops don't look closely enough to care, but this is a boy his own age and he needs to get everything absolutely right. The first real test he's faced.

"I'm Alfie," he says, and moves over to make room.

Noah's an erratic digger, flinging sand so wildly that half of it falls back in. Alfie wonders whether he should correct Noah's technique, explain that if he's slower and more careful, the hole will grow more quickly and they'll both stay cleaner. He settles for quietly demonstrating his own method, and feels a thrill of joy when Noah watches and adapts. The sand's wetter now, making streaks and teardrops against their skin and clothes.

"It looks gross," Noah says, picking a long worm of half-dried sand off his forearm. His movements are jerky and restless. Alfie's spent years learning to look fluid, boneless, effortless. Will he have to unlearn it all again?

"Like poo," Alfie says, and glances at Noah.

"Bird shit." Noah glances back. They laugh together, then look guiltily upwards, where the grown-ups might be listening.

"Is that your dad?" Noah asks.

"My dad and my grandad."

"I'm with my mum and my sister." Noah jabs at the sand with a spade. "My mum and dad split up over the summer. So now we've got to come to my grandma's for Christmas for some reason." He shakes his hair away from his face. "And I'll see my dad on Boxing Day and we'll have, like, two Christmases, so who cares?" He wipes sand from his cheek, leaves more behind than he gets off.

"Mine have split up too," Alfie says, startled by the tightness in his throat, because he's only saying out loud what he already knows. "I think they have, anyway. My mum's cleared off somewhere for a bit." He can't cry, he won't cry, that's one thing he knows he's not supposed to do.

Noah looks tactfully away. Glances up at the top of the hole, which is almost as high as their heads. "This is getting boring. Shall we look for crabs?"

"Okay."

Alfie's made sure the sides slope inwards towards the bottom as instructed, but getting out is still a challenge. Noah claws out handfuls of sand to make niches, then scales the side like a monkey. Without really thinking about it, Alfie gathers his legs beneath him and propels himself straight upwards, high enough to hook his hips over the edge of the hole and wriggle out. Noah watches in reluctant admiration.

"That was mad," he says. "Do you do a lot of, like, weights or something?"

If he says *dancing*, will he blow his cover? He settles for a shrug, because it seems like something Noah would do.

"We're going to look for crabs," Noah declares to the adults.

"Is that all right?" Alfie asks.

His dad's put on his mirrored sunglasses, making his face even less readable than usual. He looks them up and down, then nods.

"Sure."

"Want me to come with you?" Frank sits up and shakes sand from his hands.

"That's okay," Noah says. "Have you got a bucket?"

As it happens, Alfie does have a bucket, bright blue with a sneering face. Is it too childish to show to Noah? Then he sees Noah collecting his own bucket, discarded in the sand-pile at the top of the hole. It's bright pink with a rainbow on the side. Alfie sighs with relief and grabs his own.

"Come on, then."

On the way down to the water, they pass a woman with long brown hair and a red cardigan, helping a small girl stick fragments of shell onto a sand-pie. Noah waves at her as they pass.

"Take care, you two. Are you looking for crabs? Put them back where you find them, okay?" Her words are shouted into Noah's back, and when he replies "We will, don't worry," he doesn't bother to turn around. Alfie used to take his mother for granted in this way too.

"She's a teacher," Noah says gloomily, as if this explains everything.

"My mum's a teaching assistant," Alfie offers. "And my dad's a soldier."

"No way!" Noah lights up. "That is so cool. Where has he been? Has he been in, like, wars and that?"

"Yep."

"That's excellent. My dad's an accountant. Does he bring all his gear home with him? Guns and stuff?"

"He's not allowed. He has to leave it at the base."

"Come on. Let's get some crabs." Noah darts off like a dragonfly, zig-zagging around two small children who squat in the shallows, blue-footed and blue-lipped as they diligently pile sand into buckets and scoop up tiny quantities of seawater with their spades.

So that's how boys move, Alfie thinks. He's spent so long trying to fit in with the girls that he hasn't paid much attention to his own kind. *This is what I'm supposed to do.* Changing direction at the drop of a hat. Moving across the surface of life like a predator. Fast and strong.

They fill their buckets with water, jeans and joggers rolled up to their knees, pretending not to mind the cold. Noah has a faint bloom of hair on his calves. The breakwater is lush and slimy with seaweed. Noah picks confidently through the fronds, but there are no crabs to be seen.

"Must all have been taken," Noah says. "You have to come early to find them."

Alfie's watching a small smooth pebble lodged in the wood. As he stares at it, the pebble stretches out a spindly leg, and then another. He reaches delicately in and extracts the tiny crab. It waves its legs in helpless protest.

"You found one," Noah says.

Alfie shrugs. "It's only small."

"Still, you got one."

"It's a bit rubbish though." (So boys, like girls, sometimes say what they know the other person's thinking. That's good to know.) Alfie drops the crab into Noah's bucket. It sidles into the crease of the bucket wall and pulls in its legs. "Maybe there's more."

They inspect the wood, studying each crevice from every angle, and find a few more miniature specimens. Despite their shells, they feel so fragile that Alfie's afraid he'll crush them. They add a few periwinkles too, with the vague idea of providing a food source. Then Noah exclaims in excitement and grabs Alfie's shoulder.

"Look at this one."

Lurking in the shadow of the breakwater, nestled behind a chunk of granite, the crab is pretending to be a stone. It's wider across its shell than either of their hands. Can it see them, peering through the silty water? Does it know they're alive, and looking back?

"Shall we pick it up?" Noah looks uncertain. "Or we could get a stick."

"You have to grab them behind the shell." Alfie bites his lip.

"What if it puts its claws out, though?"

"We could do it together."

The water plays tricks on their depth perception, and the crab's further away than they thought. It stirs slightly on its base, but doesn't attack. They feel their way closer, hands wavering through the water. When their fingertips touch down on the rough-brick surface of its shell, they both sigh at the same moment.

"It's massive," Noah says.

"Maybe we should leave it."

"No, let's get it. We could get it out together. If we slide our hands underneath…"

It's a good idea, but the crab's large and intimidating, and for all Noah's tough confidence, it's clear he doesn't have the courage. Alfie thinks about the intricately folded network of legs and joints, the spidery way they move. He will do this. He will not fail.

Underneath feels like living pipework. Alfie feels it moving against his palm, alien and disturbing. If he waits much longer it will simply get up and walk away. A moment of hesitation, and then he's bringing the crab up through the water, grabbing and juggling to stop it from sliding off, willing himself not to shriek when it moves. Noah's yelling encouragingly in his ear.

"Put the bucket in the water," Alfie gasps. "I don't want

154

to drop it; we might crack its shell… No, not your one, my one, it's deeper."

Noah slides the bucket below the surface. A fat glop of water slurps in, and one of the tiny crabs floats out.

"Doesn't matter," Alfie says, as Noah grabs for it. "We've got the big one." He tips the crab gingerly in. Its claws catch on the side and he thinks he's lost it, but then Noah gives the bucket a brisk little shake and the crab slips inside. Instantly it pulls its arms and legs back in and hunkers down.

"We got it," says Noah.

"Yep," Alfie replies, breathless with excitement.

"That was really cool."

"Thanks."

"Shall we go and show everyone?"

Something's shifted in their relationship, and now Alfie's the one in charge. He tries not to let his grin grow too obvious.

"If you like," he says, and leads the triumphal march back up the beach.

"Alfie got a massive crab," Noah calls out as soon as his mother's in earshot. "It's really big. Grace, do you want to look?"

A little girl who looks disconcertingly like Noah stumps across the sand and peers into the bucket.

"It's big," she says, and pokes a curious hand into the water.

"Don't touch it." Alfie and Noah speak together. Grace's hand instantly withdraws.

"It's just it might try and pinch your fingers," Alfie explains, seeing Grace look crestfallen.

Grace blinks. "Can we keep it?"

"We can't keep him. Crabs belong in the sea." Noah's mother has arrived to inspect their treasure. "Very well done, you boys, that's a massive one. Might even be a world record. No, I'm serious, you never know. Want a photograph? Put your hands round the bucket so we can compare sizes… There you are. Make sure you put him back where you found him, though. He'll want to be near his home."

155

"How do you know it's a he?" Grace asks.

"Well, it looks like a *he* to me," their mother says. "Alfie, are you going to show it to anyone before you both put it back?"

Alfie's dad is lying on the sand, but he sits up as Alfie and Noah approach. Alfie can see the awe, verging on fear, in Noah's eyes as he takes in the straight back, the unsmiling face, the smooth movements, the low-key, curiously adult nature of his praise ("Good job you two, that's a decent size. Take it steady when you put him back"). His grandad is more effusive, and pokes at the shell with a stick to persuade it to move. The crab, stoic, presses against the bottom of the bucket and keeps still. Then the moment's over, the glory's used up, and they wander away with their bucket, Alfie wondering what they might do next, once the crab's been sent home to the breakwater.

"I need a pee," Noah says, and nods towards the toilet block at the top of the beach. "D'you mind if I go while you take the crab back?"

Is this Noah's way of getting out of a boring job? Or is he looking for an excuse to end this sudden friendship and go back to his family? "Me too."

"What shall we do with the crab, though?"

"He can wait in the bucket."

Noah sighs. "All right. I might have to go back to my mum and sister afterwards though. I've got to help Grace make a sandcastle."

Alfie puts the bucket carefully down in the shade of the toilet block. *Gentlemen*, the sign on the door reads. He takes a deep breath.

The walk down to the water has grown longer. He isn't imagining this, the tide's going out. The breakwater where they found the crab is fully exposed, the sand around the base thick and gloopy. Should he put the crab down here even though the water's drained away? Or should he put it in the sea? Which is its real home? Alfie stands and debates this with himself, focusing as hard as he can on this critical decision so he won't have to think about anything else. Up on the beach, Noah's returned to his family. Alfie was careful not to look at them as he walked past. He had to fight the impulse to put his hands over his ears.

In the water, he decides, and dips the bucket below the surface, tipping the crab out. It looks so fierce, but if he threw it against the wall, it would shatter and die. The outer shell's only a cover.

"Go on," he says out loud, and tips the bucket further. The crab slides out and sinks to the bottom. Perhaps they've killed it by taking it out and parading it around. Why did they even catch it in the first place? It only wanted to be left alone to live its life.

Now he has to go back up the beach. This is what he has to do next so that's what's going to happen. His dad has to do stuff he doesn't want to all the time, but he does it anyway because life can't always be fun. Alfie squares his shoulders and marches up the beach without looking left or right. He has an invisible shell that he carries on his back and nothing and nobody can get through it. He's passing the place where Noah's family are, and now he decides his shell has a special shape that means he can't see out of the sides, he can't see them so they're not there, and they're nothing to do with him anyway. There's his grandad, looking troubled. Where's his dad?

His dad's talking to Noah's mother. She's angry. She knows. She knows. But why does she care? What's his dad saying in return? His dad's arms are folded and he's standing very still. Please let him stay like that. Please let him not lose his temper on the beach and shout at a strange woman the way he shouts at Mum sometimes. Please let him not do anything scary. The woman's stopped talking now. Maybe his dad's talking instead. What's he saying? Alfie wants to believe his dad is defending him, but he can't be sure he will.

"Woman's got a bee in her bonnet." His grandad greets Alfie with a gloomy smile, and pats the sand beside him. "Wanted to talk to your dad in private. You didn't hit that young lad or anything, did you?" Alfie shakes his head. "Ah, well, don't worry about it then."

He won't cry. He's a boy, and boys don't cry. He has an invisible shell around him that protects him from the outside world. Today is not ruined. Today he dug the deepest hole he's ever dug and he caught the biggest crab that's ever been caught and he's wearing his new trackie bottoms and his new t-shirt with a VW camper van on it and his hair is short and he knows who he is and he is not going to

CHAPTER SIXTEEN

(2016)

going to come home to us any day now. We all sense it, even without official notice. How do we know? It's a sweet mystery. Maybe our men send out a chemical signal. *Get the kettle on, love, we'll be back soon.* There's a flush in my skin, an awakening of parts of my brain that have lain dormant. For weeks and weeks, stretching into months, I've shuttled between school and home, home and school. I've been *Mother* to Alannah and *Homemaker* to our house and *Miss* to the kids in the class. In the silent moments of the night, bending my will to the task of keeping Liam alive, I've been something else, something secret. I've even, occasionally, been simply *Emma.* Now it's time to be *Wife* and *Lover.* I need to remember this is a good thing.

There's the journey to the train station, collecting my man from wherever they've left him this time. In the early days he liked to surprise me, walking in through the front door like any other husband home from work. A few times he got home before I did, waited in the lounge for me with a cup of tea. I knew the drill for these occasions and I did what was expected, don't get me wrong. The glad scream. The leap. The passionate snog. The swift undressing, the shag that began in the hallway and sometimes didn't make it all the way up the stairs. (I did what was expected, but I also enjoyed it. Does that make sense? That a duty can also be a pleasure?) But as time went on and our lives grew richer and more complicated, sex not the only thing on our minds at the moment of reunion, I found I liked it better when I went to collect him. The journey helped me get into the right mode.

So, yes: the getting ready process begins with that taste in the air that warns me (not *warns*, that's not the right word, let's try *brings me the wonderful news*) that he's coming home soon. Sometimes it's a false alarm, and after a few days it goes away again. But not this time. Not this time.

The school are understanding. They know I need to abandon my teaching-assistant duties for a day to fetch my husband, which is a higher duty. It's the same as when one of your children is sick. Some things you simply have to do, no matter what it costs you or anyone else. Of course, I want to do this, I want to bring Liam home. But there's still a feeling of disruption. My life had fallen into a certain shape, formed around certain expectations. Now someone's forced a rearrangement. It hasn't sunk in yet. It will sink in eventually.

I'm helped by the faint background hum of excitement that hovers over the station. When I park the car, I feel the same pleasurable skip of my heart that I get when we go on holiday. In a couple of hours, I'll be back in the place I left, but it will be different, because Liam will be there with me. My man is coming home. Coming home to me. How many women have stood in doorways or on hilltops or by the side of roads, waiting for this same moment? Now it's my turn.

There's a minute when I see him and I'm afraid in case I've picked out the wrong man. I'm afraid he won't recognise me. I'm afraid he won't *like* me. I'm afraid I'll feel the same about him. I see him searching, and his expression makes me ache because it reminds me I'm part of his team, he needs me. If I wasn't here, doing my bit, what would become of him?

But I am here. We're both here and then he sees me and

there's no stopping us, we come together and cling. No kiss at first. Only the fierce tight clutch of two bodies, separated for too long. He presses his face against my hair. I dig my nose into his chest. It must look romantic. Lovers reunited. What's happening is more primal; we're smelling each other. In his kit bag, Liam takes a special can of body spray, the same scent each time, always full, taken from the stash under the bed. I'm careful with the shampoo I choose and never change my perfume. We haven't told each other these things. It's simply what we know to do.

And once our limbic systems have done their job for us, confirmed that yes, this is the partner we love and not some convincing imposter, we can kiss.

That kiss. It always feels both staged and real. We're practicing love, but we're also performing it. There's no other circumstance when we'd press our open mouths together, tongues touching, in front of strangers.

Then there's the walk to the car, my boot filled with a man's things, the unfamiliar bulk of a man-sized passenger to my left. He offers to drive, and I tell him no, because he's had a long journey home. This is code for *because you just got out of a war zone and I don't trust your reactions.* He doesn't argue, which is how I know he knows I'm right. I drive extra carefully, because I want to impress him. I want to live up to the men and women who have driven him around in much more dangerous conditions. I know this is ridiculous. I do it anyway.

As we drive, he comments on peculiar things. *Oh look, Boots the chemist*, he says, and then, *hey, there's a toothpaste advert. Oh, wow, a traffic light!* I'm not sure if he knows he's talking aloud. It seems half-conscious, the twitches of his nervous system as he readapts to a civilian, civilised world.

If I drove quickly enough, we could go home and have sex before collecting Alannah from dance class, but the thought unsettles me. Desire takes time to accommodate. Would you want to jump into bed with someone you hadn't seen for months? So instead I take the slow road from the station, and we drive to the dance studio and collect Alannah together. The other parents look sideways at Liam, unsure. He's unfamiliar, and he walks and moves like what he's only recently stopped being, which is a soldier on active duty. It's strange that in a place where good posture is so emphasised, a place of sweat and pain and hard work and mindless repetition, my husband the soldier stands out as an oddity.

We drive to the restaurant where his mother waits to buy us dinner. This is the silent compromise Jane and I have reached over the years: I'll be the one who sees him first, but she'll feed him his first meal. Jane and I don't love each other exactly but we have love in common, and we get on best when we acknowledge this and work around it. Liam's beginning to lose the dazed look he always wears when he comes home, settling back into his chair and eating with gusto. Alannah eats more than she usually would, although less than Jane would like her to eat, and swallows three ostentatious bites of cake. She's making compromises too. She's dropping with tiredness, and this is the first moment I feel irritated, because while Liam can sleep late and enjoy his time off, tomorrow morning Alannah and I will have to drag ourselves out of bed and slip back into the groove of our routines. *Who is this man who thinks he can turn up and disrupt our lives like this? Why can't he have some consideration?* I don't like this thought, but I can't stop it coming to me. I let it arrive, examine it, then push it away again. The moment passes.

We say goodnight, Jane and I promising we'll see each other at the weekend, suddenly remembering to turn to Liam and say, *if that's all right with you, I mean*. When Liam's home, I have to check with someone else before allocating my free time. How long will it take to get used to this again? The thought travels with me on the journey home. I want to be distracted by Liam's hand resting at the top of my thigh, but I can't quite make it happen. It takes the look on Liam's face as he walks in through the door, the subtle sag of his shoulders, the deep inhale and the brief controlled spasm of emotion on his face, before I can recover my fierce bright gladness.

My man is home. He's safe. At least one of my jobs is done right. I take the coffee mug from behind the picture in the hall and put it in the dishwasher. Take the t-shirt from beneath my pillow and add it to the washing pile. So many rituals I can let go of for now, until the next time he's called away. We snuggle on the sofa, Alannah flushed and sleepy between us. When I tell her it's bedtime, she slips upstairs without arguing. Liam goes after her to tuck her in.

I go through the hall to fetch a couple of beers, and fall over Liam's boots.

He's not messy. I can't pin that one on him. They're arranged side-by-side, next to the shoe rack. They're not in the shoe rack because the shoe rack's full of my and Alannah's footwear. Shoes and boots and wellies and sandals, neatly arranged and pretty to look at, no room for a giant pair of lace-up industrial things, so they have to stand on the carpet, where I've fallen over them. Has he left them here as a small protest? Does he feel excluded because there's no room for his boots? Or am I overthinking it?

I haven't decluttered since last summer. There are pairs here that won't fit Alannah anymore. I've only held onto them because they're so sweet. I don't want to say goodbye to the shiny patent Mary Janes, the bee wellies, the glittery low-heeled strappy ballroom shoes. They're so perfect, and hardly worn. I could keep them simply to look at. But this is why there's no room for Liam's boots. I fetch a carrier bag, stack the outgrown shoes away. Tomorrow I'll take them to the charity shop.

(Or maybe I could ask Liam to do it.)

(No, that's not fair, it's his first day back. He's entitled to one day off.)

(And when do you get your one day off?)

(And when do you have to go into a war zone?)

(You only need to go to a charity shop because you need to make room for his boots. If he…)

I leave the hallway before this train of thought carries me into enemy territory.

With Alannah in bed, we sip our beer and watch television for a while. Liam takes control of the remote, the way men always do; and I let him, the way women always do. If I want to watch anything different, all I have to do is ask. I don't ask, so obviously I don't care. Left to myself, I'll watch the same six movies on rotation night after night, or else fill up the planner with trashy, comforting nonsense. Wedding dresses. Make-over shows. Home redecorations. Anything where ugliness becomes beauty and a happy ending's guaranteed. It's good that Liam's back, making me watch news and documentaries. It doesn't matter what we watch, we're simply filling in the time until we're confident Alannah is asleep.

"God, Persil," Liam murmurs. He's still decompressing, still in the stage where small visual or sonic cues seem like miracles, re-anchoring him in his true life. He reaches absently behind him and pulls out a Union Jack cushion, drops it on the floor beside his feet.

He doesn't throw things around, doesn't make a mess, doesn't wreck everything. It's just that I made the cover for that cushion, pieced out each stripe on the flag, sewed them together, then added the zip and the backing. I made it because I thought he'd like it. Then, because I'd had that thought, it became a talisman of his safety. *I'll arrange that cushion on his spot on the sofa every morning, and as long as it's still there at night, I'll know he's safe.*

Now he's home. The cushion's done its job. It doesn't matter now if it goes on the floor. And all I can think of is how careful I was to always put the flag the right way up, in case God was watching and taking notice. That, and how hard it was to get the corners crisp. Acute angles are hard to sew accurately. But I did it.

And when Liam looks at the cushion, he sees one more piece of clutter.

"There's a new Ribena ad," Liam says, almost as if he thinks I should have told him about this. "You warm enough?"

On the back of every chair and all along the sofa are hand-pieced quilts and hand-knitted blankets. When I'm alone, I take them down and wrap myself in them. Tonight, Liam's here, and I don't need them.

"That one new?" he asks, nodding towards the quilt I made with pair after pair of upcycled jeans, carefully chosen from a succession of charity shops. I took pleasure in preserving the pockets, the networks of stitching, the worn places where keys or wallets had been carried.

"Yes."

"Don't we have enough yet?" The question's mild enough, a little teasing, but behind it is a difference so fundamental that for a moment, I feel as if I'm falling into a pit. I like prettiness. He likes order. We're different people. And somehow, we have to live together.

Then it's bedtime, the moment we've both been waiting for. Why not go to bed earlier, bring the moment forward? It's not because we're enjoying the delay, we've already been apart for too long. It's more that we need this time to remember that we do actually know each other, and we're not about to leap between the sheets with a stranger. (Has Liam done exactly this while he's been away? How would I ever know if he had? If I played away, someone would notice and bring me back into line; but the rules are different for the men.) Or maybe we're afraid of waking Alannah.

There are cushions on the bed, balanced on their points against carefully plumped pillows. There's yet another quilt, neatly folded, for the nights when the heat of a single body isn't enough to warm the corners of our king-sized bed. He pushes the quilt and the cushions to the floor, not in an angry way, more as if this is where they really belong. I try not to mind. Then I really don't mind, because he's taking off his shirt, and I see the smooth muscled contours of his chest, and my hand aches to touch the skin. His body is exactly the same as I remember it, sturdy and masculine, delicious. Have I done as good a job as he has at staying in shape? What if he doesn't like what he sees?

His eyes are dark and wanting as he watches me unfasten the buttons of my blouse, taking my time, pretending to be a little slower and less skilled than I am. I can see him thinking about tearing it off. I wonder if I'd like it if he did. But tonight, he's content to watch. Perhaps he's seen enough violent acts in the last few months to last a lifetime, and now all he craves is the slow sweetness of a woman undressing for him. Or perhaps he's long past thought, focused only on his body's need. How will I ever know what goes on in his head?

We come together, slowly at first, then faster. He hasn't forgotten how to please me; he hasn't forgotten what I like. This is one thing we never forget. This is the one thing that will save us. This one thing we do with each other and no one else. This ordinary piece of marital magic. In the next room, our daughter slumbers. Should we have another? Will tonight be the night we make our second child? When we talked about it last, he said he wasn't too bothered either way, that he'd welcome another if we had one, but it was fine if I wanted to stop at one. He said these exact words: *if you want to, you can come off the pill, any time you want mind you, and we'll see what happens. Don't tell me. Just surprise me with it. Or don't. That's fine too.*

So, the ball's in my court. It's another decision I'm expected to make, for this man who spends his working life making critical choices that mean life or death for him and for those around him, and who's now come home and expects me to do all the heavy lifting. No, that's not fair. This isn't like *what shall we have for dinner* or *do you think Alannah needs new shoes yet* or *shall we repaint the kitchen?* He's not burdening me with the responsibility. He's giving me the power. Making me his equal. I can choose, too. I can choose life, or not life.

But now I'm not making any kind of choice, I'm nothing but flesh and sensation, and I forget about the boots in the hall, the cushions on the floor, the strangeness of having a man in the house again. Sex is neither ordered nor pretty, but it is vital for both of us. The glue that holds us together. For this moment, we are held in the same place. If only we could simply do *this* forever, alone in this bed where I can finally lose the feeling of being outside myself, watching as we stroke and squeeze and nibble and lick and whisper to each other, *yes, like that, I can't wait, hurry*

CHAPTER SEVENTEEN

(DECEMBER, NOW)

hurry things up and get their order into the kitchen, he's going to walk out. How can it take so long to write down three bloody meals on a notepad? Liam feels his fists clench inside his pockets.

"Okay. So that's… three Full Englishes… two teas… one tap water." She's staring at her pad as if someone else wrote the words there in a foreign language and now it's her job to decipher them.

"One English without the beans." *Why can't you people fucking listen?*

"One without beans." The woman nods but makes no amendments that he can see. *If you send out my order with fucking beans on the side I will fucking kill you.* "Anything else?"

"That's the lot." *I will not say thank you. I will not say thank you. Just do your fucking job.*

The woman looks at him, unsmiling.

"That's thirty-one pounds."

He can see her swallowing the word *please*. He can hardly complain. She's giving back exactly what he's giving out. *Try and push me, bitch. Do it.* He's spoiling for a fight, itching to have a go at someone, anyone, so he can let loose the rage squatting in his stomach. *Go on. Tell me manners don't cost anything. Do it. Do it now and I will rain down on you like the fires of the apocalypse...*

"Let me get these." Now his dad's there, jostling and rustling and holding out two twenty-pound notes, and so great is Liam's fury – *how dare you undermine me like that how dare you emasculate me I can buy my own fucking lunch and your lunch and my kid's too while I'm at it don't you fucking dare* – that for a minute he thinks he might push his dad through a wall. In the moment when he gets his temper back into its lair, his dad has completed the transaction, pocketed the five-pound note, dropped the coins into the tip jar. The woman rewards him with a smile.

You're not supposed to tip in advance, they haven't fucking done anything yet. What's their incentive to do a decent job? You fucking moron. If anyone around him could see the spool of hate unravelling in his brain, they'd be appalled. No, not appalled, he's not a monster. If anyone around him could see the spool of hate unravelling in his brain, they'd be impressed, by how much he's managing to keep inside. *You think I'm being rude to you, you stupid fat greasy cow? You have no fucking idea how rude I could be...* He sits down at their table, willing himself to move carefully, not to jostle the rack of condiments or send the knives and forks tumbling.

"You doing okay, mate?" He thinks his dad is talking to him, actually draws breath ready to reply, but of course he means Alfie, no, *Alannah*, damn it, this nonsense has gone on long enough. Alannah's huddled deep inside her fleece, posture slumped, exactly as if she hasn't spent years training herself to hold herself up from her hips, keep her spine straight and true. He wants to tell her to sit up straight and stop sulking, but then he'll have to see the look on her face and he'll have one more thing to be angry about, one more thing to keep bottled up, and he's not sure he's got room for one more thing. It doesn't help that they're wedged in tight amongst a clutter of fellow diners, crammed around flimsy tables with ugly metal legs that wobble if you lean on them. What a shithole this place is, what a pitiful excuse for a place of enjoyment. He's sat in field canteens that had better appointments, eaten cold stuff from cans that tasted better than the shite they're serving. Fuck this. Fuck the world. And fuck that smug bitch on the beach, who had the fucking audacity to say to him—

"You all right there in that corner? Need some more room?" His dad's doing the things Liam should do himself, taking over in a way that makes Liam want to jam a fork in his dad's eye. Alannah shakes her head. "Never much room in places like this, is there?" Alannah offers a small smile, but curls in on herself, as if she's proving how little room she needs. "Looking forward to your food?"

Will you shut up, Liam thinks. Of course Alannah's not looking forward to her food, she never does. *Shut up, shut up, shut up. Stop talking so I can think. No, that's not right. I don't want to think...*

("Noah was very confused." That woman's righteous face, worse because she was actually quite pretty and in different circumstances he'd have fancied her. No, let's be honest, he *did* fancy her, and he'd filled the boredom of watching their boys roam the beach by imagining what it would feel like to have sex with her, whether she'd go on top or underneath, how hard she'd suck his cock, whether she'd let him finish in her mouth. "In future, you ought to warn people before letting your child go off with other people's kids. I don't know how I'll explain this to him.")

Don't think, don't think, don't think. There's a little wire pot crammed with packets of sugar and sweetener. Long white sticks for the white sugar. Long brown sticks for the brown sugar. And the sweetener in little thin tubes, too narrow for the weave of the wire, sticking out all over like hedgehog spines. All the packets jammed together, untidy and crumpled. He begins to rearrange them, building an outer wall of brown sugar (the most robust of the three, thanks to the coarser grain) so the rest can shelter safely inside.

("Have you thought about the damage you're doing? Making her think wanting short hair and trousers makes her a boy?" That long finger, not quite touching him but nonetheless an invasion. "She doesn't have to be a princess to be female. Being a girl isn't about what you wear, it's a biological reality." It had taken everything he had not to tear her throat out.)

"That looks neat." His dad, nodding approvingly at Liam's sugar fortress, as if Liam's six years old and still in need of his dad's admiration. He wants to tell his dad to shut up, that he's not playing around here, he's organising things the way they ought to be organised so everything can stay neat and ordered and not spill out of the sides and make a mess on the table (*look* at it, *look* at that soggy packet of sweetener, lying in the pool of a melting ice cube, leaking its guts across the surface). He keeps quiet because he knows saying it would sound childish. Outmanoeuvred, again. But he'll find a way. He'll fucking show them all.

("Anyway." She'd even chosen when their interaction ended, for fuck's sake, she hadn't even given him a chance at the last word. "She's your child, so it's your decision. But what will you say to her if she gets to adulthood and realises it was all a mistake?" And then she'd gone back to her own little kingdom, borders marked out by bags and spades and rows of sand-pies, and settled back down with her book, and the unmistakable air of a woman well-satisfied with her day's work. Thinking she was unassailable, that he'd be bound by the rules of convention and stay out of her space. Whereas in fact she was utterly vulnerable, he could have been over there in five or six strides, put his hands around her neck and twisted, one quick short jerk and she'd have been dead on the sand, her stupid face blank and empty, her tongue lolling out like a necktie… The fact that he didn't do any of that, that he turned around and walked back to his own patch of sand, that was something he could be truly proud of.)

"Two teas, one tap water." The woman smiles at Frank and Alannah but not at Liam, and he feels a flare of anger. There's no excuse for being unprofessional. He tries to catch her eye so he can give her an intimidating stare, but she's not having it. Fucking bitch. He sips his tea moodily.

"Food shouldn't be long," says Frank. "You hungry, Alfie?"

She's a girl and she's not called fucking Alfie. That's the worst part – that stupid bitch *assuming* he was going along with some gender-identity transition bullshit. But how could he have explained? *My daughter thinks we need to hide because I told her that her mother's gone a bit mad, and she's pretending to be a boy so we'll be harder to find?* Would that have sounded any less insane? The million little questions, the million little judgements to make. *Why have you taken her away from her mother? Why did you tell a little girl her mother's gone mad? Can't you get her some help, sort things out like an adult? Why doesn't she want to be around you, what did you do that's so terrible anyway? Did you hit her?* As if. He's never laid a finger on Emma in that way, never has and never would. He's never touched her with anything but love. Never even wanted to, no matter how bad things got between them. Not like that stupid bitch on the beach. Beach bitch. He could have hit that beach bitch straight into next week.

"Mind if I take a couple?" Frank's fingers hover over the sugar packets.

"Go for it."

"I don't want to mess up your design."

God's *sake*, what does his dad think's going on here? He's not playing with the sugar packets, he's *tidying* the sugar packets, and he's only doing that because he's bored out of his bloody mind. How long can it take to make a Full English? It's not like they've got an extensive menu. The kitchen's nothing more than a production line, piling stuff onto plates and shipping them out. The serving hatch provides a glimpse inwards. It looks exactly as greasy and unpleasant as he's imagined. There are two plates waiting on the hatch. As he watches, they're joined by a third. Is that theirs?

"Three Full Englishes," the woman intones, putting plates down.

Get this right, you bitch.

"One without beans," she adds, putting it in front of Alannah without asking who it's for. Liam swaps the plates over without comment. He will not give in to her fucking pathetic attempts to needle him. He's better than this. Alannah turns over the shrivelly slice of black pudding with her knife.

"Black pudding," Frank says. "Don't eat it if you don't like it."

"Do you like it, Dad?"

"It's all right." He's angry with Alannah too. That confrontation on the beach was her fault. What was she thinking, going into the boys toilets? How hard would it have been to tell that lad Noah, *actually I'm a girl*? Alannah studies her black pudding a moment longer, then cuts off a thin sliver and pops a piece into her mouth.

"What do you think?" Frank is watching in amusement.

"It's all right." Her voice is an eerie echo of her father's. "What's it made of?"

"Generally best not to ask that about sausages," Frank says, just as Liam says "Blood."

"Blood?" Alannah swallows hard and looks at her father. He looks back steadily, waiting to see what she'll do. She looks back at him, then takes a second, larger slice. Raises it to her mouth. Puts it inside. Chews.

"Tough cookie," Frank says, and Liam can't tell if he's admiring or appalled. "Like his dad."

But he's a she, Liam thinks, *Girls can be tough too. I fucking know that; I don't have any expectations.* Where did that stupid woman get off, thinking she could tell Liam what *being a woman* was about? He'd seen evidence of women's toughness that would make that beach bitch sick to her stomach. This was Emma's fault. What chance did Alannah have, raised by a woman whose main hobby was making things to dress herself in? All those dance lessons, those endless exhortations, *be graceful, be light, be skinny, be fragile.* (Okay, maybe he'd made up the last one... He knew there was nothing fragile about dancers.)

Emma's fault, not his. He'd been away, earning the money that kept a roof over their head and food in their belly. And once he'd seen what was happening, he'd come home, been practically a stay-at-home parent, trying his best to undo the damage Emma had done.

God, if only Emma was here. If he could say all this to her face, watch her fucking crumple. Tell her once and for all. He jabs at a tomato.

"Look," Alannah says. She's pushing her food around her plate but not really eating it, the way she always does. Sometimes he thinks her bones will split her skin.

"Eat it, don't play with it."

Alannah cuts a fragment of bacon from a rasher. "Sorry." She's not concentrating, distracted by something over Liam's shoulder.

"Don't be sorry. Just eat your food." Maybe the beach bitch has come in. If she wants a fight, he'll give her one.

"What can you see?" Frank, the eternal good guy, always trying to be *nice*. It's a good thing he left Liam and Jane when he did. What kind of a snowflake would Liam have turned out otherwise?

"Police," says Alannah.

There's no way they're here looking for him, but Liam feels a twitch in his spine anyway. Moving slowly, he reaches for his mug of tea, takes a long hot swallow. He doesn't need to worry. He's done nothing wrong. Emma walked out on *him*, not the other way around. He's entitled to make whatever parenting decisions he thinks are best.

(Unless Emma's somehow guessed what he's up to, what

he's planning. Unless those creepy fucking spells of hers actually *work*, and she can see what he's doing, see inside his head. No, that's ridiculous, of course they don't work. There's no such thing as bloody witchcraft. All that shit proves is that she's completely insane.)

She can be convincing, though. She's in the wrong, she's the mad one, but she has weapons. Her words and her charm and her way of twisting things around. He can hear her now. ("Yes, officer, I do have reason to be concerned. He's an ex-soldier. He was discharged for medical reasons. He's had treatment in the past for his mental health.") Ignoring the fact that he was fine, he was coping perfectly well. The truth wouldn't matter in the face of Emma's story.

"It's all right," he says to Alannah. The tension in his voice irritates him. What's he getting wound up about? "Coppers have to eat too. They'll be on their coffee break."

"But what if they're not?" Alannah's hoarse whisper is astonishingly loud. The two officers are being handed mugs of coffee and bacon rolls. Can they hear her? He plasters a smile to his face in case they can. *See my daughter? Mad as a box of frogs. She actually thinks the police are after her because she dropped a sweet wrapper on the seafront.* He points this expression in the direction of Frank, trying it out before he presents it to anyone else. To his utter astonishment, Frank is watching the police officers the way a bird watches a cat sleeping in the sunshine.

"What?" Liam demands. "What's the matter?"

"Nothing. Nothing at all." Frank's smile is ghastly. "Finish your lunch, son, it's getting cold."

Of course it's something. Grown men don't react that way to police officers. Not unless they have something to feel guilty about. Or unless they're feeling guilty on behalf of someone else. With deliberate casualness, Frank turns his gaze back to his plate. Cuts off a careful slice of sausage. Puts it in his mouth.

"It's all right," Alannah says, her whisper surely audible

from space. "They're standing at the counter and talking and eating their sandwiches."

The woman on the next table is listening in. Liam can see it in the set of her shoulders, the angle of her neck. Is she laughing at Alannah's nonsense? Or is she taking mental notes, time and place and accent and words spoken, in case she's a witness to important information?

"Why? What have you done, Alfie?" Frank's trying to sound as if he thinks it's funny. It's working pretty well. Liam can hear the difference, but Liam's been trained to listen properly. "Did you rob a bank? Are you raising a bank robber, son?"

It's as if Frank can see into Liam's head, see the fears there, all the things Liam hasn't told him. As if his dad knows far more than he's letting on.

They're not looking for us. And if they were they'd be looking for a man with a girl, not two men with a boy. But they'd have a photograph, they'd know what Liam looks like and they can put two and two together. A haircut doesn't make that much of a difference. No, of course they're not looking for them. Unless they are, unless Emma's gone to the police with her sob story. He's been round this loop already, it's pointless.

"Or maybe you stole a horse," Liam says. The woman at the next table drops a teaspoon. Or did she throw it, ensuring it landed to the side of her, so she could turn around in her seat and make faux-accidental eye contact with Liam, her eyes moving quickly over his face? He keeps his expression blank and neutral, then realises he's missed a chance to get her on his side. He should have smiled, rolled his eyes at the irrational fears of young children. Except he doesn't *need* to get her on his side because he's done nothing *wrong*, Emma walked out on *him* and left him in charge, *Emma* is the one who's a danger, only that's not the way she'll explain it to the police, she'll put her own spin on it and God knows she'll be convincing...

No, no, no, not this again. This is ridiculous. Too much to think about, too much to hold in his head. What's going on with his face? Does anything show? He's starting to panic now, even though there's nothing to panic about. God, what if he loses it? Right here in this café? No, it won't happen, he won't let it.

It's Alannah's face that's doing it, those pleading eyes, that short hair, that illusion that she's somehow become her own brother, the second child they never had. Before she was born he'd secretly hoped for a son. Of course he'd stamped that thought out the second he held her. But it wasn't until he got home from that final trip, seen her wide eyes and pretty face, stroked his hand over her long hair, that he'd been truly glad and grateful that the universe had sent him a girl. He won't come apart in here, not in broad daylight, he absolutely won't.

"You feeling okay?" Frank's hand on his arm. "It's all right, son, take it easy."

He wants to slap his father's hand away. But what could draw more attention than a grown man picking a fight in a café? He has no choice but to let it happen, the gentle caress, the soothing voice.

"I'm fine. It's hot, that's all."

"Want to get out of here?"

He wants to check if the police officers are still here, but that will draw their eyes over. He forces himself to stand up, willing his knees to hold him. Alannah slides off her chair and slithers between the furniture, joggling the table and collapsing Liam's sugar fort. He doesn't care about that. It doesn't matter. No one's looking because he's simply a man walking out of a café. He risks a single side-eyed glance. No bulky shapes in high-vis body armour at the counter. Have they moved? He can't look round, he can't. The door to the café is a million miles away but growing closer. They're through the door. They're out of the door. The clean air's fresh against his cheek.

"The police have gone," Alannah says.

"Why are you so worried about the police?" Frank's indulgent smile is very, very good, very convincing indeed. If Liam hadn't seen him in that vulnerable moment before he got his game face on and transformed into twinkly-grandad, he would have believed it utterly. "No, it's all right, you don't have to explain. Just think of them like wasps. They look scary, but if you leave them alone, they'll leave you alone. Flapping around draws attention."

He was scared of the police too. Liam's knowledge is absolute. But why? Frank is still talking about wasps and police officers, trying for a connection between the stripes of a wasp and the stripes that show how high-ranking an officer is. He's trying to be funny, to lift the mood, to resurrect something from a day that's already had too much going on, and it's not really working but Alannah's playing along anyway. They walk back in a quiet little group along the promenade, their mouths full of all the words they don't dare say out loud.

Three little liars, Liam thinks, *three little liars, all in a row. Who'll be the first to get caught? Who'll be the first to stop pretending?* Or is he going mad, imagining threats where none exist, inventing monsters? *Please*, he thinks, *don't let me lose my marbles on top of everything else I've lost, don't let me go mad*

CHAPTER EIGHTEEN

(DECEMBER, NOW)

go mad from lack of sleep, but I'm inching my way back to sanity now. Each night in my room, my head touches the pillow and I'm gone, lulled by a silence so profound I can hear the blood swishing through the arteries in my neck. Each afternoon I creep upstairs for a nap, wrapped in the heavy velvet throw from the end of the bed, waking only when it's time to eat. You'd think I'd have my fill after ten days of this, that I'd be tired of silence and stillness and the long dark nothingness of being unconscious for fourteen hours. You'd think.

The truth is, this is what I dreamed of, all those fierce cold coping days and hot tear-soaked nights. To be oblivious. To forget.

And now I'm face-down on an oddly comfortable table in a warm room with no windows, formless music twirling in my ears, flat hot polished stones balanced along the line of my spine, and I'm falling asleep, again. It's too much, I really have to stop sleeping so much, I'm getting greedy for it. But I can't resist it, that seductive downward pull into a place where nothing touches me. Besides, who could stay awake in a room like this? It's abloom with oily scents, the air quivering with music that twines and twines and goes nowhere, each note melting into the next, a low ecstatic throb of nothingness. The lights are dim, the air is warm, the stones press comfortingly against my skin like small animals taking a nap. It's too much to resist. I begin to drift, sinking into the comfort of the moment, and it's almost enough to keep me anaesthetised, almost enough so I can't hear the sound of the alarm that's beginning to ring, far away but growing closer, in the deepest places of my gut.

You need to go back. You need to go home now. Do it now. Now. Now. Now. NOW.

And like that – as if someone's shouted my name, as if I've been slapped – I'm awake. I sit up in confusion, clutching the towel against me. The hot stones tumble from my back and clatter to the floor. Within moments, the beautician's back in the room, her reassuring smile not quite hiding her concern. I wonder if I've broken anything.

"Everything all right?" Her voice is bright and perky. "Did you fall asleep by any chance?"

"Yes," I say, and then, "no, I don't think so. I just – I don't know – oh God—"

"It's all right, breathe deeply. You're coming round from being very relaxed, that's all."

"Yes, that sounds…" Bands of heat travel over my skin. Am I going to be sick?

"Would you like some water?" She's anxious, wondering if I'm going to cause a fuss.

"Yes, please." I peer about, worried about the fate of the dislodged stones, about the beautiful tiles of the beautiful heated floor.

"Everything's fine, don't worry." I notice she takes a little look herself before saying this. "Only a couple of things dropped. No harm done. Let me get you that water."

The beautician's a very nice girl, but she's a liar. Things do come to harm from being dropped. There are things in this world that are fragile and breakable and prone to damage, and when we're not careful enough, they all come to pieces. And look what I've done; look at what I've thrown away. I left Liam on his own. *I left him on his own.* I saw Alannah going back to that house and Liam was in it on his own *and I stayed on the bus and left them to it.* What the fuck was I thinking?

I sit on the edge of the table and tell myself it's all right. Try to feel my way back into my cocoon of denial. It's not happening, it's no good, I'm awake now and I have to face the consequences. It's like the exact and perfect opposite of one of those dreams where you commit a murder and wake up sweating with horror, only then the dream fades away again, and instead you have this profound sense of relief that you haven't actually done what you thought you had.

I left Liam alone. I saw Alannah walking back to the house. And I did nothing. Oh God oh God oh God. My towel's trying to unpeel itself. I tuck it under my armpits and wish I had one of those beautiful fluffy robes people keep offering you here.

"Here we are." The beautician brings a glass of iced water on a little black tray. She's even added a slice of lemon. I take it gratefully, try not to gulp. My hands are surprisingly steady.

"Now," says the beautician, and I can see how young she is. (How could I let someone so *young* take care of me? Surely this is the wrong way round?) "You have ten minutes of this treatment left, so I can wrap you back up and leave you to finish off the relaxation part of the session. Although if you're feeling a bit light-headed, that might not be the best idea."

"Maybe you're right," I say. She looks relieved. This must be the right thing to say.

"Okay, so instead, I could give you a hand massage, to help you reground yourself and let everything in your body equalise a bit."

I don't want a hand massage. I don't *deserve* a hand massage. I've done something terrible. I need to start putting it right. But I can't upset this poor young girl.

"That sounds wonderful," I lie, and she looks relieved.

She must have been worried I'd complain. "If you're sure you don't mind."

"Of course not! I mean, it's a pleasure." She's still young enough to blush when she deviates from the script they've drummed into her. "Let me fetch you a robe, and if you'd like to take a seat in that chair, we'll get you nice and relaxed…"

Nice and relaxed. That's the entire goal of this place, to get women (and men as well, of course, but let's face it, this is primarily a place for women) *nice and relaxed*. As if wandering around in a trance, gazing out from behind your eyeballs like a cow in a field, is something we should all aspire to. I thought this was what I wanted. It *was* what I wanted. I wanted to be somewhere with no demands made on me, where I could let go of everything, be entirely selfish and free. And, lucky me, I got exactly what I wanted. The classic fairy tale curse. So now I have to sit here and have my hands massaged by a young girl, because if I run away I'll hurt her feelings. No, that's not right, I can leave, I *ought* to leave, I have to get back to the house and—

No. Don't panic. If I panic I'm admitting something might be wrong. Everything is fine. I don't need to feel guilty.

The girl's hands are firm and strong, moving over the muscles of my palm with a deft and clever touch.

"You carry quite a lot of tension in your hands."

"Sorry."

"Don't be!" Her smile is warm and beguiling. Male guests will misinterpret it. Is she old enough to know how to get out of something like that safely? "That's what we're here for, isn't it? To help you release all that tension and feel totally relaxed."

I don't need to panic. I don't need to panic. I haven't done anything wrong. I glance at the watch that rests over the girl's heart. Seven minutes to go. I can get through this.

"Which oil would you like? I have basil and olive, vanilla and rose water, or orange and bergamot."

"They all sound lovely… um, basil and olive, maybe?"

"That's my favourite," the girl says.

Six and a half minutes to go.

"And could I ask why you're leaving early?" The receptionist, older and wiser than the sweet beautician girl, gives me a warm smile, inviting me to share whatever negative feedback I have. "If there's any problem we'd much rather hear about it so we can put it right."

"No, it's all been lovely. Absolutely perfect. Thank you all so much. Something's come up at home, that's all."

"Oh, I am sorry." She's mastered the art of looking genuinely sorry while maintaining a professional distance. "It's tough when life gets in the way, isn't it?"

"It is." What a stupid phrase that is, *life* getting in the way of things. As if there are things we have or things we want that are somehow not life, and that life stops us from having. What would that even be? Death?

Don't say that word. Don't even think it. I force my feet not to tap on the floor as she makes up my bill, force my hands not to clutch at the house keys in my pocket. I should have taken the car. Instead I'm stuck waiting for a taxi, and then a train, and then a bus, dependent on the efficiency of strangers.

Are you watching, God? Please let me off the hook for this one. I'll go straight back home and I'll run up the front path and I'll face whatever awaits me on the other side of the door and I will be brave, I promise, I swear. And I will devote my life to Alannah, even more than I have done, everything for her, whatever she needs, whatever it takes, if you'll please forgive me for the one moment when I was weak. Is that a deal? Please say it's a deal. "Thank you so much, that's brilliant."

"Now, because you booked your break as a package, we wouldn't normally be able to offer any refund, but as this is your first visit, I've put the balance on a gift card that you can redeem against another package, any time in the next twelve months."

183

"Oh! That's so kind of you." Even though I'll go to my grave without setting foot here again, my eyes sting with tears. "Thank you so much."

"It's a pleasure. Can I ask how you'll be travelling today? Do you need a taxi calling?"

"I've already called one, he should be here any minute. But thank you."

"It's a pleasure. And do you need your luggage bringing down from your room?"

"I've got it here with me already, but thanks."

"It's a pleasure." It's only when you engage them in a long conversation that the mechanics begin to show. Mostly it sounds spontaneous and sincere. "Oh – I think I can see him coming in at the door right now – yes, that's him. Hello, Steve, good to see you."

So the taxi driver's part of the team. That must be a sign of something, but I'm not sure if it's good or bad. He takes my suitcase with a cheery smile and waves goodbye to the nice receptionist. I clutch my voucher in a pocket that's already growing hot and sweaty.

The traffic's good, and we reach the station in plenty of time. That's a good sign. The train is ten minutes late. That's a bad sign. Or wait, maybe it's a good sign, maybe it's a sign that even if we'd been held up in traffic, God would still be on my side. The first train arrives late but they've held the connection for us. I get a seat on the second train. Two more good signs. Three buses come that aren't my bus. Bad sign. My heart's pounding out of my chest. That's the worst sign of all.

Stop this, I tell myself sternly. *You've done what you've done. You didn't know. No one can blame you.*

Here are the streets I know like the contours of my daughter's face, everything in its own familiar groove. The same sun sinking over the same houses, the same rain forming puddles in that place by the bus stop. The cars parked outside the houses and on the driveways, the ones I recognise without even realising I've taken notice. Dogs on their walks, the same routes, the same time. But I'm someone new and different, so everything seems strange.

This always happens after time away. You leave your place and go somewhere else, and when you return, you wonder if you'll ever feel comfortable again. Within a day or two you're rubbed smooth again by the friction of everyday living. But first, there's that odd discomfort that comes from the ways you don't quite fit.

This must be how Liam felt, every time he returned home. That dazed look he'd get, staring around at the walls, noting each detail that had stayed the same, each one that was different. The way the bathroom door swelled in the summer and shrank in the winter. The noise of the boiler when the hot water switched on. Next door's cat, pouring over the fence to hunt mice at the bottom of the garden. That one time I got my hair cut in a slightly different style and he teased me about it all evening, and it was only when we went to bed that night and I couldn't sleep that I realised the teasing was his way of coping.

This was what I wanted – to force a change, in both of us. But what if we've both changed for the worse? There's a black smear across my palm where my sweat's dissolved the ink from the hotel's voucher.

The house looks closed and secret, as if it's trying to pretend I'm not here. The garden gate's shut. I push it open. My key slides smoothly into the lock of the front door. I breathe in. Breathe out. Push on the door.

The door opens. I lift my suitcase in over the threshold. I've done it. I've made it. I'm home.

What am I expecting? Something I can't quite bring into focus, the inside of my own head a temporary mystery. I have to deduce it from the way I'm behaving. I call out, but it's a tentative "Hello," as if I know there'll be no answer. I'm holding my breath, trying not to taste the air, but when I finally have to inhale, it only smells a little musty, a little unoccupied.

Thank you, God, I find myself thinking, and wonder if I dare to understand what I'm thanking Him for.

I can hear the house's emptiness. Liam must be out, which is a legitimate thing for him to be. He wasn't expecting me home. It's all right.

Why am I checking the hall table, then the kitchen table, then the coffee table in the living room? Why am I looking for a note? There won't be a note because Liam *wasn't expecting me*. I've come home early. Everything's fine and Liam will be back soon and I only need to wait for his arrival.

How shall I fill the time? I'll make a cup of tea. I fill the kettle, take down a mug, put in a teabag. There's milk in the fridge, on the point of turning but just about acceptable. Why has Liam not bought fresh milk?

Without really knowing why, I wander out of the kitchen and upstairs. Maybe it's to do with reclaiming my territory, making sure all of this is still mine. I open the door to our bedroom. The bed is made. Liam's even put the cushions against the pillows, something he always swore he'd never do. How strange. Maybe this is a peace offering. Maybe, now he's the one who has to stay and wait, he's evolved his own rituals to bring me home safely to him. I wonder what kind of bargain he might have made in the darkness of the night. But perhaps men don't bargain. Perhaps they simply believe they can impose their will on the universe.

Now I'm home, I can have my mobile phone again. I've missed it in the days I've been away. Leaving it was an act of defiance, but also a way of shoring up my defences against my own weaker nature. If I'd taken it with me, I would never have held onto my silence. There it is, in the drawer of my bedside table. The screen's black and dead, but I still enjoy the weight of it in my hand, the rubbery feel of the case against my fingers. I plug it in to charge and feel pleased that I'll soon be reconnected to the outside world.

Now what? I haven't even taken off my coat or my shoes. My feet are swollen with travelling, glad to be set free. I leave my coat on the bed, then pick it up to hang in the wardrobe. It's my best coat; I don't wear it very often. It has its own hanger. There's something not quite right about the wardrobe, but I don't let myself see it yet. I tell myself the clench in my stomach is only because I'm hungry.

Now I have my phone back, I can call Liam. Even if he won't take the call, he'll know this means I've come home again. I switch my phone on, wait impatiently for it to boot up. Enter my passcode. A red bloom of notifications – missed calls, voicemails, Instagram posts, Facebook news – beg for my attention, but I ignore them. Recent phone calls. Liam at the top of the list. I picture him taking his phone out of his pocket and looking at the name, *Emma Mobile*, deciding whether to answer.

My picture's wrong. His phone goes straight to voicemail. Maybe he's out of range. Or maybe, maybe he's switched it off because he's in an interview. That's a good thought, a brilliant thought. How shall I fill the time until I can get hold of him? I bring up my call log, see I have two voicemail messages and four missed calls from *Mrs Baxter Dancing*.

Oh fuck. Oh fuck oh fuck oh fuck. Something's happened to Alannah, she's hurt, she's injured. Or what if it's not that, what if she's heard something, been told something, what if Liam… What if he…

No. No no no no no. I'm not thinking about this, I'm not. Thoughts have power, so I'm not letting this one take shape. He wouldn't. He hasn't. The house is empty. It's fine. It's all going to be fine.

I'm roaming the rooms now, opening doors and closing them as if Liam might be hiding in the airing cupboard or my sewing room, putting off the moment when I'll have to listen to my voicemail. I have to stop my wandering, I've got to face up to this, I've got to look it right in its ugly little eyes. How bad is this? How bad could it get?

My phone lies on my bedside table, waiting for me to discover what other people already know. I think about the fairy tale of the good sister who spilled gold and jewels whenever she spoke, the bad sister who could produce only toads. Which will I be greeted with? It must be an injury, a fall maybe, something strained or sprained, maybe even broken. That would be awful but I could accept it, that's something I could live with. Maybe that's where Liam is? That could be it, he could be looking after Alannah. That could definitely be it. *Dear God, I'll accept you giving Alannah an injury as long as she—*

No. I need to stop bargaining and woman up and find out what's happened.

I press the screen, lift the phone to my ear.

"This is Mrs Baxter. I'm calling to say what a disappointment it was to get your husband's text saying Alannah's had to withdraw from *The Nutcracker*. It is extremely short notice, so we'll have to ask you to pay her accommodation costs regardless. I could really do with talking to one of you about this, so if you or Alannah's dad could give me a call…"

The words go on and on, dripping with passive-aggressive professionalism. My ears sing with shock. Liam has done this. Liam has plucked Alannah from her haven. So where are they?

"This is Mrs Baxter again. I'm quite surprised not to have heard from you. I'm just checking you got my earlier message. Obviously we'll have to think very carefully about whether we put Alannah forward for opportunities like this in future…"

So Liam has sent one curt text, and then no further communication. Why would he do that? He's efficient but he's not rude, not intentionally. Is it because he's a man and he's bad at social etiquette? Or is it because…

Because…

Please God, if you…

But it's too late. It's too late. What's been done has been done. Where is he? Where's he gone? What has he…

He'll have gone to Jane's house, I tell myself, *he's clearly not here and neither is Alannah but he's gone to stay with Jane, that's all that's going on here. He'll be with Jane, sulking. I'll call her and she'll tell me they're both safe.*

I've brought this on myself. My fingers tremble as I dial.

"Hello?" Jane always takes a while to answer. In the time it takes her to pick up the phone I've imagined a dozen different ways this could go. "Emma, is that you, love?"

"Yes, it's me." My voice is oddly calm. "I'm just checking, are Liam and Alannah there with you?"

A little pause.

"No, they're not. Were you expecting them to be? I thought Alannah was in rehearsals all week? And I haven't heard from Liam since—"

"Sorry, I'm getting confused," I say. My heart is pounding so loudly I can hardly hear my own words. "Ignore me, Jane, I'm getting muddled, I rang the wrong number, that's all, I thought you were someone else."

"Emma, are you all right? What's going on?"

"Nothing, everything's fine, sorry, oh, I can hear the door going, Liam must be back after all—"

"But what's going on, Emma? Have you had an argument or something?"

"Yes," I say, brilliant with relief that she's handed me a temporary cover story. "That's it. I'm so sorry. We had a massive barney and he stormed out, I mean, I sort of deserved it to be honest, but I can hear him back now. I'll call you tomorrow, all right? Sorry again."

I hang up the phone on her confusion. The more I say, the worse I'll make things for myself.

I can't find Liam. I can't find Liam and I have to call the police. Will they listen? They'll have to listen. I'll tell them in a way they'll have to hear. *My husband has my daughter and I think he might...* I can hardly finish the sentence, even in my head.

Liam has taken Alannah. Oh God, he has Alannah, and I don't know what kind of mess

CHAPTER NINETEEN

(DECEMBER, NOW)

mess coagulating around him like thick glue. Liam takes a deep breath and tells himself that he only needs to keep going, clean up, maintain freedom of movement. This is nothing, only a temporary thing, nothing to worry about. He's strong and resilient. Working hard is how he copes. What he needs is a challenge. The kitchen's driving him mad.

He begins with the cutlery drawer, taking out the tray, tipping the contents onto the countertop. The mess will have to be worse for a while before it can get better. He's fine with that, how can anyone think there's something wrong with him when he's prepared to make more mess first? Someone who was properly mental would never cope. He squirts washing-up liquid into the bowl, adds hot water. Scrubs at the tray compartments. How can anyone live like this?

"Dad." Alannah stands in the doorway in that sloppy, half-in-half-out way that makes Liam's teeth itch.

"What's up, Alannah?" See? He's not shouting even though he wants to. He's got everything locked down.

"Alfie."

"No, Alannah. It's time we stopped this."

"My name's Alfie." Alannah actually looks like Alfie

as she says this. He can see the identity settling on her like dandruff. The short hair. The boy's clothes. Jesus. He's losing the plot here.

His hands clench tight under the water. He will not lose his temper. He will not lose his temper. He will keep it together.

"What do you want?"

"Are you feeling all right?"

The question pierces him. He hates being taken by surprise.

"Why are you asking?" Answer a question with a question. Go on the offensive. Keep the other person guessing. "Is there something you want to tell me?"

"You're cleaning the cutlery drawer."

"That's right. And do you know why?"

"No."

"Because it's filthy," Liam says, and gives it one final rinse. "That's what happens when people don't look after stuff properly."

"Can I help?"

"I don't know. Can you help?" Answer a question with a question; keep the other guy guessing. It works every time, with his wife, with his child, with that knobhead he saw for a few weeks, tall skinny weedy bloke who looked like his mam never let him out the house without a coat on. Keep the other guy guessing and they'll never get inside your head, where you keep the private things no one gets to see.

"What needs doing?"

"What do you think needs doing?"

Alannah creeps into the kitchen, slinky like a scared dog, none of the poise he's used to seeing. What's the matter with her? She's had training, the same as he has. Why is she letting herself slouch? She peers uncertainly into the drawer.

"It's a bit crumby in the back," she says.

"So, what needs doing?" Alannah reaches cautiously for the dishcloth. "No, not that one, that's for washing-up. Get a new one. Under the sink. That's right. No, wet it first. Here, use this spray. What are you doing now?"

"Not suitable for non-washable surfaces," Alannah reads, slowly and infuriatingly. "Is the drawer a non-washable surface?"

"Do you think people make drawers that aren't meant to be cleaned? Should we put clean cutlery in a mucky drawer?"

He's half-hoping Alannah will fight back, the way Emma sometimes fights back, but Alannah is eleven years old and conditioned to behave. Has he made her cry? He's not sure he can stand to see tears right now. She looks a bit rigid in her shoulders, a bit pink in the face, but she's holding it together, spraying into the corners of the drawer, wiping carefully.

"Good job." What he wants to say to her is *stop looking so miserable*, but he knows he mustn't. *You don't get to control what everyone around you feels* – something Emma flings in his face regularly. "Looks better." Alannah gives him a wobbly smile. He busies himself with drying off the cutlery rack. The plastic's discoloured and brittle. Must be as old as the hills. Maybe even as old as the kitchen. They're always saying plastic lasts forever, but look at this thing, it's falling apart. What do scientists know anyway? They're just as dumb as the rest of the human race. Alannah's still busy with the drawer.

"That's it. Wipe right into the joins." What he'd really like is an old toothbrush to scrub at the dark places, but this is fine. He puts the cutlery tray back, relieved to see that it doesn't quite touch the sides. As long as they're careful when they close the drawer, the tray won't ever make contact with the unscrubbed corners. "Now put the cutlery in."

"Do we need to wash it first?"

"Does it look dirty to you?" Alannah shakes her head. "Why are you asking, then?" Her voice is only a little above a whisper. It's hard to make out her words. "Why are you talking in that stupid quiet voice?"

"I thought it might need doing."

"Do you still think it might need doing? No? Why are you asking, then? Put them away. No, neatly. *Neatly.* Don't you know what *neatly* means?" He nestles the spoons against each other, bowls pressed together, handles aligned. "Like this. That's better."

Alannah finishes the spoons, begins on the forks. The tension in his head's fading. This is how the world's supposed to be. Neat and orderly. Everyone knowing how to behave. Nothing out of place. This is right. It's all right. They're going to be fine.

"Liam?" Now his dad's at it, hovering in the doorway as if he's standing at the entrance to the cage of a dangerous animal. "Can I borrow you for a... What are you doing?"

"Cleaning the drawers," says Alannah.

"Oh? Well, um, thanks, Alfie, that's very kind. Liam, would you mind—?"

He minds a lot, but he's a guest and he doesn't have a choice. Damn it. He needs to sort out his own place, or he'll lose his marbles completely. Somewhere quiet, a long way from Emma, where he can get work. No chance of that happening at home. Thanks to Emma, everyone knew his history. All he got was pitying looks and platitudes from his back-to-work adviser. He needs to start again, somewhere nobody knows him. His dad's paused the television to show him something. For God's sake, he's got things to *do*.

"Um," says Frank.

"What?"

"Look, you need to see this," Frank says, sounding as if he doesn't think anything of the sort. "But I don't judge you at all, okay? Not for any of it."

"There something you ought to be telling me?"

"Just watch this," Frank says.

"*—minister said in a statement earlier today that there had been no change in the government's position—*"

"Sorry." Frank is pressing the fast-forward button. "Had to rewind a bit. Here we are."

"*—for the safety of Liam Wright and his eleven-year-old daughter Alannah. Mr Wright – a former soldier who was*

194

discharged from service after suffering with post-traumatic stress disorder – and his daughter have not been seen at their house for almost two weeks. Mrs Emma Wright, who was away at the time of her husband's disappearance, this afternoon made an emotional plea for Mr Wright to get in—"

He's not aware of taking the remote control from his father's hand, not aware of pressing the button. The picture freezes on a shot of some conference room somewhere, a table and two police officers and two giant photographs and a woman coming in to take her place between the officers. The woman is, of course, Emma, but she hasn't yet turned her face to the camera, so he won't have to smash the television screen after all. Thank God for small mercies.

"She's making it up," Liam says. Why is he trying to justify himself? Go on the offensive; keep the other guy guessing. "She's lying. She doesn't want me to leave her."

"I didn't realise," Frank says. "I mean, that Alfie's – that he hasn't – I mean, that he's – I mean, I *knew*, of course I did, but I thought it was sort of official that he—"

"That's the bit you're going to worry about?" Here's his way in, the point of weakness. "My wife's spreading lies about me on television, getting the police on my back, and you're concerned about a bit of play-acting from a *kid*?"

"There's no need to shout." Frank's voice is infuriatingly calm, maddeningly smooth. "I'm not shouting at you, son. Why are you shouting at me?"

"I'm not fucking shouting!" Even Liam can hear how ridiculous this is. He brings his voice down by several decibels and half an octave. "I'm not shouting, okay? I'm only frustrated because there are lies being spread about me and I don't like it. But I haven't done anything wrong. I'm Alf—I'm Alannah's dad, I'm entitled to have her."

"So why are the police looking for you?"

"You heard what she said. All that bollocks about me being off my nut. Women make up shit like that all the time. Parental alienation. Getting kids to hate their dads so their mums can have them. But it's *Emma* that's the mad one, I'm not even kidding, she needs fucking *help*."

"But why would they believe her?"

"I don't know why the police believe what they believe, do I? I suppose she must have been convincing."

"It's nothing to be ashamed of. It's like any other injury—"

"I'm fine!" He's shouting again, he can hear himself doing it. Deep breath. Lower voice. He can do this. "I'm fine. Emma's deflecting, that's all." Go on the offensive. Think, Liam. "Did you know about this already?"

"What are you talking about?"

"The other day in the café. When those two coppers came in. And you hustled us all out of there at top speed. Have you been talking to her? Does she know where I am?"

"No, of course not! How could I possibly—? I don't even know where you live, Liam, I don't know anything about your life except what you've told me. Please, calm down, son. We'll find a solution."

If there's one thing he can't stand it's being patronised. There is no *solution*, there is no *we*, there's just Liam on his own and he'll have to find the answers by himself. Fine, he doesn't mind that, but he won't stand for fools pissing on his shoes and telling him it's raining.

"Dad." Now Alannah's there by his side, tugging at his arm. Why can't everyone leave him alone? "Dad, do you want to come and see the drawer? I put the knives in but I don't know if I did them right…" She glances at the television and her eyes go wide. "Is that *Mum*? Is Mum on the television? With the police?"

"It's nothing to worry about," Frank says, and Liam snorts with laughter. "Alfie, why don't you go and have a bath? It's nearly bedtime, I think."

"Ignore him," says Liam. "It's a quarter past six. Of course it's not bedtime."

"Why is Mum on the news?"

"Your mum," Liam says, deliberately talking over Frank's

anxious reassurances, "is on the news because she's told the police a bunch of lies about me."

"Really, Alfie, it's fine, don't worry about it. Everything's all right—"

"She'll have told them I'm mentally unstable." It's hard to say this even though he's vowed to tell her the truth. "She'll have said she thinks I might hurt you."

"Shush, Liam, you're frightening him. Alfie, your mum's all right, you can see she's all right. Look, she's right there on the telly, see?"

"Alannah." Liam isn't shouting, he doesn't like shouting, but he is using the full power of his vocal range. "Stop calling her Alfie. She's a girl and her name's Alannah. And now it *is* time to go for a bath, isn't it, Alannah?"

"I'm Alfie," Alannah whispers.

"No, you're not, you're Alannah, you can stop pretending now. Look, he's known all along, all right? Your grandad's not an idiot, he knows what a girl looks like. Stop staring at me like that and get in the bath."

Alannah turns her face towards Frank.

"You knew?"

"Um." Frank glances from Alannah, suet-coloured and reproachful, to Liam. "Well, I thought at first – and then I – look, it doesn't matter really, does it? If you want to be Alfie for me, you can be Alfie, all right? I'm so pleased I got to meet you at all."

"Her name is Alannah." Liam is proud of himself for how in control he's being, in the face of all this utter nonsense. "She's a girl, and you can call her by her right name from now on. Alannah, run yourself a bath and get in it. Come back when you're clean. We need to talk about what's going to happen next."

"That was cruel," says Frank, as soon as Alannah has crept out of the room. "Why not let him be Alfie for a while if he wants?"

"Because *she* doesn't really want… She's going through a

phase, that's all it is. It's that bloody show she was supposed to be in, she was dancing a boy's part. Or maybe it's, I don't know, dancers get so obsessed with having the right body, she's that age when they get confused – look, what makes you think I give a damn about your opinion?"

"Because," says Frank, very gently, "you came to me for help."

The world rocks beneath Liam's feet. He can hear sirens in his ears, feel the air swooping around him, trying to knock him off balance. He steadies himself. He's strong enough to withstand this. He will not give in. He will look his dad full in the face and take whatever's waiting there. Even if it's pity. Even if it's love.

"Emma's telling the truth, isn't she?" Frank says. "About the PTSD, I mean."

"She thinks it's true. She thinks a lot of things. Doesn't mean she's right."

"But why would she think it if—?"

"It was nothing. Cutbacks, that's all. They make up any old shite to get the numbers where they want them."

"The Army's lying? About you being ill?"

"Course they were! They tried the same thing on three or four mates. I let them do it cos I was about ready to come out anyway. Emma wasn't doing the best job as a parent. You've seen the way Alannah is. All that ballet, all that obsession with being *pretty* and *light* and *graceful*. Bloody recipe for an eating disorder." He's kept these words inside him for so long. It feels good to get them out. That beardy twat was a waste of a skin, but maybe he had a point about this one. Liam will give him this one moment of being right. "I mean, it's not right, is it? A kid, worrying about how she looks?" His pretty wife Emma, who he loved so much, and who's turned on him so viciously. He should never have married her. Next time he'll pick a plain girl, someone who'll be so damn grateful for the attention she'll think he's perfect…

"So you came out of the Army to look after… after your child?"

"Yes," he says, and then winces. Lies are for the weak, and weakness is one flaw he's never had. "Okay, it wasn't *just* that, but yeah, that was part of it. And I am not fucking mad, all right? I am not fucking mad. If anyone's mad it's *Emma*, the shit she was up to while I was away—"

"What about the nightmares?"

"What?"

"You get up in the night and wander around."

"So do you!" Liam can see himself in the mirror over the fireplace. He looks insane. No wonder. His wife, his daughter and now his bloody *father*, conspiring to wind him up… "It's not me that sits out in the garden with weed and an umbrella, is it? Do you think you might have a problem with that, by the way? Does it seem normal to you to get up in the night and get stoned in the rain?"

"It's not weakness to need help."

"I do *not* need fucking help." His father isn't saying *I got up because you got up, I was keeping an eye on you,* but he doesn't need to. Fuck's sake. It's time to move on anyway. If Emma's talked to the police then she's definitely talked to his mother, and while Emma might not know his dad exists, his mum certainly bloody does. "We needed somewhere to stay, and, thank you for that. It was good of you. I appreciate it." *See? There's nothing wrong with me, I know how to behave, I can do it even when all I want to do is rip someone's throat out. That's the difference between madness and sanity. Being able to do the right thing even when all you can think of are the wrong ones.* "But we'll be off now."

He's expecting his father to argue with him, but Frank is nodding to himself.

"I understand. I mean, God knows I don't *want* you to go, but if you have to…"

"We're not on the run," Liam says. "As soon as we're sorted, I'll get in touch with Emma, let her know. And she can see Alannah. I wouldn't keep her from that. But I'll be the main parent from now on."

"Will you manage?"

"Of *course* I—yes, we'll manage. I'll get Alannah into a decent school for New Year. Make sure she's settled." He has only the vaguest idea of how to get Alannah into a school, but the dimwits at the school gates manage it even though he wouldn't have thought they could find their own front doors, so how hard can it be? "We'll make a go of it." He can't resist the chance to be cruel, take a jab at his dad in return. "Whatever it takes, right? I won't have her growing up without me."

He watches with half-shameful satisfaction as the blow goes home. He sees Frank wince in pain, gather himself back together.

"I can help you out with money."

"Sorry, what?"

"I wasn't much of a father. Still not much of one. But that's one thing I always got right."

"I don't need money."

"Yes, you do. Your mum never admitted it either, but she needed it, and I sent it. That's what being a good dad *was* in those days, you see. The bad dads disappeared and didn't pay, and the good dads disappeared and did pay. But the kids belonged with their mothers. That's how it worked."

Ah, the good old days, back in the eighties. Liam knows what his dad's saying isn't right. He remembers his friends whose parents had split, going for weekend visits. His dad must have told himself this lie so often he's come to believe it. He could tell his dad this, take another swipe, push the knife in a little bit deeper – but he won't. His dad's a poor old man now. The best revenge is to not make the same mistakes.

"Anyway. I can help you out with cash. How much do you need? Ten? Twenty?"

Ten or *twenty*? His dad can't possibly mean what this sounds like.

"Sorry, I mean thousand, obviously. Not twenty quid, that wouldn't get you your bus fare these days."

Liam's face feels numb.

"No. *Jesus*, what are you—? Of course I can't take that, that's way too much."

"It's fine, I can afford it. It'll all be yours one day anyway, you might as well have it now. It's in cash, I know it's a bit of a pain but as long as you're not buying a house or a car you'll be all right." His dad wipes fiercely at the corner of his eye, and his face crumples up. "And once everything's settled down you'll come back and see me, maybe? Only once in a while."

"And what will they say at the bank? They'll be watching, the police will have told them. What will you say you want with twenty thousand quid in cash?"

"I don't have it at the bank, I've got it in the house."

Liam looks at his father. His father looks back.

"And what," Liam says at last, "what the hell are you doing with twenty thousand quid lying around the house?"

"You know perfectly well what I'm doing with it," says Frank. "We're both of us shit at keeping secrets." He smiles. "Quite good at turning a blind eye, though."

"Jesus, Dad." Those people who came round the night he spent out on the seafront. "For fuck's *sake*." That horsey man on the beach, the expert way they got rid of both him and Alannah, the sense that he'd turned around just too late to see something being whisked out of sight. "You have got to be kidding me." The money he'd grown up taking for granted, the cash they'd never been short of. "You do *not* sell drugs out of the house where my daughter's been sleeping. You did *not* put Alannah in danger like that."

"Of course I don't... Well, I *do*, but not like that, okay? I don't sell to users. I'm a middleman. Take things in and pass them on."

"How long have you been..." He doesn't want to admit to not knowing; he can work this out for himself if he's clever enough. "Seriously, Dad, *all those years*? Even when I was a *kid*? That's how you bought this place, isn't it? That's *why* you bought this place. Fuck me—"

"Language," says Frank, with another ghastly smile.

"Fuck off."

"It was a joke."

"Jokes are funny."

"Did Mum know?"

"What do you think?"

This is why his dad was never allowed to see him. This was what his mother was shielding him from. She took him away from danger, kept him safe and clean. She hid him from his dad, using the threat of *I'll send the police round* to keep him at a distance. She wasn't too proud to take the money, though.

"I don't blame her," Frank says. "You shouldn't, either."

"You had a proper job. You could have lived off that. You could have quit the other."

"No, I couldn't. That's not how it works. They like me, you see. I look respectable and I don't draw attention and I don't get caught, not ever. Wouldn't let me go without a fight."

"And you like doing it."

Frank hesitates, then shrugs.

"Yes. And I like doing it."

"You like getting away with it."

"I do. I'm sorry, son. But you can have the money if you want it." His face has a hint of skull-ness around the eyes. "Why mess with a winning formula, hey?"

"Do you fucking swear," Liam says, "do you swear on your fucking life, that Alannah has never been in any kind of danger?" Frank hesitates. "If you've put her onto their radar, if they've got, I don't know, fucking *photographs* of her, if they know her name or anything about her—"

"No, of course they haven't. They met Alfie that day on the beach, remember?" His dad's trying to sound convincing, but he's not making a great job of it. "But you've got to

202

understand, son, there's always danger. It's dangerous simply being alive."

What the hell would this stupid old fool know about danger anyway? That's the thing with civilians; they don't know what the world's really like, how dangerous

CHAPTER TWENTY

(2014)

dangerous pleasures in those long quiet hours when my bed becomes an infinite space and the world turns silently around me. Insomnia is a curse for some, but I'm finding an odd comfort in it. My sleepless nights without Liam are not some passing influence of imbalanced chemicals or excess caffeine or a lack of fresh air. I'm awake because I need to be awake. I'm awake because I'm needed. I'm awake because I've been summoned.

On the nights when I can't sleep, God lies on the pillow beside me and murmurs in my ear.

This is not a kindly visitation. The *God* I talk to is a definite person, with an agenda of His / Her own (oh, it's *Him*, who am I kidding, as if any female God would ever put other women through this shit), and a job of work to do. He does not come to me with words of comfort, telling me He holds us all in the cradle of His hand. When He comes, He's here to ask the hard questions, the questions that come to us when our loved ones are in danger. When God lies in bed beside me and strokes my cheek, He's here to bargain.

If I were to do something to hurt your husband, God whispers, *how much could you stand before you'd prefer him dead? Let's begin with the easy ones. What if I were to take half a leg?*

Yes, of course. Yes, I could deal with that. I could deal with him losing half a leg below the knee. Dear God (I don't think there's anything *dear* about God, but it's important to observe the niceties), if you bring Liam home to me alive, I will gladly accept the sacrifice of one leg, below the knee. He'll recover. He'll do the rehab. He'll be provided with a prosthetic. He will get out alive and come home to me and we will live good lives and he will have an interesting feature to show to people at parties.

And God replies:

Ah, but we've barely got started here, have we? A prosthetic leg's not nothing, but it's nothing to what I could do. Both arms intact, no damage to the fingers. No ugly rebuilding of approximate pincer grips; no awkward moments during handshakes. Still able to walk, talk, think, work, fuck. No damage to the face. What if I demand more? How much will you let me take in return for keeping him alive? You know I'm a greedy bastard sometimes, and cunning. Which is worse: both legs below the knee, or one leg above it?

Prosthetics are harder without the knee joint. Motion becomes stiffer, more painful, and the strain on the back's increased. Wear and tear become a significant concern. The chances of longer-term disability, of a painful middle-age and a premature retirement, increase. Liam doesn't do well with pain (if we're honest, who does?). His temper would fray and flare. We'd pick and bicker at each other, not from a lack of love but because some things are just hard to deal with, and that would be how we'd cope.

So you're saying you'd choose both legs below the knee, then?

I flinch, because God, who knows the secrets of everybody's hearts, most surely knows the secrets of mine. I really, really like that Liam's taller than me. It's shallow, but when your natural body type is slightly farm-girly, you appreciate the chance to feel dainty. If he lost both legs below the knee, when he took off the prosthetics... It's shameful but it's the truth. I don't know how I...

You're saying you wouldn't want your husband back if he lost both legs below the knee?

Of course I want him back, I think hastily. *I would want him back no matter what happened to his legs. You're not getting Your hands on him that easily.*

Ah yes, let's talk about hands! And while we're at it, how about arms? How much of him can I hack off before you stop wanting him? How damaged can I make him before you'll give up? You love that body of his, don't you, that firm, strong, powerful body. You love that face. How much scarring can I paint across his skin before you'd prefer him dead?

I don't know, I admit, and God rests His hand against my breast.

It's all right. I see everyone's hearts. Why not admit you couldn't cope with a disabling injury? You wouldn't be the first woman to make that prayer. Ask me to keep him safe, go on. Ask me to send him home to you whole. I promise I'll keep my word.

Oh, but God's a sneaky bastard, always looking for a loophole, and this is a classic. It sounds so tempting. But we have our stories to remind us:

There was a woman once who had a son. She had a son and her son joined up and he did well, he was born for this life. She knew her son, knew how much he loved the strength that lived in his arms and legs, the power of the heartbeat behind the long white fingers of his ribs. She talked to God in the watches of the night, and they reached what she thought was an agreement. *My boy, he'd never cope with being disabled. Don't you do it to him, please. Let him come home to me walking and talking, all his limbs intact, all his parts working. Don't make him a prisoner inside a cage of his own flesh.*

And God took her at her word.

Her son was on patrol and there was an IED and his mates

got the worst of it, but not her son. Instead, he took a splinter of shrapnel in the tender flesh of his eyeball, straight through and out the back and into the secret cave of his skull. They called his survival a miracle, because people often confuse *miracles* with the merely unlikely. A miracle is an act of grace, an impossible kindness from the universe. What happened to her son was neither impossible nor kind.

When he woke up from the coma and yelled at the nurses for looking at him funny, they laughed, because they were so damn glad to see him awake. When he ate like a horse, always hungry no matter how much food they put in front of him, they said his body was recovering, he needed fuel to get well. He came home a shambling, disinhibited wreck, violent and dangerous, no control over his actions. Throwing plates and mugs and dishes at the wall, not out of rage but because he found the sound of their breaking hilariously funny, and he couldn't understand why he shouldn't. Stripping off his clothes. Roaming the house with his cock erect, demanding his parents and carers wank him off, threatening violence when they told him no. And constantly eating, eating, eating, three times the size he'd been and still growing. He lived at home for three unbearable years. Now he lives in residential care, and his mother divides her time between visiting, and drinking.

You're not getting me that way, God. Fuck your bargain. I'm not committing to anything yet. I need to think some more.

You know, God purrs into my ear, *you're really being quite selfish. Making it all about what you want. What would Liam choose? It's his body. He's the one who'll be in it. And I should probably tell you, I'm more likely to listen to a prayer that's a little less selfish.*

What would Liam want? How much damage could he take before he'd prefer death? I bite my lip and consider. So much of Liam's training is about switching off parts of his mind, switching on parts of his body. He's learned to withstand cold and heat and hunger and thirst and tiredness and pain. He's wired in new routines and procedures, to do with weapons and actions and unthinking discipline. He keeps going long past the point when most of us would give up, because he's learned that his mind will quit long before his muscles. What would it do to him, being trapped in a body that's weaker than his mind?

Have I ever asked him? Of course I haven't. God's always listening, to Liam as well as to me. *Think you can live without a leg? Good to know. Now guess what's waiting for you out in that dry sandy hell-place; that and a side order of neuropathic pain and a phantom limb that endlessly burns with an itch you'll never, ever be able to scratch.* I can't let Liam expose himself like that. Instead I have to watch for clues, try and guess what he might be able to manage.

Liam doesn't mind disfigurement or ugliness, he's far less shallow than I am. I like prettiness, he likes order. But he's not good with any kind of physical failing, any kind of clumsiness. Part of why he likes me is because I'm good with my hands. I can make things that require discipline and care and a steady touch. He approves of the fact that I rarely drop things, that if I spend money on a nice set of plates, all those plates will still be intact years later. He has no patience with people who fumble with wrong keys or misplaced purses, who drop things or bump into things or dither or hesitate. He would hate, hate, hate the long, inevitable period when he'd be one of them. Would he be tough enough to get through and find his new normal? I want the answer to be *yes*, but there's enough doubt for me to hesitate. How much of him can he lose before he's not *himself* anymore? How long before the pain he's in turns him into a man I can't love? How long before he stopped loving me?

Oh, my dear. It's so hard, isn't it? Wouldn't it be easier to give everything over to My care? You'll sleep so much better once you give up this foolish idea that you can influence anything.

And it's so tempting to give it all over to God, to leave everything in His unknowable hands. I'm sure there are many who do exactly that. But there's something in me that won't believe I can do nothing to keep my man safe while he's away from me. I have to believe I can make a difference.

This is how I find myself becoming a witch.

Such an old-fashioned word, but what else can I call it? I've uncovered the first and only true requirement for casting a spell: the belief that you can make a difference. Sometimes I lie awake at night and wonder what the world would be if all the women like me – the women who mutter and hoard and save and bind, the women who mark the boundaries and keep the taboos – were to gather together on some dusty plain somewhere, the way our men do. Me and my sisters from this side of the conflict, all those other women from the opposing side. Would we change the world for the better? Or would we tear each other apart?

Here's the first spell I cast in order to keep my husband alive:

It starts with sex, which seems right for the first time. It starts unintentionally, which also seems right. Becoming a witch isn't something you choose, more something you discover you already are. It happens the night before he leaves me for a place where there are guns and enemies and the possibility, at least, of battle.

So, we have sex. It's not impossible that this will be the last time, and we both know it. Because it could be the last time, it's not simple, efficient, we-both-know-what-we-like sex, but the challenging, complex kind that takes effort and commitment. We take our time getting each other warmed up. We demand. We make each other wait. Time slows down, then stutters to a halt.

And alongside all the licking and sucking and probing, this is the part that matters, although I don't realise it until afterwards. I take off his sweat-soaked t-shirt and, between a gasp and a touch, stash it beneath my pillow. I don't think about it. It's simply instinct.

And then it's midnight, and then it's morning, and then

he's leaving me and we're carefully not crying, carefully not saying anything too prophetic or portentous *just in case*, and then it's three days later and I'm changing the bedding, and I find that t-shirt. When I bring it to my face, it smells of him. Of us. And I feel the thought take shape in my mind:

As long as I keep this t-shirt, unwashed, underneath my pillow, Liam will be safe.

Any spell contains its own undoing. If Liam is safe as long as I have his sweat on his t-shirt beneath my pillow each night, then letting that t-shirt be washed would mean his doom. There's no cheating, no alteration of the rules. If I hide the t-shirt somewhere else, the spell will fail entirely and he will die.

And so, for the whole of that tour, when I change the bedding, that week and every week afterwards, I endlessly check to make sure Liam's t-shirt hasn't crawled inside a pillow case or duvet cover. The second the new bedding is on the bed, I fold it up, replace it where it belongs. Each night before I sleep, I slide my hand beneath my pillow and whisper, as if Liam's beside me, *sweet dreams, I love you.* It only goes in the wash when he comes home again, triumphant and exhausted, unharmed and invincible, and we can finally reverse the ritual, reconnect our bodies and remind ourselves of who we are.

Before you think I'm insane: I'm well aware that his safe return is not only because of what I did. He's alive because of the actions of hundreds of other men and women, perhaps thousands. The actions and inactions of those on his side, and those on the other side, a spiderweb of things done and undone, a sticky net that caught some, but not Liam. Not Liam. Not my Liam. Because I did my part too. I kept his t-shirt beneath my pillow and whispered to it each night, reminding him of where his true place is. I've become one of the hidden ones, keeping the combatants alive through the power of our will alone. Ignore anyone who tells you that casting a spell doesn't have power. When he came back, I held my man in my arms and in the dark places of my head, I let the thought take shape: *He's still alive because of me.*

And then, the thought that follows. *And now I can never not do it.*

As time passes, my rituals begin to grow.

One so-early-it's-barely-morning when Liam departs, I find his dirty coffee cup on the kitchen table – unusual for him, he hates leaving a mess. It's because I distracted him, pulling him into one final fierce hug so he forgot to tidy it away. And there's the thought, waiting to pounce, the spell making itself out of coffee stains and thin air. *Leave it unwashed. As long as it's unwashed, he'll be fine.* There's something not quite right about this, and it takes me a minute to see the true shape of my thought: *if you wash that coffee cup, he will surely die.*

Am I allowed to move it? I don't let myself stop to think about this. I can't leave it on the kitchen table, it's too dangerous. The chances are great that Jane or Alannah will see it and wash it, not understanding its significance. Before I can let the prohibition take hold, I pick up the cup and put it at the back of the cupboard. But no, now I've cheated, I've made it too difficult. God will be angry, and an angry God has the power to tip over the gameboard and scatter the pieces to the wind. Every spell must be made with the potential for its unmaking. Anything less is an attempt to trick the universe.

I carry the empty coffee cup around my house, experimenting with places I can put it. I try the mantelpiece. The bookshelf. My bedside table. The table in my sewing room. A windowsill. The right place turns out to be on a little shelf in the hallway, beside the framed photo of our wedding.

There. Now it's slightly out of reach, but prominent enough for a busybody to move it if I don't guard it well enough. The conjunction of the two objects – the public memory and the private, the sacred icon and the secret fetish – strikes me with a mysterious rightness. Now there are two rituals keeping

Liam alive: his t-shirt under my pillow, and the coffee cup by our wedding photo. Will I be able to replicate this in future? I'll find a way. If I don't, who knows what will happen?

This is the curse of becoming a witch. Once you start bending the universe to your will, you can't stop. There's no putting down the burden.

And so the list of things I have to do grows. I press his t-shirt to my face, breathing in his scent before I whisper my goodnights. I keep his unwashed coffee cup safe beside the photograph. In my coat pocket, always, is a pebble he picked up on a beach and gave to me for safekeeping. I have scraps of his handwriting, clippings from his hair and even his toenails (disgusting, but I couldn't help myself, you can't afford to flinch when you feel that compulsion inside you). I have scraps of herbs that have dried to a crisp, reels of red thread that have been used to make clothes for him and now carry his essence as surely as anything else. The house is full of scraps and fragments of Liam, stored safely-but-not-too-safely, in places where their finding is unlikely, but not impossible. I ceaselessly patrol the borders, of my house and of myself.

Because, as well as the rituals, the secret things you do, you have to watch your words. You have to remember, always, that God is listening, and His agenda is never the same as yours. You want to keep your man safe. He wants permission to kill him. When I put it like that, I realise how far from most people's concept of *God* the God I talk to has managed to get.

Here are some of the things God can do to you if you say the wrong words at the wrong time:

A woman was sick of her husband rushing off to the pub to see his mates. "Been away for weeks and he can't even stop in the house five minutes," she said to her best friend. "Why can't he sit still and be quiet for a bit?" Three months later, he stepped on an IED and lost both his legs, a part of his jaw, half of one of his arms. Now he sits very, very still indeed, and speaks only rarely.

Another woman was looking forward to her husband's discharge. He'd been an engineer, his skills were in demand, and they were excited about the future. She was thinking about the things we all think about: where they'd live after he came out, what sort of house they'd be able to buy, whether they'd put some roots down at last. She said, "I was thinking about that new estate they're building. You know the one I mean, that Coney Chase place…" (or Harriers Field, or Loxley Park, or Summermeadow – the exact name isn't important, it never is in fairy tales). And then, the fatal words: "I'm probably kidding myself, those places cost an arm and a leg." She knew what she'd said as soon as the words were out of her mouth, but it was too late.

Or the woman who found her husband's dirty boxers thrown carelessly beside the laundry basket and declared, only half-joking, "Oi, if I have to pick up your boxers one more time this week I'm going to pay someone to shoot you the next time you ship out."

Or the woman who refused to kiss her husband goodbye because they'd been fighting, a toxic fight that lasted for most of his leave.

Or the woman who saw the barman smiling at her and let herself smile back, let herself imagine she was single once more.

These women don't exist. They're the stories we tell ourselves, to maintain our delusion that we can influence the universe. This is what I know on my sanest days. But my gut knows the opposite. These women have the bedrock reality of a fairy tale. They are the collective wisdom of every woman who's gone before us. They are the awful warnings, existing for us to learn from. They're the women we'll become if we don't watch ourselves.

Once you start, once you uncover a thing you can do to protect your man, you have to *keep doing that thing* for all time. When you cast a spell, you're disturbing the universe, making it mould, by however little, to your will. When we cast a spell, we place limits on what God can do. It goes without saying that He doesn't like this. God has a great dislike of female power. And once God notices you, you can guarantee He'll always be watching. Waiting for you to forget. Because however much you do, it can never be quite enough

CHAPTER TWENTY-ONE

(DECEMBER, NOW)

enough to kill him if he let it, the way his son's looking at him. The sheer *judgement* in his face, as if Frank has confessed to robbing old ladies, to beating his mother, to serial murder. What's he done that's so terrible? It's supply and demand, nothing more. That's all it's ever been.

"You," Liam says, almost wondering, almost impressed, "are a drug dealer. I brought Alannah to stay in a house with a drug dealer. I am an actual fucking moron."

"Stop saying that," Frank says.

"You think I'm *not* a moron?"

"I mean I'm not a drug dealer! I don't sell to, you know, junkies or anything. I just take stuff and pass it on."

"And you're not responsible for where it ends up."

"Look, people take drugs whether I'm in business or not. It's pointless trying to stop it, we're meeting a market need is all. I don't hurt anyone, I don't cause any trouble, I—"

"Pay taxes?"

"Well, if I could then I would, all right? If I could declare it as income then I'd happily do that. Ten years from now it'll all be legal and no one will care. I'm not doing any harm—"

"You're breaking the law," Liam says, and goes into Alfie's

room. Pulls his rucksack from beneath the bed. Opens up the drawers where his scant selection of clothes lies waiting.

Go after him, Frank tells himself. *Talk to your son.* He makes it as far as the doorway.

"Let me help," he says. Where's Alfie got to? He must be in the bathroom. *Keep your voice down; no kid likes to hear grown-ups shouting. See, Jane, see what a good father I could have been if you'd only have let me?*

"What do you think you could do that would help?"

"I've told you. I've got money—"

"And I've told you, I don't want it." Liam's an efficient packer. He's already pulling closed the top of his rucksack, moving on to Alfie's stuff, folding and stuffing and neatening in a smooth mechanical rhythm.

"Don't go like this. We can't leave it like this. It's been so good seeing you."

"Has it?"

Does *good* describe what it's been like, having his son under his roof? Feeling as if they're building or rebuilding something, some connection? Seeing Alfie, his really-not-really-yes-God-damn-it-really grandson? What has that been like? He's felt alive, at least. He's lived more in the last few days than in the last few decades.

"Yes. Yes, it has. It's been *great*."

And there's a minute, before the shutters come down, that he thinks Liam almost believes it. A minute when...

Then, Liam squares off his shoulders, straightens his spine, goes back to what he was doing, and Frank thinks he might vomit with how much Liam looks like Jane. Because he doesn't know what else to do, he goes to the kitchen and puts on the kettle.

Jane, you stole him from me. You got what you needed from me, and then you took him away and turned him into a male version of you.

Jane would say she hadn't done anything, that Liam was made the way he was and neither of them could change it.

Was that true? He remembers Liam starting school, the shock of realising how little intersection there was between their experiences. Frank's school memories were of patches of expansive freedom, interspersed with periods when adults confusingly insisted he did something he didn't see any point at all in doing. *Sit in this classroom. Write your name. Write it again. Now write it again. Write it this way. Count these buttons. Count those bears. Hold your pencil differently. Sit on the carpet while we read a story you haven't chosen.* He did these things, because it was easier than being told off for not doing them, and spent every second he could dreaming of escape.

Liam, on the other hand, had *liked* school. Not because he was particularly clever – he was solidly middle-of-the-pack, hitting all his targets, missing and exceeding none – but because of the scheduling, the timetable, the imposed sense of order. No, by the time Liam went to school he was already Jane's creature.

How about before? There was a summer evening when Liam was three, and Jane was out for some reason, a rare event indeed. Rather than following the routine of half an hour of television and bath and stories and bed, Frank took Liam down the road to the locked playground and showed him how to crawl under a fence so they could play on the swings. A grand adventure. What could be more fun?

Apparently, almost anything. "But won't we get into trouble?" Liam kept asking, over and over, his face anxious and taut, exactly like Jane's. Frank did his best to reassure him – "I'm with you, it'll be me in trouble, not you, and we can get away long before anyone catches us, no one's checking." Still there was no shaking that look on his son's face, the anxiety that gradually melted into something else: the realisation that his father was breaking the rules and there was nothing Liam could do about it. Liam's disapproval would have been funny if it hadn't been so heart-breaking. His discomfort came not from a fear of being caught, but from a dislike of rules being broken at all.

And so Frank let the swing slow to a stop, and lifted Liam from the seat, and led the way back under the fence, and they went home and watched half an hour of television and then did bathtime and stories and bedtime, and then he went downstairs and stared unseeingly at the TV screen and thought, *where did I go wrong? Why isn't he more like me?*

Because the truth is that the angry man flinging clothes into backpacks in the spare bedroom isn't his son, has never been his son; Liam was always, always Jane's creature. Jane arranged his schedule, seemingly within ten minutes of their son's delivery. Wake, change, feed, cuddle, sleep. Wake, change, feed, cuddle, sleep. Bath at six thirty. Cuddles, stories, into the cot. Wake, change, feed, cuddle, sleep. In the night Frank would hear Jane moving about in the semi-darkness and beg her to put the light on so she wouldn't fall over, but she refused, saying it would help Liam learn the difference between day and night. Wake, change, feed, cuddle, sleep.

After a few months, Frank rebelled against Jane's edicts and made alterations, such as bringing Liam downstairs after his bath, to snuggle and snuffle on his father's shoulder as they watched the news. A few evenings filled with piercing shrieks and hours of pacing the floor, and he was forced to admit that Jane did, in fact, know best. But what if he'd been braver at the start? What if he'd put his foot down and—?

You stole my son from me, Jane, Frank thinks. It's not a new thought but it has a new power. *He came back to me and I almost had him for a while and now I'm losing him again and it's your fault. I could kill you. I could kill you. If I ever see you again, perhaps that's what I'll do.*

It's dark in the kitchen. He reaches for the light switch and thinks, *you'll get through this, this is not the worst thing*

CHAPTER TWENTY-TWO

(DECEMBER, NOW)

worst thing about phone calls is not being able to see the other person. I hate talking on the phone to strangers. I'm not thrilled about it when it's someone I know. I can just about stand it when it's family. But really, what a weird way to communicate. Why did we ever invent it? Why would we want to talk to people we can't see? Apart from tonight. I look at my phone that's ringing, ringing, ringing, and think, the best thing about phone calls is not having to see the other person. *Come on, Emma*, I tell myself. *Pick up the phone and answer.*

The house phone rings, rings, rings. I already know it's Jane, I can see her number on my caller ID. I know why she's calling. She's seen the news. I could *not answer*, that's a thing that I could do. Maybe she'll think I'm out, or with the police.

No, of course she doesn't think I'm out. She knows I'm sitting here, at my kitchen table, staring at the shrilling phone. She knows perfectly well I won't dare leave, in case Liam calls. Fifteen years is a long time. She's seen me go from a young girl who thought she knew everything (my God, I wasn't even thirty when we got married! What was I thinking!) to a woman knocking on the door of forty who's finally starting to realise she knows hardly anything. And what's changed in Jane, in that time? I don't really know.

"Emma?" Jane's voice sounds old today. It's nothing that suggests she's ill, only that slight worn-out hoarseness that comes on gradually and then does not leave. "I saw the news."

"I'm sorry."

"I saw my son on the *news*, Emma, on the news. I put on the news and there you were, talking to the cameras, and a big photo of Liam in the background. I thought for a minute he was…" Jane swallows hard. "Why didn't you tell me? What were you thinking?"

What was I thinking? My recent thoughts are all in there somewhere, but I don't want to go looking, any more than you'd want to go poking around in an attic without a torch. Who knows what damage you might do, blundering around in the dark?

"I'm sorry," I repeat weakly.

What is Jane thinking, all alone in her neat little house? I didn't call her because she's Liam's mother, and I knew she'd be on Liam's side. Whatever happens, Jane will assume it's all my fault.

"I'm coming over," Jane says at last, not asking but telling, and hangs up.

I had to answer her call, and if I hadn't, she would have come anyway. Jane believes in action, in shaping the universe to suit your will. Still, I can't help a twinge of discomfort, as if I've accidentally made the first fatal move in a long series of events that will ultimately lead to my unravelling.

I fill the hour until she arrives with small acts of reclamation, left undone since my return and now long overdue. I unpack my suitcase and put my dirty clothes in the washing machine. I empty the sour contents of the fridge and leave the door open for ten minutes (the motor hums and whirs in protest and I know it's a waste of electricity, but I hate the way it smells, and this is the best way I know to get rid of it). I throw out the cheap supermarket flowers that I put on the table the day before I left, and rinse the slimy water down the sink (the chrysanthemums are still in reasonable shape and I ought to pick them out and put them in a smaller vase with fresher water, but I can't be bothered, and besides, I don't want Jane to think I'm being frivolous). I put on the kettle and make myself a cup of black coffee, the bitterness taken off with two fat spoons of sugar. I look at myself in the mirror. Do I look the right kind of harrowed? Not really. I've gone a night and a day without sleep, but I spent ten days before that in a cocoon of near-silent luxury, and it shows. Jane's going to be angry. What will that be like? She's never been angry with me before. But then, I've never hurt her son before.

The doorbell rings. She must have driven like a maniac. She's normally so controlled and careful in her driving. I glance again at the mirror. Will I do? I'll have to do. I open the door.

The first thing she does is the first thing she always does. She stands on the threshold of my house and her arms go around me and I feel the strength of her, the straightness of her spine, and feel comforted and protected. Then she lets go and looks me up and down, and I see the look in her eyes, as if I'm not the real Emma anymore, and I do the same to her and realise she's not the real Jane anymore either. Or maybe it's not that at all. Maybe it's that we've dropped our façades, and become our truer, uglier selves.

"Would you like coffee? Let me make you a coffee. Oh, and your coat, I'll take it for you." With two participants missing, our rituals are disrupted. What's supposed to happen is that Liam takes Jane's coat and hangs it on its special hook in the hall, Alannah leads Jane into the living room and drags the footstool over towards Jane's feet so she can sit close to her grandmother without squashing into the same chair, while I go to the kitchen and fill the kettle and brew the first of many mugs of tea. "I can't make tea; the milk was off and I didn't like to go to the shop in case you came while I was there but I've got coffee and coffee whitener so I can make you—"

"Let *me* make *you* a coffee." Jane cuts across my babble the way teachers always can. Does this mean she's not angry? "Tell me what's been going on."

"I don't know where to start," I say, partly because I really don't know where to start but mostly because I want time to think. Liam was always telling me how important it was to have a plan – no, don't think about Liam, that won't help you now. "Can you find everything? The coffee whitener's in the—"

"I know where everything is." Jane takes my cold and half-drunk mug of coffee, tips away the remainder, rinses it out, leaves it upside down on the draining board. She's particular in the way she makes her coffee. I would have spooned the granules into the dirty cup and let them begin to melt. "Now tell me. Did you two really have a row?"

"Yes," I say. It's the least titanic word for what we've had, but I'll accept it for now.

"Did you throw him out?"

"No! No, of course not."

"But you told him you want to leave him."

"No, I didn't, of course I didn't—"

"Don't say *of course I didn't* when we both know it's been on the cards for months." Jane's lack of emotion makes her words even more devastating. "You've thought about it a lot, haven't you?"

"I wouldn't," I say. Is this the truth? I hope it's the truth. "I wouldn't do that to him."

"He thinks you're going to."

"Has he told you that?"

The kettle boils. Jane spoons coffee into the mugs and fills them.

"No. My son doesn't talk about his feelings. You ought to know that by now. But it's what he's afraid of."

My son. It's a warning. She's telling me, *be on your guard, because I am not on your side anymore.*

"We did have a row," I say. "We've been arguing a lot."

"I've noticed."

"What? How have you noticed? We don't argue in front of you, we've never argued in front of you."

"Alannah told me." Jane is stirring her coffee very fast and energetically, creating a vortex that sucks down the thick layer of creamy powder into the heart of the mug. "It frightens her."

"He can't help shouting. It's not his fault. He's…"

And here it is, the shameful truth we've both been trying to keep secret. How would it feel to hear that about your son on the news? It was cruel to keep it from Jane.

"He's not well," I whisper, as if whispering will make a difference.

"I know that. Don't you think I already know that?" The contempt in her voice makes me cringe. "He's *my son*."

And he's my husband, I think but do not quite dare to say. Apart from anything else, I don't know if it's still true.

"And what about you?" Jane puts the coffee spoon down and turns her gaze onto me like a searchlight. "Why do you shout back, Emma?"

So it's going to be like that, then. This is how we're going to be.

"You should try living with him for a week," I say. "I bet you'd shout too if you had to put up with how he is sometimes."

"I probably would." Jane is endlessly surprising tonight, not saying what I think she'll say, constantly shifting her attack. "I'm sure he hasn't been easy. But that doesn't mean he's always in the wrong."

"You think he hasn't been *easy*?" For a moment I find it genuinely funny. "You think living with Liam… hasn't been easy. You have no clue…"

"Emma, he's ill. He wants to get better."

"So why doesn't he try?"

223

"Because helping him get better is your job!" This is what people mean when they say *if looks could kill*. Jane's look is so powerful I think it will burn me up. I recognise the passion in her face, words pouring out of her like spilled salt. She's been holding onto them for a long time. "He needs you to look after him. And you haven't."

"I…" Jane is so wrong I don't know where to begin. "How can you possibly think…" If Liam had cancer, would it be my job to cure him? Why is it any better because the sickness is inside his head? "It's not—"

"That's the promise you made, Emma. You promised for better, for worse. You promised you'd be by his side for always. You married a soldier; you knew what you were taking on. And now it *has* got worse, he's been injured, and you haven't stuck by what you promised."

I can hardly believe the hypocrisy of a divorced woman lecturing me about the sanctity of marriage. I shouldn't laugh, but I don't know if I can stop myself. I keep it to a choked splutter, and wonder if Jane can see what I'm thinking.

"You can't be serious," I say at last, as a compromise.

"Of course I'm serious. I'm furious about this, Emma. How dare you do this to him? He left you sitting in this pretty house, all warm and safe and taken care of, while he went off to that hellhole to serve his country, and he came home and he needed your help and you didn't help him, not the way you should have done, and now you tell me that Liam's walked out on you and *you don't know why*?"

"What would you know about what it was like?" It's almost appalling, how quickly we've torn away the façade of love that we both thought, until now, was how we really felt about each other. This is what happens when two mothers are left alone and unchecked. "You have no *bloody* idea how hard it was, looking after Alannah by myself, no calls, no letters, never knowing if I'd see that car pull up outside my house." Now I'm the hypocrite (what can I tell Jane about being a single parent?), but I don't care. I'm not right, but

I'm not entirely wrong either. "And then when I finally got him back—"

"So that's how much you love my son, is it?" Jane's face is white and tense. "You love him while he's well and healthy and able to keep you—"

"I bloody *work*, Jane, I work every single day."

"Emma, you're a teaching assistant. You cut shapes out of paper and stick pictures on walls with a staple gun. And while you're doing craft projects all day long—"

"And what if I wasn't there doing all that? Who would have looked after Alannah if I hadn't been at home? Whose income do you think we've been surviving off while Liam's been out of work?"

"So you live off your TA's salary, then? You don't get benefits? Support from the state? Money from a system Liam paid into? You got off lightly in my opinion, you've seen the state of some of those poor boys. What would you have done if he'd come back with no limbs?"

As if I haven't had that thought myself a million times. The bargain I made, the deal I struck. *Please let him still be happy in his body. Please let him still be able to be a good dad to Alannah. I'll accept absolutely anything else.* Be careful what you wish for. Sometimes God gives you exactly what you asked.

"That would have been easier," I say.

"How can you say that?"

"Because he would still have been *Liam*. The man he is now – the person who's in this house every day, waiting to pounce – this, this fucking *stranger* who gets into bed with me every night – that's not the man I married." None of this is getting through to her. "Look, what do you *want* from me? What do you want me to say?"

"I want you to stop feeling sorry for yourself and think about Liam. I want you to call him, right now, and tell him you're sorry and you want him to come home so you can talk

225

about how you'll do better in the future. And then you two can damn well talk this through."

"I can't do that."

"Yes, you can. Get on with it."

"He's not taking my calls. I think he's switched it off, it's not even ringing."

Jane frowns, but recovers quickly. "So we'll wait for him to come home. How long's he been gone?"

"I don't know. I wasn't here when he left."

"But you must have some idea."

"I don't know! The most it can be is nine days, but I don't know for sure."

"Nine days! He could have been gone for *nine days*? Where the hell were you?"

I don't know why she's asking. We both know there's no answer I can give that she'll find acceptable. That said, *I was at a luxury hotel* isn't something I'm going to share with her. And as I fumble for the right thing to say, I see what's been missing from our conversation so far, the piece of information she must have seen, but has not yet processed. It must have been a shock to turn on the television and see Liam's face. She's a mother, she wouldn't have been thinking about anyone else.

"Why do you keep saying *him*? It's not him. It's *them*."

"What do you mean?" Jane blinks. "Did you go to the police because your husband ran off with someone?"

"He's got Alannah with him," I say, and the quiver in my voice is uglier than I knew anything could be. Terror makes its own space in your head; there's still room left over for everything else too. Like triumph. Like the mean pleasure of suddenly having the upper hand. "He took Alannah."

"What?" Jane is shrinking before my eyes, her strength spilling out of her, her bones crumbling.

"I've got messages from the dance teacher. He rang her up and said Alannah couldn't do the show after all, I don't know exactly how but he did it, all right? That's why I rang the police. Because of Alannah."

"But he would have come to me. He would have come to me. Wouldn't he? If you have to leave home isn't that where you'd go? Back to your mother?"

How selfish we can be, even at the worst of moments. Why isn't Jane thinking about Alannah?

"A hotel." Jane bites her lip. "Could he afford a hotel? I thought things were tight for you both."

They have been tight. Especially since I've been siphoning off money to pay for my escape, stacking up debt onto the credit card to keep the household afloat. The bills all went out the day before I ran. Of course they're not in a hotel.

Jane's on her feet now, striding up and down the kitchen. "Could he have some money you don't know about?"

I shake my head.

"So… He could have been gone over a week. He's got no money. So where—"

And then she sees it. I've been hoping she wouldn't, because if Jane doesn't see it, it's still something lurking, unformed, in the back of my head. The police mentioned it, of course they did, it's the reason they're looking. But it's their job to see the worst in people. Jane is his mother. She knows him.

"No. No, he wouldn't. He wouldn't do that. Not with Alannah. Would he?"

"I don't know."

"He's a good father. He loves Alannah. He *loves* her. He wouldn't hurt her."

"I keep telling you," I whisper. "He's not the same person he used to be. I don't know what he might do."

Then why the hell did you leave him alone? Jane doesn't ask this aloud, but she doesn't need to. Why did I leave him alone? Why did I do that?

I know the answer. Because I was tired of the work, the effort, the mental strain it took to try and keep him alive.

227

I wanted him (and everyone else too, but mostly him) to understand and appreciate how much I was doing for him. I wanted to rest.

There's a darker answer too. But I won't look at it. I will not.

I wait for Jane to turn on me the way her son has so often done in the last couple of years, to tell me all the ways I've failed as a wife and a mother. Or maybe she'll be kind? Liam was kind too, once, and it must have come to him from somewhere.

Jane points at me with a bony finger.

"If anything's happened to my son and my granddaughter," she says, "I don't know how you'll ever live

CHAPTER TWENTY-THREE

(DECEMBER, NOW)

live like this? How is he supposed to do it? Alfie stands before the tall bathroom mirror and forces himself to face his own reflection.

He'd begun to feel more comfortable recently. Each time someone called him by his true name, each time his grandfather said *Alfie* and not *Alannah*, each time a shopkeeper said *there you go mate* or *good lad* or some other casual reminder, he felt himself settle a little more comfortably into his new shape. He knows, really, that most of it's the clothes; but still, it felt good. Tonight is the first time he's made himself look at his naked reflection.

He starts with the face. Bright eyes, prominent cheekbones, the skin hairless and soft. He can get away with this because he's eleven, but what will happen in the next year or two? His cheeks will stay smooth, his neck slender. He'll look like a girl. A girl with a boy's haircut. Oh God.

Next, the chest. He flicks his eyes downwards, then away again, then forces himself to look, to feel. There's no escaping it. It's starting. There are two round little buds there, and no matter how hard he works, how diligently he tries to starve them out of existence, they'll only grow more visible. He's growing boobs and there's nothing he can do to stop it.

Downwards, and everything there is still the way it's always been, not ugly but simply *wrong*, the wrong configuration. He remembers being small, seeing his mum naked when they took baths together. He'd been startled and confused by his mother's insistence that they'd look the same when he was older, convinced there'd been a mistake. (His mother was pretty; he could see that. It wasn't that there was anything wrong with girl's bodies. He just didn't want to live in one himself.) Then he'd seen his dad coming out of the shower one day and for a second, before he'd managed to stop himself, he'd thought: *that's what I'm supposed to grow into.*

He remembers the first time he had *The Nutcracker* read to him, that Christmas morning when Granny Jane gave him the book, and his first term of lessons. The Nutcracker Prince, stiff and rigid, trapped in a body that was not truly his. And then, by an act of magic, he was set free, becoming his true self. He'd been enthralled by that possibility without knowing why, his whole heart ablaze at the idea that, if you waited long enough and willed it hard enough, you could be remade into your true form.

He knows the word for who he is. He's watched a lot of YouTube videos, trying to make sense of the inside of his head; he's sat through the excruciating awkwardness of the school puberty talk. He's come across people who seem to be like him. Some of the stories make him feel hopeful – *there are things they can do! I can be myself! I can make people call me by my right name!* Others fill him with despair. (*What if my mum throws me out? What if Granny Jane doesn't love me anymore? What if people beat me up? What if nobody ever loves me?*) He's gone through long periods of pretending none of it's real, of letting his mother dress him in the prettiest frocks she can devise, of begging her for complicated hairstyles and ridiculous shoes. The pleasure his mother takes in indulging these moments hurts him in a way he can't quite name. He wants to make her happy, but what about *her* wanting to make *him* happy? Why doesn't she ever see who he really is?

"Stop it," he says to his reflection. When he cries, his face softens and he looks more like the girl they're always telling him he is, the girl whose body he's accidentally ended up with. Is his female twin out there somewhere, doing exactly this, from the inside of Alfie's body? Why can't someone invent a machine so you can go inside one part of it and the other person goes in another part and when you come out, you've swapped bodies and you're both happy at last? That would be a good thing to do.

But then, how could you actually swap bodies? Your body is who you are. How can your body be wrong? *What are you talking about? You don't look wrong, you look perfect. Wait until you grow up a bit and then you'll see.* That's what his mum's told him, over and over. *Your body's fine, it's strong and healthy and does everything you want it to.* That's his dad. That's what Alfie's told himself in the dance studio, over and over and over. His body does everything he wants it to. Everything except look and feel like he belongs inside it.

He can hear his dad and his grandad in the living room. They're arguing about something. If he listened harder he could probably make out what it is they're yelling about, but he's afraid to, in case it's about him. He'd really thought his dad was going to be all right about it. He'd honestly thought, these last few days… And now he's crying again, and he won't let himself do this because he's a boy, on his way to being a man, and he's never seen his dad cry and he's going to be like his dad and everything's going to be all right, somehow, in the end.

It's lonely in the bathroom, and his skin is cold and goose-pimply, and he knows in his bones that he's in this one on his own.

Get on with it, he tells himself. *Get it done and then it's over, and there won't be anything anyone can do about it afterwards.*

He'd thought about a knife, but his mother's scissors feel like the right tool for the job. She's used them so many times to make him look like the person she thinks he ought to be. And that's what's happening here. He's going to make some improvements.

It's going to hurt, he knows that; but he's been in a different kind of pain for such a long time. Maybe he'll have built up a tolerance. He thinks about the horses on the beach. They had bits chopped off them, and they were fine afterwards, weren't they? They got rid of some bits they didn't need, and then they were happy, not tormented anymore by the feeling that there were other things they were supposed to be doing. They were healthy and strong, running across the sand in a flowing stream, snorting and tossing their heads like children. They were happy in their skins…

His dad and his grandad are still arguing, but it won't be long before one of them wonders where he's got to. He's got this moment, and a mirror. And his mother's scissors, growing warm in his hand, ready and willing to do what needs to be done.

Now all he needs is to find the courage. He fits his fingers into the grip of the scissors. The blades part like lips. He takes a deep breath, closes his eyes, opens them again, and in that moment becomes ready.

Then there is nothing but redness and pain and a high shriek coming from far, far away, and he knows the bathroom floor will be hard when he hits it but it feels soft beneath him and he lets it take him, imagining he's being held by someone who loves him, pretending

CHAPTER TWENTY-FOUR

(2019)

pretending Liam and I are going to be all right. For the first week after his discharge, we're so good at it, we almost fool ourselves.

That first week's a strange honeymoon period, walking around each other as if we're both made of spun glass and a harsh word or movement will see us smashed on the floor. I take a week of emergency leave, even though money's tight and will only get tighter until Liam finds work. We don't discuss money, or Liam finding a job. We don't talk about the future. Liam never mentions his recent past.

Instead, we make food and drinks for each other. We do laundry. We hold doors open and hold coats out and put things away and step back to give each other room, cleaning up the slightest mess as soon as it's made. Three mornings out of the seven, we go back to bed and have sex, concentrating on what the other one wants rather than thinking of ourselves, not rushing, not demanding. If sex can be *polite*, then that's the kind of sex we have. We're silently competing to see who can be the best human being out of the two of us.

When Alannah comes home, she plays along too. She's absorbed the new rules: Dad and Mum both at home, Dad not going away anymore, but the reasons why must never be approached. When she's in the house, we both switch gears, becoming the world's most Instagrammable parents. Sometimes Liam gets in first, declaring in a loud voice that "Mum deserves a break", and driving Alannah to class. Sometimes I'm quicker, declaring that we (which means Alannah and I: this time it's Liam's turn for the enforced rest) need to do some baking, but before we can do any *baking* we need to do some *shopping*, and then it's into the car for both of us, off for a wild trawl around the supermarket, collecting flour and butter and eggs and sugar and overpriced sugar-shapes and sickly buttercream mixes to plaster onto our (slightly misshapen) buns.

Alannah gets through it the same way she gets through everything. She smiles in the right places, submits to all the activities we impose, eats as little as possible, and shows absolutely no sign that she's enjoying any of it. I start to get irritated with how little appreciation I'm getting, as I strive to keep everything normal and happy and maybe even a little bit festive. I remind myself that Liam is trying hard, too. He's ill, even though he doesn't look it. Ill enough for a medical discharge. But how do they know? How can they tell? He seems fine. Absolutely fine. What if they've made a mistake?

Perhaps it's all a mistake and in a week or so, everything will go back to normal.

Then, the night before I have to go back to work, I get my first glimpse of what I'm really dealing with here, what it is I've signed up to.

It begins with a mug on the coffee table. I make a late-night herbal tea and, feeling lazy and ready for bed, decide not to put it in the dishwasher. But this is the first time, and I'm not prepared. I'm a fast learner, it won't take me long to understand that I can't do this anymore.

I go upstairs, take a shower, wash my hair. Towel myself dry. Vaguely register that something isn't quite as it should be. Blow dry my hair (I should do this in the morning, it'll lose its shape overnight, but tomorrow's my first day back and I don't want the rush). Hang up my dressing gown. Put on my pyjamas. Realise something still isn't quite right. Notice Liam isn't in the bedroom. Hear the sounds coming from the kitchen. Go downstairs to investigate.

My first thought is that there's a leak, because Liam's pulled out everything from underneath the sink and is half inside the cupboard. Then he backs out and sinks a sponge into a steaming bowl of soapy water, and I realise he's cleaning. He's cleaning the cupboard. The cupboard where we keep the cleaning things. At a quarter to eleven at night.

"It's filthy," he says, and even though his voice is low and controlled, the back of my neck prickles with something I'll later identify as fear.

"It's late." I want to sound light-hearted, maybe even a bit pissed off. But the muscles of my throat must know something I don't, because I sound nervous, placatory. "Why don't we sort it out in the morning?"

"It can't wait."

"Of course it can. Why were you even looking in there, anyway?"

"That bloody mug!" The transition from calm to fury is like a switch. Then the switch flicks off and he's calm again. "That mug. The one you left out. With a herbal teabag in it. If you leave it like that, it stains. So it needs bleaching. And when I looked for the bleach, everything in here was a mess. So I started tidying. And when I took everything out, it was filthy."

"Liam." The switch is about to flick again, I can sense it. Whatever I say next runs the risk of being wrong. And I don't know what to do. I'm prepared for upset and tears, but I don't know what to do with his rage. I can comfort a small hurt boy, but what do you do with a man so angry he's barely keeping control?

"It's all right." His smile shows his teeth. "Everyone makes

235

mistakes. But next time, can we make sure there aren't mugs left everywhere with teabags staining them bright purple?"

Can he hear himself? Does he realise how insane he… No. Get it together. Of course he sounds… not right. This is his illness talking.

"You're not well," I say. This is another mistake I won't make again.

"There is nothing fucking wrong with me!" He's not being violent, he's not making any kind of threatening gesture, I have absolutely no reason to think he'll hurt me. This is what he'd say if I could replay this moment to him. What he doesn't realise is that he, all by himself – *just him, shouting* – is terrifying. Except it's not him. That's what I have to remember. This isn't him, it's his illness. I have to take care of him, the same as if he'd lost a leg.

"I'm sorry. I didn't mean to upset you."

And the switch flicks off again. "Never mind. Everyone makes mistakes."

"Shall I help you put everything back?"

"I'll do it. Good thing you've got me here though, isn't it? Come and watch. Then you'll know how it's supposed to be."

I want to tell him to stop being so stupid, go upstairs, and flounce under the duvet. An acceptable compromise would be to tease him out of it, work my fingers along his spine until he gives in and leaves the cupboard for tomorrow. If he was well, I could choose to do this. But he's not well, and I don't know what will happen if I try. So I sit on the kitchen floor as he re-stacks the freshly scrubbed cupboard. *See how much better this is*, he keeps asking, and I alternate between seeing him as a patronising tosser who thinks he can mansplain the contents of my own kitchen to me, and as a small boy looking for validation of how clever he's been. I know how wrong both of these are. It's *our* kitchen, not *my* kitchen, and he's not a mansplainer or a child, but a man, wrestling with something terrible.

"There," he says, and closes the cupboard door. "Now we're living like humans again."

I glance around the neat, pretty, welcoming, homely space that I've poured so much time and love into creating, and manage not to cry. My feet prickle with pins and needles.

"Steady on." He takes my shoulders and squeezes them affectionately. "You been drinking, love?"

"Only herbal tea," I say, and then instantly wish I hadn't, because I've flicked the switch again. How long will it take me to learn? He peers disapprovingly into the cup. There's a thick half-inch of bleach in the bottom: I can smell it when he swirls it around.

"That's better," he says grudgingly. "But we can't live in a shit-tip, all right? We're not animals."

"I'm sorry." I'm not sorry, but I don't know a word for what I am. What is the word for what I am? "I won't do it again."

He's washing the bleach from the cup. Scrubbing even though it's already spotless. Can I tell him to come to bed? Will that be okay? I'm still trying to decide when he reaches for the tea towel. He dries the mug until it squeaks, puts it in the cupboard.

"Now we can sleep," he says, and suddenly he looks exhausted.

"Come on then." I can do this; I've had more than a decade of practice. I know how to cherish, to nurture, to mother. "Upstairs and into bed."

He follows me obediently upstairs. I wonder if I'll have to help him undress, clean his teeth, remind him to pee, but some sort of autopilot kicks in and I lie in bed and hear him rattling around like a machine completing an automatic cycle before shut down. He comes back into the bedroom. Are we going to talk about what happened? He climbs under the duvet. Scoots down, ready for sleep.

"Night." His kiss is quick and perfunctory, his breathing slow and rhythmic. I feel the gradual relaxing of his muscles. Clearly, there will be no talking tonight. A good thing, since I've got to be up for work in the morning. I don't have the energy for a long, impassioned discussion about what his symptoms mean, how I can help him manage them, what we can do differently in future. Soon this lack of conversation will become a torment. Tonight, this first time, it's a relief to let sleep take me.

Half an hour later I'm woken by someone yelling. Whoever it is, they're either in terrible pain or terrible danger. I'm upright instantly, adrenaline like an electric shock up my spine, but it's dark and I'm disoriented and I don't know what's going on. *Alannah*, is my first thought, but this is a man's voice and not a girl's, and they're in the bed beside me, and of course it's Liam, it's Liam and he's having a nightmare.

"It's all right." I try to put my arms around him. He flings me off, scrabbles out of bed and towards the door. I follow him, convinced that if I can get my hands on him, only get my arms around him, he'll be calm again. "Liam. Liam! It's all right. You're safe. I'm here. You're safe."

He comes back to me slowly, awakening like the sleeper he is. I have to remember this: he's dreaming. Like Alannah waking in the night, eyes wide and glassy, shrieking about something only she could see. Come the morning, he probably won't even remember.

"It's all right," I say, stroking, patting. His muscles are like rocks. "It's all right. You're safe."

"What are you doing out of bed?" He's fully present with me now, we're in the same place once more. "Is Alannah all right?"

"Yes, she's fine. But you had a—"

"Back into bed, then. You've got work tomorrow, remember?"

I almost want to laugh – he thinks *he's* comforting *me*! – but if I laugh, I'll have to explain, and surely it's better to get everything smoothed over, everyone back in their right places. "Okay."

"Did you set an alarm?" He doesn't wait for my answer: he's already fumbling with the bedside clock. "Seven fifteen.

Don't you want to be up earlier? You said you wanted to be up earlier."

He's right. I forgot to change the alarm. He mutters and fumbles with the buttons. Six thirty is earlier than I'd planned, but I don't want to argue, so apparently six thirty is the time I'm getting up now.

"Good thing I'm here," he says, and although he's teasing me, something darker lurks behind his eyes. I swallow and look down.

"Thank you," I say, meekly.

"Night." The same quick kiss. The same turn onto his side. The same deep breathing. It's almost funny. For a while I think it *is* funny, allow myself to smile up at the ceiling before closing my eyes. *You've got to laugh, haven't you? Got to laugh or you'd never get through.* And laughing to myself, or at least smiling to myself, gets me through the barriers of sleep and into the welcoming darkness, where I stay for a whole forty minutes until it happens again.

The next morning, we're both zombies. I drink two cups of coffee instead of my usual one, and pack a can of Red Bull for lunchtime. Thank God for caffeine. Liam sits at the table in white-faced silence. I don't feel right leaving him. But what else can I do?

"Right." I bend over to kiss his mouth. "I'll see you tonight."

"Have a good day."

"Will you be all right?"

"Yes, of course." Liam frowns. "How about you? Will *you* be all right?"

"Why wouldn't I be?"

"You were up half the night roaming around the bedroom," he says, and I can hear the accusation in his voice. "Kept waking me up. What was the matter with you?"

The switch is about to flip. My finger's hovering over it. I fumble for the right words. The honest answer is *I was awake because you were awake, you were having nightmares*. But *honest* is not the same as *right*, not anymore.

"I was worried about today," I say at last. "Sorry. I'll try not to do it again."

"Why didn't you try the relaxation technique I showed you?"

"I forgot about it."

"You never listen," he says. We're still on the edge, the switch still live. "Why don't you listen?"

"I'm sorry," I say, because that seems easiest. "I'll try it tonight, okay? Promise."

I have a full day's work ahead of me and I'm already exhausted. On the short walk to school, Alannah's quiet to the point of sulkiness. I should try and coax her out of it, but I don't have the energy.

It'll get better, I tell myself. *It has to get better. He'll get better soon. This is only for a little while. You can do this, Emma, you can. Concentrate on what he needs, not what you need. Oh God, if I could only go back to bed for a couple of hours, just a little more sleep. Just a little bit more would be enough. Oh God, I want to scream*

CHAPTER TWENTY-FIVE

(DECEMBER, NOW)

scream is inside his head only. He won't make a noise. He'll concentrate instead.

The seventeen leaflets arranged in the rack are of varying sizes and styles. Eleven are in what's presumably a standard NHS format, the same logo across the top, the same font size and typeface. The other six are a mishmash, destroying any potential for true order. Some are slotted in neatly, corners squared off, pictures upright. Some have clearly been briefly skim-read then jammed back into the wrong place. He will not rearrange them. He will not touch them.

What else, what else, what else? Leave the leaflets alone, he can't be rearranging leaflets, he'll look mad. *Leave them.* He'll count the ceiling tiles instead. He'll count the ceiling tiles and then he'll stand up and walk down the corridor and back again, each pace perfectly measured, and then he'll know how long the corridor is and from this he will be able to calculate the rough size of each ceiling tile and when he has done all these things, another few minutes will have passed and he will be that much closer to the surgeon coming through the doors and telling him his daughter's fate.

(The blood. The blood on the floor. Her face. The noise

she was making. The slow understanding of what he was seeing, what she'd done to herself. Those scissors, the ones she'd stolen from Emma, little scraps of flesh clinging to the blades.)

Twenty-one ceiling tiles long. Five tiles wide. Twenty times five is a hundred, add on five is a hundred and five... The door's opening. He's ready, he's ready to face whatever's coming, he will not, *will not* flinch. Then it's only his dad, carrying two tall paper cups, and he's furious because he was ready for news, he was *ready*, and now he has to wait again, and it takes all he has left not to take the coffee cup and fling it against the wall.

(The blood, spurting out of her.)

"No news yet, then?" His dad, trying to be kind but with no idea what he's going through. It's Liam's fault. Going along with all that *Alfie* nonsense. Letting her cut her hair. No, it's not only him, it's Emma, too. Alannah was in trouble long before this, they both knew it, but they were so focused on each other, Emma so absorbed in trying to fix Liam even though he was *fine*. And even if he hadn't been fine, what kind of a mother puts her husband above her...

("We've stabilised the bleeding, and now we need to operate so we can patch up some of the damage. You're Dad, aren't you? Excellent, so if you can sign these forms for us and we'll get up to theatre straight away.")

How could she do it? How? He thought the pictures in his head from that last tour were the worst things he'd ever have to look at, but now there's a new horror to contemplate, another mutilated child. And once again, where was Emma? Why isn't she here to look at what she's done? He should have taken out his phone, taken pictures of the mess, so she can look at what she's done to their daughter and then *she* can be the one who wakes up in the night sick with disgust at herself—

"Liam." Frank is talking to him, breaking in on his train of thought. "Liam. I need to tell you something."

"I'm listening."

"I know you won't like this but I had to do it."

Fuck's *sake*. "Fine, just tell me."

"I'm so sorry, son. But it had to be done."

"Tell me." One more delaying apology and he'll hit him. He'll hit his own dad right in the mouth and then there will be more blood for him to think about, more pictures to hold in his head. He can't take much more; he's going to burst. His head's going to split right open and spil! onto the linoleum.

"I got in touch with Emma and let her know what's going on."

"No, you didn't." He hadn't thought he would ever laugh again, but somehow that's what's happening, that's the noise coming out of his face at this moment. "Don't be fucking stupid."

"Yes, I did, I knew you wouldn't like it but I did. She needs to be here too. She needs to know what's happening."

"You don't even know where she lives. How can you possibly—?"

"I called the police hotline and told them where we were and they're getting in touch with Emma. She'll be on her way now. That's why I was so long getting the coffee."

"You called the police?"

"It doesn't matter, you haven't committed a crime, they were worried about you, son, that's all. They only wanted to make sure you were both safe."

"Well, Alannah's not fucking safe! She's lying on an operating table while some surgeon tries to stitch her back together after she's… she's…" He's not going to be sick, he's not, he's a soldier and he's seen things other people don't even want to think about. He's not going to be sick. Then suddenly he is going to be sick, and there's nowhere good to do this, no convenient bin or handy corner, but he does the best he can, keeping still so it'll all go into one place, bending well forward so he'll miss his shoes. Frank puts a hand on Liam's back and rubs gently. One more thing for him to resist: the urge to slap his father's hand away.

"Don't worry. You sit still and I'll find someone to clean up."

He's not worried. He's certainly not worried about puking. This is a hospital; they deal with this stuff all the time. He's furious, is what he is. Furious with his dad for calling the police, furious with the police for sticking their beaks in, furious with Emma for fucking everything. His daughter, Alannah, with those goddamned *scissors* sticking out of her... The spasm comes over him again, so quickly he can barely catch his breath. He won't choke, he won't. He's a soldier and he's dealt with worse than this.

"It's all right. Take it easy. There you go." He wants to be alone, but the corridor's suddenly full of people. His dad, and a nurse offering him a grey cardboard thing like a sombrero, and now the surgeon's materialised out of nowhere and is sitting beside him, and they're all looking at him with compassion and tenderness in their eyes and he's never wanted to punch a set of strangers more in his life. "The operation went fine. We're out in recovery now."

"She's going to be okay?"

"It all went very well. Breathing well, waking up nicely from the anaesthetic. We'll talk about the rest later. You can visit for a couple of minutes. Only you for now, Dad, but we can sort out other visitors once we've got settled on the ward. As soon as you feel ready. No rush."

"It's fine, I'm ready now."

"Are you sure? Do you want some water first?"

Why won't everyone just leave him *alone*? Who does he have to beat to a pulp to get people to listen? "I told you, I'm fine. Let's go."

He keeps his head high and his breathing even. The door opens.

Alannah lies beneath a white sheet and a single blue blanket, both tucked around her waist. He'd worry about her being warm enough, but the temperature in here's enough to cook an egg. What happens next? Will she really be sent up to a ward? Made to lie in a bed with half a dozen other kids? Forced to explain why she's there? She'll hate that so much; she's never liked being with strangers.

Her chest is bandaged. Is she bandaged down below as well? How's she going to… Wait, there are tubes coming out of her from all sorts of places, one of them must be a catheter. He remembers the scissors, pushes the image away. God, she's so little in that bed. The skinniness of her, taut muscle over sharp bone. He wants to cover her up, keep her safe from the judgement of others.

"Hey." He wants to kneel at her bedside, press his cheek against hers. He wants to grab her by the shoulders and yell into her face, forcing her to explain how on earth she could be so utterly stupid. "How are you feeling?"

"Did they take it all away?" She's barely awake, eyes rolling, face contorted. This is how she used to look when she was little and they had to wake her up for some reason. Holidays. Long journeys. That first day of school. "Is it all gone now?"

"You're going to be fine. Don't worry. They can fix anything these days." Two fat tears gather at the corners of Alannah's eyes. "Hey, what are you crying for? Does it hurt?"

"—sick," Alannah manages, and then there's a nurse beside her, expertly lifting and positioning, holding another grey sombrero thing to Alannah's mouth, stroking her hair. It should be Emma doing this. It should be *him* doing this. How dare that strange woman touch his daughter? He swallows down the rage, feels it souring the lining of his empty stomach.

"There you go," he says as soon as the nurse has gone. "Better out than in, hey?" His hand, so big and awkward on the pillow beside Alannah's cheek. How does he touch her? How does he know where she hurts? Why hasn't anyone told him this stuff? Does he have to do everything around here? "Still feeling sleepy?"

"Did they take it all away?" Alannah squints at him through reddened eyelids. "Did I get rid of everything?"

"Don't upset yourself." He's aware of the nurses watching, the surgeon waiting in the background, a group of people who he's guessing are nurses but who no one has bothered to introduce to him. Human clutter. So many strangers, all staring at his naked and mutilated daughter. Do they think *he* did this to her? "It'll all be okay." Is he lying to her? He has no idea what's happening, doesn't even want to picture the damage she's managed to do. How long will she have the scars? How bad will they be? Will everything still work? Still grow the way it should? What if it can't be fixed? She's crying again, too tired to keep her eyes open, certainly no energy for wailing or sobs, only those fat tears rolling down, spreading into the cotton of the pillowcase. "Alannah, can you hear me?"

"Don't call me Alannah," she mutters, and then she's gone, eyes closed, somewhere he can't reach her, and he wants to shake her awake again, to check she's not dead.

"Nothing to worry about," says one of the nurses. God, there are so many of them in here, where are they all coming from, how's he supposed to keep track? "It takes a while to wake up completely. You pop outside for a bit and we'll give you a shout when we've got up to the ward." And then, as if he's very old or very sick himself, he's turned away from Alannah's bed and guided back into the corridor and there's a woman in a white coat getting right in his face, holding out a hand to him as if he's supposed to know what to do with it, directing him to sit down.

"We weren't introduced before. I'm Doctor Adams."

"Is she going to be okay?" he demands.

"I've spoken to my colleagues in the surgical team and there's no immediate danger from the injuries."

"But is she going to be okay?"

"We need to have a chat about what happened."

"Jesus, isn't it obvious? She went for herself with a pair of scissors, okay? Her mother's scissors, sewing shears or

246

something they're called. She keeps them extra sharp for fabric cutting."

"Is her mother on her way?"

"I… Yes, I suppose so. We're separated. Temporarily. Well, I mean, I don't know what's going to happen. Why do you want to know, anyway? It's none of your business." He knows he's being rude and irrational. He can damn well *feel* her humouring him. How dare she?

"That's good. Well, when Mum gets here, we'll need to chat about what led up to these injuries."

"I – you can't think I – she did it *herself*, I would never – God, I feel sick just *thinking* about it."

"It's all right. Take some deep breaths. Put your head between your knees."

His ears are singing. "I'm fine, don't fucking bully me."

"No one's bullying you, Mr Wright. I'm trying to look after you. Put your head between your knees now."

Because he's used to being told what to do, he does it. The world rocks and rolls around him, then steadies. He sits up slowly.

"Better? Good. Now, can you tell me exactly what happened?"

"She did it to herself!" He can't believe the howl that comes out of him. "She did it to herself. My little girl. She did that. She did that to herself with scissors. Fuck off, don't you dare look at me, how dare you look at me, leave me alone—"

"Mr Wright. Liam. It's all right. It's normal to be upset. It's normal, do you hear me? You've had a tremendous shock and it's absolutely all right to cry."

"I am not fucking crying!" Her hands on his shoulders are the heaviest thing he's ever had to lift, pressing him into the ground like a full backpack at the end of a day's hike. Still, he finds the strength, flinging them off, holding his arms out wide, making himself as big as he possibly can. "I am absolutely fine! I don't need anyone looking after me! I am all right! Now get the fuck off me and leave me alone!"

And then there's a flurry of activity and some burly men in blue uniforms who have that indefinable look of fellow soldiers are there beside him, taking hold of him and marching him away into a room by himself, and the word *police* is mentioned but he doesn't care, he doesn't care at all what happens next. Nothing can ever be right again.

He sits in the room long enough to need to pee, to go outside and find the bathroom and fill a cup of water on the way back. To drink the water. To wonder if he's hungry. To decide he may never be hungry again. Then there's someone in the doorway and he knows he ought to recognise her. Is it one of the doctors? The receptionist? He'll have it in a minute.

She looks a bit like Emma. Christ, it *is* Emma. Emma's here, and she's a mess.

"Why'd you take so long to get here?" Get yours in first, get the opponent on the back foot.

"Liam, don't." She looks as if she's been crying all the way here. Her eyes are swollen. Could she even see to drive? "We can't fight now. We need to think about Alannah."

"Was that what you were thinking about when you went off and left us?" The words *this is your fault* float between them, ready to be snatched by the first claimer. "About Alannah?"

"They want to talk to us," Emma says. She's not rising to the bait. Does she not care anymore? If she argues back, he'll know she still cares what he thinks.

"Who's *they*?"

"Someone from the psychiatric team," Emma says wearily.

It's the same doctor who called security on him in the corridor, but she doesn't seem inclined to mention this now. Is she holding it in reserve, ready to unleash it later? She's a woman so she'll be on Emma's side. He has time to think all of this in the few moments it takes them both to sit down in the doctor's office.

"So am I right that you were caring for your child when the incident happened?" Doctor Adams turns her face towards Liam.

"Most of the time she's with me." Emma is butting in, anxious and flushed.

"That's right." He won't look at Emma, that's how little she matters to him right now. "We were staying with my dad." His dad the drug dealer. Will that come out in the investigations? Emma reaches a hand towards him, then lets it drop again. "But the scissors are Emma's."

"Why don't you tell me about it?"

He hates feeling like a child, hates the feeling that he's being managed. "Okay. She was in the bathroom. I thought she was just, you know, getting in the bath. She was in there for a while. I was talking to my dad. Then I heard this..." He has to swallow. "This screaming. And when we broke the door open she was, she was..."

"Has your child ever said they think they might have been born in the wrong body? Told you they're actually a boy, or they want to be a boy? Anything like that?"

Emma gasps. Liam has to stop himself from grinning. He's ahead of the game here. He already knew this was coming. He knows Alannah better than Emma does. He's got his answers all ready.

"No," Emma says.

"Yes," says Liam, quicker and louder. "But it's all a mistake. She's a dancer, she thinks about her body a lot, and she's been rehearsing for a boy's part—"

"She was fine until you took her off with you!" Emma is hissing like a cat, fingers spikey and witchy, her voice low and furious. "She was fine until you were discharged for being a *fucking nutcase*."

"That is not relevant, that has absolutely nothing to do with—"

"Oh, you think living with you isn't part of the problem? She sees the way you treat me, an unpaid skivvy with shag privileges tacked on, and you wonder why she's confused about whether she wants to be a girl? And don't pretend you wouldn't have preferred a boy. Another little boy to play soldiers with you. You even cut her hair—"

"She did that herself! First chance she got!"

"If you could both calm down a little, please." Doctor Adams looks as if she's seen all of this before, seen it so many times she can hardly muster the will to deal with it yet again. "We're here to talk about your child. Did you know that the ambulance crew brought them in under the name Alfie? That was the name they asked the crew to use."

"Stop saying *them*. She's a girl."

"That's one possibility. It's too early to make any diagnosis yet. But when they were brought in, they were very insistent to all the medical team that their name was Alfie. And when they came round from the anaesthetic, their first question was *is it all gone now?* It's important that we listen to what's being said here."

Emma's settled back in her chair. Her focus has turned inwards: she's searching for the answers she wants, the solution that will unlock everything and put it back the way it's supposed to be. He recognises the look even though he doesn't want to.

"Emma." Without needing to look, Doctor Adams reaches for a box of tissues, passes them over. "You're aware of the nature of the injuries, aren't you?"

Emma swallows. "Yes."

"Inflicting that degree of harm on those specific parts of the body is a very strong indication of unhappiness with their assigned gender. You need to be open to the possibility that your child is a trans boy."

"But she's a girl," Emma sobs.

"You're not turning my child into a surgical freak," Liam says.

When he closes his eyes all he can see is the scissors, the bright blades and the bright blood splashing eagerly out across the floor. He may never eat again, never sleep again, because Alannah has cut her breasts and stabbed herself in her vagina and he had to look at it and see his failure as a parent spilled out across his own father's bathroom floor, and who cares what happens next? How can there be any coming back from this? *No more cutting*, he thinks, *no more damage, no more blood. I won't have it, I won't allow*

CHAPTER TWENTY-SIX

(DECEMBER, NOW)

won't allow myself to flinch as Emma and I walk through the sliding doors of the hospital, walking in step as if we're still on the same side. As if she hasn't hurt my son so badly I'll never forgive her.

I've imagined this before, if not the details then the broad shape of it. For families like ours, Death always stands a little bit closer. You don't want to think about it but you can't help yourself sometimes, any more than you can resist poking at a wound.

So, yes; I've imagined sitting beside my daughter-in-law in a car on the way to a hospital, not knowing quite what we'll find when we get there. It's just that… It's just that…

We both knew, when the phone rang, that it wouldn't be Death. They don't break that news with a phone call. Instead you get the car at the roadside, two figures walking up the path. I got to the phone first even though it was Emma's house, because I'm used to being in charge and because I wanted to look as if I was helping while simultaneously taking what I wanted. Secretively, in the disguise of helping. The way women of my generation have learned to take power. And besides, Liam is my son.

And then it wasn't Liam at all, it was…

Hospital lights, hospital smell. Hospital confusion. Why do they make these buildings so bewildering? Ward names that make no sense, lifts that go to some floors but not to others. Signs that point you in a certain direction, then abandon you to your fate. We ask at desks, scurry and bounce from one place to another, not looking at each other.

Finally, finally, we find a receptionist who wants us to get to where we're going. He leaves his desk and shows us the correct lift, presses the button for us, tells us to turn right when we get out and then take the third double doors on the left. Now we're here. A thin windowless corridor. Right in the heart of the maze. How long will it be until we're free to find our way out again? Who will we all be when we do? I'm thinking about leaving because I don't want to imagine everything I'm going to have to face before we can.

Yet another reception desk, staffed by a woman wearing that uniquely dowdy uniform that must have been chosen by a man. She says Liam's name, then Alannah's, but I can't process anything else. She takes Emma by the arm, leaves me behind with a look that's firmly apologetic, and I want to shout, *I'm a mother too, Emma's not the only mother here*, but I know it will do no good.

I could kill Emma for all of this. If I thought I could get away with it, I would have done it already. Maybe that's what I'll do with the rest of my life after this is over. Maybe I'll devote it to killing Emma, for whatever it is she drove my son to do.

But Liam wouldn't hurt Alannah. I know he wouldn't. My son is a good man.

Now what happens, now what happens, now what happens? I'm unneeded but I daren't leave. Partly because someone could come with news at any moment. Partly because I'm afraid I'll get lost and never find my way back again. There's an old man here too, shuffling around the leaflet rack, picking them up and putting them down again. I wonder who he's waiting for, what he's doing here. If he's a patient, or simply another lost soul, the same as me. He glances at me, looks me briefly up and down, looks away. Goes back to his leaflets. Looks me over again at the same moment that I, too, circle back for a second look.

What's the word for a reunion when the two people involved are the opposite of lovers?

I hate him and he hates me, we can both feel it pouring off the other one, like scent, or like smoke. I hate him and he hates me, which is odd because after all this time you'd think it would have faded away into indifference, but as it turns out, we're still capable of a bit of passion towards each other. I hate him and he hates me but he buys me a coffee anyway, and we sit beside each other and juggle the cups between our fingers because they're almost too hot to hold and it feels as if the plastic is melting in our hands. Or maybe the cups are responding to the rage that still flows between us both, even after all this time. It could always be that.

He looks so much older. I almost didn't recognise him, until I did. I suppose I look so much older too. That's how these things work, of course.

"So how did you—?" It makes me furious that he somehow knows more about what's going on than I do, but that's how it is. Strange that even with the panic over, what's happening to Alannah bubbling away in my stomach, I can still find room for other feelings too.

"I was there." Is that a sly flash of triumph in his eyes? I can hardly blame him if it is. He *has* beaten me on this one, briefly and temporarily, but nonetheless it's a point to him. "They came to stay with me. After his wife, whatshername—"

"Emma. She's a lovely girl." Even though I don't think this anymore, the words come out convincingly.

"—after she gave him his marching orders. He came to

stay with me for a bit." Now he's definitely looking a little triumphant. "Still remembered where I'd be after all those years. It was great to see him again. Never thought I would."

If I'd had my way, he never would have done. Why did Liam go there? Why not come to me? Wasn't I the one he knew he could rely on? A door opens down the corridor and we both go tense, waiting for news, but the nurse is a stranger to both of us, and he walks right past without acknowledging our presence.

"How about you?" Frank takes a mouthful of coffee, swallows slowly.

"I was at Emma's. The police called her. Said she needed to get here. I drove her, she wasn't in any state."

I still don't know exactly what's happened, but I can see from the wince of Frank's face that he does, and that whatever it is, it's something he wishes he hadn't seen.

"Poor little chap," he mutters into his cup, and I can see the quiver of his hands in the surface of his coffee.

"How is he?" Another burst of fury, that I have to ask for news of my son – *my son* – from this man sitting at my side.

"They haven't let me see him yet," Frank says, which I find confusing, and then, even more bafflingly, "I think he's out of surgery though."

"In surgery? What was he doing in there? They let him – they didn't let him – watch?"

"What?"

"What?"

We stare at each other in confusion.

"How the fuck could you do it, Jane?" Frank says suddenly.

"Don't swear at me."

"Why the fuck shouldn't I swear? You took him away from me. Our son. You took him off me, and now I want to know, how could you even do that?"

"You know why I had to." Is this really what we're going to talk about, at this time, in this place? "It was your own fault, and besides, you never even tried to see him, you never made any sort of effort—"

"You wouldn't have let me see him if I did try!" He's spilling his coffee. He licks a splash from the side of his hand, then puts the cup carefully down on the table. His tongue is as pink and clean as I remember it. "You weren't too fucking proud to take the fucking money though."

"You didn't have to send it. What was I supposed to do? Send it back?"

"You didn't even tell him I sent it," he says. "You let him believe you did everything."

"That's because I did do everything!" I'm actually hissing at him, I realise in surprise. This man I used to be married to has the power to make me hiss. "Even before I left you, I did everything. I got up with him in the night, I fed him, I changed him, I dressed him—"

"I would have done more if you'd let me!"

I laugh, realise how inappropriate it is to laugh in a hospital, make myself stop. "No you wouldn't. You never did, not once. Not the hard stuff. You only ever wanted to do the fun bits. Going to the park, playing football, reading bedtime stories once in a blue moon. How many nappies did you change? How many times did you mop up after he was sick? How many tantrums did you sort out? How many—" I was going to say, *How many nights did you get up with him when he was sobbing his heart out because he missed you*, but I manage to stop myself, because that doesn't help my case, and I don't like thinking about those times, even though they were for Liam's own good, always.

"And still," Frank says, as if he can see what's going on inside my head, "despite all of that, when he needed somewhere to go, he came to me."

And there's nothing I can say in response, because it's true. For whatever reason, when he needed to run, Liam didn't come home to his mother, who raised him single-handed for half his life. He picked his feckless, drug dealing father who he hadn't seen since he was ten years old. The depth of the hurt this causes me is astonishing.

All right, then. If Frank wants to see if he can hurt me, I'll let him see that he's hurt me. I'll give him that. Maybe if I do, he'll stop trying to hurt me anymore. Who knows what else he might have in his arsenal? Who knows what he and Liam might have been talking about, two men together, off by themselves when I couldn't see? It's a tactical decision to turn my face towards him and show him the tears brimming in my eyes. Men are so easily undone by the tears of women. Making them feel powerful is one of the best ways to take that power from them.

"Jane," Frank says, as I knew he would. (Is it strange that I still know him so well, even though now we're basically strangers?) "I'm sorry."

"Don't be. You're only telling the truth." (Tell him what he wants to hear, do a bit of grovelling so he'll say you don't have to. Is it still a game if you also believe it?)

"I know, but I didn't want to make you cry. I'm sorry."

"It's not you." He looks so hurt that I can't help but correct myself. "Not only you. It's… well." I can feel the sob making my face ugly, wrestle against my own throat for a moment. "My poor little granddaughter."

Frank's face is soft with surprise.

"Um," he says.

"What? What do you know? Did they give you some news? Is she all right? Tell me." I don't want to beg him. I hate that I'm begging him. But for Alannah, I'll do it.

"I…" He swallows. "I don't know if I'm supposed to—"

"Oh for God's sake Frank, man up and talk to me. Unless you're keeping quiet to try and bloody torture me. I mean, if that *is* it then I can't really make you—"

"Of course I'm not. I wouldn't. Is that really what you think of me?"

"How do I know what you might be like? I haven't seen you for decades."

"I haven't changed that much."

"Yes, well, you would say that, wouldn't you." I'm not even making sense to myself anymore. I'm talking out loud so I won't have to hear the voice in my head, pointing out all the ways this sad gentle man in the seat beside me is different to the vision I used to conjure each night. Used it like a shield to defend me from the treachery of wondering if I did the right thing when I kept Liam from him.

"It's just that," Frank says, very gently. "Look, I might have got this wrong, okay? I might have got it all wrong. It might only be a temporary sort of a thing. You know how kids are these days."

"For God's sake, *what*?"

"Well," Frank says, "when I first met him. Her. Um. This is really strange…"

If he doesn't tell me soon, I'm going to throw coffee all over him. (How did he stand it, all those years when I knew things he didn't? How has he not killed me? Is his kindness to me now a sign of his weakness? Or is it strength?)

"The thing is," Frank says, all in a rush, "I didn't meet a little girl called Alannah. I met a little boy called Alfie."

"I don't know what you're talking about."

"Yes, you do. You live in the same world I do; you see it on the television and in the papers. He introduced himself to me, and said his name was Alfie. You know what I'm saying."

"So she was playing a game. She's still little, she pretends to be all sorts."

"I think he really meant it, Jane."

"Don't be silly, you can't possibly know something like that, you've only known her a few days. I've known her all her life and she's—"

"He. Um. He. He's in here because he…" The surface of Frank's coffee is shimmering beneath the lights. His hand's shaking. "Jane, he's a boy. There's no way he could have done what he – what he did – if he didn't mean it, it was horrific."

"No. *No*. Not Alannah." How can I even still feel this

as a shock on top of everything else that's happened to me today? "She's not... No, I don't believe you."

"I know it must be strange for you. Like you said, you've known him all your life. But I'm telling you, he introduced himself to me as Alfie and he *is*, Jane, that's who he *is*."

"It's not right. She's a *girl*, I've seen her in her bath a million times, she's a little girl. Her body's absolutely perfect. She's pretty and dainty and she dances like a fairy. She's a girl. Why would she want to change that?"

Frank reaches out a hand towards me, then hastily pulls it back again. "Does it really matter so much?"

"Of course it matters! You can't change your sex. It's not possible. It's in the genes. It's a law of Nature. There are men and women, and you can't swap from one to the other, nobody can."

"What if he's not swapping? Maybe he's putting things right?"

"There's nothing to put right. She's not one of those poor in-between kids with something wrong with them, she's perfect..."

"But if it makes him happy, then who is it harming?"

It matters because there are *rules*. There are things that cannot and should not be changed, things that are fundamental to the way the world is. Alannah is a girl and I am her grandmother and the X chromosome that made her a girl and not a boy came to her from me, via my son. She is my granddaughter. Frank's grandson, this *Alfie* person he's talking about, is simply an illusion.

He's looking at me sideways, shy as a boy on his first date, afraid to show his heart in case I sink my teeth into it. "It's... It's honestly sort of nice to see you again. I always hoped... I mean. Not like this. But I wanted to say."

I want him to shut up. I don't want to hear this. For all these years I've been so desperate to believe I did the right thing, that I was right to leave and he was worthless, reciting it like

259

an incantation. I don't think I can take hearing Frank's version of events where he is, somehow, in some way, a good person.

"I always took care of you both. That's why I sent the money. Keeping up my side of the bargain. And I always did, didn't I? Even though you never let me—"

Another door opens. A woman in a white coat walks down the corridor. We watch her for clues. She's wearing a trouser suit and heels, so I assume she's not the surgeon. Is she here for us? We tense, readying ourselves. She assesses us with a brief sweep of her dark eyes. But we're not who she's looking for. She gives us the kind of half-smile that tells you you're not needed but you're not being criticised for that, and moves on. We both breathe again.

When I come back to myself, I realise I've instinctively reached out to Frank, and he's reached for me in return. How long has it been since we last touched? Between my palms, his hands feel

CHAPTER TWENTY-SEVEN

(DECEMBER, NOW)

his hands feel like his again, and he can move his feet. He's been awake before, but those moments were like the nightmares where you can see and hear, but not move (strangers surrounding the bed, confusing noises, pain everywhere). This time Alfie's fully in his body, fully in control, every part belonging to him.

"Dad." He isn't prepared for his own tears. "Dad. Are you mad with me?"

"Oh, love." His mum's on the other side of the bed, an unexpected bonus. Alfie reaches out one hand to each of them and feels cocooned.

"How are you feeling?" His mum strokes his hair, and Alfie remembers with remorse that he's cut it short.

He moves experimentally in the bed, feels sharp fingers of pain coming for him in all the places where the scissors did their work. Did he do enough? He knows he can't carve out the body he belongs in, but he can at least get rid of the parts he doesn't want. "Hurts."

"Do you want some painkillers? I'll get the nurse." His mother can't sit still, she's already off and roaming the ward. She can never rest if she thinks someone wants something, even if they don't actually want it. He doesn't mind the pain, but it's no good saying that, his mum's off now, and he'll go along with whatever she brings back because he loves her. He catches his dad watching him, having the same thought, and they smile shyly at each other.

"She never could sit still," his dad says, and Alfie lets himself savour their mutual knowledge. "Look, Alannah…"

Alfie shuts his eyes tight.

"No, I know you're awake. Listen to me. This is important."

I'm Alfie. I'm Alfie. I'm Alfie. Why can't you see that?

"We need to have a chat. While your mum's not here."

Call me my proper name. Please.

"I know it's not been easy for you. I mean, me and your mum. Things haven't been good recently. And I know I wasn't around much. Before, I mean."

But his dad was at work. He knows that, he understands that. The school has loads of Forces kids, they all know how it works. How can his dad possibly think *that's* got anything to do with it?

"And your mum… well, she loves you to bits, okay? But you know what she's like. She likes dressing things up to look pretty. And that's not you really, is it?"

"But Dad—"

"But, Alannah…"

Does this hurt more than the stabbing between his legs? Or does one pain make the other worse?

"…you can cut your hair short and wear trousers and, I don't know, play football and climb trees and all those things, and still be a girl."

It's not about what I look like or how I dress, it's about who I am inside. And I'm rubbish at football and I've never climbed a tree, nobody I know has ever climbed a tree, why would anyone even do that?

"And it doesn't matter if you – if you don't want – I mean – look, you don't have to dance if you don't want to, okay? All those smiles and pretty tutus. It's a bit of a stereotype, isn't it? But, I mean, girls can be tough and strong and aggressive if they want to be. Trust me on this."

Has his dad ever thought about the effort that goes into becoming a dancer? A trickle of sweat crawls between Alfie's buttocks. He wants to scratch but he's afraid of how much it will hurt him to move.

"My God, if you met some of the women I served with… But they're still women, is the point. You can be a girl and do anything you want. There's no limits. Alannah? Are you listening to me?"

"Alfie."

"No, Alannah. We picked your name and it's a girl's name and that's because you're a girl. You're Alannah."

"I'm Alfie."

"Alannah, you can't be a boy any more than you can be a dog. Okay? It's simply not possible. Who you are comes from your jeans."

It takes Alfie a minute to realise his dad's saying *genes*. In that minute, he's missed his chance to speak.

"Do you know what I mean? Like, DNA. Chromosomes. Have you done that in science yet?"

"A bit. But, Dad—"

"So you're never going to be a boy. I mean, if I grew my hair long and wore a dress and make-up, I'd still be a bloke. And that's how it is. It doesn't matter what you do with the outside part, you're still you *inside*."

"Yes. I know." He has to make his dad understand this, has to get him to see. "And I'm me on the inside. I'm Alfie, I'm *me*. It's the outside that's wrong."

"See? I knew you'd get it. You don't have to change who you are; you can dress and act and look however you want. But you can't go trying to change what sex you are, see? You're you. You're Alannah."

"No I'm not!" He wants to yell it but his throat's sore and his voice cracks and disappears. "I'm not Alannah. I'm—"

"Is this about girls? Do you like girls? Because that's okay, you know. There's nothing wrong with fancying girls. But a girl who likes girls isn't a boy, she's a lesbian. All right?"

He's spent so much of his life trying to work out who *he* is, how he can fix the wrongness he's always felt inside himself, that he hasn't even considered who he might want to go out with one day. How could he ask someone else to like him when he doesn't like himself?

"It's not that," Alfie manages.

"It doesn't matter if it *is* that. Look at, what's her name, that Ruby Rose girl. You know the one. She's got short hair and dresses butch and she looks amazing. If that's your thing, then bloody go for it, okay? I will absolutely support you and I'll make sure your mum does too. She'll not like it but she'll get used to it. And if you end up bringing a girlfriend home, that's not a problem either."

"Dad, I'm *eleven*, I don't go on dates and stuff yet."

"But you've got to promise me," his dad says, and he's clutching Alfie's hand tightly now, so hard he's crushing the little plastic tube thing they've shoved into one of his veins for some reason, and he can feel the plastic moving against the bone and the sensation makes him feel sick. "No more cutting. You can't do this to yourself. You might have..." His dad's throat moves as he swallows. "I mean, you'll be all right. Scars fade when you're young. But if you do it again, you might do some permanent damage, and then you'd have to live with it for the rest of your life—"

"But that's what I wanted!"

This may be the first time ever he's successfully interrupted his dad.

"I want it to be permanent. I want to get rid of my, my..." he doesn't know the words to use, all he has is a conglomerate of swear words he's afraid to say out loud. "I don't want my body to be like this. I want it to match."

"Match what?"

"Match *me*. I'm a boy and I want a boy's body."

"Well, you're never going to have one!" His dad's rage is

264

sudden and terrifying. "No matter how much anyone hacks away at you, you'll still be a girl, do you understand? One day soon you'll grow breasts and pubic hair, and you'll have periods and maybe have babies and that's how you're going to turn out. Because that's what your body is made to do. There's nothing wrong with it."

"There *is*, I don't *like* it, it doesn't feel *right*—"

"And you'll never pass," his dad continues. "It doesn't matter how much surgery you have, people will tell. People can always tell. They'll know what you are."

Why would that matter? Why would that be so awful? I'm not trying to fool anyone. He wants to say this out loud but his dad is so big, so big and terrifying, and Alfie is so frightened and so sore.

"And you'll not have a partner, either," his dad continues. "If you want a girl she won't want you because she'll want a proper bloke, not someone dressed up as one. And don't think the lesbians will have you either. And gay men won't fancy you because they like cock, okay? Look at any gay website and that's all you'll see, wall-to-wall cock."

It's like his dad's forgotten he's even there. Alfie wills himself not to cry. His dad looks down at him, and forces himself to sit again.

"Look, I don't want to frighten you."

But you are frightening me.

"But I don't want you living your life as a freak. Your body's fine, it works, it does everything you want it to. Why would you want to carve it up, put fake hormones into it, all of that so you'll end up looking like a freak?"

Because then I'll be me. If people think I'm a freak then I'll have to get used to it. But I won't be a freak to myself anymore. If he says this out loud, will he be heard?

"Here comes your mum."

His dad's attention is like a searchlight. Now it's focused on his mum, and Alfie's in the dark again, gathering strength for his next move. His mum looks exhausted and old. *I did that to her*, he thinks, and squirms with guilt. She's not looking at him, she's looking at his dad. Are they going to fight? They never used to fight in front of him, but maybe that's going to change.

"The nurse is bringing Calpol," she says. "That's what they're starting with, but if it keeps hurting you let me know, okay? This is a hospital; they have all the good drugs here." She's petting and fussing at Alfie again, and he sort of likes it but also sort of doesn't, because he's pretty sure she's doing it so she won't have to look at his dad. "Oh, baby girl. You look so small in that bed."

Please don't call me a girl, he thinks wearily.

"Why did you do it?"

"Why do you think she did it?" asks Liam, before Alfie can get a word out.

"I want to hear what Alannah's got to say."

Alannah's not here, she's never been here. There's only me.
Liam looks at him and shakes his head.

"Do you think the way you treat her might have something to do with it?" His dad's doing that thing he always does, the thing where he asks questions as a way of winning arguments. "Do you think it's the way you behave that makes her not want to be a girl?"

"The way I behave? You mean all the shit I take from you, day in and day out—"

"All those dance costumes. All those clothes. Fussing about how pretty she is. The way you dress her up."

"This is my fault for dressing her wrong?" His mother's laughter is terrifying. "You're out of your mind, well, we already knew that, didn't we? Whose watch did she do it on, though? Did she hurt herself when it was me and her? Or did she wait until it was the two of you?"

Unless Alfie changes something, this is how it's always going to be. They're going to argue and argue and argue, round and round in circles about whose fault it is. Why can't they like him the way he is? Is the person he is so dreadful?

"I wish you'd let me talk," he whispers. They're not listening, so he tries again, a little louder. "I wish you'd let me talk."

"Alannah, your mum and I are having a conversation here. Wait a minute, please."

"You're talking about me!" If he shouts too loudly, will the nurses hear? Will he be in trouble? "I want to talk too!"

The look his parents turn on him is identical. For the first time in what feels like a lifetime, they're on the same side again.

"Don't be cross," he says, feeling his fierce resistance already melting away.

They're still looking at him, waiting to hear what he's going to say.

"It's not because of either of you," he says. If he doesn't look at them, it gets easier to speak. "It's the way I am, that's all. How I'm made. I'm made like this. I'm made wrong, and I wanted to fix it."

"But you're not broken," his mum says, very gently. "Your body's perfect."

"Not to me." If he can only make her understand this. If he can only make *one* of them understand this. "I don't feel right."

"Then the problem's inside your head," his dad says.

"No! It's not *me*, I don't want to change *me*. Only the outside."

"And that's why you need to talk to someone!" His dad is white-faced with rage and frustration, trying to keep his voice quiet but not really managing it. "So you can feel better about yourself! For God's sake, what's the matter with you?"

Alfie clenches his fists. "Talking about it won't change anything."

"Now, where do you think she might have heard that one?" his mother asks, and she's doing it again, she's talking to his dad and not to him. Can't they focus on him for a minute?

"What the... What the hell is that supposed to mean?" His

dad's rage is terrifying even though it's not directed at him, even though Alfie can see now the fear that lies behind it.

"You know as well as I do."

"For God's sake, Emma." His dad's hands are fists. "Would you please, for once in your life, just... just bloody well leave well alone?"

"Because that's worked out so *fucking* marvellously for all of us," Emma hisses, and then, incredibly, she's gone, stalking out of the ward with her head held high, not caring that everyone else in the ward who's got the energy to look is looking at her, not caring that the nurses are watching her warily, not caring, not caring, not caring.

"Jesus Christ," his dad whispers. His hand is on Alfie's shoulder, and it hurts but Alfie doesn't dare ask him to move. "Jesus Christ. Is she ever coming back, do you think?"

What on earth is he supposed to say? Not flinching at the pain in his wounds is taking everything he's got.

"I'll tell you what." He's never seen his dad cry, not ever. Is he going to see it now? "Being a man is an absolute crock. Why would you ever want to be like me, mate? Why would you want to be a man when it's so unbearably fucking lonely?"

And then his dad's leaving him too, back straight, head high, gaze forward, and he's alone with all the interested faces of people who have clearly been listening in to every single word, because who can blame them? Will they come back? They have to come back. Even if it's only to be angry again. At least if they're here, there's a chance they'll hear what he's trying so hard

CHAPTER TWENTY-EIGHT

(DECEMBER)

trying so hard to keep going, to keep looping around the same course day after changeless day. Five days a week, all three of us get up together. Alannah and I escape to school, leaving Liam to do whatever it is he does. When I come home, the house is scrubbed clean, things hidden away in places I'll never guess, but that Liam insists are logical. His general attitude is that he can't understand how I ever coped without him here to take care of things, that he's not sure how I'll manage when (when!) he goes back to work.

Once, he tidies my sewing room. This is the only time I let him see me cry.

This is also the day I give up trying to fix Liam, start thinking about how I can fix myself instead.

It starts with an image that I conjure on the nights I can't sleep. The nights I can't sleep means *most nights*, because I know what I'm in for. Liam would tell you he's a very good sleeper – they taught him some special technique and he still uses it to this day – but *good sleeper* depends on what you're measuring. What he's truly good at is falling asleep. *Staying* asleep – as opposed to lying there like a log for anywhere between forty minutes and three hours, then leaping from the bed with a wild shriek – is something he's currently working on. I ought to rest whenever I can, survive on short bursts of oblivion in the same way I did when Alannah was a newborn. But as my exhaustion grows, being dragged from slumber seems worse than lying awake and waiting. So I lie awake, and wait, and let myself imagine:

The bed will be large, king-sized, maybe bigger. The sheets and duvet cover will be crisp, white and heavy. There will be many pillows, at least six, and they will be filled with goose down so soft that putting my head on them will make me feel slightly dizzy. All I have to do is climb in, pull up the covers and finally, finally sleep

sleep, Liam thinks, Emma's obsessed with sleep. Always complaining about how tired she is. She ought to try a couple of weeks out on Dartmoor, yomping through bogs and sleeping in ditches. Then she'd know about tired.

And the mess the house is in, Jesus. Shoes all over the hallway, coats left on chairs and on beds, Emma's sewing everywhere, in various states of completion. He spends his days trying to impose some sort of order, but it feels as if Emma's trying to crowd him out of the house. Cramming it full of her stuff so there's no room for him. He can hardly sit on the sofa for the quilts she's smothered it in, hardly get in the bed for the cushions that have got there first. Some days he thinks his head might burst with it.

But he's going to fight. He won't be squeezed out of his own home by fucking craft projects. If Emma thinks she'll get away with this, she's got another thing coming

coming for her, Alannah can feel it. Part of her longs for it, this change she can feel singing through her blood. They won't let her go up on pointe until her bones harden, and they won't harden until she goes through puberty, and so she'll have to…

But when she imagines her new body – pouches of flesh on her chest, a curve to her waist, hair spreading out in that weird *down there* place she can go for months without thinking about – all she can muster is a cold terror. Who knows what she'll end up with? Who knows what her body will be like once it's all over?

She tries to talk to her mother, desperate for someone to understand. *Mum, I'm scared. My body doesn't feel right. I don't want boobs and hips and all that, it's not right. I think I want…*

Her mother hears her, but she doesn't seem to listen. She's off in a world of her own, worrying about her dad. Alannah doesn't blame her. She's worried about him too

too much money to consider, so I don't let myself consider it. I forget about the total and think instead about small steps.

Each time I think about buying myself a coffee, treating myself to some hand cream or a book for my kindle, I write down the amount in a notebook. Each day, I transfer these small amounts over – no less, no more – to my savings account. I'm meticulous in stealing only from myself. If Liam looked closely at our finances, he'd spot it in an instant, but balancing the books is one more task on my list, so I know I'm safe. For months, the amount in my account is pitiful. I keep going anyway. It's only a dream, something pleasant to think about

think about, behind that beautiful face of hers? Liam used to know his wife but now he doesn't. *I'm worried about you*, she tells him over and over, which drives him insane because he can't stand being treated like an invalid and besides, he's not the one she should worry about. She needs to focus on Alannah, they both do, because what the fuck is happening to their daughter? She's creeping around the house like her own ghost.

He knows this is his responsibility too. He doesn't expect Emma to sort Alannah out on her own. He's an equal partner in this, in everything. He'll do his part in raising their daughter and running the house and while he's not yet found a permanent job, he's found plenty of temporary ones and when he's been given the chance he's worked like a dog and he's asked her for nothing and never let his fear show and, seriously, what more does Emma want from him?

Still, those big shadowy eyes that follow him everywhere. His two girls, watching him like he's the one they're frightened for.

Is Emma blaming him for how tight things are financially? She must know he's doing his best. Every day like clockwork, on all the websites, making phone calls, going to interviews. Picking up scraps of work where he can. And he's still doing his bit. He knows about teamwork; he knows how to pull his weight. The kitchen, sparkling. The bathroom, gleaming. The floors, scrubbed and vacuumed. The shopping (from the cheap supermarket that takes him an hour and a half round trip because it's further away but that's all right, he can take that), done and put away. Still, she looks at him.

And when he asks her what the matter is, what else she *wants* from him (keeping a lid on what he really wants to say, which is *can you for fuck's sweet sake leave me alone, can you please stop walking in the door and instantly undoing all the fucking work I've done today*), she blinks at him like a cow in a field and says, *I'm worried about you. You need to see someone.*

Some days he has to breathe deeply and remind himself not to punch through a wall. If he wasn't so good at holding on to his temper, he could be frightened of the rage that lives inside

"...inside the nutcracker was an enchanted prince, who'd been cursed by a wicked sorcerer. And that's the end of Act One."

Of course, they all know this already. Alannah's seen it performed countless times, in Christmas theatres and on Christmas televisions. She's pored over the dance programmes in her bedroom. Been given copies of the story by distant relatives. A good half of her classmates found their way to the studio solely because when they were small, they sat on a red velvet seat in a darkened amphitheatre and watched the shimmering grace of the Sugar Plum Fairy. Still, they listen. They know what's coming next. The teachers have been trying to keep it a secret but a dance school leaks gossip like a sieve. Alannah sits still and quiet, hands in her lap, back straight, shoulders relaxed, neck long. She needs to look as if she's listening. Just in case she's lucky enough…

Now more than ever, it's important to hold on to her present size and shape. Sudden transformations are only acceptable in stories. She can't afford a growth spurt if she's going to pass as one of Clara's brothers. If she's lucky enough to be one of those chosen…

She doesn't dare think about why she wants to be one of the brothers, and not Clara herself.

"And so," says the teacher, and Alannah brings her attention back to what she's saying. "Those of you who've been working *really hard*

hard to admit, but he's good at the difficult stuff and he'll look this one right in the face without flinching. Emma's starting to slip away from him. She thinks he can't tell but he can, and this knowledge would kill him if he let it, but he's survived everything else the universe has chosen to throw at him and he'll get through this too.

Of course things aren't good right now, he's not an idiot, he knows that, but this is simply how life *is*. Sometimes it's marvellous and sometimes it's shit, and when you get to the shit parts you don't complain, you simply dig in and hold on and keep going.

And yes, he knows he's not exactly the same as he used to be, but then – and this is the part that really riles him – *neither is she*. He used to be a man who went away and did Impressive Man Things and returned as a conquering hero. She used to be a sultry vixen who kept his home warm and welcomed him back. Now he's… well, he's between identities right now, but that's normal, that's something that happens to people, and she's become a nagging shrew of a woman who doesn't appreciate how hard he's working, and who seems to make it her mission in life to undo whatever small achievements he can manage, and guess what? He still loves her. Has never even thought about leaving.

She loved him once, but that was when he was strong and successful. Now he's still strong, and he will be successful again, but her love for him is fading. How can she be so willing to let go of everything they once had?

How fucking dare she? Things are hard now, but they'll get better

will get better. I pray that *I* will get better, as in *become a better person and stop hiding money away from my family for a holiday I don't deserve*. Instead, I get worse. I implement a new policy. Every time Liam blames me for something that's not my fault – picks holes in a task done in a perfectly okay way, argues over something petty and pointless – I pay myself a reward. Five pounds from our household budget, into my secret account. Now I'm making a hole in our finances. I let the credit card soak up the slack, debt mushrooming in the darkness. It's only a short-term thing. It won't be forever. My goal's in sight. (Not that I'm going through with it: I wouldn't do that, it's just a dream. But still, now there are those two weeks before Christmas when Alannah will be in another city, dancing, so I could.)

Then suddenly, dizzyingly, I'm there. I'm there. I'm

actually at my goal. I've saved enough money. I've robbed Peter. Now it's time to pay Paul.

I open the website. Click the buttons. Make the payment. Merry Christmas to me.

God, the shame, the utter, utter shame; but still I do it. I'm tired of holding up the sky. Let's see what happens when I let go. Let's see what happens when I slip away from him. Then he'll have to see

see clearly now there's something wrong with Emma, something wrong inside of her head.

He first notices one evening when he comes home from the pub (a rare night out, he only went on the vague promise of work from an old friend. The promise came to nothing, but he wasn't to know that when he went, was he?). He walks in with a confident tread, ready to tell Emma straight away that the job's no good after all. He won't hide from her. He won't keep secrets.

In the living room, Emma has Alannah on her knee, winding long wet strips of hair around strips of soft pink cotton, tying each into a tiny knot on the top of Alannah's head. Alannah sits patiently, not complaining even though it must hurt to have your hair literally tied in knots like that. Even though the skin of her face is pulled thin and tight with it.

Emma looks blissed-out but also feral, as if grooming their child unlocks a part of her she can't access any other way. She looks as if she can hardly keep herself from licking the top of her daughter's head. For all he knows, she might have actually licked Alannah's head.

"Mum," Alannah murmurs.

"Yes, baby?"

"Is Dad all right?"

"Your dad's fine, baby," Emma murmurs. "You don't have to worry. You only have to concentrate on dancing. That's all that matters."

"Can I tell you something?"

"Of course." Emma's fingers caress Alannah's neck. "Sweet baby. So beautiful."

"No I'm not. I don't like the way I look. My body's not right."

"You don't need to worry about a thing. You're going to be beautiful and you're going to succeed and you're going to have all your dreams come true, do you hear me?"

"But Mum—"

"Listen to me." Emma looks almost drunk. (Could she have been drinking? He didn't think they had anything in the house.) "You're going to be beautiful." She kisses the top of Alannah's head. "You're going to succeed." Another kiss. "And all your dreams will come true."

"How do you know that?"

"Because I'm a witch," Emma says, very calm, very normal. "I can cast spells. And I'm telling you this, all right? You're going to be beautiful, and you're going to succeed, and all your dreams will come true. There now. I said it three times, so it's bound to happen."

What the hell is going on? What has he stumbled upon? Does Emma do this a lot? Is this why Alannah looks so taut, so stretched, so anxious? Because she knows her mother's going mad? He should say something, but he doesn't know how

doesn't know how to pray. Would it even do any good? Would God listen to a prayer that goes, *please don't let anything bad happen before Christmas so I can still dance in* The Nutcracker? Alannah remembers Granny Jane reading to her from the programme all those years ago, that interview with the very first Sugar Plum Fairy she ever fell in love with. She still has it somewhere. *If you're going to be a dancer, you have to be a bit selfish.* And that's what she's being right now: selfish. Hiding in her own little world while her mum and her dad go through some sort of awful crisis.

But what else can she do? She's eleven years old and she's got no power at all. She can only wait and see what happens next. And pray, in her selfish little heart, that whatever's coming won't get here until *after.* It's the very first engagement of her professional life, and it will fix everything, everything that's wrong with her, because her mother's cast a spell and it has to work, it has to. If she can just get onto that stage, and stand there under the lights and hear the applause from the audience. It's the only thing she dares to let herself want

want – no, not what I want, what I *need* – is for Liam to do something big. We've been bickering all day, the way we always bicker – I've left a coffee mug in the sink, I didn't clean my hair from the shower trap – but it's not enough. I need something big enough to provoke my response, so he'll understand that there's a cause and effect at work here. He will do *this awful thing*, whatever it might be, I will go off to a nice hotel for two weeks, and he will...

He will...

I don't let myself think about what he'll do.

How much time left? I've got a train to catch. I've packed my bag. Packed Alannah's bag. Given her the charm I've made, something to keep her safe. I've done everything I can. Now I only need Liam to do his part, to do the thing that sets me free.

The doorbell rings. It's Alannah's friend Lucy, come to collect her so they can walk round to Lucy's house. Liam and I hug Alannah on the doorstep, wish her luck, tell her we can't wait to hear how it goes, can't wait to see for ourselves. They vanish into the dark. My baby girl's going away from me. Will she be safe? How will she manage? No, don't think about that, concentrate on what needs doing.

I'm so used to absorbing and deflecting that I've forgotten how to pick a fight, but I should have known not to fret. When it comes to the crunch, Liam doesn't let me down. As soon as Alannah's out of the door, as soon as we're safely on our own, as if he's been waiting for this too, he turns to me and says, "Now we're alone, do you mind telling me what the actual fuck this is?"

Liam takes a savage satisfaction in the look on Emma's face. Being able to surprise each other is supposed to be good for a marriage. Maybe this is where things finally turn around for them both. They're alone now, the gloves can be off.

They can battle through what's between them, find

find her mother's gift to her. Where is it? She's supposed to have it with her, have it with her all the time. *Hold onto this, and as long as you have it you'll know how beautiful you are.* She'll be spending two weeks surrounded by perfect, professional dancers. *I'm a witch,* her mother said, *and I can cast spells.* She needs her mother's charm to keep her terrors at bay. How is she going to manage without it?

Does she have time to go back for it? How fast can she go? Alannah bites her lip and considers. It took them almost half an hour to walk it, but if she's running

running through my mind is the old terror: *it won't work if anyone disturbs it. It's something you have to keep secret, something you don't tell anyone about. If anyone but me touches it, it will all come apart.* And now Liam holds it in his hands.

"Where did you find that?" I whisper.

It's one of my more elaborate protections. A hank of his hair, trimmed from his head one night in the brief moments when he slept. A twist of thread, taken from the same reel I used to make the raglan t-shirt I welcomed him home with, his first new garment as a civilian. A scrap taken from a letter he once sent me, where the words "get well" have been torn from their original context of *going to get well and truly drunk, but not until I've had a chance to take you to bed* and repurposed. A secret, shameful thing. An intimacy I'm not ready for with anyone, never mind with this angry stranger who I once thought I

thought I must be imagining it. But they were all over the fucking *house*, Emma, they were everywhere." Liam doesn't look at her as he empties his pockets, not wanting to see the hurt and the shame in her face. It can't be easy to be confronted with your own acts of utter lunacy. "Mad little scraps of leaves and bits of paper and fucking, fucking bits of hair and toenails in jars – what the hell's wrong with you? What *is* all this stuff? What the hell were you thinking?"

"How dare you touch them! How fucking dare you touch my stuff!"

She's like a banshee, but that's all right, that's good, that's a good thing. If they don't speak, how will they ever get better? A good row, that's what they need. To raise the roof with all the ugly words they've kept inside them, then to fuck like animals and patch themselves back together.

"You don't know what it's like," she whispers, and for a moment she's not the madwoman he's somehow ended up living with, she's the girl he met all those years ago, that night in the pub when he gave her his heart with gladness. He makes himself drop his own voice to match.

"Look, I know it's been hard for you. Whatever's happening to you, we can sort it out. We'll get you some help. Get you fixed up. Okay?"

"You're going to get me fixed up?"

Her laughter makes her sound mad, but that's all right, people can go mad and then get better again. It's the strain, that's all. The strain of him being out of work and around a lot more than she's used to. She's not as strong as he is and that's okay. She needs his help, this woman he loves. She

279

needs him to protect her. He can feel himself growing taller, his breathing easy and free

free from him at last, from the tyranny of knowing I have to somehow hold him together. With his own hands Liam has taken away the spells I've cast to try and protect him, exposed their secrets and unravelled whatever strength they may have had. It's not my job to look after him anymore.

The depth of his delusion is almost glorious. All the time I've wasted cleaning surfaces that are already clean, all the shoes I've put away even though I'd want them again two minutes later, all the books I've left on shelves, unread, because he gets antsy when he sees gaps in the shelves. All the nights I've held him through the shuddering terror of his dreams. After all of that, he thinks I'm mad. He thinks I'm the one who needs to see a

a *Nutcracker* overture runs through her head to the same rhythm of her feet. She knows exactly where she left it

left it alone, but I've started now so I'm going to finish, tell Liam what I've held inside me for so long. "I know you've got it all worked out in your head, you had to come home to look after me and Alannah because I wasn't coping. But what story do you tell yourself about why they let you go?"

This must be how it feels to kill a man. No wonder Liam found it so hard to leave behind. I wait for him to respond, but he's got nothing. He's just looking at me as if he can barely understand who I am.

"I wish you'd lost a leg," I say to him. "Or even an arm. That would have been easier than all of this."

"There is nothing wrong with me." He clenches his fists, his jaw, then relaxes them again. "I am absolutely fine. It's *you* that needs sorting out. You know it and I know it. All this voodoo nonsense, whatever it is. And the stuff you tell Alannah! I saw you the other night. Fucking hell."

A few months ago I'd have been terrified he might hit me, but now I know he never, ever would. This isn't a grown man in a rage. He's an angry child caught out in a lie, desperate to make his version the true one.

"Right, then," I say, and I feel cold now, cold and smooth and powerful. "If I'm the one who needs help, I'd better

better than this, it's pathetic. She's eleven years old and she ought to remember the important things. But if she's quick enough, maybe she can get into the house and back out again before they even notice she's there. She promised Lucy she wouldn't be long, and she's making good time. She can get in the back way; her mum has a bad habit of leaving

leaving me, Emma, don't you dare. You don't get to walk out of here and leave me—"

"Why not? You left me, over and over and over. Don't worry. I promise I'll come back. But for the next two weeks, I'll be gone, and there'll be absolutely nothing you can do about it."

How's he taking it? I don't let myself look at him for more than a couple of seconds at a time. Instead I concentrate on getting my overnight bag out from the hallway cupboard where I've stashed it away.

"You packed a *bag*?"

"Yep."

"How long have you been planning this?"

He's been

been outmanoeuvred and he knows it. Liam's been beaten by a superior force, or rather, by a better-prepared force who knows exactly how to make the most of their resources.

"A while." Emma's at the front door. It's happening so fast. "See you in two weeks."

"You're not coming back."

"Of course I'm coming back."

"Don't lie to me. I know what's happening here. You coward, Emma, you *coward*, don't you dare walk out on me." God, he's begging, no wonder she's leaving him. How can he get on the front foot? *Attack from a position of strength: look for an advantage and use it.* "You're not getting our daughter; do you hear me?"

"What did you say?"

"You heard." *Stay with me.* "I'm the stay-at-home parent now and that means I'll get Alannah. She's staying with me." *Stay with me. Stay. Stay.*

"You are fucking not getting Alannah."

Yes. That's it. Stop walking. Stand there. Fight back. Fight back and then we can make up and it will all be all right again.

"I'll tell them," he says. "I'll tell them you're mad, I'll tell them what I saw. I saw you tell our daughter you're a *witch*, for God's sake, what kind of woman believes in that shit?"

Her blush is so deep she looks like someone else for a minute. Then the tide ebbs away from her skin and she's looking at him, defiant.

"You know what? You're right. I'm not a witch. I can't fix you. And I'm bloody well done trying. I can't do it anymore, Liam. Maybe you're right and I am mad. Because you've driven me to it."

And then she's gone. She's gone. She's gone. Emma has gone and Alannah has gone and he's on his own and what the hell is he supposed to do now?

He wants to give up but he won't, that's not how he is. The car's in the garage and he has the keys

the keys might be in the back door and it might be locked and if it is she'll have to go to the front because she can't get in with the spare key from the shed and they'll know she forgot something and her dad will be angry and she might even have to tell him what she forgot and she doesn't know if he knows what her mum can do

is that her mum on the bus yes it's her mum on the bus right at the front looking out of the front window what if she sees her no she hasn't seen her she looks so strange like she's not really there what's happened how is her mum not seeing her is she ill what's going on never mind get back to the house

and if the keys aren't in the back door then she *can* get in without them knowing and she's only a few streets away now only another five minutes or so and she'll be there and she'll get the spell her mum made for her and get back to Lucy's house and it's going to be okay

going to be okay, of course he is. The walk to the bus stop took all the adrenaline out of my system and now I'm safe on the top deck and it's empty apart from me and I'm calm. We're not moving yet because it's here early and it won't leave until it's time but that doesn't matter, I'm doing my plan and I'm safe. Liam's a grown man and he's going to be fine. Why was I so worried about this? We're taking some time apart, that's all. That's a healthy thing to do, a good thing to do. Especially for a couple who've been living in such claustrophobic proximity.

The spells aren't important anymore. He doesn't need my protection. He's home from the Army and he's not in a war zone and there are no more people trying to kill him and he's going to be fine. He doesn't even have Alannah to worry about, not like me all the times he was the one leaving and I was the one left behind. He can be as selfish as he likes, he can be

be careful. He doesn't want to spook Emma into getting off the bus early. But he is going to follow it, watch each stop,

283

find out where she's going. A plan, that's what he needs, and now that's what he has. A mediocre man with a plan beats a brilliant man with no plan ninety-nine times out of a hundred. Does that mean he's mediocre? It doesn't matter. He knows what to do. He'll follow his wife from a discreet distance as she gets on the bus, find out where it is that she thinks she's going without him.

So that's the plan. He's going to follow the bus. And to follow the bus he needs the car. He needs the car so he has to take the keys and go into the garage. Go into the garage and climb into the driver's seat. Climb into the driver's seat and turn on the engine. Turn on the engine and register vaguely that something's a little different

different somehow, a strange smell that's also familiar. Alannah almost ignores it, because a strange smell in the house isn't something she's supposed to be worried about. She's come to get her gift and nothing else matters. *If you're going to be a dancer, you have to be a bit selfish.* She creeps upstairs.

There it is on her bedside table. She's had it there every night, clutched it between her fingers, whispering *please, please let me see what Mum sees, let me be the girl Mum wants me to be, stop me feeling like I don't belong in my body.* She grabs the gauzy bag with its collection of things inside. *Don't open it,* her mother cautioned her, *you mustn't look inside.* Breathes a sigh of relief that she's somehow, *somehow* not been caught.

Goes back down the stairs. The smell's stronger now, demanding her attention. Is something on fire in the kitchen? What will happen if her dad's in there and sees her?

She listens at the door. Not a sound, which is weird because her dad isn't in the living room either and he's nowhere upstairs. Maybe her dad was on the bus too? Maybe they've gone out together? That would be nice. Maybe they've gone for a drink, maybe they're going to be all right from now on. She almost doesn't open the kitchen door. She almost turns away.

There's a lot of weird stuff on the table, stuff she's seen her mum playing with sometimes. One of the many things she's never dared ask about (*I've said it three times so it's bound to come true*, her mother murmurs in her ear). There's no fire. What there is, is something creeping around the doorway that leads to the garage, and that smell, she recognises it now, it's the smell of

smell of diesel fumes could be the scent of salvation? I'm making my escape. It's happening. I don't need to worry about anything. I only need to think about myself.

Liam will be fine. I'm the mad one, he told me so himself. I'm the mad one and that means I'm allowed to be selfish (just as he's been selfish) and focus on myself (just as he's been focusing on himself) and I can sit here on this bus that's finally moving and lean my head against the window and not flinch as it takes me back along the road I walked up, past our house that looks different somehow. Something to do with the garage. Something hazy about it, something creeping out from around the edges of the door. There's a tug of worry there but I dismiss it. The top of the bus feels so peaceful

so peaceful, sitting in the driver's seat of the car. It's quite weird really, Liam thinks, that anything could feel this relaxing. He's been a bit tired lately. Not quite thinking straight. What's he doing in the car again? There was something he was going to do…

And then there's someone screaming, not Emma, but Alannah, and what the hell is she doing here? She's supposed to be at her friend's house, what's her name, Lucy Something-or-other. Instead she's here in the garage, scrabbling at the car key, coughing and coughing, and he suddenly realises what this looks like

looks like her dad might already be dead, but then he's moving, he's coming with her, half-falling out of the car, but she's a dancer and she's strong and she drags him out somehow, and the engine's off but she can't stop coughing and he's so heavy, so *heavy*, but that doesn't matter, this is her dad and she's going to get him out of this. She can hear herself yelling, can hear her dad yelling back, both of them clutching at each other as he bellows into her face, "Alannah, for fuck's sake, what are you

you have to believe me. I saw our garage, I saw the fumes, but I didn't realise – I *didn't understand what I was looking at*, what it might mean. What Liam might have...

I really didn't know. Didn't even suspect. I swear. If I'd known what it meant I would never have stayed on the bus. I'd have got off it and ran back down the road and gone to drag him out of that car, I would

would have been fine." Liam can hardly finish a sentence. "I'm all right, Alannah. Okay? I'm fine. I just. Put the engine on. Wasn't thinking. Was about to. Open the door. The garage door. I'm fine. Don't worry about me."

"You were in the car." Alannah's face is grey and sick. "You were in the car. The garage door was shut."

"I would have been fine. All right? I was only. Feeling a bit. Wasn't thinking. Me and your mum. Had a row, that's all. I was going after her." It's vital Alannah believes him. He can't have his daughter thinking both her parents are off their nuts.

Besides, he's not lying. He wasn't trying to... do that.

That's the act of a coward, and he's never been a coward. It was truly an accident. Probably a good thing Alannah came back, though.

That's his way out, of course. The best defence is a good offence.

"What are you doing back here, anyway? You're supposed to be at Lucy's."

She's not really looking at him. She's looking at the litter of rubbish all over the table, then down at her own hand. Slowly, she unfolds her fingers to reveal a little bag full of something, tied with white ribbon.

"Were those for you?" She's whispering, as if she's talking about something secret and shameful. And, Liam thinks weakly, she's not fucking wrong.

"Yep."

"She does it to you too?"

"Yep."

"She made me this one." Alannah is picking at the ribbon, unravelling Emma's work. Spilling out the contents. A scrap of hair, a few words scribbled on paper, a tiny figure made from twigs and wrapped in a scrap of gauze and a length of ribbon. Such a small thing. "She wants me to be perfect."

She only likes things when they're perfect. Liam bites his lip against the words. *She wants me to be perfect too.*

"It doesn't work. I don't like being me." Alannah's face is almost ugly with its intensity. "I don't want to be me."

He's a man. How is he supposed to know what to say?

"You don't have to be what your mum wants," Liam tries. "You can be whatever *you* want, okay? Whatever that turns out to be. You don't have to be pretty and girly and so on."

Alannah's eyes are brimming with tears. He ought to put his arms around her, let her sob. But then Alannah turns away, straightens her shoulders, shoves something deep back down inside herself. Her body language is a neon sign: *I don't want to talk about this. Leave it alone.* He knows how she feels because that's how he feels too.

And now, look at them both here. All ready for an adventure. Emma thought she'd been so clever, their daughter safely out of the way, but the universe has another plan.

"Tell you what," he says to Alannah's quivering face, "do you feel like an adventure? By ourselves, just

CHAPTER TWENTY-NINE

(CHRISTMAS EVE, NOW)

just Liam by himself, out here in the sunshine, wrung out dry and light. His dad's left; his mum's talking to Emma; his child's asleep. There's nothing he needs to be doing. Or rather, there's a million things he needs to be doing, but none of them need doing right now.

The hospital steps are deceptively comfortable. There are five altogether, more than necessary for the degree of the slope but then, it's a hospital. There's a wide concrete ramp to one side. (Why didn't they get rid of the steps and make the ramp wider?) The ramp's narrower than the steps, would probably fit into them somewhere between two and two and a half times…

No, he thinks. *You're trying to stop yourself thinking, but you can't do that now. Time to stop deflecting. You won't get better if you don't admit there's a problem.*

Why would Alannah want to be a boy, anyway? Masculinity is an absolute fucking shower. He's sick of hearing how privileged men are. Yes, you might get paid a bit more for doing the same work and they listen to you down at the garage. But how's that compensation for the downsides? Like not being able to admit to weakness, ever. Like not being allowed to talk about your feelings, whole swathes of emotions locked away completely, stuff you're not even supposed to *experience*. Or not being allowed to confess that, even though what you did was completely within the rules – even though what you did probably saved the lives of dozens of your mates – *even though it was your duty*, you still don't know how to live with it. Not knowing how you'll cope with having a son rather than a daughter. Not daring to admit you need help with any of this…

He hears the slow shuffle and squeak of someone approaching, presumably with a walking aid. It's an old man, or rather a man who looks old but could be anywhere from late fifties to early nineties, totally bald, bone-skinny but with a surprisingly healthy glow, in too-big pyjamas and a thick burgundy dressing gown. The squeak is from the tall frame that holds his drip bag, its clear plastic tube like an extra vein. Should he help? Does the man want his help? And where's he going, anyway? Is he going to bump that IV stand down the steps? The man stops.

"Mind if I join you?"

"Sure."

With infinite care, the man lowers himself down. He is so thin his bones must ache against the concrete.

"Wanted to see some sunshine," he explains to Liam, who nods cautiously. "Gets boring in there." He takes cigarettes and a lighter from his pocket. "Plus they won't let you do *this* on the ward."

Liam watches the man fumble a cigarette from the packet. The inside of his arm is stained with old bruises.

"Miserable sods," Liam offers, and the man laughs.

"Aren't they, though? Like it'll make a difference now. Want one?"

"No thanks, I don't."

The man hesitates, his lighter halfway to his mouth. "Mind if I do?"

"Go for it."

"Cheers." The man lights up, takes a luxurious breath in,

holds it. Lets it go again. The smoke is blue and frail in the slight breeze.

"It's not lung cancer, by the way," the man says suddenly.

"No?"

"Prostate. Bad one. Some of them you can live with for years. Some of them get out of hand." He takes another deep drag, holds it. Closes his eyes in pleasure. "Nothing to do with smoking."

Liam isn't sure this is right, but he's not about to argue with a dying stranger.

"Why not," he says. For a minute he almost wishes he smoked too, so he could join the rebellion.

"Should have seen the doctor earlier," the man says. "My wife, Sarah, she told me and told me. Always listen to your wife when she tells you to see the doctor. Women always know. No wonder they all bloody outlive us."

"You're not wrong," says Liam.

"You married?"

"Yep."

"Best thing you can do, I reckon. She nag you about going to the doctors?"

"Yes."

"Mind me asking—?"

"I'm here with my kid."

"Oh. Sorry. That's rotten luck."

"We'll be okay. Bit of an accident with…" He swallows once, steadies his voice. "…with some scissors."

"Goes right through you when it's them, doesn't it," the man says sympathetically. "I've got two. Some months it felt like we lived at A&E." He stubs out his cigarette. "They're grown up now but you never stop worrying. In your head they're always that little wriggler you saw come out in the delivery room, aren't they?"

"Yep."

"You just got the one?"

"So far."

"One's good, we're not running out of humans any time soon. Boy or girl?"

He hesitates. Goes for it.

"Boy. Alfie."

"That's a good name. Good to have a son. We're not supposed to say that, are we."

"Probably not," says Liam. Dizzy with the weight of his own words.

The man's struggling to his feet, a delicate manoeuvre because of the IV line. Liam gets to his feet and hovers, helping as much as he dares. For a moment, their hands are linked and he feels the other man's pulse beneath his fingers, the surprising strength in his grip as he clings to Liam's palms. Maybe he could talk to this man. Maybe they could talk to each other. Maybe them both coming out here is a sign. Maybe it really could be this simple. Spill his guts to a man who's dying and will take every word to the grave and then he'll be fixed and he'll be able to fix Alannah too and everything will go back to normal.

Then the man lets go, takes hold of the wobbly stalk of his IV stand, and the moment's passed.

"Nice chatting to you," he says. "Good luck with everything. Hope you get out soon."

"You too," Liam says.

The man's face works as if there are worms crawling under his skin. "You know, that's all I want now. To die at home. Sarah's promised to look after me. Hope I can get it over with quick before she gets too tired. You know?" The man's cheeks are wet and he swipes fiercely at them with his sleeve. "Don't know where I'd be without her. We've had our arguments and there's been days when we wanted to kill each other, but she's a bloody angel, putting up with me all these years." He takes a deep breath. "Right. See you again maybe."

And then he's walking away from Liam, his movements slow and careful, the squeak of the IV stand following in his wake. Liam's chest is about to crack.

He's never believed in a higher power, but he's always believed in his wife. He and Emma are connected. If he sits here long enough, wills it hard enough, she'll hear him.

Emma, he thinks. *Help me. I need you. You were right and I was wrong. I need you and I love you and I can't do this on my own.*

She doesn't come to him straight away, but he's patient and willing to wait, and the hospital steps in the sunshine are a nice place to be. Refusing to check his watch, letting go of the count in his head, he marks the passage of time by the infinitely slow curving of the sunbeams as they cross the patch of scraggly grass and stubborn trees, screening off the busy road beyond. When he finally hears her, he has to make himself carry on sitting still and not leap up and grab on, burying himself against her while her arms wrap around him like a life jacket.

"I've been looking for you everywhere," she says. He can't tell if this is a reproach or only an observation.

"I've been here a while."

"Al – she…" Emma frowns. "I mean, Alfie's asleep."

The name sounds strange on her tongue. He wonders if the man he spoke to earlier noticed anything odd in the way Liam pronounced it.

"I don't get it," Emma says. "I mean, how can she be a boy? If she'd got, I don't know, some sort of chromosome condition or something, or if she was, whatsit, not hermaphrodite, there's another word…" She clicks her fingers. "Intersexed, that's it. If she was that, then I could understand. But she's completely normal. So how can she be a boy?"

"I don't know."

"Maybe she's not. Maybe it's just a phase."

"Could be." He's saying the words, but he doesn't believe them. What Alannah… Alfie… did in that bathroom seemed pretty conclusive to him. Liam's used to enduring discomfort and even pain, been taught to ignore it so he can do his job (*pain with a purpose*, which is what those annoying lentil-weaving childbirth people called the pain of labour, but he likes the phrase so he's stealing it). But he can't imagine the strength of will required for an eleven-year-old child to lift those scissors and – and then, while the pain of those first cuts still sang in their ears – no, he still can't bear to think about it.

"Maybe she's a lesbian."

"Maybe." *Or maybe he's a boy, living in a girl's body.* How could that even happen? How was it possible? Was this something he'd ever understand?

"You were right, you know." Emma is looking straight at him now, not letting herself flinch away from his gaze. "I was so happy when she was born and she was a girl. I did want a daughter. Not because of the clothes, but, well, because, because you do, don't you? You want one that's the same as you. Like you wanted a son."

"I didn't mind either way."

"But if you got them from the supermarket, and if I'd sent you down there without me and told you to pick out the one you wanted, you'd have gone to the boys aisle. Wouldn't you?"

"What does it matter? We don't get to pick them out, we get what we're given."

He wants to touch her. Wonders if he dares risk it. Reaches out and presses her fingers with his. Feels his heart skip a beat when she doesn't take her hand away.

"What do we do about school?" Emma is frowning. "If she – if *they* want to go in and – and present as a boy, what will the kids make of it?"

"Don't you get training about all that?"

"*We* get training. Not the kids. No one's ever done it at our school."

"But isn't there that kid in your class? Little boy who wears skirts? And he came as Elsa on World Book Day?"

"He's still a boy. He just likes skirts. And he's always done it, no one's ever known him any other way. This is different."

"We can't not do this because we're worried about what other kids think."

"Oh God." Emma's face is blurry with sadness. "It's going to be so hard, isn't it? All those people who'll judge. Even the nice ones, not just the meatheads. They'll ask so many questions, and it won't make any difference what the answers are, they'll already have made their minds up."

"It'll be worse for Alannah."

"I *meant* for Alannah. She – he, I mean – he's going to have a lifetime of people asking him about his body and how it feels and whether he regrets it. He – no, I'll never get used to it. She's our daughter, she's our *daughter.* How can she be our son?"

"I don't get it either," he says.

"And what if she changes her mind? What if we agree to treatment and she takes hormones and has surgery and whatever and then she realises it's all a mistake and she wants to go back?"

He wants to tell her the answers, but he can't because he doesn't know himself what the answers might be. Maybe there aren't any answers. Maybe he simply has to learn to live with it. Maybe this is his life's work from now on. Learning to live with things he can't understand.

And besides, how much of this is up to them? If they ignore what their child's saying, shout louder and use their adult privilege to refuse any treatment, what changes might be made in other locked rooms, with other cutting edges? Could anything the doctors might do be worse than those scissors?

"I don't know what we're supposed to do," Emma mutters.

Suddenly, Liam doesn't want to talk about Alfie. He knows this is selfish but he can't help himself, he's waited so long to do this and surely it must be his turn, now? Surely with Alfie asleep they can concentrate on him for a minute? "Emma, can I say something to you?"

She looks at him warily. "Go on then."

Her eyes are so wise and lovely. His wife is so wise and lovely. She's all he needs. What was it that man said about his wife? *A bloody angel.* And she is, she is. She's an angel. Once he's well again, he'll spend the rest of his life making everything up to her.

"I'm going to get treatment," he says.

"Okay."

"No, really, I mean it. I'll go back to therapy and I'll do it. Properly. I won't walk away this time. I understand now, that I'm... that I need help. I didn't want to admit it." He wants to stop but he won't. He won't shy away from this because it's hard. This is what being a man means. Doing the hard things, the things you don't want to do, to protect the ones you love. "I mean, I hate not being strong enough, you know? But it's not a sign of weakness to ask for help, is it?"

"Is that what you're asking me for? Help?"

"No!" He's shouting, he can hear it now. Shouting, and not being honest. Emma was right, she was always right. Christ, this is tough. So many bad habits to unlearn. "I mean, yes. *Yes.* I'm asking for help. I *need* help, I get it, I do. I was trying to fix myself on my own and I get now how awful it must have been for you. But I understand now. I'll do everything you wanted. I promise."

"That's good." He can't read her expression. He can feel the anger rising in him, the way it always does when she doesn't do what he wants...

No. No. He's not going to be angry. He'll feel the emotion he's trying to bury with his anger. He'll face what's really happening inside his head. What is it that he feels? Fear, that's it. Fear this isn't going to work.

"So, what do you think?"

"I think that's really good. I'm so glad."

"I don't mean about me." Don't get angry. Don't get angry. The anger's simply a habit. Habits can be broken. Feel what you're really feeling. Fear. Fear. He's terrified. "I mean about us. I understand why you left me."

"God, I wish I did. I'm sorry, Liam, I shouldn't have—"

"No, you don't need to be sorry, *I* need to be sorry. I was a shit husband. You're an angel for putting up with it."

"I'm not an angel."

"Yes, you are. I was talking to some bloke this morning—"

"You had a conversation? With a stranger?" He loves her smile. Her smile must be a good sign.

"Right? He looked about ready to die, to be honest. Wasn't sure he'd make it back to the ward. But it was… well, it was good. I don't know. He helped me get things sorted. In my head."

"I'm so glad." Her eyes are wet. "Liam, I do love you."

"I love you too." He reaches out for her, for the familiarity of her skin. It's the feeling of coming back from deployment. As if he won't properly drop back into his body until he's held her against his chest and inhaled the scent of her shampoo. The magic trick that's brought him home so many times before. It didn't work that last time, and he's been waiting ever since then, holding his breath, trapped in the place that broke him. But all he needs now is to put his arms around her and—

"But I can't do this," Emma continues.

"Can't do what? You don't have to do anything. Only hold on while I—"

"I can't. Not anymore."

"You don't have to do *anything*, except wait for me. That's all. Be strong a little bit longer and wait for me. That's all I want."

"Liam. Please. Stop talking over me and listen."

"And then we'll be happy again, okay? It'll be better than before because I'll be here every night. I'll find a job; we'll have enough money. We'll buy a new house. It'll be great."

"Shut up!" Emma leaps to her feet, presses her hands over her ears, shuts her eyes. "Shut up, shut up, shut up."

Making himself stop talking is almost beyond him, because

he's terrified of what Emma might say. On an ordinary day, he'd say that shutting up and letting her speak is the hardest thing he's ever done. But today has been nothing but a succession of unbearably hard things. He forces the bubbling of words back down inside. Waits for Emma to sit down. Waits. Is this the last moment of his life when he'll be truly happy? Perhaps.

"Liam, I can't—"

"Don't say that."

"Don't talk over me, don't you dare. If you say one more word I'll walk away from you right now and never come back, do you hear me?"

He knows now that it's possible she might actually do this, but it's not fear keeping him quiet. It's because he knows that if he fails at this task, there will be no more tasks for him ever, and he doesn't know how he'll bear it.

"Since you came home," she says. "It's been like... like I've been the only one who's all right. The one who had to keep everyone else together. I didn't dare not be okay, I couldn't risk thinking about myself or what I wanted. Do you know what I mean?"

Is he allowed to speak? Will it be worse to keep his mouth shut, or to say something? Normally he'd be angry about being boxed into a corner like this, but today he can't afford the luxury of anger. He risks a nod, hopes this will be enough.

"Every time I went out I was afraid I'd come home again and find you dead. Every single day I'd walk out of the front door and think, *what if I come home this evening and he's bled out in the bathtub? Or he's hanged himself in the garage? Or he's taken a load of pills and gone to bed?* And then I'd think, *how will I tell Alannah I let her dad die?*"

Her eyes are wet. He wants to put his arms around her and crush her face against his shoulder, let all the words inside her melt against his flesh.

"No, let me talk, let me *talk*, this is important. I had to leave you; do you see? Because I couldn't fix you. I'd tried

298

everything I knew and I couldn't do it. And while I was thinking about you, I was ignoring what Alannah – what was happening – what she was trying to tell me."

He listens without flinching. He's been trained to absorb pain and move past it, keep moving forwards towards his goal. *Pain is weakness leaving the body.* But Emma is far from weak. She's the strongest person he knows.

"Secondary school," Emma says next. He can't follow the train of her thoughts. "Secondary school, next September. Who knows what that's going to be like? And there'll be hospital appointments and psychiatric appointments, and she – *he*, damn it – he'll get bullied, and he'll fall in love and they won't want him back, and there'll be people calling him the wrong name and people telling him he's a freak. And they'll judge me, too, I know they will. Whatever decisions I make, whatever treatments, there'll be someone telling me I'm doing it wrong."

He wants to tell her it'll be all right, that she doesn't have to do it by herself because they'll be in this one together, but if he says one word to her she'll walk away and never come back.

"And the thing is, I can do all that." He believes her. She looks like a Valkyrie, all flashing eyes and powerful chin. "I know I can. And I could do it for you, too. It'll be the same for both of you, won't it? There'll be appointments and treatments and nights when you come home in bits and setbacks and breakthroughs, and all that stuff... I know I can do it. But I can't do it for both of you." She's on the verge of tears, but she's holding them back. "Liam, are you listening to me? I can't keep both of you alive. Not anymore. I've got to choose. And I choose our child."

His chest is collapsing, he's a hollow shell and the sides are caving in. If he lets her see that, will it change anything? If he'd let her see all of this before, would they be in a different place now? But it doesn't matter; he's made his choices and mistakes, and now he has to live with them. He keeps his face turned towards hers. Gives her a brisk nod of acknowledgement.

"You're so brave," Emma whispers, and touches his face gently. "You look like a little boy. A soldier boy. I wish I could look after both of you, but I can't. You'll have to manage on your own now."

"But you'll let me see Alfie." He's not afraid she'll walk away; she's already done that. All he can do now is cope with what's left behind. Hold on to what he can still keep hold of. Find a reason to keep going.

"Yes, of course. I'd never stop you seeing her."

"Him." He's not correcting her, more trying it out to see how it sounds. It feels strange in his mouth, but in time it will become familiar.

"Our child." Emma kisses him, softly, on the mouth. "I'm going back to the ward. I'll see you up there, okay?"

Liam chooses not to watch her go. It's hard enough to hear the click of her shoes as she walks away from him.

Now he's alone again, and this time it's final. No, not alone, not ever alone. He has a son. Not a daughter, but a son. He's got a new job to do. He has to show his boy how to be a good man.

What kind of man will Alfie be? A better one than him, hopefully. Kinder. More tender. Able to get in touch with his feelings. Able to actually *have* feelings, other than his own default setting of *rage* and his own occasional relief of *lust*. Some combination of masculine and feminine, the perfect blend of his (few) good traits with Emma's (much more abundant) ones. A good person. A happy person. Someone who lives a worthwhile life. That's all any parent can hope for.

His legs have almost gone to sleep with sitting on hard concrete, but he's a soldier and he's used to coping with physical discomfort. He'll get past it, and he'll find his way into the future.

He straightens his shoulders, and marches back towards the building where his child is waiting

CHAPTER THIRTY

(2018)

waiting for the time to pass. Filling the time with weights and measures, small observations. The ground's twenty feet below him: further from the heat radiating upwards. He's wearing his vest: more weight and insulation. He's under a tarp: shade makes a bit of difference, not much but a bit. He's surrounded by sandbags, which give shade when the Sun's in the right direction but also absorb and radiate heat, so that one goes both ways. Something trickles down his forehead. Could be sweat. Could be water from the wet paper towels he's packed his helmet with. Liam stands in the heat and stares through sunglasses at the dusty road, and parses degrees of discomfort.

They're supposed to wear body armour at all times, but plenty of lads simply refuse, preferring to take their chances with a stray bullet. Forget the locals, the biggest enemy's the temperature. He considers this thought, then amends it. *Usually* the biggest enemy's the temperature. *Right now*, it's the gut-rot blazing through the camp like, like… like an attack of gut-rot blazing through the camp. Utterly resistant to Loperamide. The brass dosed everyone up, sent them up to sentry duty anyway. A couple of hours in, it was disgustingly clear that wouldn't work. So, for now, protocol's been adapted. As one of the seemingly immune, he's up here on his own.

A crust of salt's forming in the seams of his uniform. Scrapes against his skin when he moves. He hasn't pissed for hours, doesn't feel any need to. Has to do some serious rehydration when he goes back down. Rehydration, and electrolytes, if there's any left thanks to the gut-rot. Could murder a bag of crisps. They all crave salt constantly. When he's trying to sleep, he doesn't fantasise about lying next to Emma. Instead he walks into McDonald's, watches the server fill the largest container in the place with thin golden fries. Falls asleep with his mouth watering, the scent of hot oil coiling around his dreams.

Sentry duty's boring. Even more boring on your own. Doesn't matter. He's an expert at boredom, smashing through the levels like a champ. Since being here he's managed to experience just three emotions; hot, bored and terrified. (Is *hot* an emotion? Or is it more of a physical state? These are the thoughts you have time for up here, thoughts you have to chase off as they lead you away from reality and into the depths of your head, because if you let yourself stop to actually *experience* the way you're feeling, you'd go mad.)

How long's he been out here? Clock in his head says thirty-eight minutes. Checks the watch on his wrist. Yep: thirty-eight. Good to know his superpower's still intact. It's not much of a skill but it's his skill, and he'd hate to think of it shrivelling away under the Sun… No, don't think about the heat, you'll go mad. Remind yourself of the measures you've taken to cool yourself down. Paper towels in your helmet. Patch of shade from the tarp. Up high to catch the non-existent breeze. Small scraps of improvement. Christ, how do human beings survive here? Are the locals even the same species? If they came to Britain, would they feel like they'd moved to the Arctic?

He shifts position. His feet are dank and swampy inside his boots. His feet will be white and shrivelly later. There's a

302

competition: who can produce the grossest feet. It's unclear what the winner gets when they finally ship home. Alcohol, probably. Keg of beer. Crate of whiskey. Shot of everything off the back of the bar in a pint glass. One minute to chug it. Personally, he'd prefer fries from McDonald's.

The base is dry apart from the odd mouthful of contraband, but he doesn't miss it. You soon lose the taste for alcohol. There's always opium, but unsurprisingly that's an instant no-tolerance ball-bust. Besides, the dead-eyed scrawny teenagers slumped on street corners, fingers twitching and eyes rolling back, put off all but the most determined. He's clean and serene, outside and in. When he gets back, he'll be off his face sniffing the bar towel. How long's it take to rebuild your drinking boots?

He forces himself to stop this line of thought. It's too close to thinking about home, and he has a superstitious belief that if he lets himself think about his wife and child out here, he'll attract the attention of the universe, draw bad luck his way. A pothole in the road he won't look at closely enough. A quick moving shadow, ready for a death-dash towards the gates. He might be missing something right now, off in his head rather than here in his body, doing his job. Focus. Do the job. It's why you're here. He scans the road again. Nothing to see. Not a bird. Not a rat. Not a snake. Nothing.

On the way out, they'd been told to treat all snakes as venomous and leave them strictly alone and not try to touch them or even approach them. He'd wondered why that even needed saying, because when you're in an actual fucking war zone with a job to do, who the fuck goes around poking strange snakes with sticks? Now he's here, the utter boredom of the place (*hot, bored, terrified*, the three things he's felt since he's come here) makes poking a snake with a stick seem quite entertaining.

The last shot of *terror* was weeks ago. That time in the convoy. Lead vehicle went over a bump-in-the-road-that-wasn't. Burst upwards like a tossed ball. Frantic minutes of terror and teamwork, each second like crossing a desert in the dark. Strange noises and screams. Did he feel something else later on? Grief? Relief? Elation? He sorts through his memories. Finds no trace. His brain's a smooth simple blank. Everything tidied away for later. *Later*, meaning a time when there's less risk of breakages.

So, yeah. Here he is. Standing in the sun. All on his own because half the camp are shitting their guts out for the next thirty-six hours. Watching the road for signs of life he can hardly believe exists. Counting down the moments on the clock until he can go back into the shade and rehydrate. Hot. Bored. Dreaming of a bit of terror to liven things up. If there was a snake up here on the platform he'd be right on it. Jabbering that slithery bastard with the tip of his gun. Just to make something happen. For a moment, he actually sees a snake, coiled against the sandbags, head raised in challenge.

Then he blinks, and it's gone again. They all see stuff from time to time. Figures in corners. Animals slinking around buildings. Slicks of oil on the floor. Could be the boredom, could be the heat. No one's sleeping well. The temperature drops at night, but not enough. They lie under sticky sheets and sweat into their pillows. Wait for the hours to pass until it's time to get up again. Maybe that's what causes the hallucinations. Can he add *tired* to his list of feelings? Not really, since he doesn't feel it. It's just something he knows he ought to be.

Something creeps down his forehead, skirts his nose. Could be sweat. Could be a fly. He takes a chance, puts out his tongue. Tastes salt. Too hot even for flies. If he wasn't too hot to think, he might manage something like, *this is a waste of time, no one's going to mount an attack on the base in these conditions.*

Good thing it's so hot, then. Fuck that shit. He's not here to think, he's here to do. Sentry duty's boring, but it's still a duty. This is a war zone, a killing zone. Never mind that it looks like someone already did all the killing, left everything empty.

It's his job to manage his boredom. Be ready for when God flicks the switch and the world flips from *boredom* to *terror*. It'll happen eventually because this is the one constant. The one thing they all have drilled into them. *When*, not *if*. At least he's out here doing something. Not lying in bed, listening to the grumble of his guts. Waiting for the next cramp. Leaping for the latrine.

Still. He'd love a snake to poke at…

Back at home, preferring work to being in bed would seem insane. Back at home, snuggling under the nice warm duvet with his nice warm wife was the best feeling in the world. He shouldn't be thinking about this but he can't stop it, he'll indulge for a moment. Getting into bed with Emma, turning towards her, finding she's reaching out for him too, her hands eager, her face soft and unfocused…

He can't make himself *be there*. He can only imagine watching. A pudgier, paler version of him climbs into the bed. A woman with Emma's hair and Emma's build takes off her t-shirt, bares her breasts. The man reaches for her, grabs a handful of hair. Pulls hard. He's watched too much porn. He's starting to forget that sex is something you do with a woman, rather than something you see on a screen.

The clip they cheered over last night. Pretty red-haired girl with silicone tits, double-teamed by two black guys. Trying to act like she loved it (couldn't quite hide her grimace when the second guy rammed inside). Twitch of interest at the memory. Maybe add *horny* to the list of things he feels. Not sure that counts as an emotion, though. Simply another primitive need experienced by this chunk of Army wetware. Like *hungry, thirsty, need a piss, need to do some exercise*. Having a wank's just another maintenance job.

Fair enough. Out here you can't afford to be complex and emotional and live a full life. That's for leave. That's why when they get back home, civilians find them all a bit nuts. Too full-on. Too eager to cram every moment. They don't understand what it's like. Having to leave your home-self behind, become the *other* person. The true version of you hanging up in your locker. Waiting for you to ship home again.

So much baggage you can't afford to bring along. The love you feel for your wife. The love you feel for your child. Being afraid something'll happen to them. Being afraid of what they'll do if something happens to you. Realising you're killing other humans, same species, totally compatible. They could walk into your life and operate there, like you could walk into theirs. You have to leave all of that behind. Become a simple cog in a complex machine.

A cog's okay. Cogs are useful and being useful matters. That's why he's standing here with the heat and the boredom and the imaginary snake. The job needs doing and not everyone can do it. But he can. So he will. He's not here to enjoy it. Only to get it done. No need to think. That's the other guy's job. The guy he'll go back to being when the tour's up. He'll check his work persona into storage and retrieve his true self, climb into their shared skin and go home to Emma and Alannah. He'll sleep deeply, wake reluctantly. Scrub himself clean in hot water, then stay in ten more minutes because it feels good. He'll stop watching porn and get lost in the beautiful haven of his wife's body, her hair tumbling about her face as she climbs on top of him and takes what she wants. But first, first, first, before he does any of that, he – both of him, the one he is here and the one he is there – the two guys who share this body and meet only in the moments of handover, will go to McDonald's and buy two, no, *three* giant boxes of fries, shower them in salt until they look like they've been snowed on, and then eat and eat and eat until his stomach hurts.

Now he's done it. He's not a cog. He can feel again. All the things his brain has packed away (stored on high shelves where they won't get broken, because war zones are filled with giant angry man-babies with guns, who flail around the place trashing everything they come into contact with, every emotion gigantic, every moment exploited for maximum destructive potential) spill out into him, filling him up. He remembers Emma's face and thinks he might dissolve with longing to kiss her lovely mouth. He thinks of Alannah, the way she looks when she's clean and warm and wrapped up in the cute little flannelette pyjamas Emma sewed for her, palest pink with a delicate print of rabbits dressed in ballerina skirts.

He remembers being on the sofa, Emma beside him and Alannah on top of him, their warmth and weight making him feel welcome and loved. The kaleidoscope fracturing of all the things he wanted. The father who wants his daughter on his knee. The husband who wants to be alone with his wife. The tired man who only wants his own bed. He remembers being clever and complex enough to *manage* those wants, to decide *okay, another half an hour and then I'll carry Alannah upstairs*, and then go downstairs to his wife and be a man for her without any feeling of ickiness, any sense of jarring as he moved between one part of his life and another. He's not a cog anymore, and even as his feet shift in his swampy boots because the skin feels sore and excoriated, even as something else trickles down the side of his nose and his tongue shoots out and this time he's unlucky and it's a fly come to drink from his sweat, even as he catches it on his tongue and feels its shape against his lips and tries to spit it out again, resisting the urge to think about where else that fly's been before he almost ate it, he's not really paying attention at all, because he's the other guy, *the home guy*, the one who doesn't belong here, who wouldn't last five minutes, not thirty seconds.

And – when he finally gets rid of the fly, recognising that it's a warning to forget about the barely-real concepts of *wife* and *child* and *home* and concentrate on what's going on *here and now* – it's at least partly that guy, that *home guy*, who peers out through his sunglasses and sees the shape on the road before the gate.

Instantly he's at attention. The binoculars that hang around his neck are against his eyes before he's even thought about it.

Is there someone there? Or is it like the snake? The binoculars are perfectly focused. There's no mistake.

Local boy. About eight? Maybe nine? Hard to tell. Kids out here are skinny and small. This one looks happy enough. Grimy and cheerful. Free-looking. Kicking a stone down the road.

He ought to radio in, let them know what he sees. That's procedure and out here, procedure's king. (Except when it *isn't*, when all procedure goes to hell and the best you can hope for is that, when they pick over the bones of what you and your mates did in that moment, the actions you took will somehow turn out to be the right ones, or at least not court-martial-ably wrong.)

Call it in. Challenge with rifle lowered. Challenge with rifle raised. If none of that works, do what needs doing. Procedure matters. They're not lone wolves or vigilantes. They're here to do, not to think. He's a cog in a machine. His radio's tucked beneath his chin. All he has to do is push the button and speak into it.

Liam stands still, binoculars pressed against his eyes, and watches.

The boy's chosen a good stone. It's smooth and rounded, skidding nicely across the dust. It's large enough and different enough to keep track of. (Liam can still remember the deep and utter importance of staying committed to Your Stone, making sure it was the chosen one and no other that you nursed along its journey.)

When the stone moves in a smooth straight line, the boy grins. When it judders against the ground, or bounces off in an unexpected direction, he frowns. When he misses the stone altogether, he glances around and shrugs, making sure the universe at large knows how little he cares about looking stupid. Liam can feel every kick and movement, every moment of joy and disappointment. He's down there with him on that road, a boy again, coming home from school, anorak tied around his shoulders, bag bouncing against his back. The boy Liam was and the boy Liam watches are different sizes, different colours, their clothes making different shapes when they move. Born into different worlds. But right now, in this moment when Liam is himself again and can access every part of his mind and heart, they're the same.

As if he feels it too, the boy looks up at the tower, and sees Liam looking down.

He can't be surprised at being watched. Liam doesn't recognise the kid (he finds the locals impossible to tell apart, and they probably feel the same way about Liam and his mates). But he's got to be from the area, because who else would come here? Who but a local boy would be out unsupervised? There's no way he could have come down this road, not knowing what he'd see at the end of it. Nevertheless, the boy looks surprised, a little apprehensive.

Well, Christ, you poor lad. How could you look any other way? He's split in two, the watcher on the tower and the watched boy below, looking up at the strange figure in combat gear and body armour, helmet-headed, eyes replaced with mirror-shades, gun nestled across his body, skin mostly hidden but the small amount that's visible a shade of reddish-bronze that's confusingly called *white*. A figure barely recognisable as human. An invader from another world, proclaiming peace and kindness, bringing chaos and destruction.

Of course, they're here with permission (although from the looks they get sometimes, it's pretty clear that *permission* hasn't come from everyone). They do their best to build connections. Food and drink that's shared. Efforts to learn the basics of *please* and *thank you* and *hello* and *goodbye*, trying not to mind when the translators endlessly correct their pronunciation. Their mission's supposedly about *empowerment*. Getting the local lads trained and ready to right their own battles. Sounds good on paper. But how can anyone sort the good locals from the bad ones, unpick the web of connections and separations that define *friend* and *enemy*? Fuck that, how are you supposed to teach, when everything you both say has to go through a third party neither of you really trust? And why is this patch of shitty desert worth risking his life for anyway? What would happen (what would happen back in his world, that is) if they all walked away? Left the locals to sort out their own shit? This is what he's thinking, and it's a home-guy thought, not a work-guy thought. Dangerous. He needs to put this guy back in his box. Get back to work.

Without taking his eyes off the boy, Liam takes off his sunglasses. For a moment he's blind, and he knows, he *knows*, he's being stupid. In a couple of seconds, that boy could get close enough to turn himself into a fireball, take out the wall. But then his sight adjusts and the boy's still down there, his stone resting against the instep of his sandal, watching Liam.

What next? He's off-script. Wandering away from the rule book. What's he trying to do?

The home-guy thoughts continue. If he's right about this kid's age, in another world, he'd be at school with Alannah. The two of them side-by-side, working out a problem concerning… What do kids learn at that age? How to grow cress on a paper towel? Whether sticks float or sink? What happens when you stick a glob of sodium in a cup of water? He's missing out on so much of Alannah's life.

What was she doing before he left? Egyptian gods, that was it. Does this kid down there in the road know about Egyptian gods? Presumably he knows there's a country called Egypt (or you'd think, anyway, but who knows what kids know these days? Especially out here). But does he know about the mental ideas humans once had about how the world works? A giant dung beetle, rolling the Sun across the sky. That whole deal with your heart being weighed after you die, to see if you go on to the afterlife or get eaten by some demon creature. (What would his heart weigh right now? The work guy doesn't really have a heart. But Liam does. It's pressed against his ribcage, expanding with all the stuff that doesn't belong here, love and anxiety and questions about morality and being afraid of dying and remembering how it feels to kick a stone along a pavement and wondering how that kid down there can stand the heat and whether he gets enough to eat and…)

The boy's arm goes up in a friendly wave.

"Do you have a pen?" he calls. Voice spiralling like a bird. "Do you have a sweets?"

Sweets and pens; pens and sweets. The currency of children in war zones everywhere. The sweets he can get his head around, but what's the deal with the pens? What good is a pen without paper to go with it? Or do they hoard them in the way of children everywhere, the way he hoarded trading cards and plastic counters and other half-forgotten shit, utterly useless and infinitely valuable? The way Emma hoards scraps of fabric that can surely not be turned into anything wearable. *I can make pants out of them*, she always says when challenged, and when he tells her *yes but you never* do *make pants out of them, and besides, is it worth it when pants are so cheap?* she gets that look on her face that tells him she's going to keep it anyway, hide it away in a cupboard where he won't look and wait until he's gone again – no, shit, he can't afford to be daydreaming about Emma. He doesn't want her anywhere near here.

The boy's come closer, his face turned upwards. His skin's as flawless as eggshell. His eyes are blue, a sight Liam never gets used to. Those huge blue eyes in that soft brown face; beautiful but, to his Western-adjusted gaze, *wrong*-looking. Like God's photoshopped a tiny piece of the world, waiting to see if you'll notice.

"Sweets?" the boy repeats, and takes another hopeful step forward. "Please do you have a sweets? Do you have a pen?"

There must be more useful phrases these kids could learn, but no, it's all about the pens and the sweets. Or maybe they know more than they're letting on. They might not always have running water and their schools are a crumbling mess, but you see satellite dishes on roofs, the blue glare of television from corners of rooms. In the city, people on the streets check smartphones, and groups of friends (okay, groups of boys or men – the women don't seem to get out much) cluster and chatter about what they're seeing. They've skipped an entire generation of technology, gone straight to the latest and the best, which kind of makes sense but also looks weird and wrong, sort of cargo-cultish. For a wild minute, he wonders what he's got in his pockets. Does he have a sweet? Does he have a pen?

"Stop." The work guy's back. Back enough to cover the basics. "Stop there. This is an Army base. You can't be here."

He's a kid.

He's a local kid.

He's still a kid.

He's still a threat.

"Please, do you have a sweets?" The boy's smile suggests Liam is some kind of god, with the power to grant any wish the boy could think of.

"Stop." One hand up in clear instruction, the other cradling his rifle. "You need to go back now. Do you understand?"

"You came to my school," the boy says then, astonishing variation from the script. "You remember? You came."

Christ, is that even true? *He* hasn't been to any school, but the brass go all the time. What do they talk about? Do they let the kids touch their guns? Try and sow the seeds of a future career in the police? (Would the teachers even let them *in*? Imagine trying to walk into a British school with a gun; imagine how terrified the kids would be. Imagine how Alannah would feel if one day she saw the other guy, the work guy, doing the things he's been trained to do and does so well...)

"You came," the boy repeats. "Please, do you have a sweets?"

But if this school visit really had taken place, wouldn't they warn the kids not to come near the base? Surely that would be something they'd drum into them. *Do not come anywhere near the Army base or we might have to—*

312

Gun at his shoulder now. Still pointing downwards but ready for use. His body remembers the drill even though his head's AWOL. What the fuck is he doing?

"Turn around and go." Even if he doesn't get the words, he must get the body language. "Stop there, turn around and walk away. Do you understand?"

"But you came to my school," the boy repeats. His eyes – eyes of a Western Madonna in the face of a little brown kid – are wide and hurt. "We're friends. The British are friends."

The gun's barrel is raised. He's pointing his gun at a kid the same age as his daughter. A skinny little kid who's turned up at one of the most dangerous places in the world, to ask for sweets.

"We're not friends," Liam calls back. "You need to go. Understand? You can't be here. It's not safe."

"Please," the boy says, and takes one more step forward. "I need help. We're friends. My dad's sick. I need help."

"Then you need to talk to another adult." This isn't what he's meant to be saying. He needs to stick to the script. "Tell your mother to talk to someone. You have an aunt or an uncle? Talk to them." This isn't right. Here's here to protect the base, not to problem-solve for one random kid. Get back on task, soldier. "Walk away now." But what if his dad's got the same gut-rot that's got in here? They're all right behind the wall, it's a matter of staying hydrated and waiting it out. But what if they were out there? Out in the field, no water or rehydration salts? "This is your last warning."

"Please," the boy says. His eyes are so big and beautiful. No wonder they lock their women away, eyes like that in the face of a woman would be absolutely—

And then the boy's face changes. His eyes turn a Hallowe'en orange. His mouth grows wider and turns up at the corners. When he smiles, Liam sees the filed points of his teeth, many more than a human could possibly have, a mouthful of white needles. He grows taller, his arms and legs shooting out from his scruffy shalwar kameez...

You're hallucinating, Liam thinks. *You're hot and you're tired and you're dehydrated and you're seeing stuff.*

But the boy's hand is going to a place on his waist as if he's reaching for something, something he can grab hold of through the layers of cloth, something that can't be a gun because he'd need to hitch up his shalwar kameez to get it out, but could most definitely be a button or a trigger...

And now there it is, the terror that breaks through the boredom, and if he had anything in his bladder he'd piss himself right now, but then...

...then, the other guy takes over.

From a small helpless place inside his head, Liam watches as the other guy raises his gun.

There's a short crackling burst.

The boy crumples to the floor.

There's a gap here that he never manages to fill – his body doing stuff, but neither Liam nor the other guy taking notes. Perhaps someone even more primitive is in charge. Perhaps he's simply so busy with what needs doing that his brain doesn't have the time to take notes. His next memory is standing beside the bomb disposal guy, a little in front of the sergeant, as the robot trundles out towards the dead child. Someone else is on the watchtower, scouring the landscape with binoculars.

To Liam – who is somehow still around, even though the whole point of the other guy is for Liam to never be here, never ever *ever*, so there'll always be a version of him that can go home and pass for human again – the moment is filled with a kind of holy dread. What he did is unforgivable. No way back. Meanwhile, the work guy – reptile-brained and focused on self-preservation – goes over his story, checking for flaws. *He ran up the road. He was coming fast. I gave him two verbals. No time for a warning shot.* Has he said this out loud? He doesn't know.

None of them speak. The bomb disposal guy's focused on driving the robot, but Liam's pretty sure that he's also carefully not looking at the man who shot a child in cold blood. The Sarge's gaze drills holes through Liam's uniform. Liam pictures marks like cigarette burns.

Remember the story. The kid was coming fast. You gave him two verbals. No time for a warning shot. He's braced for what's coming. The robot will probe cautiously beneath the edge of the boy's clothing (soaked maroon now, like the dusty pool the robot trundled through) and find only torn brown skin. Skin that used to be soft and silky, stretched taut over bones that are slender like Alannah's. Skin that will never turn coarser, grow hairy, press against the bare flesh of a woman. The food that will never be eaten, the work that will never be done. The words that will never be spoken. The children who will never be born. The long marching lines of possibility, snapped off at the roots. He did that. He's made a broken place in the world.

"Yep," says the bomb disposal guy.

Liam forces himself to hold still.

"Kid's got a vest on." The bomb guy clicks his tongue. "Good spot, mate."

Liam wants to sag at the knees in relief, but the other guy won't let him. Instead he nods in curt acknowledgement. Of course the kid was wearing a vest. That's why he...

Liam feels sick. The other guy swallows it back down.

"Okay," the Sarge tells him. "Take fifteen. Get some water inside you. Then we'll debrief properly. Dismissed."

He salutes. Turns. Walks away. Makes his way to the mess room, then to the bathroom, which stinks of disinfectant but at least he'll be left alone in here. Takes on water. Stands up as he does it, because if he sits down he might never get up again. Tries to send his home-self away.

So the broken place was already made. The lines of possibility had already been snapped. All he did was anticipate the inevitable by perhaps five seconds. Oh, and save his own life. And the lives of his mates. He did his job.

He repeats this several times, then forces himself to recall the version of events he gave to the Sarge. The boy was running. Gave him two verbals. No time for a warning shot. Plus, he was right. Did he see something that made him suspicious? An outline under the clothes? No. Best to keep it simple. *I felt suspicious. Knew something was wrong. Had to make a judgement. Glad it was the right one.*

Okay. Story straight. Fifteen minutes are up. Time to go and see the Sarge, make his story official. He checks the time against his wristwatch. Puts the plastic bottle in the bin.

For an instant, the rattle of the bottle against the bin becomes the rattle of the boy's stone. For an instant, he's back on the tower, the heat pressing down on him like a weight he has to resist. *That's normal*, he tells himself. *It's only just happened.* He checks his reflection. Smart enough.

He takes a deep breath and walks out, not knowing yet that for him, it will always have only just happened, he will never leave this room, some part of him will always be standing in the bright light and harsh disinfectant scent of the grimy toilet block, staring at his reflection in the mirror

ACKNOWLEDGEMENTS

Thank you, as always, to my wonderful editor Lauren Parsons, to Tom Chalmers, and to all of the Legend team, for trusting that my slightly manic and over-excited pitch to you in the Legend offices would turn into a finished novel. Your faith means the world to me.

Thank you to my sisters-in-writing – the Women of Words Lynda Harrison, Michelle Dee and Louise Beech, and the amazing Dr Kate Fox. The lightstick that was snapped for our "Queens of the North" show in 2017 is still shining.

Thank you to all the wonderful bloggers and reviewers who support the writing community with the endlessly precious gift of your time, your thoughts and your reviews.

Thank you to my lovely, lovely family and friends, for loving me, for supporting my work, for reminding me to leave the house occasionally and maybe talk to someone who isn't either a cat or someone I'm related to, and for putting up with really quite a lot of nonsense from me in general.

Thank you to Harry, for permission to dedicate this book to you. You're courageous and inspiring, and I wish you a million bright tomorrows.

Most of all, thank you so, so much to all the men and women who opened up and shared their experiences with me so I could write *Soldier Boy*. Your stories are not mine to tell, so I haven't told them; but I hope I've done justice to everything you trusted me with.

My "thank you" list means even more this time because I'm writing it in the middle of lockdown. I can't wait for the day when I see you all in person. In the meantime, much love; be well; stay safe.

IF YOU ENJOYED WHAT YOU READ,
DON'T KEEP IT A SECRET.

REVIEW THE BOOK ONLINE AND TELL
ANYONE WHO WILL LISTEN.

THANKS FOR YOUR SUPPORT
SPREADING THE WORD ABOUT
LEGEND PRESS.

FOLLOW US ON TWITTER
@LEGEND_PRESS

FOLLOW US ON INSTAGRAM
@LEGENDPRESS